A DUBLIN INK NOVEL

SIENNA BLAKE

Dirty Ink: a novel / by Sienna Blake. – 1st Ed.
First Edition: July 2022
Published by SB Publishing

Stock images: shutterstock
Editing services by Proof Positive: http://proofpositivepro.com.

DIRTY INK

A DUBLIN INK NOVEL

SIENNA BLAKE

For all those dirty-mouthed boys

who give good aural...

1

RACHEL

Getting married was supposed to be romantic.

So far all I could say about it was that it involved a lot of waiting in lines, a lot of filling out forms, a lot of unpleasant forms.

"It smells like piss in here," JoJo complained as she spun the pen on its chain round and round. "At least on the subway, you get a little whiff of pizza now and then. They don't even let you eat in here. And why? Because someone might spill something on these pristine yellow laminate floors? Because someone might actually have fun in this hell hole?"

I smiled pleasantly at the woman behind the smeared glass window when she looked up from the top of her glasses.

"What my vocal friend means to say," I explained while tugging the pen from JoJo's hand and setting it carefully back in the holder, "is that we're very grateful for your help. And that civil servants such as yourself are the reason why this great city keeps running. And your offices here at city hall are only a tiny bit dirty because of how many people you help on a daily basis. Did I say we're grateful?"

The woman pursed her lips and narrowed her eyes. “I need to go double-check something,” she said in a bored monotone.

She pushed back her chair and disappeared into the aisles upon aisles of file folders. I groaned and let my head flop over my arms on the counter. My feet hurt, stuffed into the cream pumps Tim preferred. I’d worn a shift dress of white linen and a cream cotton blazer and despite it being all natural materials, all the finest natural materials (I was assured) it felt stifling in the unmoving air of the records basement. My hair was done up in the tight, tidy bun (Tim said it showed off my neck, but I suspected he found my hair down too wild, too untamed, too...*Brooklyn*) and I could feel each and every pin jamming into my skull.

I dragged my head back up with a tired sigh and found JoJo giving me *that* look.

“Don’t,” I said.

“Don’t what?” she said, batting innocent neon-green eyelashes.

“Don’t say what you were about to say.”

She cupped her cheeks, which caught the florescent light and glowed lavender, and smiled.

“All I was going to say was, ‘Darling, shall we have the pinot grigio or the pinot bigio for lunch with Mother?’”

I rolled my eyes. “There’s no such thing as a pinot bigio.”

JoJo jabbed me in the chest. She was always more violent than she needed to be. Probably something to do with the fact that she was only a hair over five feet on a good day. She compensated with four-inch platform boots and painful displays of superior strength.

I licked my thumb and swiped at the stain of pink eyeliner she’d smudged on my dress.

“That’s my point!” She flailed dramatically against the

counter. "The Rachel I know would never say, 'There's no such thing as a pinot bigio.'"

"But there isn't."

JoJo rolled her eyes this time. "But there could be—"

"There's not."

"But there *could* be," she said. "And the Rachel I know wouldn't just say with her nose in the air—"

"My nose wasn't up in the air."

"With her nose *all up* in the air, 'There's no such thing as a pinot bigio', she would say, 'What is a pinot bigio? I want to hear more. Is it sweet? Is it tart? Can I have it right here on my tongue because I love life and living and being loud and dancing and shining like a star and making up shit with my best friend instead of waiting in this stupid line for a sheet of paper that says I can marry this boring, vanilla-white average Joe.'"

"His name is Tim," I said before leaning across the counter to spy where the woman had gone. The faster she came back, the sooner I could escape JoJo and her inconvenient, annoying questions like, "So, like, why do you even want to marry this guy?"

JoJo's fingers drumming on the counter brought my eyes warily back to hers. Her chin jutted up at me as her nails tapped, tapped, tapped.

"What?" I said in exasperation.

"You know that I know his name ain't Joe," she said. "You know that I know his name is Tim."

"So?"

JoJo balled a fist. I wasn't fast enough to avoid it colliding against my arm, all tiny, bony knuckles and fury.

"*So*," she said, "you could have said, 'I love Tim,' or 'Get off his case, JoJo. I'm marrying him and I'm fucking happy' or 'Shut the fuck up, JoJo. You don't know shit.'"

I drew my tongue along my teeth. Tapped my nails against the counter.

"And?"

"And you said, 'His name is Tim'."

I bit back an aggravated exhale and said through teeth I hoped weren't clenched too tightly, "I love Tim. Happy?"

JoJo rested her hand against mine, her smile soft.

"I'm happy," she said quietly. "Are you?"

I tugged my hand away on the pretext of resecuring one of the bobby pins holding my bun. I cleared my throat and again searched the office behind the empty window.

"Goddamn, what is taking so long?" JoJo complained beside me. "I thought people come here all drunk and fucked up all the time to get hitched. We're cold-ass sober—your fault by the way, my friend, I said we should sneak in a bottle of champagne or two—and I can hardly wait any longer."

I didn't say it, but I was thankful as I stretched up onto my tiptoes and pressed my nose against the glass. Behaviour Tim would call "unrefined". JoJo was the nosiest, loudest, most brutally honest friend a girl could have, but she also knew when to step back. To give me space. To not be the nosy, loud, brutally honest friend, but just the friend. There for me. No matter what. Stupid, life-ruining decisions or not. JoJo knew there were things I kept from her. Things about my past. Things I didn't want coming out. Couldn't have coming out. Not for the life I was living at least. Or about to live. And she was okay with it. Okay with me having secrets. Okay with not opening that closet. The one with the skeletons.

"If you're going to be late for your audition," I started.

JoJo waved her hand to dismiss me. "Please," she said, laughing, "Pierre still hasn't paid me back from that last show I did for him. I'll show up whenever I'd good and ready please and thank you."

I draped my arm over JoJo's shoulders (something she hated and something I loved, because I knew how much she hated it) and squeezed her in tight. She squirmed away and straightened beside me, lifting her chin just a little too high.

"You know, you can still audition, too," she said. "There's this part that you'd be—"

I interrupted by saying, "Yeah, Pierre already has enough people he owes."

JoJo eyed me, clearly wanting to say something more but dropped it. Maybe she knew it was just an excuse. Maybe she knew Tim expected a certain image for his wife, and a small (probably unpaid) role in a (far, far off) off-Broadway play about disco aliens was not exactly what he was looking for.

"Seriously," JoJo complained again. "How do people pay Elvis to stick around while they wait all this time? Do they get him drugs or something? If I were Elvis I wouldn't be chilling on some sad bench at city hall waiting for all this nonsense for a shotgun wedding. They must give him something, don't you think?"

I laughed.

"I wouldn't have the faintest clue," I said.

JoJo eyed some of the couples waiting to get their marriage certificates. Girls in tea-length dresses big with tulle. Guys in t-shirts laser printed with a bowtie and black vest. An old woman in a fur coat with a slicked-haired twenty-something. Wet, sloppy kisses. Bodega bouquets going limp by the second. Sprays of cheap perfume against sweaty necks.

Tim and I were going to get married in a cathedral. With white lilies of the valley. And a train of lace so long...it was going to be...nice.

Every girl's dream.

My dream, I mean.

"But you lived in Vegas," JoJo said after a few minutes, the civil servant still lost in the aisles of file folders. "You did the whole..."

She waved her hand vaguely, because all the information I'd given her about my time there was vague. She was pretty sure I'd danced. Pretty sure I'd been in entertainment. Pretty sure I'd left in a hurry. It was all mostly right.

I laughed as I turned around to knock on the glass.

"Just 'cause I was in Vegas doesn't mean I got drunk, found some guy, and dragged him off to the Little White Chapel to get hitched by Elvis," I said. "Where did she go? Tim said it took him like thirty seconds to get his."

I knocked on the window. "Hello?"

JoJo went back to twirling around the pen on its chain. It was then that I heard, amongst the din of people talking, a deep voice. It was the accent that set it apart. The accent that sent my heart racing. The accent that made me turn around.

A pair of lips crashed into mine. Before I knew it I was being swept low, a strong hand at the small of my back.

It was *him*.

He'd found me—how the hell had he found me?—there in the basement of city hall.

For half a second, I kissed him back, because that's all I'd wanted for all those years was to brush my lips against his just one more time.

Just in case you didn't know, half a second goes by pretty damn fast.

I realised that mouth—reeking of cheap whiskey and cigarettes—was *not* his.

"Get the fuck off me!" I shouted as I pushed away the complete stranger.

JoJo was hitting him with her little tie-dye purse. The man stumbled back and laughed.

"Ah shite!" he slurred. "I t'ink I got the wrong lass!"

Security arrived just as a woman stumbled down the stairs shouting, "I'm ready! I'm ready!"

When everything was sorted, the two drunk idiots went off to get married (for how long, I'll let you guess). I went about scrubbing my lips of any trace of the bastard.

What really made me the most upset wasn't that I'd stupidly mistaken the voice or that I'd been kissed against my will or that the guy stunk to high heaven. It was that I could still hear him: laughing, kissing his woman, having a grand ol' time while I stood there still waiting.

"Who knew today was going to turn into such a shit show," I grumbled as I tried to straighten the wrinkles out of my dress.

JoJo practised a few punches, I guess just in case we were assaulted again during our stay in purgatory. "You know, for a second I thought you were kissing him back."

I blanched. "Of course not."

JoJo grinned. "Not getting the nasty from Tim?"

I groaned. "I'm getting plenty of the— Tim and I have a perfectly fine sex life."

"'Perfectly fine', tell me more," JoJo teased, chin cupped in her hands.

Just when I thought my day couldn't possibly get worse, the woman returned to her chair. She seemed in no hurry whatsoever as she rearranged herself in her chair. No hurry as she scooted back up to her desk. Inch. By. Painful. Inch. No hurry as she tidied the stack of documents in her hands and cleared her phlegmy throat.

"Well?" I asked impatiently as a bad feeling swelled in my stomach.

The woman looked up at me from above her glasses.

"Miss Garcia, I'm afraid you are not legally qualified to get married."

She slid a piece of paper across to me that I ignored.

"Why?" I demanded.

The woman tapped a nail to the sheet of paper.

"Because," she said in a tone like she was reading me the weather forecast for the weekend and not ruining my goddamn life, "you're *already* married."

2

MASON

To be young and free was the only thing that mattered in life.

To dance with girls, fight your way to the bar for pints, and yell along with the whole bar singing as a single crush of bodies was what life was all about. To leave with whoever you wanted, fuck whoever you wanted, and say goodbye in the morning to do whatever you wanted the next night was the most important thing to being happy.

No strings. No attachments. No tomorrows.

Just the night. The music. The alcohol. Hell, even the drugs every once in a while.

And the women. Oh God, the women.

I loved them and they loved me. The boys at Dublin Ink liked to say that I went “fishing” at night, that I got dressed up for the club to go “hunt”.

It was never as complicated as all that. I know fuck all about fishing (Dublin is wild enough for me, I don’t need the actual wild), but I do know you need a tackle box, string or whatever they call it, bait, maybe a little hat. That’s all before you’re even close to eating what you may or may not catch.

No, what I do is more like room service. I open the doors of the club like a menu. I pursue. I select. I enjoy my delicacy du jour in bed an hour later, give or take.

Also, hunting would mean hurting. And I don't hurt.

Or at least, I never try to.

I always tell the women I go home with that all I'm offering is a fun time for one night and one night only. My cock is a carnival tent pole and I make it abundantly clear to the lovely ladies that the next morning it's getting packed up and moving on. Same city. New attractions.

Sure, there have been some tears. Nobody likes to see the magic go, ye know? I get it. I do.

That night I was alone because Conor was working late with Aurnia. (Right, so I'm degraded with "fishing" and "hunting", but Conor gets to call it "work"? The perils of being a playboy, I guess.) And Rian...well, who the fuck knew where Rian was. Physically. Mentally. Astroplain-ly. That night I was alone, but not for all that long.

Not long enough to realise that I knew all the songs. Recognised all the patrons. Had memorised the bar menu. Not long enough to get that uncomfortable sense of deja vu. Of time standing still. Of the four walls of the club I called freedom feeling a little bit...claustrophobic.

The girl was gorgeous, but weren't they all? Don't get me wrong, I wasn't complaining. Of course not. Pouty lips painted blood-red. Seductive cat eyes blinking beneath a razor-sharp line of inky black liner. A pair of holy fuck, hallelujah, "God, is it good to be alive" tits peaking up from the top of a skin-tight little sequined thing I could easily imagine on the floor of my bedroom or wrapped around her neck.

The music was loud enough that neither of us could really hear what the other was saying. What did that matter in the end? *"Where you from?" "Dublin." "Oh cool, cool. Me too." "What do you do?" "Tattoo artist. Own a place actually." "Oh I love tattoos. Want to see mine?"* A cab ride. Falling up the stairs. Fucking.

Or *"Where you from?" "Dublin." "Best place on earth." "Yeah, yeah. Want a smoke?"* A cab ride. Falling up the stairs. Clothes on floor. Her on top. Bed post banging against the wall.

Or *"Where you from?" "Limerick." "Oh really?" "Just here for the weekend." "I see... Can I show you the best sight in Dublin?"* A cab ride. Falling up the stairs. Her bent over as I gave her a taste of Dublin for the scrapbook memories.

There was only one way the night would end. The details were lost in the bass.

We danced for a few songs. Sometimes that's nice. Like foreplay. Sometimes that's nice, too. Her ass against my cock. Trying not to get hard in public. Mostly succeeding. Her hands stretching back to curl around my neck. Her nails against my scalp as she ground herself against me mostly to the beat. Sometimes that's nice as well. A little change from the direct approach: panties down, zipper down, deep and fast and hard and quick. Her nibbling at my jawline as the song ends and another begins. Spice of life and all that.

The girl then shouted up at me, "Want to see my tattoo?" Or maybe it was, "Want a smoke?" Or then again maybe it was, "You know I'm leaving Dublin tomorrow."

Like I said, it didn't really matter, because her hand on my cock (mostly not hard) was words enough for what she wanted. What we wanted. Getting back through the crowd to the stairs up was the hardest part. Girls got lost easily. Another man with another drink. Boys got lost easily. Another girl ready to take another drink. Maybe what I did was more like fishing than I realised. This was the reeling-in part. It was always a crap shoot what you ended up with when you popped up onto the sidewalk, fresh air hitting you like a semi truck.

"So, should we like call a cab or something?" my fish said as

I blinked drunkenly at the night. Always too early. Always too late.

I whipped around and nearly fell over. The girl laughed and said something about which one of us was drunker.

"You're American?" I asked. Accused, more like. She didn't seem to pick up on it.

"What's round on both sides and high in the middle?" She giggled.

"What?"

"What's round on both sides—"

"I heard you, love, but come 'ere, are you American?"

The girl tossed her long blonde curls from her shoulder and threw her hands into the air while shouting, "Ohio!"

I leaned heavily against the brick wall outside the club and sighed. "You're from Ohio?"

The girl nodded eagerly, all curls and dimples and fuck me.

"Born and raised. Cheered at Ohio State. Want me to show you one of our dances?"

God, did I. The way she was wagging her hips like a puppy who just wanted to play. The way her bottom lip was held in her teeth like a leash at the front door. The way she made these little whining noises, all bottled up delira and excira and Jesus, Mary and Joseph, I was certain we could have gone at it till morning.

Before the girl could raise her arms, before she could start her cheer and win my heart over, I put my hands on her shoulders. She knew by my heavy sigh that something was up.

"Listen," I said, "you have no idea how much I want to take you home and hear you...cheer. Cheer my name, cheer your shitty ex's name, hell, cheer whatever bleedin' name you like. However loud. Wake up the neighbours."

The American girl pouted out her bottom lip as she looked up at me. "...but?"

I held her chin between my thumb and pointer finger and swore under my breath.

"But I can't."

Her eyes sparked mischievously up at me.

"Why not?" she asked, voice all smoke and seduction. The sweetness gone. Replaced with lust. Replaced with need.

I tried to exhale steadily.

"I've got a rule."

"No one-night stands?" she asked.

I laughed. "Quite the contrary."

"No girls with massive, *real* tits?"

"See previous response."

The girl drew her nails down my chest. Walked me back till my shoulders collided with the brick wall. Her lips curled up as she pressed herself against me.

"Then what? Because I'm American?"

I grinned down at her. "I'm very xenophobic."

Her eyes darted between mine. She licked her lips.

"Hate fuck me then," she said. "Take out all your pent-up rage on me. I can take it. I like it rough, you know? And with those big ol' muscles of yours..."

I hit the back of my head against the wall and held back a frustrated growl. My fingers tightened around the back of her dress. I wanted to draw her closer. Ride her right there on the sidewalk against the brick wall of the club. Feel the back of her head scrape the brick as I pinned her to it with my cock.

But then she would end up in my bed. And morning would come. I'd have my eyes closed, sleep with half its hold on me and I'd hear that accent. I'd be vulnerable. Helpless. Unprepared. It'd crush me all over again.

I looked down at the girl, all sex appeal and eagerness, all the things I wanted. I brushed my thumb over her cheek.

"It's not hate that I feel," I said softly. "Not rage either."

"Then what?" the girl asked, nails sinking into my skin.

As an answer, I lowered my lips to hers and kissed her. I kissed her like she had wild hair the colour of dark honey. Like the sequins of her dress were at the corners of her sparkling hazel eyes. I kissed her like it was the goodbye I never got. The goodbye I never wanted.

I kissed her like I'd found her. Like *she* was there. Like her lips were the only lips I would ever kiss again.

The girl was breathless when I pulled away. Her lids were heavy, drunk on what they poured in the club. Drunk on me.

Her forehead fell against my chest and she sighed. When she looked up at me, she said, "Fuck," first and then, "The one who got away, huh?"

"You've got one of those, too?"

She shook her head.

"No," she said and then grinned. "Though maybe I do now."

I called her a cab and waited till the red lights disappeared down the street. Then I went back into the club. Back down the stairs. Back into the life I wanted. The good life. The free life. The life of no strings. No attachments. Back to fishing. Back to hunting. Back to shouting at someone who couldn't possibly hear me.

What more could I ever want, right?

3

RACHEL

I was pacing across rugs that cost more than I'd made in my entire lifetime combined. More than years' worth of crumby singles thrown at my feet or the dollar signs that came from my name in lights. More than all my tips at the cafe, though that's probably the least surprising of all.

I was pacing over wood floors that were a part of a building in a part of town where if I tried to walk in ten years ago the doorman would call the police. I was pacing in front of windows that overlooked Central Park. Pacing in shoes with red bottoms bought with a black card, stored in a white walk-in closet bigger than any of my previous apartments. I was pacing in a silk robe that was actually silk, actually goddamn, fucking silk.

All around me was security and money and ease and it was all going to be mine and I was digging a hole in it, pacing back and forth, back and forth.

After asking for the woman's manager at city hall and then her manager and then his manager and after being told that there were no more managers to ask for, after being told the marriage license was real, after being assured it wasn't some stupid joke, JoJo and I came back to the apartment.

Tim was at work and I was in a panic. JoJo was asking questions I never thought I'd ever have to answer:

"Who the fuck is Mason Donovan?" "When did you meet him?" "How did you know him?" "How long did you know him?" "What happened to him?" "Where is he?" "Why aren't you two still together, Rachel? Rachel, hello?"

And that was all before she got to the questions I *couldn't* answer:

"When did you get married?" "What do you mean you don't know?" "You don't remember getting married?" "Rachel, how could you not remember getting *married*?"

There was lots of tea. Lots of crying. Lots of "Fuck, fuck, *fuck*, JoJo, what am I going to do?" There was whiskey. There was more tea. More "fucks". Tissues. More damn tissues. Screams. More whiskey.

And then there was Google.

JoJo typed quickly. Her pinkie hitting Enter felt like someone pulling the pin out of a grenade and throwing it at my feet. I slapped my hands over my eyes.

"Well, hello, Mr Mason Donovan."

My hands were still over my eyes. They were there until JoJo forcibly tugged them away.

And then there he was.

Mason.

The one who got away.

The one who apparently didn't get all the way away.

There he was on the computer screen. Chiselled jaw. Cheeky smile. Tousled hair. Tattoos all down his muscular arms. All my best choices and worst mistakes rolled up into one god of a man.

He'd started a tattoo parlour, JoJo was saying. He was in Dublin. He was so fucking sexy, she was saying. He was looking for a three-way with two American chicks.

"What?" I blurted out.

JoJo laughed. "Oh, so now you're listening."

"You were joking?"

JoJo just rolled her eyes. When she saw me distraught, she twisted around in the office chair and extended her arms. I was probably double her size, but still I sat on her lap like a little baby.

"What am I going to do?" I moaned into her cropped hair, blue today, who knew what colour tomorrow.

"Well," she said, rocking me like I wasn't crushing her alive, "you could move to Utah and join the Mormon faith."

"JoJo."

"Or you can pick."

I pulled away from her.

"Pick?"

She looked confused at my confusion.

"Yeah, pick," she said, searching the room for a picture of Tim, my fiancé. "Joe or—"

"His name isn't Joe."

JoJo grinned.

"Pick either Isn't-Joe or the sexy, hunky Irish tattoo artist."

I laughed even though it wasn't fucking funny.

"That's not a choice," I said.

JoJo nodded.

"I agree," she said. "Mason all the way."

"I'm marrying Joe— I mean, Tim. Goddammit, JoJo. I love Tim. He's given me all of this."

I waved my arm at the massive Upper East Side apartment.

"He's going to take care of me. Provide for me," I said. "He's nice. And he's never hurt me. And..."

"And you're married to someone else," JoJo said, tapping the picture of Mason on the computer which I still didn't really want to look at all that much. "Someone very different, it seems."

I glanced at Mason out of the corner of my eye. A face I hadn't seen in years. A lifetime ago. He was someone different. But so was I. Someone very different.

"That doesn't mean I have a choice," I said to JoJo, sniffling.

And yet there I was, pacing.

JoJo had left and I was alone and I was pacing. Pacing like I had a decision to make. Pacing like I had a choice.

The elevator at the front of the apartment dinged and I froze. What was I to do? Run to Tim and laugh and tell him all about this silly mistake from my youth? Set his team (army) of attorneys to fixing the problem? Move on like this was a simple accounting error on our taxes and open a bottle of pinot grigio, a real wine, from the *real* world?

Why did I even ask myself the question, because of course that was what I should do. If I wanted to marry Tim and if I loved Tim and if I trusted Tim enough not to leave me if he found out about this "indiscretion" (that's what he would call it, I was sure), then there shouldn't be any question at all.

And yet, I stood there. Frozen. Frozen even as the elevator doors parted and he walked inside. Even as he walked by me, leafing through the mail. Even as he went into the kitchen and said after a quiet moment, "You've been drinking?"

I was frozen but my heart was beating. Beating like I had a decision to make. Like I had a choice.

"Rachel?"

Tim's voice came sharp from the kitchen. Like a displeased father. Not that I knew anything about good parenting.

Before Tim could call my name again, I kicked off my slippers. It was hardly anything, kicking off my slippers. Hardly anything at all. But it felt like leaping off a cliff. The floors were warm from the late afternoon sun, sure and steady beneath my feet, but it felt like I was suspended over open air. As I hurried toward the bedroom I tugged at the sash round my waist. I let the silk robe fall from my shoulders in the living room, let it pool behind me as I tiptoed down the long hallway lined with priceless art.

"Rachel?" Tim's voice came echoing down to me as I wiggled out of my pyjama shorts lined with lace.

I wasn't sure what I was doing. Wasn't even really sure why. But for some reason I knew I had to. Had to tug the French designer camisole over my head. Had to let it flutter to the floor behind me as I hurried. Had to unclip the mother-of-pearl clasp from my hair and drop it at the edge of the bedroom as my hair cascaded around my naked shoulders.

I wasn't sure what choice I was making. What decision there even was. But I knew I had to dart over to the bed as Tim muttered a, "What the hell?" in the living room. Had to messy my hair with my fingernails as I heard his footsteps getting closer down the hallway. Had to arrange myself for him as he (I imagined) paused to scoop up my panties with a finger. To study them in the dying light, all amber and gold and ruby. To continue on toward the bedroom slowly...

My heart was racing in a way that I didn't quite understand. Tim had seen me naked before. Of course he had. He'd drawn his tongue against my nipples. Never his teeth. He'd unzipped my dresses in the soft glow of the streetlamps. Never tore it, clawed at it or ripped it. He'd fucked me in bed. Never against the wall, never outside the Upper East Side apartment, never in the glow of neon.

Tim was my fiancé. I loved Tim. I wanted to be with Tim for the rest of my life. So why was my heart racing like this was going to decide something? Like there was a choice and the choice was now?

I tried not to squirm as I waited for Tim to enter the

bedroom, the end of his trail of crumbs, very expensive, very exclusive, very shouldn't-be-on-the-floor-Rachel crumbs. I knew this was how I wanted him to see me, this was how I wanted to be seen: rounded hip high and prominent and cast in light, hair a wild cascade across my shoulders, eyes smouldering in the shadows. I tried to look at ease. Calm. Sexy. Not freaking the fuck out for no reason at all.

I inhaled shakily. Then Tim was there in the doorway. Nothing in his hands as I had thought. As I had expected. As I had wanted? His breath did not catch as I had thought it might. As I had maybe been naive to expect. As I was childish to want. He frowned at me like I was a small inconsistency on a loan application.

"Did you forget about Invig? It's already past six," he said, crossing to the closet.

Not getting within six feet of me. Not getting anywhere near close enough to reach out to me. Not getting anywhere near close enough for me to reach out to him. I heard him rustling through the closet, moving the hangers apart, brushing his fingers across his custom suit jackets, but not touching me.

"It wouldn't be the end of the world if we were a little late, would it?" I asked.

My voice was sweet, gentle. It was the voice I used with Tim. The voice JoJo made fun of me for. The voice I hardly remembered anymore wasn't my own.

"I don't think they'd appreciate that," came Tim's voice from the closet.

He emerged with his fingers on his lapels, his fingers on his buttons. Ivory. Imported from France. With his fingers everywhere but on me.

"You know," I said, trying to smile seductively, playfully. "We could have ourselves dinner in tonight."

I ran my hand along the curve of my waist, trying to not be

embarrassed that I was naked. That I had thrown myself out there like a fool. That Tim was checking out the time on his watch, but not checking out *me*.

"Rachel," he said, levelling his eyes at me, not like I was his to-be wife naked and eager on his bed, but like I was a client who hadn't brought in the correct documentation *again*, "we've been waiting months for a reservation."

No, not *we*. Him. What did I care for fancy new restaurants in the city? What did I care, except that I was supposed to? Because this was to be my life: waiting around for reservations at restaurants that left you with a bill the size of a normal person's monthly Manhattan rent and an empty stomach. No spontaneity. No losing track of time between the sheets. Appearances. Appearances. Appearances, Rachel.

Just like that, the decision that I didn't know was a decision was made. The choice that I hadn't known was even a choice was fixed upon.

"Tim," I said as I slipped out of bed and tidied the covers behind me. "I meant to tell you."

He admired himself in the full-length mirror. While I got dressed like his sweet little fiancée. While I put my hair back in a chignon the way he liked it, appropriate for the image of innocence, of virginity, even if he could forget long enough that he sometimes fucked me. I grabbed my shoes from the closet. The ones not too tall. Not too flashy. Not too slutty. Sweet. Innocent. Tim's little rescued orphan.

"Is it about the alcohol in the kitchen?" he asked.

Had he forgotten about my trip to city hall? Perhaps not. Perhaps he just assumed I was legally allowed to marry him. How could I possibly have a past? And a dirty one at that?

"No," I said, turning around so that he could zip up my dress, the one he selected for our dinner. "No, it's... I got an audition."

"Rachel—"

"I know, I know," I said. "But it's a good role. Shakespeare. On one of the big stages."

Tim exhaled slowly. I knew what he was thinking: how would that look to his finance friends? How would that look to our old money acquaintances? Would his boss be impressed or find it distasteful when considering promotions?

"Well," was all Tim said.

Mild approval. That was all I was ever going to get for my "little hobby".

"Yeah," I said. "The only thing is...well, it's in Dublin."

Tim patted my back to signal that he was finished.

"Just remember we have those reservations at Viande next month with the Strausses," was all he said.

"Right," I said, still facing away from him.

"My assistant will book your flight."

I nodded.

"Now, really, Rachel," Tim, my fiancé, my love said. "We're going to be late. You know how I hate that."

He stepped over my silk camisole still on the floor. I guess he supposed the maid would take care of it after all. What did it have to do with him? After all.

4

MASON

I had hoped for lashing rain.

Not that I wanted the weather to match my shite mood or any nonsense like that. My mood was going to be shite regardless. What did I care if everyone else in Dublin enjoyed a bit of sunshine? I wasn't going to sit against the big window downstairs and watch the drops streak the window all day. I wasn't going to run outside and throw my head up to the sky and scream as the rain splattered against my cheeks. I wasn't even going to go outside even. I hadn't even decided whether I would get out of bed really. It was entirely possible that the blinds would stay closed all bleedin' day long, so what the fuck did I care if it rained or not outside?

No, the only reason I hoped for rain was so that I could have a few more hours of blissful unconsciousness before the day began. A few more hours for it not to be today. A few more hours for it to be last night. Tearing off clothes. Slamming each other against the walls. Falling off the bed and not even bothering to climb back up. A few more hours for it to be *that* night. All those years ago. Glitter on my chest from *her* cheek. Neon light cascading down her spine, pooling in the small of her back like water. Long honey hair over my shoulder, over my throat...

Anyway, I didn't get rain. I got a fucking bright-ass ray of morning sunshine straight to the eye through the blinds that couldn't have been closed more tightly. Go figure.

With a groan I raised an arm to block the light. My other arm was stuck beneath Miss Last Night.

Come 'ere, it wasn't me who started calling my lady friends this. Go give out to Conor. Or maybe it was Rian. It wasn't me. If I was to call them anything I would call them "Miss Wants to Have a Good Time and Understands Fully Because It's Been Agreed to Beforehand That It Will Just be a Good Time for One Night and One Night Only." Bit of a mouthful though. I can admit Miss Last Night is snappier.

As I pulled my arm from beneath her, Miss Last Night stirred a little before sighing and nestling in closer to me. Not a great sign. Any other morning and I would have kissed her on the forehead, crawled out of bed, and gone to the shower (locking the door behind me, a lesson I'd learned the hard—very, very hard—way). But it wasn't any other morning and I had more pressing needs.

Closing my eyes against the intrusive light, I patted around the bed. My head was pounding. A killer hangover was surely on its way. I wasn't too worried. Not with what I had planned for this day. This shite, shite, always shite day.

I slapped at the sheets and found a couple of torn condom packages, a thong, a second thong (which confused me until I vaguely remembered ripping the thing in two the night before), a little velvety purse, and none of that was what I was looking for. I squinted one eye open against the sun and scanned the crumpled sheets. I glanced over my shoulder at Miss Last Night.

Shite. I started with her hair. There couldn't be anything misconstrued about checking around under someone's hair.

There wasn't anything sexy about lifting some dark, kinky curls from the pillow. I stretched over Miss Last Night to check the other side. Curls lifted. Nose peeked under. Nothing.

"You want your fingers all up in there again?" came a thick voice, muffled slightly by the pillow.

I dropped the curl and retreated.

"It was just itching my nose," I said, drumming my fingers impatiently on either side of me.

"You can pull on it again," Miss Last Night mumbled sleepily. "You know I like it rough."

"Listen, Miss—um..." Well, damn, I couldn't call her Miss Last Night to her face, now could I? "Listen, *love*, like I said last night—"

"Right, right," Miss Last Night said even as her fingers walked across the sheets toward me. "One-time thing."

I grabbed her hand before her fingers could slip beneath the sheet toward my groin and quickly hoisted it up to check beneath her arm. Nope. Nothing.

Miss Last Night grinned against the pillow and said, "Oh, you want me to turn over, do you?"

"Well, actually, I wouldn't mind seeing if—"

"Didn't get enough of these last night, huh?"

Miss Last Night shifted onto her side and cupped her tit. My attention, however, was not on her (admittedly) lovely nipples, but rather on the exposed bit of sheet she'd been sleeping on.

Dammit. There was still nothing there. I scanned around the room. The floor. The top of my armoire. Even the pile of laundry that hadn't quite made it to the hamper. The hamper. No. Nothing there. Nothing anywhere.

With an irritated grumble, I kicked back the sheets to check at our feet. Not only was there nothing down there either, but this elicited a low growl from Miss Last Night.

"You going downtown, baby?" she purred.

She pressed my head down. Before I was forced to her hips, waggling at me like an eager pup, I gathered her wrists together in my hand and pressed a kiss to her palms.

"Downtown was last night, love," I told her. "This morning is—"

"I see," Miss Last Night said, nodding seriously. "I got you, baby. I got you."

Miss Last Night sat up and I greedily ran my hands over the warm sheets. I cursed when I found nothing. I cursed when I realised Miss Last Night had only sat up so that she could scoot down to *my* hips.

"Woah, woah, woah," I said, pulling my cock away just before she wrapped her lips around it. "That's not what I meant."

"No?" Miss Last Night said, long, dark eyelashes batting up at me, lips pursed.

"Can you just, I don't know, can you just stand up for a second," I said, patting wildly about the bed again.

It had to be somewhere. It had to be fucking *somewhere*.

Miss Last Night stood on the bed, giggling as she shook her tits at me. I looked where she'd just been lying. But it hadn't been beneath her hips. Nor her thighs.

I was so busy digging around beneath my own back that I didn't pay attention to her stepping one foot over my hip. Didn't pay attention to her whispering seductively, "Oh, you want it like *that*, baby?" Didn't pay attention to her lowering herself to her knees, straddled atop me.

Miss Last Night was halfway to guiding my hard cock (yes, hard—morning wood, so sue me) into her pussy before I could grab ahold of her hips, roll her over, and get on top of her.

"Yes, yes," she moaned, clawing her fingers through her hair and squirming in delight beneath me. "Yes!"

I threw aside the sheets and flung pillows. Miss Last Night

unfortunately misconstrued all of this as a wild desire to fuck, and fuck hard, instead of what it really was, what it had all always been: me trying to find that goddamn bottle of whiskey.

Beneath me, Miss Last Night dragged her hands up and down her body, squealing as she pinched her own nipples, bucking her hips up at me like I was balls-deep in her.

"Yes, yes," she moaned. "Let's do this all morning. All day!"

I leaned over Miss Last Night to wriggle my fingers beneath the mattress and the wall and yelped because of two things at the same time: one, because Miss Last Night had sucked my balls into her mouth when I stretched over her and two, because I'd found the bottle of whiskey at long last! See, perseverance does pay off, kids!

Miss Last Night groaned in disappointment when I pried my balls from between her lips. I groaned in disappointment when I saw that I'd left myself no more (but no less) than three drops of whiskey.

"Bollocks," I muttered as I crawled out of bed.

Not only was I not able to sleep in, to avoid the day, *that* day, but now I was also not able to just stay in bed and drink the hours away. If I wanted to get to the forgetting part (which I did, I absolutely did), then I would have to go downstairs. The way the day had started I wouldn't have been surprised to have to go out to get a bottle from the liquor store either. To have to see all those happy faces in the sun. To remember for way longer than I ever intended.

"Look, like, are we having sex or what?" Miss Last Night said from the bed.

I glanced over at her as I tugged on a pair of sweatpants. She was propped up on her elbows. One leg folded seductively over the other. Pouting at me. I saw it in her hooded, hungry eyes: she was a naughty Miss Last Night. She was the kind who swore all she wanted was a good fuck and a quick goodbye, but heard wedding bells when she closed her eyes. She was the kind who lied about yoga in the morning anyway, a busy day anyway, "I have better things to do than lie around with you all day" anyway, but had plans as clear as a bright blue day. She was the kind who complicated the simple. The kind who would not go easily.

"Come here, love," I said, holding out my arms, half inside a jacket, half out, "come, come."

Miss Last Night hesitated half a second. For half a second, she worried it was a trap (it was). But I smiled my charming, disarming, winning smile and half a second later she was pressed against me.

Lips against her warm hair, I said, "I think your dress is on the chair there."

The cursing started then. She stomped into her dress. Yanked it up. The zipper broke halfway, she tugged it so violently. Those three drops of whiskey went fast. And didn't go far. I rubbed at my temples and let loose a few curses under my own breath.

"Love," I said, "would you just look at me for a second?"

Miss Last Night pushed her thick curls from her face and glared at me.

"You've got your dress on inside out."

Miss Last Night growled and stomped out of my room. I followed with my hands stuffed into my pockets. All that mattered was that she leave. Angry or not, I didn't really care. Not today at least. All I cared about today was getting that bottle of whiskey. Getting back to my room. And forgetting. That was it.

Miss Last Night was almost to the top of the staircase when she turned around abruptly. Shite.

Voices came from downstairs, the shop already up and running for the day, but they might as well have been on Mars, because there was no getting past Miss Last Night in that narrow hallway.

"No," she whispered dramatically, hands on my chest. "No, I can't just let this go."

"Let what go?" I whispered back.

"*This*," she exhaled.

"This?"

"*Us*."

She jammed her lips against mine and I gently pushed her back.

"What we have," she whispered, "it's special."

"It's really not."

"And I won't let your fear of commitment keep us from something special."

"Love, we fucked once and it was average," I said before trying and failing to guide Miss Last Night back toward the stairs.

"You're afraid," she gasped, pressing me back till my shoulders collided with the wall.

Looking down at her, I nodded side to side.

"Yeah," I said. "A little."

"You've been hurt. I'll heal you. I'll *heal* you."

Downstairs I could make out amongst the voices that of an American. It was rare enough that we got clients in the shop, let alone foreigners, so it was enough to make my heart jump. Dublin Ink had been a way to find her. To call out to her wherever she was. But the time had long ago passed where I thought it was actually possible.

"Look," I said to Miss Last Night, "today is a hard enough day for me. And you're making it harder because you're in the way of my whiskey. And now apparently an American is in the way of my whiskey. So if you don't mind?"

I gestured toward the stairs. Miss Last Night listened as the

American asked something I couldn't quite make out. She sounded angry. Rian was my best guess, mostly by process of elimination. Conor already had a woman to make angry. Aurnia wasn't American.

Miss Last Night's face was indignant as she looked back at me.

"You're fucking her too, huh?" she growled.

"What?"

Before I could stop her, Miss Last Night took off again toward the stairs.

"You think you can just sleep around on me?" she called back. "You think I'm just a piece of meat you can use up and then go on right to another piece of meat? You think I don't know my worth as a woman?!"

I ran after Miss Last Night to try to avoid a scene.

"I don't even know who she is," I said as I jumped down two stairs at a time.

Miss Last Night snorted derisively.

"How many times have you fucked her?" she shouted.

I lost it. "I have no idea in bleedin' hell who that bleedin' woman—"

My words bit off when I saw who was there at the bottom of my stairs. The woman who looked up at me. The woman there at the bottom of my stairs, there in person, at Dublin Ink, there at the bottom of my fucking stairs *glared* at me.

The one who got away.

She glared at me. "You have no idea in bleedin' hell who your *wife* is?"

5

RACHEL

hen…

I WAS at the bottom of the stairs waiting for a guy I didn't like in a dress I didn't like, and the worst part was that it wasn't the first fucking time.

It felt like all my life I'd been there, shifting uncomfortably in shoes that didn't fit. That weren't quite right for me. Felt like all my life I'd been waiting. Waiting around to be someone for someone else. Waiting around for the curtains to part and for the audience to clap. Waiting around to say my lines, walk where I should, stop where I was told, look this way or that, smile, smile, always smile, and then take a bow. It felt like the bottom of those stairs, waiting, uncomfortable, was where I would always be.

I couldn't do a goddamn thing about it. And I didn't know why.

"Are you coming?" I called up into the darkness. "This was your idea."

"Yeah, yeah, yeah," Fitz shouted back down. "Don't get your panties in a bunch, Rach. This last line isn't going to snort itself."

I sighed and leaned against the wall. Tugged down a dress that was too short. Pulled at a top that was too low. It wasn't that I didn't like showing my body. I had a burlesque show in Vegas, for God's sake. But something about the clothes Fitz picked for me made me feel dirty in a way that sequined pasties never did. When I danced, I danced for myself. When I dressed, it was for Fitz. Or Robby. Or Mick. Or Paul.

"Fitz!" I shouted.

"Bitch, stop yelling at me! I'm coming."

I knocked the back of my head against the wall. How many times I'd waited at the bottom of stairs just like those. Shitty carpeted stairs. Dark and small and old. How many times I'd hoped that someone else would come walking down them. Someone different. How many times I'd wished someone else would come walking down the stairs and see me as different. As someone different. As someone else. As someone who I could be proud to be. Whoever that goddamn was.

In the end it was always the same. Always Fitz. Or Robby. Or Mick. Or Paul. Always a shaky finger run beneath a white-powdered nose. Always a slap on the ass and a jangle of keys. Always a promise of big money, big futures, big lives. Always a shitty car I had to open myself. Always playing a role. Always feeling alone.

For Fitz I was the Bonnie, he the Clyde. The Showgirl and the Thief. He was going to game the system in Vegas and we were going to ride out of there in a storm of dust and find some beach somewhere to bask in the sun. I wasn't even sure I wanted a beach somewhere. I wasn't sure I wanted a Clyde. But still, I swore like a sailor for him. I said, "Fuck the system" with him. I added more eyeliner and snarled at security guards and learned how to shoot a gun for him. I played the role. Played it well. Like always.

"Rach, honey doll."

A hand on my elbow and I was reaching for my purse before I even thought about it. I was at the bar at the casino and Fitz was at my side. He'd already run out of money to gamble with. He was just warming up. The house wouldn't know what hit 'em. We were going to own the fucking place, baby. I'd heard it all. Bought it all. I handed Fitz a stack of twenties and he licked my neck. Love, am I right?

The casino was busy as always. But I knew the bartender and he knew to keep my mojitos coming. This was my big night out. The one night a week I didn't perform. And this was how I was spending it. I would get drunker and Fitz would get higher. He'd keep losing and I'd keep giving. We'd leave out of our heads and out of our cash. Nix that. *My* cash. We'd fuck and go to sleep and in the morning, I'd go to practise and he'd go to score weed. With my money.

Bonnie and fucking Clyde, my ass.

But there he was again tapping my elbow. And there I was yet again opening my purse, handing over the cash, smiling when he smiled because I was supposed to. Because Bonnie loved Clyde. Because she wanted that adventure. Because she was happy. Because she was Bonnie.

I don't know what got into me that night. It should have been like any other night. Pretending to be happy should have made me happy enough. I was pretty good at believing myself when I told myself enough times.

But I was irritable. Every time Fitz came to my elbow, "Rach, sugar tits", "Rach, honey bun", "Rach, Rach, Rach", I got madder and madder. Maybe the bartender wasn't making the drinks strong enough. Maybe I wasn't drinking them fast enough.

Maybe my period was coming early. Or maybe it was that guy in the crowd the night before.

The stage lights had gone down just enough for me to see. Only for a moment or two. Blinking against the glare. Blinking against the white heat. It had just been a moment. A chance glance. A pause between the numbers. A moment to breathe and catch my breath. And it had all gone wrong.

Because I'd locked eyes with a man in the audience. Instead of catching my breath, I lost it. Instead of a reprieve from the glare, from the heat, his gaze blinded me even more, made sweat drip down my bare back. Instead of it being just a moment, there and gone, it was a memory. It lingered. *He* lingered.

I couldn't help but wonder about him. Wonder what it would be like if he came down the stairs instead of Fitz. Wonder who I would be with him. Wonder if I might even be me.

It wasn't really Fitz's fault that I blew up at him. We'd done this enough times out at the casinos that he thought I liked it. Thought we were having fun. Thought there was nothing to blow up about.

I'd been leading him on just as much as myself. I'd been playing a role for him for so long that when my true self showed up, I'm sure he had a right to wonder what the hell got into me.

I shouldn't have yelled at him. Barked at him. Lost my cool at him. But I was so caught up in the memory of that man from the audience. In the heat. In the glare.

I just couldn't take it. I just couldn't.

I lost it. I fucking lost it. Fitz came back for more money and his hand was at my elbow again and I just fucking lost it. I couldn't remember being that mad. That infuriated. That pissed at him. And me. And life. And whatever goddamn road had brought me to that point.

The whole fucking casino bar went silent when Fitz touched

my elbow and I squeezed my eyes shut and shouted way too loud, "Goddammit, no! No more. No fucking more! No. No. NO!"

I opened my eyes and turned to tell Fitz exactly where I thought he should go and there was that heat again. That glare on my burning red cheeks. Because it wasn't Fitz with his hand on my elbow. It wasn't Fitz sliding into the bar stool beside me. Fitz was nowhere in sight.

There was just *him*.

6

MASON

hen...

THE FIRST TIME I saw her had been in an explosion of lights. Lights so bright that they blinded me. Lights I had to shield my eyes against.

I saw her there on the stage. Feathers extending from behind her like Venus's clamshell. Sequins on her face like dazzling, sunlit scales. Tangled, wild hair caught up with tinsel like she'd been dragged up from some distant sea. Maybe halfway across the world. Maybe from halfway across the universe.

The second time I saw her was in another explosion. An explosion of words. A violent, frustrated, end-of-her-rope explosion. Eyes screwed up tight like she was strangling someone. Or coming. Fists clenched like there was a dying pulse against her fingertips. Or a racing one. An erratically beating one. One that was going to explode itself. Her voice shouting like it was only her and me. No one else. Like there had never been anyone else.

I didn't know why she was exploding. Why she was yelling. Why she felt that everything that had been pent up inside of her had to escape then, right in that very moment. All I knew was that I was in love.

Whoever she was, this woman I had seen only twice. This woman who I'd never uttered a single word to except maybe to utter in the theatre under my breath, "She'll be the death of me."

This woman who I couldn't even be sure had truly laid eyes on me. The first time blocked by the glare of the stage lights. The second time blocked by her rage and fury. This woman who lived life violently. Thrived in explosions. Dazzled in them. Attracted them to her like a magnet. This woman who I knew, just *knew*, had to be mine.

The woman stopped screaming with this delicious heavy pant. It made me think of the early hours of the morning. It made me think of sweat-soaked sheets. It made me think of gritting my teeth to try to stave off coming for just a minute or two more. Just a minute or two more.

The woman sagged in her bar stool like she'd found her release. Like she was about to fall atop me. Breasts slick. Heart struggling to return to a semblance of normal beating. Fingers slipping into the hair at the nape of my neck. The woman opened her eyes like she knew exactly who would be there at her elbow. The dynamite to her explosion. The kindling to her fire.

Her surprise aroused me more than I could say. The slight widening of her seductive, cat-like eyes. The parting of her pillowy lips. The small exhale like my thumb had just brushed across her erect nipple under that skin-tight latex.

"Oh," was the first word she gasped at me.

I imagined a thousand "ohs". Each different. Each beautiful. Each worthy of making me collapse to my knees in front of her.

"Oh" when I wrapped my arms around her at the kitchen sink. "Oh" when I lifted her and put her on the counter. "Oh" when I lowered myself between her legs as the pasta water boiled over. "Oh" when she felt my tongue on her throat. On her navel. On her clit.

"Oh" when we made the bedframe rattle. "Oh, oh, oh" when I fucked her hard enough to drive the posts through the wall. "Oh" just before we both laughed because there was no way we were getting our security deposit back at that point.

A life of "ohs". A world of "ohs". A future of "ohs".

Her and me. This woman who so far had said only one word to me. And that one word more of a sound than anything else. A delicious, beautiful, irresistible sound.

"I thought you were someone else," the woman said before turning away and returning those lips to the straw of her mojito.

She didn't apologise. Didn't invite me to sit. Didn't acknowledge me any further. I was not the man (sure an assumption, but one I was fairly certain making) she had meant to yell at in a very public place. Despite realising her mistake, there was still... tension in the way she sat. In the way she drank with her fingers gripping her glass. The way her narrowed eyes darted quickly toward me and away from me.

"Are you mad at me?" I asked, holding back laughter from my lips.

The woman flipped her long honey-coloured hair from her shoulder and glared at me in the mirror at the back of the bar.

"Yes," she said and then, "No."

I drummed my fingers on the polished countertop. "But yes?"

This drew the woman's face toward me. She tucked her hair behind her ear and studied my face. I could see in the way she was looking at me that it wasn't to see me for the first time. It was like she was checking something. Checking against something. Like I'd somehow existed in her mind and she was comparing the images. The me of her head. The me of real life. Probably too close.

Only then did she pull her elbow away from my hand. Like she'd only just realised my fingers were still on her bare skin.

Had she liked my touch? Or was it somehow already so familiar to her that she'd not thought to pull away? Like a lover's chest against your back at night. Night after night.

"Yes," she said irritably, again returning to her drink.

Her straw slurped. Before she could raise her hand, I caught the bartender's attention and ordered her another. A whiskey for me. Anything Irish, I told him.

"Bit of a cliche, no?" the woman grumbled at me, her eyes darting toward me in the mirror.

"When it's good, it's good," I said with a shrug and a smile as I lowered myself into the bar stool beside her.

The woman looked at my reflection. "No, I mean inviting yourself to drink with a woman who clearly wants nothing to do with you."

"What can I say," I told her, "I'm curious."

She didn't wait to cheers with me before hunching over her fresh mojito.

"Curious about what?" she said a moment later, almost too low for me to hear it.

"Why it is that you don't know me from Adam, why it is that I clearly wasn't the intended recipient of your little...explosion—"

The woman snorted.

"—and yet everything about you makes me feel like you know every little deep, dark secret about me, like I was exactly who you meant to—"

"Explode at?" she finished for me, turning her face and levelling her eyes on me.

I grinned. This just seemed to piss her off.

"If I tell you, will you leave me alone?" she asked.

"I think I'd rather you not tell me then."

She looked surprised. I scooted closer despite the obvious disdain written across her face when I did so.

"The way I see it," I said, "is that you're like this burning fire right now. And well, I sort of like the heat. I don't know what's fuelled it, sure, but I like it. The way I see it, you're offering to give me the answer and then send me into the cold. I'd rather have the heat and the mystery."

The corners of the woman's lips had begun to curl up. Almost imperceptibly. But I was looking for it. Wanting it.

I sipped at my whiskey and then added, "So, if you don't mind, I'd prefer that you don't tell me what's gotten you so angry."

The woman's finger circled playfully around the rim of her glass. "Now I want to tell you."

"Not good." I shook my head.

"Not good?" she repeated, arching a dark eyebrow.

"Not at all," I told her, leaning in conspiratorially. She eyed me warily but did not move away. "Because what you want and what I want are now at odds with one another. Now we're basically in a war with one another."

The woman grinned. I watched her lips as she formed the softly spoken word, "And?"

My hand came to her knee. She did not push me away. Like she liked it. Or like it was so familiar to her that she didn't even think to push me away.

"And I'm quite afraid I'll win," I whispered to her.

The woman's bright, clever eyes bounced between mine.

"I'm angry that you're real," she said.

"That I'm real?"

"That you're real," she said, grabbing ahold of my thigh. Far enough up that I couldn't misinterpret. Low enough down that I couldn't keep myself from squirming.

"I saw you in the crowd at the show last night and— It was only for a second, but I saw you. I see dozens of faces a night—just for a second—but I *saw* you. You stayed with me like a flash of light that stays on the inside of your eyelids."

The woman's fingers curled in the material of my pants. Tightening. Squeezing. Her eyes did not leave mine.

"And I thought about you. I thought about you being with me. About you kicking my asshole boyfriend to the curb. He thinks he's Clyde. He thinks I'm Bonnie. He thinks he's robbing the strip, but really he's just robbing me. When he came down the stairs tonight, I thought about you coming down the stairs instead. I thought about you being different. I thought about me being different."

The woman sighed and removed her hand from my thigh. I immediately missed its warmth. Its pressure. The blood it was sending straight to my cock.

There was a sudden flash of sadness in her eyes as she took my whiskey and downed it in one go. Tipping it back. Letting the heat roll down the back of her throat. I watched her as she slammed the glass back on the bar. As she leaned back. As she stared up at the ceiling.

"It ruins everything if you're real," she muttered. "And that's why I'm mad at you. That's why I wish you never came over here. That why I'm going to leave."

She stood.

I caught her by the wrist. Her eyes flashed like daggers, but I met her violent gaze undisturbed. Unfazed. Unafraid.

"Let me go," she hissed.

I knew she'd scream again. I knew she'd have no qualms about making another scene. I knew that if she truly wanted me to let go that she would get exactly that. Noisily. Messily. Probably law involving-ly...

"You said he thinks he's Clyde," I said.

It was enough to catch her off guard. Maybe she was expecting a "Don't go." A "But I don't even know your name." Maybe she didn't know me as well as she thought in that pretty little head of hers.

"Well?" I pressed when she just stared at me in half angry, half trying-to-be-angry silence.

"Yes," she said.

She spit the word out at me almost spitefully.

"And that makes you his Bonnie."

"I already told you."

"Who do you want to be?" I asked.

I could feel her pulse beneath my thumb. Feel it pounding against me.

"That's a stupid question," she said, trying to tug away. Or at least trying to want to try and tug away.

"You don't want to be Bonnie," I said, holding her in place. "You don't want to play this silly little role with this silly little man."

She glared at me.

"And you said you hate me because I'm real, because if I'm real I can't be what you imagined in your mind when you saw me watching you last night," I said, my words quicker than I intended. More desperate than I ever would have wanted. "But what if I wasn't real? What if I could be exactly who you wanted when you thought of me? What if I could see you exactly the way you wanted me to see you when you thought of me walking down those stairs?"

The noise of the bar seemed to fade away. The music. The drone of the crowd. The clinging and clanging from the distant slot machines. All I could feel was the woman's pulse against my thumb. Loud like rapids. Roaring. All I could hear was her breathing, almost panting, her breath hitching.

She remained half pulled away from me. Half ready to leave. Half wanting to turn away from me and never lay eyes on me ever again. I'd go back to Ireland. To the place I'd called home until I saw her up there on stage. She'd go back to being Bonnie, whoever the fuck Bonnie was. Half ready to leave us both without homes. Both without identities. Both without knowing who or what the fuck we even were.

She licked her lips. I watched her tongue slide over the high ridges I longed to climb with my own tongue. To trace with my dick as she looked up at me with those eyes. Those damn eyes.

"How do you want me to see you?" I asked. I begged. I fucking *begged*.

She hesitated. Studied me in that strange way again. Like there was nothing at all to study. Like she already had me memorised.

She stepped closer. And closer still. Stepped close enough that her thigh was against my thigh. Her shoulder was against my shoulder. Her lips were just inches from my lips. She bit that lip. That lip that was just inches away from mine.

"Like this," she said, her voice low. Thick. Syrupy.

"Like this?" I echoed back. Stupidly. Dumbly. It was all I could manage with her so close.

She twisted her hand around in my now loose grip so that it was she holding onto me. Her fingers intertwined with mine, her touch sending electricity up my arm. I inhaled sharply.

"I want to be seen just the way you're seeing me right now… I want to try that."

"How do I see you?" I asked, voice barely a whisper.

The woman smiled. She leaned in closer than I thought was possible. Her breath was hot against my ear.

"Like I'm beautiful. Like I'm real."

It was she who tugged at me this time. Tugged me away from the bar. A couple twenties thrown over her shoulder like pennies into a wishing well. Tugged me toward the neon glow of the emergency exit. Toward the night filled with flashing lights and none flashing brighter than her.

We were in a bar. And then we were in each other's arms. And it was as if there had never been a bar at all. Never anything but us.

7

RACHEL

ow...

We were in a bar. A fucking bar of all places. A fucking bar!

"I don't need a drink," I growled, trying to tug my arm free from Mason's hand. "I just need you to sign these papers."

It was stupid of me to come to Dublin. I knew that now.

In my head everything had been different. I'd find Mason at the tattoo shop, at the shop I dreamed up. But that he created.

I'd walk in and he'd be there with a notepad across his knees. Drawing like he once drew me. Like he once drew on me. He'd lift his face and our eyes would meet and I'd know that I made the right decision. The right choice. Flying across an ocean. Lying to Tim. Seeing if there was still something. Seeing if maybe not everything had been lost.

Mason would walk over to me. Slowly. And then quickly. So quickly. I'd be in his arms. My mouth against his. We'd grab at each other's clothes. Trying to get fistfuls. Fistfuls of one another. Because I'd made the right decision. The right choice.

Instead I arrived at Dublin Ink, stood at the base of the stairs and watched the man I was married to carry a half-naked chick down the stairs who was shouting at the top of her lungs exactly who Mason was. Had always been. Would always be. A womaniser. A user. A fuck boy. A playboy. A *boy*. An immature boy who ran from commitment. Who played games. Who would never grow the fuck up. Ever.

In the end his eyes did meet mine. They sure as fuck did. And I saw alright. I saw this was a huge fucking mistake...

"Unless this bar also sells pens, I don't see what in God's name we are doing here," I shouted as Mason tugged me roughly toward the bar. "All I need is your goddamn signature, you asshole."

It was some shithole bar like all the other shithole bars all over the world. There was a sign, as Mason had bundled me inside, that said "The Jar". It wasn't like reading the name of some shithole bar was high up on my priority list. The signature of some shithole person on my goddamn divorce papers was the only thing I truly cared about.

The bar stool screeched against the sticky, peanut-shell covered floor as Mason yanked it back and pushed me unceremoniously into it. The place was nearly empty given that it wasn't even noon on a goddamn Wednesday. The only light was from the window, half covered in grime, half covered in band stickers, probably shitty, shitty band stickers, too.

I slapped the divorce papers on the counter and they immediately soaked up some liquid from the night before. Beer probably. Beer hopefully.

"It's really nice to see you, too, Rachel," Mason said, slouched over in the bar stool next to me. "You're looking great. Yes, yes, thank you. I'm looking great as well, I appreciate you saying that."

I ignored him as I rooted around in my purse.

"You say we're married then?" he continued. "You say, calmly, of course, and politely, of course, that we got hitched all those years ago? That we're bound in blissful matrimony? That we're bound in the eyes of God and the church and whatever witness was present at this love ceremony of ours?"

My words hadn't been quite so poetic. Mason had come down the stairs. Or halfway down the stairs really since he froze when he saw me. Some woman's ass against his cheek. Some woman's heels kicking against his cock.

I'd said, "Hello, Mason. I want a fucking divorce."

That's what I'd said. That's what I'd said before finding the folder. Jamming it up toward him, frozen there on the stairs. That's what I'd said before I truly freaked the fuck out.

"Sign it," was what I said as Mason put that random woman down. "Sign it," as he smiled at his co-workers, a tiny girl and a monstrous man. Both confused. Both concerned. Neither uttering a single word.

"Sign it," I said as Mason tried to put his arm around me and said, "Let's go talk, eh?" "Sign it!" was what I shouted as he ushered me out the door, tugging on a pair of sneakers on the way out.

"Sign it, sign it, sign it!" was what I yelled over the traffic as he pushed me down the sidewalk muttering, "Today of all fucking days..."

Half the contents of my purse was scattered across the dirty bar top before I realised that I hadn't brought a pen for Mason to sign with. Maybe that had been the jet lag. Maybe I was so focused on remembering all the documents that it was simply an oversight.

Or maybe I'd done that stupid thing where I got a little play stuck in my head and purposefully left the pen on the hotel desk. A role for me: the one he left, but never forgot. A role for him: the idiot who was getting a second chance. The ending:

there was no need for a pen. Because we still loved each other. Because we'd always loved each other. Because we could make it work. We could. This time we could...

"So tell me," Mason said, leaning over the bar to grab a bottle of Jameson whiskey, "how was your flight?"

"I don't want a drink," I told him.

"I need a drink," he said.

Just as he was rummaging around for a glass, a man came out from the back office of the bar. Attractive, tall, like an Irish Thor. He seemed surprised to see anyone there so early.

"I usually do that part, you know," he said as he nodded at the bottle in front of Mason.

"Noah," Mason said, sinking back into his stool to drag his fingers wearily through his hair, "this is Rachel..."

Noah set two shot glasses in front of us. "What's the craic, Rachel?"

"...my wife."

Noah's eyebrows disappeared into his wavy blond hair. "Oh. Right." He took the shot glasses back and replaced them with full-sized glasses.

I pushed mine away and exhaled irritably.

"Well, then," Noah said awkwardly in the heavy silence, "I think I'll just...hmm, that sounds like the, er, phone in the office? I better go get it. It's probably Aubrey or my accountant... or someone who needs me for a very long time."

Noah disappeared back through the door he came from. Seconds later there came a blaring of Irish music that made my nails dig into my palms.

Mason poured himself a drink, a full four fingers. He was about to pour one for me when I pushed the bottle away. Whiskey sloshed onto the divorce papers and I cursed. Mason didn't seem to give a damn as I flapped the wet papers over the edge of the bar.

"Mason, we don't need to make this complicated," I said and then added after glancing over at him, "or difficult."

"You should have had that drink," he muttered.

"All I need is your signature," I told him.

I didn't tell him that I didn't drink whiskey anymore. Not since Vegas.

"Today isn't really a great day for me," Mason said.

I rolled my eyes. Like it was a great day for me?

"Then let me make it better," I tried. "Sign these papers and I'll leave you all alone. Then you can get back to whatever it was —*who*ever it was—that you planned on doing today."

Mason finished his drink and poured another. He poured slowly. Not rushed at all. I realised that my toe was tapping on the footrest of the bar stool. Being angry with Mason had distracted me. Given me a shot of adrenaline. Numbed me almost.

But now I was coming down. Now I was faced with reality. I was there. On a bar stool. Next to Mason. The man I'd loved. The man I thought I'd spend my life with. The man who I'd apparently married.

I tried to remember that woman's ass. The one that had been against Mason's cheek. I tried to remember it and hold onto it. In my mind, I tried to think of it naked. Of Mason's hand on it. Of his fingers digging into its soft flesh.

I tried to remember my anger. My hurt. I tried to hold onto it. That adrenaline. That numbing rush.

But the bar was so silent. It was too obvious that it was just him and me. And all I could remember was that bar in Vegas. His fingers around my wrist. His words on my heart. His eyes on mine.

"Can't you just sign the damn papers, Mason?" I asked, my voice suddenly dry. My throat tight.

Mason was running his finger along the lip of his glass.

"No good."

I scoffed. But it was just an act. I no longer had the indignation for it. The annoyance for it. It sounded hollow even to my own ears. An act. And not a good one.

"What do you mean 'no good'?"

"It seems to be that you want to bother me with signing and I want to be bothered with drinking and those two things are opposed to one another."

"So we're at war then?" I said, remembering a different bar. A different time.

Mason's eyes were on me in the mirror behind the bar. This was one was dirtier. Smokier. Smudged and covered in hasty rag streaks. But his eyes cut through it all. Cut through right to me. He smiled at me in the mirror.

"You think you'll win?" I said to him.

His eyes on me were driving me crazier. It was making that anger, so bright and red and hot just seconds ago, feel like dying embers I couldn't possibly hold onto. I wanted to jam the papers against his chest.

I also wanted him to jam me against his chest. Against the bar. To sign his name, but not on the papers. On me, with his tongue.

"I think I'll take that drink," I said, swallowing heavily.

Mason grinned and poured me two fingers of whiskey. Not enough, I was sure. Not nearly enough.

8

MASON

hen...

"YOU CALL THAT TWO FINGERS!" I shouted at the bartender, who rolled his eyes and walked away to serve more drunk customers. "That's not enough! Not nearly enough."

I stood up on the stool, stretching out over the bar, when suddenly someone had me by the back of my pants and was dragging me back down. I flopped to my seat. I would have fallen right out of it if she hadn't caught me. Pulled my face to hers. Crashed her lips against mine. Laughter and whiskey and me on her lips.

Rachel. Her name was Rachel.

Or at least that's what she told me. I didn't care if it was her real name or not. I'd call her whatever she wanted to be called. Anything in the world.

Rachel nipped at my bottom lip playfully and then pulled away. Her glass collided with mine, whiskey spilling over. The glass was so wet that it nearly slipped from my fingers as I raised it to my lips.

"I think this is plenty," she said after the shot, collecting stray drops of whiskey around the edges of her glistening mouth before sucking it off her finger with an audible pop.

The string of Christmas lights hung above the bar sparkled in her eyes as she broke out into laughter. "Until the next shot, that is."

I couldn't have been with Rachel for more than a couple hours (Or was it a couple years? Had I known her my whole goddamn life?), but I never wanted to leave her side. Her energy was infectious. Her smile both innocent and wildly naughty. She was charming and loud and sweet and bold and greedy, greedy, greedy for life. She wanted all of it. All of it and more.

I wanted to give it to her. I wanted to be there with her when she took it. I wanted to drain the whole world for her. To help her run away with it all.

Okay, so I might have been a little drunk. There was the whiskey at the first bar. And there was the whiskey at the second bar. I was fairly sure this was the third bar. But it might have been the fourth. Definitely not the fifth. Absolutely certainly definitely not the fifth...

Okay, okay, so I might have been a little more than a little drunk. But Rachel had her legs draped over mine, her arm on the back of her bar stool, and she was looking at me with these hooded cat-eyes and a devilish grin and if anything at all can sober up a drunk man, it was his whole goddamn future staring at me. There. In the flesh. Everything he never knew he always wanted.

Does that make sense?

"Does that make sense?" Rachel was saying as she handed me a magically refilled glass.

Her toes were painted a bright lavender and they wiggled

atop my lap like we were casually at home on the couch. Five years into our relationship. Ten even. I shook my head and laughed.

"I'm sorry," I said, "I honestly wasn't listening."

Rachel chewed on a bar straw and wiggled her toes.

"I was saying that I think we're going to get married and fight about hand towels and shit in the grocery store one day and that I kind of can't wait," she said. "And I asked you if that made sense."

I tapped my glass against hers and smiled, saying, "I'm not sure anything has ever made more sense to me in my entire fucking life!"

There might have been another bar or two. There might have been some tripping down the sidewalk on the strip, arms draped over one another's shoulders like age-old friends. There might have been hands on chests and stumbling steps backwards and backs colliding with streetlamps or bus station posts or stop signs and sloppy, wet kisses as cars whipped by, horns laid on loud and heavy. There might have been intense eye contact, stupid promises, slurred vows. There might have been laughing and singing and making fun of each other's accents. And then there might have been one more bar after all that. Or two.

There was definitely a Denny's.

On the table in the booth there were two massive cups of black coffee, two platters of pancakes dripping with maple syrup, a plate with crispy bacon, scrambled eggs, and sausages, a pot of more maple syrup (why?), more varieties of hot sauce than I even knew existed, and a host of condiments like mustard and ketchup and honey and green salsa and God knows what else. All of that didn't stop Rachel. I was fairly certain that nothing would have stopped Rachel.

That's why I loved her. Loved her more than I had loved

anyone else. Loved her like I didn't even think I was capable of loving.

Love. You might think that sounds ridiculous. Loving someone after a few hours. Loving someone after a few drinks. Or even more ridiculous, "loving" someone after a *lot* of drinks.

But you didn't see the way that Rachel hopped up onto her side of the booth after darting over to the jukebox. How she stepped up onto the table like it was the grand stage at the Bellagio. How she ignored the shouts from our waitress, "Hey, hey, *hey*!", ignored the clattering of the cups and plates and jars of hot sauce, how she ignored everyone else in that Denny's, everyone else on that flashing neon street, everyone else in the whole damn world except for me.

Rachel stood tall above me and gave me a wicked wink before closing her eyes as the music began. She swept her hands down low and then raised them up, up, up. She sang along and danced. She got dirty looks from the other customers and threats from the waitress and catcalls from out on the sidewalk, but she didn't hear any of it, see any of it. She was dancing. Dancing for me.

She saw only my eyes on her. She saw only my mouth stupidly open. My arms limp at my sides like I no longer had any use for them. My head shaking slowly side to side because I couldn't believe that I'd found her.

Rachel saw me fall in love. I was sure of it. Sure of it from the way she smiled down at me as she danced. Like she knew. Like she'd always known. She saw my heart open to her. Unfold for her. Break into a million pieces for her.

Rachel danced up there on that table and I sat below her on that red vinyl booth and she saw me imagine our lives together. Our future together. She wiggled her hips and she saw me imagining the words I'd say to her when I proposed. She shouted the lyrics at the top of her lungs and she saw me imagining the dress she'd wear as she walked down the aisle toward me. She kicked her long, tanned legs, one and then the other, and she saw me imagining the children we'd have together. The colour of their eyes. The shape of their tiny lips. The texture of their delicate curls.

I was drunk and she was drunk and it was obvious to everyone around us. They would have called us fools. Idiots. They would have said what we had couldn't possibly be real. Be true. They would say this is what annulments are for: people who rush in when they have no business at all rushing in. People who can't see past the alcohol. People who are just pretending for a night or two.

But they didn't see Rachel looking down at them as she danced her burlesque dance on the table. They didn't see me looking at her as I watched, transfixed, hypnotised, struck dumb by dumb, dumb love.

They didn't know. They didn't know like we knew.

The song ended and the manager told us the police were on their way. A few customers gave a few confused claps, but I just smiled and stared at Rachel. She swept into a low bow. Her face was there just above mine. Her lips sticky with maple syrup. Her cheeks bright. Her eyes catching the neon lights from outside.

"Well?" she asked. "What did you think?"

I was silent for a moment, the chaos of the restaurant and the busy strip outside disappearing for a moment as I stared into her eyes and she stared into mine. At first I think she meant the question simply. What did I think of her dance? But the longer our eyes remained locked on one another, it became more and more clear that the question was growing.

Her in her sweet little curtsey up on the table. Me at the edge of the booth with my heart leaping up toward her. The question hung between us. Her eyes searched mine and mine hers.

"Well," I said at last because the question had become everything, a gap between us that I wanted to cross. "I think I love you."

Rachel's sharp inhale was the last thing that was in silence. I grabbed her round the waist and pulled her into my lap. She yelped gleefully and all the noise came crashing back in. The waitress's bellowing. The manager's angry threats. The customers all laughing or cheering or returning to their own drunken late-night antics. The cars out on the street, the pedestrians stumbling down the sidewalk, the music pounding from nightclubs. The rattle of the dishes as Rachel's foot caught the side of one of the coffee cups and sent it crashing.

There was noise and life and Rachel in my arms, smiling up at me. Laughing wildly. Kicking her feet and draping her arms around my neck and pulling me into a kiss.

The coffee spilled and dripped off the table onto the floor, but I didn't care.

Because I was in love. I was sure that I always would be. Then and forever.

9

RACHEL

ow...

COFFEE SLOSHED over the edge of the cup. The waitress who set them down hadn't exactly been the pinnacle of fine service. She hadn't tried to hide at all that she was pissed about having to work the late shift again at the BoBos Burgers (a funny name for a burger joint until you were told *Bo* was Gaelic for cow), a Dublin institution on Wexford St that stayed open late. The waitress's loud sigh was meant to be heard. Meant to be interpreted exactly as: fuck you. Fuck your drunken selves. If you fuck with me and my peace and my magazines, I will fuck. you. up.

As she walked away, I eyed her warily as I slumped in the booth across from Mason. Arms crossed petulantly across my chest. Toes tapping on the sticky floors beneath the table.

"A wonderful country," I grumbled. "Really just a lovely place. With lovely people."

Mason and I had been talking (and drinking) all day long. It was now dark. Probably somewhere around midnight. My phone was long dead. My vision long past being capable of focusing on the little clock on the wall across the diner. My sense of time and place so fucked up that I guessed it was midnight, midnight later that night, but it could very well have been midnight ten years in the future. Or ten years in the past.

I'm not sure Mason and I had really gotten anywhere in our long, antagonistic discussions except for wasted. Very wasted. My head buzzed. Bitter laughter came easily to my lips like bubbles to the top of a glass of champagne.

"Tell me something," Mason said, dragging his finger through the spilled coffee.

I'd told him everything already. Everything that he needed to know at least. We were married. I didn't want to be married. He needed to put his signature here, here and here. What else was there to know?

To know why electricity still snapped between us so we were forced to avoid each other's eyes most of the night?

To know why every glance at him brought me back to Vegas? To his hands all over my body? To the way he made me feel? Alive. Free. *Me.*

To know why after all this time we had been thrown back together after we'd been ripped apart? After *he* ripped us apart?

I don't think either of us wanted to know any of that. I don't think it was smart, asking those questions. I don't think it was safe, looking each other straight in the face and answering those questions.

I slurped at the coffee like it could sober me up. Like sobering up would give me clarity. Like I wasn't already ready to leave that burger joint and find another bar. Another drink. Another shot of whiskey. Another chance to go back. To be back.

"Tell you what?" I said, probably slurring. Definitely not

caring.

It was kind of nice actually. With Tim I had to watch what I said. How I said it. When I said it. Decorum was important, not feeling. I had my role to play. Innocent. Sweet. Someone, something to be saved. It was kind of nice to curse at Mason. To grumble and complain and annoy Mason. To be hurt and confused and loud and filthy. To be honest.

"Look, does this place sell beer?" I asked before Mason could answer, craning over my shoulder to spy the waitress and her "don't fuck with me" eyes. "Or something stronger? Anything stronger?"

"Tell me something," Mason repeated, still playing with the mess on the table.

"You already said that."

"Tell me how you found out," he said.

I was sober enough to realise that I'd walked into a trap. And drunk enough to not really know how in the hell to get out of it.

Mason's eyes darted up to mine and I saw: he knew there was an answer there. Maybe an answer he'd been avoiding since the very moment I told him that we'd been married this whole time. Maybe an answer he feared. Maybe an answer he didn't really want to hear. An answer the whiskey made him want to hear. Or stupid enough to hear.

A trap, a trap, my mind was shouting. *No way out, no way out*, my heart was pounding.

"How did I...?" I asked stupidly, buying time even though it was pointless.

There was only one reason why someone would find out that they were secretly and unexpectedly married. It was, of course, the only reason I found out: I was trying to marry someone else.

I knew this. But did Mason? Was that why he'd waited so long to ask? Was that why he'd asked it with just a dart of the eyes at me? Was that why he wasn't looking at me any longer, but circling his finger round and round in the spilled coffee which was dripping now off the edge of the table?

"How did you find out that we were married," Mason answered. Softly. Almost sadly.

His eyes darted again to mine when I remained silent. Silent too long. The answer hanging there between us. The answer I didn't want to speak. The answer it seemed Mason didn't want to hear.

But it was stupid, wasn't it? It was silly. I should just come out and say it: *I'm engaged to someone else, Mason. He provides for me. He's there for me. He wants to marry me. His name is Tim.* JoJo's voice came into my head as I stared across the booth at Mason, *And you love him...right?* Why didn't I just say it? Why couldn't I just say it? I love Tim, Mason. I love the man I am engaged to be married to. I love him and I want to marry him and that is how I found out that we were, all this time, all this long time, tied to one another.

The dripping coffee marked out the passing seconds which grew longer and slower.

Shit. I didn't want to tell Mason the truth. I didn't want him to know that I was engaged. That this was how I found out, in the process of marrying someone else.

"That's a stupid question," I said, because I was angry. Angry at myself. Angry at the situation. Angry that I didn't have a way out. "That's a really fucking stupid question, Mason."

This made him laugh. Angrily. Bitterly. Drunkenly. I wasn't sure. He laughed and he looked up at me and he crossed his own arms petulantly across his chest.

"Yeah?" he said in that Irish accent that undid me. "Yeah, and why is that, Rachel?"

"Because it is," I said.

I sounded stupid. Didn't we all when we were desperate?

When we were cornered?

"Were you always this immature?" Mason asked, laughing again, which made me want to lunge across the table and throttle him.

"Did you always ask such stupid questions?" I answered.

"Tell me why it's a stupid question," Mason said. "How about you do that, Rachel? Tell me why it's a stupid question. *Prove* to me it's a stupid question."

He knew. I was sure of it. From the way he was looking at me. The diner was silent except for the drip, drip, drip of the coffee.

I could hear him over the silence. I could hear his accusations. His indignation. His stupid hurt which wasn't fair at all. At fucking all. *He* destroyed what we had. Not me. So why did I fucking care? Why did I care if he knew?

Why did I want so fucking much for him not to know?

My voice was raised as I said, "Because it's obvious."

"It's obvious?"

Mason's voice was raised now, too. The waitress lowered her eyes at us over the top of her glasses but did not move from her place behind the counter. There was no one else in the place. No one to hear us yell but each other.

"Yeah!" I shouted.

"Yeah?" he shouted back.

He and I both stood up at the same time, knees knocking against the table. The coffee cups tipped over and coffee went everywhere.

"Hey!" the waitress shouted, and it wasn't an Irish accent that I heard but an American one. The street outside the diner wasn't dark but dazzling with a rainbow of flashing lights. Mason wasn't glaring across at me with a heaving chest but smiling up at me, his eyes dazzling not with that rainbow of flashing lights but with me.

"Why?" Mason shouted. "Why is it so stupid to ask a simple question. A simple question, Rachel."

"Because it is!" I shouted back, fists balled angrily at my sides.

"How did you find out, Rachel?"

No longer yelling. And that terrified me.

My mind searched and searched for another explanation. For a way that I would have found out that about the marriage certificate that didn't involve a diamond ring, a lowered knee, a bottle of the most expensive champagne money could buy. My cheeks grew red because I was getting angrier. Angrier because I was getting more and more desperate. Angrier because I didn't quite understand why I was so desperate. Why I couldn't just tell him the truth.

"Goddammit," I cursed, tugging at my hair.

"Just tell me," Mason said, and I was more desperate because he wasn't yelling.

I wanted him to yell. I wanted him to scream. It was stupid and pathetic, but I didn't want him to give up on me. On us. Fuck, fuck, *fuck*, my mind screamed.

"Rachel," Mason said, and the way he said my name was familiar.

It took me back. To a time he had said it before. To a time when he said it and I was certain that it was the first time in my life that someone had ever truly called me by my name.

"I remember," I said. Mostly to myself. Mostly under my own breath.

But Mason heard.

"What?" he asked.

Was it hope I heard? Or was it hope that I wished to hear?

I looked up at Mason like I was coming out of a daze. The answer was so obvious. So simple. I'd almost missed it. Almost completely missed it.

"It's a stupid question," I said, all my confidence and bravado surging back, "because I never 'found out'."

Mason stared at me warily. Mistrustfully maybe. I was sure he wanted to trust me. Almost sure.

"What are you saying?" he asked.

I flipped my hair over my shoulder and raised my chin. "Are you telling me that you don't remember our wedding?"

Mason hesitated a moment. Then he scoffed.

"Are you telling me you do?" he asked.

Again mistrust. Again hope. Or at least that's what I wanted to believe.

"Of course I remember getting married," I said. I *lied*. "How could I forget?"

The truth was I remembered nothing of any marriage ceremony, any marriage license or certificate or dress, any marriage vows or kiss or walk down the aisle. I remembered the sex. And I remembered the tattoo. One I was able to hide. The other still haunted me. And my dreams. And my happiness.

Mason stared at me a moment longer and then threw some bills on the messy table.

"I guess I owe you another round then," he said, eyeing me quickly over his shoulder. "Nobody should have to remember that."

I laughed because he was laughing.

"Yeah," I said as we left. "It was a real shit show alright."

Mason held the door for me. But as I went to step through, he blocked me. It meant I was close. Too close.

"You remember?" he whispered, his lips close. Too close.

I nodded. Throat too dry to speak. I had to lie. No, I didn't have to lie. I wanted to lie.

"Are you sure?" he asked.

I didn't dare breathe.

"Yes."

10

RACHEL

hen...

I TOOK Mason through the theatre back to my dressing room. I knew the way well, of course. I ran it every night before my show. Every night after. I could run it in the dark. Run it in towering heels. Run it with a million different people shouting for me.

But moving down that corridor with Mason, our mouths clashing, bodies ricocheting off the walls like pinballs, giggles and groans echoing down the hall, I felt like all those other times had been a charade. This was the real way. With Mason. With our hearts pounding in rhythm. With our needs rising up in us, as inescapable as the tides.

We tumbled into my dressing room, my legs wrapped around Mason's waist, my skirt lost somewhere in the hallway. The floor lamp in the corner cast a soft pink glow over the room. Mason didn't seem to notice as he yanked down my top, sending my breasts spilling out. "Fuck, your tits are perfect."

I didn't correct him. Didn't say that they weren't as perky without a bra. Didn't say that my nipples could be smaller, the skin tauter, not to mention my stretch marks and the freckles on my cleavage from too much time in the hot Nevada sun. Because in that moment, as he groaned into my cleavage, as he lapped at my nipples, they felt perfect. They *were* perfect.

Blinded by my breasts in his face, Mason ran us into a rack of boas in shades of rose and lavender and citrus. Knocked over racks of tulle dresses. He was wrecking the place. But I didn't care one bit. My giggle was lost in a groan as he gently bit my nipple, testing my limits.

He let out a low hum. "You like that, baby?" His rough Irish accent making my head spin.

"Harder," I begged in response.

This time, his growl came from the depths of his throat. He lowered his head again, licking and biting harder so that flashes of pain came like lightning in a storm of pleasure.

My big mirror reflected the two of us amongst it all. Amongst the sequins and glitter. Amongst the velvet and leather. Amongst the fishnet and the lace and the masks on silk strings. The sight of us sent a rush of heat through me.

Fuck, I needed him naked—now.

I slid my hands down his chest, revealing in the hard muscular plains, down the defined bumps of his abs, a new wave of need coursing through me as I followed the V down. Jesus Christ, this man was an Irish god. I slid my hand lower and found his thick hard length. My head spun. Lucky Irish. Lucky me.

I stroked at his length, wondering if um, *now* was too early to pull it out, drop to my knees and suck it.

"Not yet." He let out a groan as I opened his zipper and slid my hand in. Jesus Christ. He was smooth and hot and perfect in my hand. "Shite. I won't last long if you—"

I grinned against his mouth, dizzy with power, and kept stroking him.

He let out a feral growl, backing me up till my back collided with a wall covered with fluffy feather fans, knocking several of them off. He pinned my wrists above my head as I thrashed against him.

"Naughty girl. I said, 'Not yet'."

I fought against Mason, but he held me there, pinned against the wall. I could feel his hard cock as he pressed himself up against me. I let out a moan, desperate to feel him in my hand, my mouth, my aching pussy. Fuck, he could claim my ass if he wanted to. I wanted all of him.

In the dim light I could just make out his wicked smile as he pressed his lips to my ear.

"I think you need to be punished."

I stopped my struggling. Stopped my fighting. "Punished?"

His eyes flashed wickedly. "So you remember who's in charge..." He backed up, tugging his jacket off as he did, his eyes never leaving mine. "Don't move."

I felt the loss of him instantly and reached for him out of instinct.

"I said. *Don't. Move.*"

The force of his words was like a blow and I fell back against the wall.

He glared at the spot above my head. At the spot where he'd pinned my hands.

I lifted my hands automatically and placed them back above my head.

That earned me a half smile. "Good girl."

My knees shook as his praise caressed me like actual touch.

"I can be a good girl," I whispered.

His gaze took in my bare legs, my breasts fallen obscenely out of my top scrunched around my waist, clinging to the wall like a doll. He watched me, just out of reach, as he undid the buttons of his shirt and shrugged it off his shoulders, revealing a body like art. There were eagles, mermaids, wooden ships crashing against rocks, and a snake curling around a skull with roses for eyes, all in bold block colours. I wanted to lick each one. To see how he tasted.

He reached for his belt, the clinking noise sending shivers and a single bolt of fear down my spine.

"Wh-what are you going to do to me?" I asked.

He slid the belt out of the loops. "I promise it won't hur—" He broke off with a deep chuckle. "No, I can't promise that. I promise you'll like it."

He stepped up to me, the size of his shoulders, the sheer heat rolling off him crowded me. He slid the belt around my wrists, looping them around until he was able to belt it up, the leather cutting into my skin in such a glorious way. Then he stepped back to admire what he'd done.

I tried to lower my hands but—

I couldn't. They were stuck on something. I glanced up to find he'd hooked part of the belt into one of the hooks that once held up a fan. It was easy enough for me to lift the belt off. But I soon realised that it wasn't meant to restrain me, but to give me something to rest my arms against.

I sucked in a breath as he moved into my space again, his whiskey breath warming my forehead.

"Until I say so, you're going to do nothing but watch," he said, his voice thick, heavy. "You're not going to move. You're not going to touch me. You're not going to touch yourself. Not your clit. Not your perfect little nipples. You're not even going to bite into that bottom lip of yours..."

I whined as he sank his teeth into my bottom lip to make a point. Hissed as he sucked a nipple into his mouth before he sank to his knees. Moaned as he flicked his tongue across the wet lace of my thong.

Mason grabbed the thin waistband with his teeth and dragged my thong over my hips. I grabbed at the wall, my nails scratching at the plaster. I arched my back as I yearned for more. I looked down between my breasts to see Mason grinning around a mouthful of my thong. Before he let it drop to the ground around my ankles. I stood there practically naked, the cold lonely air like a cruel sting against my aching pussy.

"And you," he said, "are *not* going to come."

What?

The first lap of his tongue caressed my clit, causing my body to jerk like he'd electrocuted me.

"Spread them," he growled into my folds.

I stepped apart on shaking legs.

"Wider."

I did as he asked, my ankles threatening to give way as I stood as wide as I could in my stilettos.

"Good girl."

I was rewarded with him burying his face into my wetness. I moaned as I tilted my hips up to meet his tongue swirling over my clit.

"Oh, perfect girl. You're so needy," he muttered as he pushed a finger inside me. "So responsive."

He curled that finger around and pressed at that delicious spot inside me. My hips bucked as I felt my orgasm rushing up to me.

"God, yes, there," I moaned as he worked me right to the—

He pulled away, his finger coming out of my pussy with a wet sound.

"No," I whined.

I was so close. So fucking close. One touch. One lick. That's all I needed.

"I need you..." I groaned, as my legs shook. "Mason, I'm so close."

He lifted a wry eyebrow.

"Mason, please," I gasped, my head hitting hard against the wall as I shook my head violently from side to side. I clenched my core, ground my hips at the air, trying to push myself over. But I wouldn't. I couldn't. I needed *him*. Bastard.

"What did I say, Rachel?"

His eyes glittered with lust, with raw power, his hot breath like torture on my sensitive thighs. This giant tattooed Irishman might be kneeling before me, but I was completely under his control.

"Don't make me repeat my question."

"I-I," I sucked in a breath as our gazes locked. I swear his eyes darkened, "am to just watch."

"And?"

"And..." I squirmed before freezing, "I am not to move."

His eyes darkened. "And?"

I felt like crying. "I'm not to come."

"And what are you trying to do?"

Fuck.

"Come," I whispered.

"So what does that make you?"

"What?"

"What. Does. That. Make. You?"

I squeezed my eyes shut. "A... a naughty girl?"

"A very naughty girl. A very bad girl." The bastard grinned at me. "I don't think you've learned your lesson yet."

I knew...

He wasn't finished torturing me.

He pushed his face into my cunt, alternating between slow swirls with the tip of his tongue and languid flat-tongued licks. He pushed two fingers into me, working my g-spot with smooth strokes. It was too fucking slow. It was fucking not enough.

"Please," I moaned, I *begged*, "fuck me."

Put me out of my misery.

He chuckled and the vibrations caused a whole other sensation to wave through my core.

"When I fuck you, I'm not going to take you slow, bit by bit, inch by inch. 'Cause that's not what you want, is it?"

I shook my head, mumbling incoherently at this point.

"You want it hard. You want my whole cock, all at once."

"God, yes." It came out as a growl. A guttural sound from deep inside of me. It came out as a plea, a prayer, a begging down on my knees.

It came out like a gasp, like I was about to go under water. Like I was about to drown. I wanted to fucking drown in him.

And I did. I drowned.

Over and over, Mason bought me to the edge with his tongue, his lips, his fingers. He held me there, dancing me on the edge. Never letting me fall.

It was divine torture.

Beautiful punishment.

A lovely hell.

I don't know how long he did it for. I stopped counting how many times he got me so close. How many times I internally cursed at him for stopping just as I was about to fall.

Through my haze, I suddenly realised my cheeks were wet. I was crying. Sobbing. And Mason was licking my tears.

I wasn't against the wall anymore. Something soft was against my back. I was lying on the old velvet couch in my dressing room, my arms by my sides, the belt gone. Mason settled between my legs, his whole body covering me, making every single one of my cells buzz and ache, his erection flush against my pussy. God, he was so close. But I knew better than to lift my hips and try to take him inside me. I knew better than to move until he told me to.

"Beautiful girl," he muttered between licks. "Have you learned your lesson yet?"

"Yes," I mumbled as my body shook, knotted up with frustration, as my pussy ached.

He chuckled. "What did you learn?"

"T-that you're in charge."

"Good girl. And?"

"I do what you say."

"And who do you belong to?"

"You," I whispered.

"Louder."

"You," I tried again.

"Scream it. I want the fucking world to hear you."

"I belong to you," I screamed.

Without another word Mason thrust into me. I cried out at the size of him. The power of him. He was too much. Too big. Too all-consuming. Too much but not enough.

He didn't stop. Didn't hesitate as he fucked me hard. I clung to him as the pressure of him overtook me. He was all that existed. All I could feel. He was everywhere inside of me. All around me.

I should have known he was dangerous. That I'd given him the power to hurt me. To destroy me. But as Mason drove his hips into me, pushing him away was the last thing on my mind.

"Fuck, you feel so fucking good around my cock."

He sounded drugged, his deep voice growling in my ear. Like he couldn't, wouldn't stop as he drove his cock in and out of me. Such intoxicating friction. Such consuming fullness and delicious pressure.

"Such a good girl. My perfect girl."

My hair fanned wildly around me. Strands clung to the

sweat on my face. I could feel it trapped beneath my drenched back, soaking into the top still bunched around my waist. I felt wild. Feral. My nails dug into his muscled back, his wide shoulders, his rounded ass. His skin was slick with sweat and it seemed every time I found purchase, only to slip again. I was sure I was tearing his skin. Leaving long, angry red marks. Drawing blood even.

But for us it didn't matter. There was nothing in the world but our bodies clashing. Nothing but our demanding rhythm. Nothing but his mouth against my ear, muttering pretty obscenities that sent shivers up and down my spine.

"This tight little pussy is going to be the end of me."

Mason was grunting and I was screaming with the effort of holding my orgasm back. He didn't make it easy for me, fucking me somehow faster, somehow harder.

"Good girl."

He reached in between us, his thumb pressing on my clit.

"Come. Come so hard, you choke on my fucking name."

There was no name but his. No name before or after. No one had ever fucked me like he was fucking me. No one had ever held my body so tight. Had ever filled me so fully. Made my fingertips and my eyelids and my lips all buzz, all tingle, all hum like I was fucking high. Made me curse and adore him.

When I came, I screamed his name. I screamed it against his throat. Against his vein pumping hot blood toward his heart as each wave of pleasure slammed into me.

Again and again, I screamed until my throat was raw and I choked.

I collapsed, limp as a rag doll as Mason's rhythm grew irregular, erratic. The way he was looking down at me, all haze and hooded eyes, I knew he was close. Gripping his shoulders, I took him by surprise by heaving us over the side of the couch. He ended up on his back and I ended up on top of him. I barely felt my knees bruising against the floor.

I bucked my hips before he could question what the fuck had happened. My tits bounced as I fucked Mason as hard and fast and rough as he'd fucked me. So that *my* name was the only one. I fucked him so he'd remember. So he'd never forget.

With my nails digging into his chest beneath me, I hissed, "Your turn to choke."

When he came he screamed my name. Screamed it like I'd never heard it screamed. Like never before. I didn't know it then, but never again.

He screamed it until he choked.

11

MASON

Now...

I SANK against the couch and the world spun wildly around me.

The low lights of the bar expanded into starbursts that twisted like pinwheels as I turned my head. The last few stragglers before the inevitable last call all had at least two heads as they bent over cheap pints of beer or fingerprint-smudged shot glasses that had seen a refill or two too many. Not that I was judging. Like I said, my own world was spinning. In more ways than one.

I rolled my head to the right and narrowed my eyes at Rachel as she clumsily scratched at the label of her beer bottle. Her hair was tucked behind her ear so I could see the fullness of her cheek, the softness of her chin. In the dim light and in the drunkenness that was making it hard to focus, I saw the woman I fell in love with all those years ago. I saw her laughing. Saw her dragging me behind her to that theatre. Saw her switching on that lamp in her dressing room.

But no matter how hard I stared, eyes all squinted, vision all wobbly, I couldn't see her extending a hand toward mine. I couldn't see her saying "Yes" in a white dress. I couldn't see her in my arms as I carried her back down the aisle.

I wanted to remember that moment. I wanted to have it forever, like Rachel had. Or at least like Rachel said she had.

"Why now?" I asked over the low blare of the single saxophonist in the practically unlit corner.

On the couch beside me Rachel looked up, rather startled. She was just as wasted as I was. If not more. Had she forgotten that I was there? Was it that easy?

"What?" she said, a little too loudly.

She laughed a little. Hiccupped. One of us was going to make a mistake tonight. That was for damned sure.

"Why now?" I asked again.

When had my hand come to rest against her knee? When had she moved in so close that her sweet whiskey-stained breath blew around my neck? When had her lips become so swollen, so wet, so alluring as she looked up at me with wide eyes?

"Why now what?" she shouted (there was no need to shout).

I knew I should scoot over. Should take my hand from her knee. Look at anything, *anything* other than her lips.

But there was my shoulder leaning against hers. My hand shifting up her thigh. My gaze fixed, absolutely fixed on Rachel's mouth in the low light.

"Why a divorce now?" I asked. "If you've known that we were married all these years like you say, then why all of a sudden do you need a divorce? Want a divorce?"

Why not when we first woke up the next morning, whatever morning it was of that whirlwind week? Why not before she left forever? Why not any time at all if she knew where to find me? There was a stab of pain in my chest upon that realisation: she knew where to find me. All this time she knew. And she hadn't come looking. Not like I had.

So why was I still moving closer to her? Why was my body doing what my heart knew it shouldn't?

"I don't know," Rachel said, for a moment averting her eyes, scratching at the condensation-soaked label, bouncing her leg, the one against mine. "I didn't need one until now."

"What does that mean?"

Rachel licked her lips and looked back at me.

"I have a new role I'm up for," she said. "A kind of big new role."

"So?"

Rachel looked a little indignant. She roused herself slightly. Sat a little taller against the old leather cushions of the couch. Separated herself from me. Something that I wasn't able to do.

"*So*," she said, "it's not like I could go on being a showgirl in Vegas, you know? I always wanted more. I always had bigger dreams than that."

Bigger dreams than me. Was that what she was trying to say and unable to?

"And the girl who is hitched to some guy in Ireland, the result of a crazy, drunken weekend on the strip, is perfectly fine for the role of a burlesque dancer. But for this new role, this bigger role, this really fucking important role, well, he— *they* expect more."

I was feeling a little indignant myself. Or maybe I was just feeling defensive. Maybe I was too drunk to tell the difference.

"So, what? You're going to completely change for this role of yours? Erase all of who you are for it?" I said, scooting away myself this time. Crossing my arms. Getting angrier than I would have thought possible with this much alcohol in my veins. "That doesn't sound like you."

Rachel laughed.

"Doesn't sound like me?" she echoed, voice leaping an octave or two and drawing more than couple of gazes who were eager for some entertainment. "You don't know me."

The words were out of my mouth before I could stop them. Before I could realise how stupid they were. How ridiculous they were. How *dangerous* they were.

"I know you," I growled, "I fucking know you."

Rachel stared in shock at me. I cleared my throat and turned away, scratching at the back of my neck in embarrassment.

I heard Rachel shout at everyone who was watching, "Mind your own fucking business, you fucking loser shitheads!"

Then she said to me, smoothing her hands down her legs, "I'm different now. Quieter. Softer. Gentler... Sweeter."

I raised an eyebrow at her, because surely she couldn't fail to see the irony given what she'd just hollered out at strangers.

Rachel rolled her eyes and huffed. "It's *you*."

I raised my eyebrows. Seriously? *I* was the bad influence?

"I mean, it's the alcohol." Her eyes darted toward mine. "I—I'm not used to whiskey anymore."

"So I don't fit into this squeaky clean little image you need for this—for this big new role of yours."

Rachel hesitated. "Our marriage doesn't fit."

"Us together doesn't fit," I said bitterly.

"But you already knew that, didn't you?"

The way she was looking at me. All fire. All rage and fury. All barely held back violence. I wanted to tell her that we fit together like whiskey and cold nights, fog and mornings in bed, sex and more fucking sex. I wanted to tell her that she was wrong. I wanted to grab her face and kiss her and shake her and curse her out and send her away forever. Because she knew where I was. And she didn't come for me. She *chose* not to come for me.

"You need me then," I said.

"I most certainly do not," Rachel spluttered, cheeks flushing. "Not anymore. Not ever actually. I never needed you. Not once. Not ever. I—I do *not* need you. No. No. Nope. You know what? Fuck you, Mason. *Fuck* you."

Rachel was breathing heavily.

I let her steam for a minute or two before tapping my toe against her purse. The file folder with the divorce papers was sticking out of it.

She noticed it. "Oh. Well, yeah. I mean...if *that's* what you mean."

I drummed my fingertips against my knees and grinned.

"Now correct me if I'm wrong, Rachel," I said. "But you need me. Did you hear me over the saxophone? You *need* me."

Rachel fumed. But she fumed in silence.

"And if you're getting something out of this, this needing of me, then I think it's only fair that I get something in return. Wouldn't you agree?"

Rachel laughed and said, "What could you possibly want from me?"

Everything, I wanted to scream. *Fucking everything. Your heart, your soul, your warmth in my bed, your smiles over breakfast every fucking morning until forever.* Wasn't that what we wanted? Wasn't that what we'd always wanted?

Instead I shrugged casually and smiled charmingly. "Oh, I don't know. I'm sure we can figure something out. So that these big new important people who are giving you this big new important role don't find out who you really are. I'm sorry—who you *used* to be. Yeah, I think we can figure something out, babe. Don't you?"

Rachel narrowed her eyes suspiciously at me.

"You know," she said warily, "if I didn't know any better and maybe if I weren't so goddamn drunk right now, I'd almost say that this is beginning to sound like blackmail."

I chuckled with my hand on my belly.

"Goodness, no," I said, wiping away a fake tear from my eye. "Blackmail? What a wretched word!"

"What do you want, Mason?" Rachel asked, her tone no-bullshite.

Ah well, maybe it was time for me to get down to business as well.

"I want you to be my wife," I said. Voice even. Assured. Confident.

Rachel nearly spit out her beer.

"What the fuck are you talking about?" she said loudly. "Mason, I'm here for a *divorce*."

My hand was back on Rachel's knee. Patting gently as I shook my head. My hip was back against hers as I scooted in conspiratorially. Her lips were back in my vision as I watched them purse irritably.

"Come 'ere," I said softly, leaning in close so that she could hear me, "I don't know if you know this, but—well, of course you know this. You're my wife. You married me."

"Get on with it," Rachel hissed.

"As you, my wife, knows full well, I am a very charming guy," I explained, continuing, "A very handsome guy. Hot even, some would say. Would my wife say that, do you think?"

Rachel grumbled under her breath, "Fine."

"Fine, what?"

Rachel rolled her eyes. "You're charming."

"And funny."

"And funny."

"And hot."

"Goddammit, Mason—"

"And because I am so charming and so funny and so hot, I attract more than my fair share of the lovelier sex."

Rachel scowled. "I'm well aware from this morning."

I lifted a finger.

"Ah! And as evidenced this morning, you might also be aware that I sometimes have a difficult time saying, how shall we say, 'Adios' to these fine beauties come morning time."

Rachel glanced over at me. Suspicion all over her face.

"I don't see how I'm going to help you be a more efficient playboy, Mason," she said.

I clicked my tongue. "I am not a playboy."

This time Rachel did spit out her beer.

I continued, unperturbed, to say, "I am not a playboy, because I do not play. There are no games involved whatsoever. If anything I'm a businessman. A deal is settled upon. Terms clearly laid out. And I only proceed when both parties—well, let's just say all parties since sometimes it's more than just the two of us—have given verbal agreement."

"You're right," Rachel said, patting at the beer on her knee. At the beer on my hand on her knee. "You're not a playboy."

"Thank you."

"You're a psychopath."

I chuckled. "However, after the fun is had, the good times rolled, the party finished, occasionally I get a business partner or two that...let's see...that hopes to 'renegotiate'."

"I still don't see how any of that has to do with me."

I smiled my most winningest smile and nestled in closer to her. "What would you do, babe, if you awoke one morning in a funny, charming and handsome man's bed and the moment you go to ask about perhaps brunch in the park, an angry, infuriated, scorned and wronged wife comes barrelling through the bedroom door?"

Rachel leapt up out of my arms, away from the heat of my body, and off of the couch, and threw the rest of her beer in my face.

"Now, now, wifey!" I stood, towering over her, and grabbed her around the waist before she could leave.

Rachel jammed her fingers against my chest. "You must be out of your goddamn mind if you think that I am going to play pretend as some angry, wronged wife of yours."

"You're doing a pretty bang-on job of it right now."

Rachel's eyes burned as she looked up at me. We were so close that I could feel her heart pounding against mine.

"Sixty days," I said. "Sixty days and no one needs to know about your past...indiscretions."

"Past *mistakes*," Rachel said through gritted teeth. "You get one week."

"I'm looking to establish a reputation here," I replied before countering, "Six weeks."

"Two. But only because I care about *my* reputation."

I smiled down at her. Drummed my fingertips against my legs. "Five weeks."

"Three."

"A month."

Rachel hesitated. "A month?"

I nodded. "Thirty days."

Rachel bit her lip. "And then you sign the papers?"

"And then you land your big new role."

Rachel considered my offer for a moment. Then stuck out her hand. I pulled a key from my back pocket before slipping my hand into hers. We shook, but instead of letting her go I drew her in closer.

"There's a room at my place, second floor of Dublin Ink," I whispered. "It's the first door on the left."

Rachel's chest was heaving. Her breath was coming in short little pants.

"It's got the biggest bed in the place."

She tried to pull away, but I held her tight. Tighter.

"The springs are mostly gone," I continued in her ear, "The thing's noisy as hell. And good lord how it bangs against the wall."

Rachel's voice was tense. "Why are you telling me this?"

"Because," I said, making sure she kept hold of the key as I slipped my hand from hers.

Rachel's eyes were dilated as she finally looked back up at me. I almost felt a little bad. A part of me could almost believe that she wanted me. Wanted me like she once had.

"Because I need you to know which bedroom *not* to go in."

I patted her cheek and brushed past her shoulder. Walked away. Found the first woman at the bar.

And said hello to Miss Last Night.

12

RACHEL

Mason walked up to the woman at the bar so easily. I sat alone on the couch. Had it been that easy with me? In Vegas in that casino on that bar stool all those years ago. Had he walked up to me like he just walked up to her? Had the conversation come easily with me the way it was coming easily with her? Had my smiles been quick like hers? My laughter fast flowing like hers? Had I fallen for him without any protest at all the way I was watching her fall?

Had it been that easy for him? When it was me?

I was out of beer and Mason's hand was at the small of the woman's back. I wasn't sure which was worse. At least the beer situation I could fix. I could get up and stalk over to the bar. I could slam my fist down. Rattle glasses. Knock over bottles. I could shout out, "Give me a goddamn beer. Right now!" But what in God's name was I supposed to do about Mason's hand there at the small of the woman's back?

I couldn't get up and stalk over there. I couldn't push the woman away and take her place on the bar stool. I couldn't slip onto the seat and face Mason's amused eyes, his eyebrow arched to show he was intrigued. I couldn't tell him that I didn't want him to leave with anyone else but me. That I didn't want anyone else in his bed but me.

That I was his wife and I wanted to be his wife and I wanted him to fuck me like I was exactly that: *his* wife. *His* lover. *His* everything.

I couldn't do that.

I couldn't do the opposite either.

I'd had all night to fess up. I'd had more than enough liquid courage to tell the truth. More than enough "fuck it" juice. My lips should have been plenty slippery enough to slip up at one point or another.

But I hadn't.

And I couldn't.

I couldn't tell Mason that I had moved on. That I was with someone else. That the reason I knew we were married was because I was engaged to someone else. That the reason I needed a divorce now was that I. Was. Marrying. Someone. Else.

Like too many times in my life, I was stuck. Trapped. Caught between two worlds. Caught acting. Caught playing yet another role.

Because I couldn't— No, because I *wouldn't* tell Mason the truth. I was forced to play the role of wife. And not just wife. Because he didn't want me to be loving. Or caring. To listen to his fears at night. To caress his hair at the nape of his neck in the morning. To be with him in sickness and in health. To love and cherish. Now and forever more.

No, I was only to be the angry wife. The cheated-upon wife. The screaming, hair tearing, bitch-chasing-off wife.

There, right in front of me, was apparently the woman I would see in Mason's bed the next morning. I cringed as I imagined having to walk in there. To see her still naked with her arm draped across his chest. To know what they had done. To try to force out the images that played in my head of the two of them all night long.

To repeat this fucking act the next day with another woman. Another pair of tits. Another perky ass. Another set of hips wiggling against Mason's groin till she laid eyes on me. There in the doorway.

I went to drain the last of my beer before re-remembering that it was already gone. All already gone.

I watched as Mason's hand came to rest on the woman's knee as he ordered them shots. It was just moments ago that his hand had been on my knee. I could have shoved it away. I could have asked him to please not touch me, because I'm with another man. Or I could have intertwined my fingers with his. I could have guided his hand up. Closer to the warmth that burned between my legs. Closer to where I wanted him.

Instead I was sitting on the couch watching. Like an understudy stuck in the eaves. My lines wouldn't come till the morning. Till after the good stuff.

On the woman's body, Mason's hand went where I wanted his hand to go on me. The woman tensed. Drew her tongue across her lip.

I knew that tensing. That bolt of electricity that straightened the spine. I knew that thrill of knowing the night would be long and hot and *good*, toe-curling good. I knew that buzz that was surely already in her fingertips because Mason was pressing his lips to her ear. Whispering God knows what. Maybe whispering something he whispered once to me. Something that made me laugh the way she was laughing.

I loved him more than anything.

And I hated him, hated him, *hated* him more than anything in the fucking world. I wanted to tell him the truth. To hurt him. I also wanted him never to find out. For my big new role to be *his* wife. Not Tim's. Never Tim's.

I was conflicted. Conflicted over what I wanted. Conflicted over who I loved. Worst of all, I was conflicted over who *I* wanted to be.

But I did know one thing, on one thing there was no conflict, my heart, my body, and my mind were all on the same fucking page for once: it hurt like fucking hell to watch Mason lean down and kiss that woman.

From across the bar on that dingy little couch I could see Mason's lips moving against hers. They would be soft still, I was sure. They would press gently. Like the brush of the first warm breeze of spring. He wouldn't press harder even though she would want it. He would make her be the first one to dart her tongue against his. To slip her fingers around his neck and draw him in closer. To suck his bottom lip into her mouth. To scrape it against her teeth. To nip at the corners of his mouth.

Only then would he give her what she wanted and really kiss her. When she'd played her hand. When she'd laid herself bare. When her need and desire and arousal was more than obvious. When it was all she thought about. When it was his to do with as he damned well pleased.

Her fingers reached up toward Mason's neck. Just as I knew she would because I had done the same.

I turned away from the sight of them. I fumbled around in my purse for a while before I knew exactly what I was looking for. At first it was just a way to distract myself. To focus on something, anything else. Then my fingers grazed my phone and I realised Tim must be worried.

I hadn't texted him since arriving at the airport earlier that morning. Or was it already yesterday morning? I probably had a million texts from him. Dozens of calls. He must be losing his—

JoJo: hottie Irish dick pic pleeeeeez

. . .

THERE WAS ALSO a message from the wedding venue confirming the dates we'd pencilled in for the ceremony, and an automated message from my dentist, time for another cleaning.

But there were no messages from Tim. No calls. Just a calendar reminder about our dinner reservation in four weeks.

I was the kind of drunk where you have to squeeze one eye shut to type anything (also known as the kind of drunk where you definitely shouldn't be texting). With the help of autocorrect and several taps of the Back button I was able to type out something that I thought was mostly coherent.

ME: Good news darling. Got the role!

AS I HIT SEND, I grumbled to myself, "Also good news: I didn't die in a fiery explosion over the Atlantic..."

I'd almost forgotten about Mason and the woman since the alcohol and the jet lag and the sleep exhaustion were all starting to catch up with me. Looking up to see them, to remember them, was like a splash of ice water to the face.

Mason threw some euros down on the bar. She collected her purse from the counter and her jacket from the hook underneath it. He pulled her in tight against his big, broad chest as she stumbled and laughed. His hands slid down her back and grabbed fistfuls of her ass. He said something and she nodded.

It was her fingers his were intertwining with. It was her neck he was leaning over to suck at before he pulled her along behind him. Her hair he was tucking behind the ear as he leaned against the exit and paused.

She slipped past him and he finally looked back toward me. He smiled. That fucker winked. Goddamn *winked.*

Then he was gone.

I sat there on the couch, alone, and watched the door fall shut behind him. Behind him and the woman.

I imagined them falling into a cab together then mounting the stairs at Dublin Ink together. I imagined them taking off each other's clothes...running their hands over each other's bodies....lowering themselves slowly to the bed to—

"Goddammit," I growled as I clenched my eyes shut. I rubbed my knuckles against them and I tried not to see anything. Anything at all.

When I reopened my eyes, I checked my phone. Nothing from Tim. Not a goddamn thing.

It would have been smart to just get a cab myself. To go to Mason's place. To sleep. But I hadn't done a single smart thing the whole night, so heck, why start now?

I stumbled (not stalked) toward the bar and slumped over it (I had neither the energy nor the will to slam my fist down on anything except for maybe my own stupid head...or heart). I ordered another round.

I kept ordering until I was sure that when I walked past the bedroom I wasn't supposed to go in—the bedroom where Mason would be fucking that woman, his cock thrusting in and out of her, the bedframe rattling noisily against the wall—I would be so drunk that there was no way in hell that I would possibly remember.

Then I ordered one more round after that.

For good measure.

13

MASON

There was no reason whatsoever that I should have stirred awake before dawn.

The night (and day) before I'd drunk enough gargle to intoxicate an elephant. I'd been sleeping like shite anyway the past week like I always did the days leading up to anniversary of the worst day of my life.

I wasn't exactly an "early bird catches the worm" kind of fella in the first place (just ask Rian or Conor). The room was grey and chilly, the sheets thick and warm, and Miss Last Night's body beside me was soft and supple. Everything pointed to the fact that I should have slept in past noon.

All except that The One Who Got Away was asleep in the next room.

I shouldn't have remembered this fact. This inescapable truth. This tear in my heart. See again, the copious amounts of alcohol for one. The tits that bounced in my face all night were decidedly lovely. But they were decidedly *not* Rachel's.

Anger and hurt swirled in my chest. Part of me wanted her gone. Part of me never wanted her to leave Dublin.

I shouldn't have awoken. And yet I did. I shouldn't have remembered. And yet I could not forget.

Miss Last Night's ass was against my groin. I had my arm draped across her breasts. Her legs were intertwined with mine beneath the covers. And yet as I blinked awake, the last thing in the world I wanted to do was close my eyes again. I didn't want to stay in the warmth. In this comfort. To stay for the inevitable morning wood and a willing pair of lips drifting farther and farther down beneath the sheets.

I didn't have a fucking clue what time it was as I slipped free from Miss Last Night. I stood at the side of my bed and waited for my swirling, pounding head to clear. Then tiptoed over the clothes thrown hastily to the floor from the night before. It didn't really seem to matter to me what time it was.

All I could think about was Rachel. If I thought about time at all it was all the time we lost together. All the time we could have had.

The door of the old house creaked as I cracked it open, but Miss Last Night didn't stir. She'd had a lot of alcohol, too. She said something about being a nurse so I'm sure she wasn't unfamiliar with a lack of sleep herself. She didn't have the person she'd loved and lost just a few feet away like I had. She'd sleep through a creaking door no problem.

The hallway was even darker than my room. Rain in the early dawn pattered on the window at the far end. The floorboards moaned slightly beneath my bare toes as I moved toward the only door that was ajar. I peeked inside to find in the dim light Rachel passed out on top of the comforter. She was still in her clothes from yesterday. The clothes she left America in. The clothes she came to me in. The clothes she was wearing when she told me we were married. When she told me she wanted a divorce.

I would always remember the costume she wore when I first

saw her in Vegas. When the curtains parted. When I blinked against the blinding lights. When she smiled and circled her lips.

But I would also always remember these clothes: a pair of khakis, well-fitting, but not form-fitting, a simple white sweater (probably some expensive material like cashmere, something I couldn't afford, that was damned sure), black boots with a heel neither high nor low, and a gold chain necklace that strangely didn't seem to catch the light. She looked elegant. Posh. Expensive. She looked nothing like Rachel.

But then there was her hair.

It was spread out wildly just the way I remembered it. The way it was on that couch in her dressing room, spilling over the sides like a waterfall. It was the way I remembered it when we were together on the strip and she turned back to look at me. Wind catching it. Lights flashing in it. Strands wiping across her face as she smiled at me and extended her hand to me. It was the way I remembered it when I got the call that changed my life. When I ran my fingers through it for what I couldn't possibly know was the last time. When I looked back at the door with my bag and passport in hand...

I had the sudden urge to creep into the room and slip off her shoes. To unclasp the gold necklace that bit into her neck, all twisted up from sleep. To lift her and guide her beneath the covers, to pull the thick sheets up around her shoulders again. Would she whimper softly and shift toward the warmth? Shift toward me like she did back then? Could it ever be like it was?

I stood there looking in and imagined that we weren't in this fucked up situation. That I didn't have Miss Last Night down the hall in another bed. That I hadn't fucked her hard and fast and rough while thinking the whole time of Rachel. That Rachel had never left, we had never fallen away, fallen apart. That all these years she had been mine.

Perhaps Rachel was passed out on the bed in her clothes because she'd gone out for a girls' night with friends. Out with Candace. And Aubrey. They'd had too many Skinny Bitches at The Jar. Rachel had performed her burlesque routine from back in the day on the bar. Guys had offered to buy her drinks. To take her home. To strip off her clothes and love her (and fuck her) like the goddess that she was. I imagined that Rachel shooed them all away because she was coming home to me. That she always came home to me.

What would it be like to go over to her and gently kiss her awake? To whisper something stupid and ridiculous and impossible like, "Hey, baby, here's an Advil. I'm making pancakes." I didn't know how to make fucking pancakes.

The fact that I didn't know how to make pancakes made me angry. The fact that I couldn't make pancakes for Rachel made me irrationally fucking angry. And the fact that I knew my anger had nothing at all to do with pancakes made it all the fucking worse.

I was probably still a little hammered. That was it. That was why I was swaying there in the doorway like a fecking eejit. Making up little fantasies like a little schoolgirl. Dreaming about what might have been when what might have been didn't exist. Couldn't exist. Wouldn't exist.

Rachel didn't just leave me for a girls' night. She left me for life. Apparently for a better life. A richer life. A life with more opportunities for big roles. A life where she didn't wear sequins at the corners of her eyes. Where she didn't dance with pasties on her nipples. Where she didn't need me. Didn't want me. A life she wanted more. Maybe always wanted more.

It wasn't the first time I hadn't been enough for someone. Hadn't been enough to stick around for.

I tripped over Rachel's purse as I stepped inside the room. The divorce papers went skidding out across the rug. I stepped on them—ah alright, maybe I ground them down with my heel —on my way to the side of the bed.

Now, how exactly does one wake one's wife? A soft, gentle hand on the shoulder. A slow rubbing of the lower back, starting with a feathery touch. A whisper in the ear. Something lovely. Something sweet.

Maybe I messed it up because I wasn't all that used to being someone's hubby. I'd apparently been one for years, but I sort of missed out on the experience part. The trial runs. The adjustment period. The real-life bollocks after the honeymoon phase, as they call it. I was rusty. Maybe that's why I startled Rachel awake, oops, rather than slowly rousing her from her drunken slumber.

Or maybe I was just a teeny, tiny bit petty. And a whole hell of a lot butt-hurt.

"Wifey!" I hissed as I shook Rachel's whole body. Palms on her back like an overeager puppy ready for his breakfast. "Wifey, hey, wifey!"

Seeing her wide, startled, searching eyes, I almost felt bad. I mean, she probably didn't know which continent she was in, let alone which country. And here was this big tattooed Irishman yelling in her face. I'd been there, too. The confusion first. The realisation second. The impending hangover third. All worse than the one before. All sucky. All unavoidable.

"Well, aren't you looking a stunner this morning?" I said as Rachel wiped a long line of drool from her mouth. A line of spit stretched from her lips to her finger and I added with a grimace, "Just absolutely stunning."

"Fuck you," Rachel grumbled. She flopped her head back down onto the pillow and tried to shove me away with all the strength of a newly birthed kitten.

"Eh, eh, eh," I said, patting her cheek as she groaned. "A good wife is never negligent in her duties."

"Make your own goddamn bacon," she muttered, eyes falling shut again.

Despite the smears of makeup and the foul alcohol, most-likely-no-teeth-brushing breath, Rachel looked like an angel with her eyes closed, hands tucked up beneath her cheek. I almost gave up and left.

Then I remembered that she'd already done that: given up and left.

I didn't feel at all bad about climbing over her and rolling her over till she fell out the bed.

"Mason, goddammit!" Rachel shouted as she glared up at me from the floor.

I grinned down at her, chin against the edge of the mattress. She let out a groan and buried her eyes into the crook of her elbow.

"It's not exactly breakfast that I'm looking for, babe," I told her, finding myself having way more fun than I should have. "I need you to serve up something a little different."

"What the fuck are you talking about?"

I plucked Rachel on the nose. She smacked my hand away.

"Our little *deal*," I reminded her. "I need you to serve matrimonial ire. Righteous indignation. Familial rage."

Rachel peered up at me from underneath her arm still flung over her face. I smiled down at her.

With a groan, Rachel sat up. With another groan, she fell back atop me in bed.

And then there we were, the two of us. In bed together. Husband and wife. Wife beginning to snore. Husband beginning to get a boner.

I climbed out of bed before anything could get too noticeable. The plan was to keep Rachel around so I could figure out what the hell I wanted. Or didn't want. The plan was not to show my hand (rod-hard cock) right off the bat.

"Wifey, darling," I said, sweetly leaning over to whisper in Rachel's ear. "You need to go get rid of my Miss Last Night. Otherwise you're not getting rid of me. Please and thank you."

Rachel's head almost collided with my nose. She blinked one eye open.

"Your *Miss Last Night*?"

"Just in the other room there. Down the hall. Can't miss it."

"But—"

Before Rachel could protest, I bounded toward the door. I ducked my head back in and winked.

"Break a leg!"

14

RACHEL

It was hard to say for sure, given the absolute pounding in my head—and the fact that I wasn't entirely sure whether I was in Dublin, New York or goddamn Mars—but I was pretty sure this was what just happened: Mason scared the fuck out of me, he called me "wifey", he instructed me to go chase off someone named "Miss Last Night", and then walked out of the room butt-ass naked (and more than aware that I could see it).

It's even harder to say for sure why I actually *did* what he told me to. There was something in the back of my mind about blackmail. Blackmail Lite. Something about my big new role. Something about not wanting to jeopardise it. About Mason (and my legal and binding marriage to him) being something that would jeopardise it.

I rolled over and sat up in the bed with a pained groan. I vaguely remembered a deal. A shaking of hands. A feeling that his body was too close. A thrill that he wasn't letting me go. A fear. A fear that I didn't *want* him to let me go.

My head collapsed into my hands and I squeezed my eyes shut. Blackmail. A deal. Break a leg. It was all so foggy. Just scraps of conversation. Just flashes of light. Different bars. Different cafes. Different glasses. Same booze. Whiskey. Irish fucking whiskey.

If it was all such a blur and if I was still piecing it together, what in the actual fuck was going on? Why in God's name did I push myself up from the edge of the bed, catch myself against the wallpapered wall before I fell over, and then heave myself toward the door to stumble down the hallway?

The only thing I could think of was: there was a woman in Mason's room. He had fucked her. And, most importantly, she was *not me*.

These thoughts alone were enough to make me squint down the hallway. Enough to make me resist the urge to flop back into bed as the rain fell against the stained-glass window. What room had he said, again?

Hmmm, this one. The one with the door ajar. I was too hungover to realise that this was not good. Scaring off some woman because I was being effectively blackmailed into doing so was one thing. Scaring off some woman because she was in a bed I somehow felt I had a right to was something else entirely. More stupid. More idiotic. More dangerous.

But that was something for sober (or sober-ish) Rachel to deal with later.

Because in that moment I had something else to deal with when I peered in: a messy, bedhead bun poking out from beneath the covers. Little strands of hair fallen from the bun draped over Mason's cheek. Mason's not-so-hidden grin as he peeked open an eye to wink at me before shutting it once more.

I was being used. This poor woman really didn't deserve what I was about to do. Mason was an asshole. A fucking, goddamn asshole. And I also knew, as I stumbled into the room, that I didn't fucking care.

"Hey!" I shouted as I grabbed the end of the comforter and yanked it down. "Who the fuck are you?!"

The woman, a Miss Last Night as Mason so charmingly referred to her, startled awake just like I supposed anyone would. Mason thrashed awake so dramatically that I knew an acting career was in his future. But I wasn't. If I could just hold onto a shred of fucking common sense for two seconds in his presence.

"What the—" Miss Last Night began, covering her tits with her arm.

"Honey," Mason interrupted, extending his arms toward me. "Now, sweetie pie—"

"Get out of here!" I shouted at Miss Last Night. "Get the fuck out right now!"

I threw her clothes at her as she ducked and squealed.

Mason, the asshole, was pretending to comfort her, saying things like, "Fuck, I thought she was out of town till Saturday" and "She wasn't supposed to be home, I swear" and "Fuck, I'm sorry, I'm sorry". For some reason that last one pissed me off more than anything. He was saying sorry to *her*? To Miss Last Night? What about *me*?

"Nobody fucks my husband but me, do you hear?" I pointed toward the door. "Now get the fuck out before I call the dogs on you!"

Okay, so I was going a little crazy. A little overboard. A tad melodramatic. I mean, we didn't even have dogs. But I was hungover. And jet lagged. Most of all I was mad that I was forced to see another woman with Mason. I mean, no, I didn't see them fuck. But I knew they did. I'd seen enough of the woman's body to imagine how her hips would have looked rolling against Mason's cock. Her tits were big enough that I knew he'd hold them as she rode him. I could practically point out where his thumb and four fingers would have been as Miss Last Night ran out past me. One heel on. The other in her hand. Clothes clutched at her naked chest. Ass bouncing as she darted down the hallway and disappeared down the stairs.

By the time Mason and I were alone, my chest was heaving. The only good thing about the whole thing was that I had momentarily forgotten what a massive headache I was going to have all day. My body slumped. I was just about to trudge back down the hall and back to bed when I heard a slow clap begin from the bed.

Oh, right. I'd chased out Miss Last Night. But there was still Mr Husband—Mr Fucking Asshole Husband. Couldn't I chase him out, too?

With a roll of my eyes, I glanced over toward him. He was sprawled out naked, completely naked, across the bed. His arms were behind his head. His toes were wiggling merrily. He was goddamn smiling at me.

"Beautiful," he said, somehow still charming despite everything. I fucking hated him. "I have to say that went exactly as planned. Exactly as planned."

I tried not to shift uncomfortably at the sight of him naked. His abs bare. The array of tattoos I remembered in that Americana style he loved, all bold colours and classic prints of sailor girls and roses, eagles and mermaids. And the ones I didn't remember because he must have added them after me.

Other women had seen them before. Miss Last Night had even seen them before. But not me. Not till now.

His long, muscular legs. And of course, his thick cock. He expected me to look away. To shield my eyes. To act demure and innocent and sweet. To act like how I told him I was now. Like the new me was.

But I didn't look away. I was not demure. Not innocent. Not sweet.

I drank in the sight of his cock like it was a big, thick glass of cold water. Oh God, how I needed fucking water.

"I'm going back to bed," I said, not reacting when I saw him grinning stupidly. "Seeing as there's clearly no other women hidden under there."

The sheets were on the floor. I'd taken care of that.

I was on my way toward the door when Mason said, "A few notes, babe."

I shouldn't have paused. Shouldn't have hesitated. I did my part. I chased off the woman Mason fucked. I earned my gold star of the day. And thirty stars equalled one set of signed divorce papers. I should have just focused on what I was there to do: get everything set to marry Tim and not die of alcohol poisoning.

I shouldn't have. So of course I fucking stopped. I turned around and crossed my arms over my chest. "*Notes?*"

Mason didn't move to cover himself. I knew he wouldn't. He instead just shrugged his shoulders. "It was a good performance, don't get me wrong. Quite effective given that you and I are presently alone."

No witnesses if I murdered him. Surely a death certificate was as good as divorce papers...

"Are you listening to me?" Mason said.

I looked across the room at him, trying not to let my cheeks flush.

"No," I said, hoping my voice didn't sound like my throat felt: tight. "No, I was not listening to you, actually."

"I said that your performance could use a little more emotion," Mason said anyway.

"Emotion?"

"Yeah," he said, still wriggling his toes, "I mean, you went just pure rage. Which is great. I mean, I bought it. Whatever big new role you're up for, I can see how it's well deserved. But I think we also need to try to pull on the heartstrings a bit. Make these super hot, super fuckable women that I'll be bringing back every night really feel bad for you, you know?"

I ground my teeth. "You want me to cry over your infidelity, my dear beloved husband?"

Mason grinned. "I'm just trying to help you achieve a more nuanced performance, baby."

I snorted.

"And I think we're lacking a bit of movement for the piece."

"I'm sorry, the 'piece'?"

Mason drummed his fingertips against his elbows behind his head. His eyes were trailing up and down my body.

"What do you think about getting a little violent with me?" he said, that devilish flash in his eyes. "You know, come over and choke me a little? Slap me for being such a bastard."

"Threaten to cut off your dick?"

Mason snapped his fingers. "Now you're thinking! See, Rachel, now we're getting the creative juices flowing. Give me more, give me more."

I gave him the middle finger.

Mason ignored it and continued, "I really want girls around town to see me as this like crazy sex-hungry prisoner, you know? And they'll want to, like, come save me from my withholding wife. This is pie-in-the-sky kind of thinking, I know, but they'll come to see it as like part of the thrill. To like sneak out early, really early in the morning before you catch them."

I narrowed my eyes at Mason. "How many more days of this did I agree to?"

"Sixty."

I snorted and turned to leave. "Nice try, asshole."

"We'll get you a robe," Mason shouted after me.

I turned back again. Damn me, I didn't keep walking. His eyes were on my body. Trailing up. Trailing down.

"Yeah," he said, licking his lips. "Something silky. Something that falls open a bit when you run in here with that wild hair of yours. Give the girls a little peek on the way out."

"Why exactly?" I asked when I absolutely shouldn't have.

Mason inhaled and exhaled slowly.

"Because it's better that way," he said, eyes locked on mine. "The sex, I mean."

I just stared at him, not understanding. He grinned and explained, "When they know I'm used to a much hotter woman. Girls will do the craziest shite when they're overcompensating."

I rolled my eyes and this time I left. Slammed the door behind me. Stormed down the hall. Slammed my door.

But he'd gotten to me. Mason, that fucker. He'd gotten to me.

The bedsheets weren't silk, but they felt like it as I squirmed to get comfortable. Nobody was there to see my nipples. Not some chick. Not Mason. But they were hard like they were. Like they'd slipped from a silk robe. Like the town of Dublin would hear all about them. And say, "Good lord almighty, Mason's wife's tits..."

Like this was all real.

Which it wasn't.

It wasn't...

15

MASON

Conor, Rian, and I all had our different styles of tattoo. Conor was all black and white and symbolism and pain here and more pain. Rian was our experimental guy: any and all styles were welcome. And encouraged.

Me, I liked big and bold. The bigger, the bolder, the better.

We also, the three of us, had different ways that we worked on our different styles. Conor worked best with churning grey clouds and a bottle of whiskey. He liked peace and quiet because there was more than enough shouting in his head, I was sure of that.

A tornado could have been sweeping through Dublin and if Rian was drawing (or even just staring at the wall) he wouldn't notice. Not even as he was lifted up from his drafting desk stool and carried away to Oz itself.

And then there was me. I was the distractable one. I got most of my best work done in the middle of the night in bed because there was no one around. Not many sounds. And little to vie for my attention.

I say all this to explain why later that day, as I was supposed to be sketching out a design for a new client, I was really watching the boys eye each other across the studio, straining to hear what they were whispering in the kitchen over tea that I was not invited to, trying to figure out what the fuck was up with them. By mid-afternoon I had gotten no work done and was going insane.

"Alright," I said at last, throwing down my unused pencil, "someone spill it."

Conor sipped at his whiskey and glanced over at Rian, who was pretending—badly—

to be engrossed in his half-finished painting of a young woman with dark hair and striking eyes; when Rian was really painting he looked lost, like a little kid, wide-eyed and distant. Even Aurnia ducked out of the room under the excuse of "emptying the trash", something she despised doing now that she was a tattoo artist "like us".

"Well?" I said. "Did someone die or what?"

"Oh God, I hope not," Rian said to the ceiling.

"And that means?" I pressed irritably.

Conor cleared his throat and set down his glass. A second later he picked it back up and drained it in one go. "Look, Mason, it's just...we're a little...worried is all."

I raised an eyebrow. "Worried?"

"Yeah," Conor said, looking over to Rian for support, who looked back up at the ceiling when I caught him spying on me. "Yeah, it's just that, you know, we hear things. Down here. When you're with your, um, lady friends. Your Miss Last Nights."

I nodded along, not understanding where this was going at all. The most unnerving part was when Conor blushed. Actually blushed. What the fuck was going on?

"We get that you're into some kind of kinky stuff, you know?" Conor continued. "I mean, who isn't?"

I beamed proudly at my drafting desk.

"And?" I said, chin raised.

"And there's nothing wrong with that," Rian finally joined in. "That bondage stuff. That rough sex stuff. We all like a little choking and such from time to time."

Choking? Well, this took an interesting turn.

"Maybe we can hurry along to the point, boys," I said.

Conor and Rian looked at each other. I could practically hear them silently shouting at one another, "You do it. No, you do it. No, you do it."

"Rian, you say it," I said with a bored sigh.

"Did you kill Miss Last Night during sex last night?" Rian finally blurted out.

I burst out laughing. My laughter died when I saw Conor and Rian's concerned faces. It died when I noticed Aurnia peeking her head around the corner from the kitchen, eyeing me.

"Look, man," Conor said. "You know we're with you through thick and thin. We're family. God knows you've been there for me through some tough times of my own, but really mate, if you fellas were having fun and the fun just went a little too far, you've got to tell us."

The tattoo parlour was dead silent as I dragged my hand over my face.

"It's just that we haven't seen Miss Last Night come down and there's underwear on the stairs so we know someone's up there and there's been like no sound, like at all, all day and, and Miss Last Night is always, *always* gone by now," Rian was saying, sounding more and more panicked. "So something has to be up, right? What's the story? Jesus, Mary and Joseph, I'm not sure I can handle a dead body."

Sighing, I let my hand fall from my face.

"Fellas," I said before looking over my shoulder to Aurnia and adding, "And lady."

All three sets of eyes were fixed on me. They might even be

holding their breath. I had half a mind to drag it out. To make them sweat a little. Have some well-earned fun after the shite I had to put up with yesterday.

"Fellas and lady," I went on, because they were, after all, my friends. My family, like Conor said. "Miss Last Night is so quiet because she's jet lagged off her head and has a hangover from hell. Miss Last Night has not left because she is staying here for a little while. Ah, and, maybe this needs mentioning, Miss Last Night is my wife."

Any relief my friends might have felt upon learning that I did not in fact accidentally kill a woman during some kinky BDSM role play in my bedroom the previous night and casually proceed to go about my day like it was nothing, was quickly eliminated by a more pressing emotion: shock.

It started slowly enough. Drawn eyebrows. Wary glances at those around them. A little nervous laughter. Because it must be a joke. Right? *Right?*

No, no. It surely has to be a joke. Mason, married? Mason, committing? Mason, finding someone he wants to give more than just his penis to (it is a very nice penis, by the way)?

It had to be a joke, said their nervous little laughs.

I didn't join in.

All the pieces fell into place. There really was no other explanation for everything. The woman upstairs. The strange appearance of an American claiming the very same thing the day before. The straightness of my face. The casualness with which I shrugged. The ease with which I drummed my fingers on the drafting desk. All adding up to the truth: Mason Donovan, their friend and most beloved (and successful) playboy, was indeed a married man.

From there, the shock turned rather loud. Behind me there was Aurnia shouting with increasing pitchiness, "Wait, what?

Wait, what, *who*? Wait, what, who, *when*? Oh my fucking God, when can I meet her?"

There was Conor who was just repeating in that low, guttural growl of his, "Are you having a laugh? Are you having a fucking laugh? Ah shite, did you knock her up?"

I smiled through it all, rather amused as my friends proceeded to absolutely lose their collective shit.

Well, all of them except Rian. Rian looked merely confused. A sort of bewilderment drew his eyebrows together as he looked about him. "Hold on, lads. Hold on...I thought you *knew*?"

Silence fell over the parlour of Dublin Ink. All attention was now not on me—the newlywed, the husband, the deprived-of-a-stag-party groom—but on Rian.

So rude.

But understandable. Because...

"What the actual fuck, Rian?" I said. "Why would anyone have known? *I* didn't fucking know."

He pointed a finger at me. "Wait, you didn't know either?"

I gripped the corners of my drafting desk till I was certain the wood was going to splinter. Aurnia sank onto the couch, head swivelling between Rian and me. She just needed popcorn. Conor joined her. It was quite the accomplishment for my shite to prove to be more complicated than theirs. Yay fucking me.

"I learned yesterday," I said slowly, eyes narrowed at Rian. "When the fuck did *you* learn of my nuptials, my dear, *dear* friend?"

The little bell above the front door rang. All four of us shouted at the poor sap who stuck his eager head in the door, "Not now!"

The sheepish head disappeared. The door closed. The attention returned to Rian. He shrugged, hands dug into his pockets.

"I don't know," he said, "I guess I learned about it when you put that candy ring on her finger in Vegas."

"Vegas?!" Conor shouted.

"Candy ring?!" Aurnia shouted.

"You got married in *Vegas*?!"

"You didn't even get her a proper ring?!"

I dismissed Conor and Aurnia with a wave of my hand and focused on Rian.

"Are you telling me that you were *there*?" I said to him.

He had the nerve to look confused. Bastard.

"Mate, *you* were there, too," he said.

"Goddammit!" I threw my hands into the air. "Am I the only feckin' one who doesn't remember this bleedin' wedding?"

"Rachel remembers?" Rian asked.

"You remember her *name*?" I bellowed.

Rian shrugged. The bastard. Have I said already he was a bastard? Have I said that yet?

"I was the witness and I was sober," he explained. "Somebody had to be. You two were plastered. Absolutely plastered. It was a beautiful ceremony though. Touching. I was Rachel's flower girl, too, by the way. She said I was the best flower girl she'd ever seen. Really, very touching all around."

I tugged at my hair.

"Rian, why didn't you tell me?"

He frowned.

"Tell you that you were married? I kind of thought you knew..."

All this time. All this time and Rian knew. Why, oh fucking why couldn't Conor have been my sober witness? He wasn't exactly a talker by any stretch of the imagination, but surely he would have brought it up after a glass or two of whiskey sometime over the years?

My head hung heavy between my shoulder blades. Through

gritted teeth, I said, "Why didn't you say anything? When I came back without this wife you knew all about? Why didn't you say fucking anything?"

"Because *you* didn't say anything. I thought...well, I thought it ended. I mean, why else wouldn't you talk about your wife?"

That was fuckin' it. I was going to take Rian's head off.

Conor leapt to his imposing height and stepped between us.

"Woah," he said, holding up his hands to me. "Hang on. Okay. So, alright. Alright. This is all kinds of banjaxed. Obviously. But look, Mason, there's a solution, right?"

I stared at him.

He shook his hands vaguely. "Ye know. Divorce papers. Some shite like that."

"Yeah," I said darkly.

"So, problem solved. Then she's gone, right?"

"Rachel has some...business in town," I said. "She'll be sticking around for a few weeks."

"Right," Conor said. "But what I mean is, it's not a big deal, right?"

I glanced toward the stairs. At the top was a hallway. At the end of which was a door. Behind which was Rachel. My wife.

"It sounds like it was just a drunken thing, right?" Conor said. "Everybody's done daft things when they've been on the gargle, you know?"

Out of the corner of my eye I could see everyone nodding. Agreeing.

Conor appeared at my side. His hand gentle on my arm. That was a lot for him. His voice was soft. Also a lot for him.

"That's all it was, right?" he asked. "A stupid, one-time drunken thing? Right?"

I turned to him and forced a smile.

"Right."

16

MASON

hen...

There was glitter on my pillow.

I blinked awake, unsure of where I was. What time it was. Even what day it was. I was unsure of everything except that there was glitter on my pillow, sunrise (or was it sunset?) peeked through the crack in the heavy drapes, and that an arm, warm and tanned and covered in bar stamps, was draped over my side. I was unsure of everything except the glitter, its colour, and the fact that I loved that arm.

I loved the delicate hairs that ran up, soft as down. I loved the delicate wrist bone at the end of it. I loved the sticky mess on the ring finger left from what must have been a candy ring. The kind you get out of gumball machines. Or win at fairs. Or buy in packets at convenience stores.

I couldn't remember when we'd gotten candy rings. I couldn't say whether she'd sucked it off her finger or whether it had been me. But I wished that the little sticky smear of colours, bright as the glitter on the pillow, could stay there forever. Perhaps I could tattoo it on her finger. Just like that. Matching the colour. Using the sticky stain as the stencil. The best stencil. The only stencil.

A hangover was on the horizon. That much I knew for certain as well. There was no avoiding it given how much we'd had to drink, half of which I was sure I wasn't even aware of consuming. It was coming. And it was going to be brutal.

But for that moment, half awake, half asleep in that unfamiliar hotel room, I felt fine. Just fine. Okay, maybe I was still a little locked. Or maybe it was the remanent of the candy colour ring and my daydreams of making it permanent that had me lightheaded.

The arm stirred. The steady breathing that had warmed my bare back changed. A long exhale. Then a stilling. I didn't know why, but it seemed like she was holding her breath. Slowly I turned over.

And *she* was there.

The reason for the glitter. The owner of the hand with the faded ring. *Rachel.*

Her wild hair was even more wild. From the hot wind on the strip. From dancing on a table at Denny's. From snagging on the bricks that I'd pressed her up against in the back alleys of a seedy dive bar. From the couch in her dressing room. From God knows where else. From life. From love. From me.

A wing of blue eyeliner was smeared at the corner of her eyes. It made her look like a rockstar. Like a warrior. Like a little girl who got into her mother's makeup. I loved all of them. All of her. Every facet. Every bright, shining spot. Every shadow.

Rachel smiled at me, skin aglow in the golden light of morning, but there was a hesitation. I got that sense again that she was holding her breath.

"Rachel."

"Mason."

We'd said each other's names at the exact same moment. Speaking over one another. Speaking in time with one another. How could one tell? We laughed that nervous laugh. That nervous laugh you exchange with a fellow office worker when you run into each other in the hallway and you both move in the same direction. Then both adjust in the same direction. Awkward. Embarrassed. Not the laughter of people who knew each other. Who knew each other's bodies. Who had spent a lifetime together in twenty-four hours. Or was it forty-eight?

"Rachel."

"Mason."

It happened again. We laughed nervously again.

"You go," I said.

Rachel's eyes were wide and earnest as she looked at me. I could see straight into her. Into her soul. Her gaze darted away and she licked her lips. When she looked at me again there was that hesitation once more. That holding of breath.

"Mason," she finally said, her voice serious, "what we did last night..."

My stomach dropped under a surge of panic. I couldn't remember the whole night. Or was it nights? What had we done that made Rachel hold her breath? Oh God. I dug through my darkened memories for something, something I didn't even know what. What had I done? What had *we* done? Was there something I wasn't remembering? Something I *should* have remembered?

Suddenly I wasn't breathing either.

"Was that, us, together, I mean, was that just a drunken thing?"

I exhaled because I hadn't forgotten anything. She meant us fucking. Us making love. Us joining ourselves together over panted breaths and sweat-slick skin. I hadn't forgotten that.

There was no way. No human way possible. I exhaled, but Rachel didn't. Because I'd gotten my answer. But she hadn't. She was still waiting. Eyes wide. Earnest again. They looked so innocent, so childlike. It was as if Rachel expected to be hurt. As if she'd been hurt all her life and she was ready for it once more. Not shielding herself. Not protecting herself. But opening her arms. Baring her heart. And ready for my dagger.

I opened my mouth to speak and words failed me. Because this was the part when I would say, "Remember what I told you last night."

When I would say, "This has been fun. And that's what I promised, right? *All* I promised."

When I would say, "I can't give you what you want. But I told you that. I told you that."

The words that I normally said failed me, because I hadn't told Rachel. I hadn't warned her I couldn't love. Hadn't made her understand that the morning was a goodbye, not a hello. Hadn't given her the speech, the "you should know what you're getting into before we get into it" speech.

I'd arrested her without reading her her rights. I'd sold her a gun without making her sign a release. I'd put her on a motorcycle racing toward a cliff without going over the brakes. How they worked. How to push them. Hard.

Rachel sensed my hesitation, my failure of words and blinked those wide, earnest eyes. She blinked and they were gone. Her eyes were seductive now. Cat eyes. Charming, alluring eyes. Hidden eyes. She smiled and laughed, this time not nervously. Not nervously at all. She smiled and laughed and leaned over to kiss me sweetly on the cheek.

"This has been fun," she said, climbing out of bed. "Really."

She gave me a cheeky smile over her shoulder. Her hip crooked to the side. The view of her ass perfect. The curve of her spine delicious. The peak of an erect nipple as she looked back at me and smiled like a postcard of her body. A memory of her. A memento. A souvenir of Vegas.

She gathered up her clothes and dress with easy chatter. She wasn't embarrassed at all. Wasn't hurt. She didn't hide her body from me behind her white dress, one she must have gotten when I ripped her other one. She let me see everything as she tugged it up over her hips. She even hopped back on the bed to have me zip it up.

"Well, I better be going," she said. "I've got a show tonight and all."

It was then that I realised it was an act. She was performing for me. A new role. The girl who didn't care. The girl who was fine with it being just a drunken thing. The girl who was perfectly fine saying goodbye. Rachel would play that girl. But she would not play the rejected girl. The distraught girl. The girl who held on too closely.

With nothing more than a kiss blown from her hand, the one with the stain from the candy ring, she was gone. The hotel room door clicked shut behind her. I was alone.

I was free.

It was exactly what I wanted. What I'd always wanted. From all my fuck arounds. From all my Miss Last Nights. From any woman that I let into my bed for a few hours, that I let into my life for a few hours. This was what I wanted of sex. Of intimacy. Of love. A few hours of passion. Heat. Bodies together. Panting breaths together. Glistening skin together. Climax. Sleep. Blissful sleep. And then goodbye.

Rachel had given me my ideal woman: the one who walks away. The one who leaves me alone. The one who spares me from hurt. From heartbreak. The one who leaves so I'm never left. Not ever again. The one who is never there long enough to miss when she is gone.

It was perfect. I'd find Conor and Rian. I'd nurse my

impending hangover with some fruity daiquiris by the pool. I'd fuck one of the cocktail waitresses tonight. I'd arrive at the airport gate just as they were closing the doors. Maybe I'd fuck the flight attendant who tsked me for being so late. For holding them up. For being naughty, naughty, *naughty*. I'd return to Dublin. To the shitty tattoo parlour I worked in. To the long line of girls waiting at the bars...at the clubs...

I knew them all. The bars. The clubs. The girls. I wanted them. Yes, I wanted them. The slipping on of shoes in the dim light. The creaking of the floorboards as they snuck out past my nan's room. The emptiness of my bed which only got emptier when their warmth on the sheets eventually faded. Disappeared. Gone forever.

That was what I wanted. Yes, that was what I wanted...

I didn't want Rachel...

I was out of the bed in a flurry of kicked-off sheets. I didn't bother with pants. I didn't even bother with a hotel keycard. I dashed to the door. Flung it open. Sprinted down the hall as I heard the elevator ding around the corner. I caught Rachel just as she was about to step through those gilded doors. Just as they were about to close on her. Just as she was about to disappear forever. Her warmth. Her arm against my side. Her finger stained with candy. Candy I was sure, sure I licked from her skin as she laughed. Both of us naked between the sheets.

"Mason," Rachel said in surprise as I stopped in front of her, panting. "Mason, you're naked."

"You didn't let me speak," I said.

She looked around the hallway. It was empty, of course. Vegas was still asleep around us. It was just her and me. And about half dozen security cameras. But who was counting?

"You didn't let me speak," I said, trying to catch my breath. Alcohol wasn't great for early morning sprints, in case ye didn't know.

Rachel glanced back when the elevator doors began to close. She reached back and stuck her hand between them. Forcing them back open. Keeping available her escape. The light from the inside spilled out over us. Golden like the sunset.

"It was pretty rude of you actually," I said as she eyed me warily. "We spoke at the same time and I politely offered for you to say what you had to say first. And you did. Which was fine. Totally fine. I'm a gentleman, as you well know."

Rachel frowned and crossed her arms over her chest.

"But the least you could do after I was so polite to let you go first is to then say, 'Oh, hey, Mason, I think you were going to say something when I rudely, very rudely interrupted. I'd really like to hear what it was that you wanted to say.'"

I was still panting, but not from running. I was panting from this sort of desperation inside of me. From this fear. I was putting myself out there in a way I hadn't ever before. And it was terrifying. I was asking to be shot down. I was begging to be wounded.

"Oh, hey, Mason, I think you were going to say something when I inter—"

"Rudely, very rudely."

A flicker of amusement flashed across Rachel's eyes and then she continued, "When I *rudely, very rudely* interrupted."

I mouthed the words for her to repeat, "I'd really like to hear what it was that you wanted to say."

Rachel eyed me for a moment and caught the closing elevator doors once more. Her look warned me that this would be the last time she held up the doors.

I could still let Rachel go. I could still get what I wanted, what I always said, what I always told myself I wanted.

"I was going to say," I said, eyes on hers, "that that wasn't just a drunken thing for me. I think I'm meant to be with you, Rachel."

This time when the elevator doors closed, Rachel did not extend her arm blindly behind her. She didn't reach back to stop them. She stood there and let them close. The light on the button went dark. The numbers above flashed lower, lower, lower. All was still in the hallway. All quiet.

Rachel and I stared at one another.

Then she said in a low, husky whisper, "I think we should go back to the room."

I patted my naked thighs and smiled.

"Yeah, about that..."

17

RACHEL

ow...

The elevator doors closed behind me and JoJo's shrieks filled the hallway of the downtown Dublin hotel. I hurried to my room and ducked inside before she summoned a pack of hounds. Or the hotel manager.

"Would you hush?" I laughed, cupping my hand over the phone's speaker like it was her lips.

"Can't a best friend be excited for a best friend?" JoJo shouted.

Her image on the screen jolted as she jumped in wild circles around her apartment back in New York City. It was apparently wine o'clock there given the massive glass of red wine she was most certainly spilling on her flea-market-find rug. I had fuck all idea what time it was there in Dublin. I just knew it was dark. And the hotel quiet. Or at least it was before I called JoJo and began telling her about all that had happened.

"I just don't get what there is to be excited about," I told her as I set up the phone on the dresser against the television. I added a pillow against the wall on second thought. My neighbour might not enjoy a 3 a.m. wakeup call from a hysterical American woman drunk on pinot and hot Irish gossip.

"Are you insane?" JoJo said, plopping back down in front of her phone. "Rachel, you're telling me he laid there butt-ass, cock-ass naked right in front of you, an Irish god descended from the rainy heavens to grace you with his tattooed perfection, and you *don't* think he still wants you?"

I rolled my eyes as I dug my suitcase out from the hotel closet.

I glanced over my shoulder. "No, I don't. I think he wants exactly what he says he wants: to fuck in peace. And I'm just a pawn on his fuckboy chessboard."

JoJo leaned in close to her phone and drawled, "No, you're his *queen*."

I stuck my tongue out at her before beginning to pack up my stuff from the dresser.

JoJo continued, "I mean, think about it, Rach. He is having you move *in* with him!"

"For ease of access," I told her. "I mean, he might have to actually talk to one of these girls, these 'Miss Last Nights' as he calls them, if I have to cab it all the way across town. He might have to, I don't know, fucking listen for once if I'm not right down the hall to wake up and push out of bed—"

"Oh, he pushed you off the bed?" JoJo interrupted, rubbing her hands excitedly together.

"No, no," I said, wagging my finger at her. "*Out* of the bed, like a parent. Like a parole officer. Not *off* the bed, like—"

"Like a hot, sexy leprechaun sex god."

I sighed and stuffed my socks into the suitcase.

"My point is," I said, "this has nothing at all to do with me. Mason is just using the situation to his advantage."

"So he won't tell Tim about you two?" JoJo said. "About your time in Vegas? And whatever it was you did before coming to New York to become the wet kitten who needed a warm home?"

I flipped JoJo the bird and she laughed.

"You really think Tim would care?" JoJo asked.

I kept my eyes on the panties I was refolding and said, somewhat under my breath, "One, yes, I think he would care. It would shatter his perfect little image of me. And two, I kind of didn't tell Mason about Tim..."

If JoJo's shrieks out in the hallway were loud, they were nothing compared to what I heard then. I was grateful for the foresight to put up the pillow, concerned it was nowhere near thick enough to save my neighbours from startling awake in terror. I tried to get JoJo to be quiet, but she just went on and on.

I put her on mute.

I left her on mute as I continued packing, even as she jabbed her thumb at me through the camera.

After several minutes I said, "Are you ready to be calm about all of this?"

JoJo gave me a demure nod. I switched back on her volume.

I was rewarded with her shouting at the top of her lungs, "Oh my God, you want him too, you fucking bitch!"

"JoJo!" I hissed, hand again cupping the speaker. "It's like the middle of the night here! Or at least I think it is. This jet lag has got me all kinds of fucked up."

"Mason has got you all kinds of fucked up," JoJo hollered gleefully. "Oh my fucking God. I'm so happy that I don't have to wear that ugly, boring beige bridesmaid's dress at your stupid wedding anymore."

"Hey, you said you liked it!"

"I can wear a purple tutu now," she went on. "I can wear a see-through top! Hey, did you say whether Mason had brothers?

Sisters? Emm, sisters with equally hot tattoos. Emm, sisters with mohawks like Mason's. Emm, emm, sisters or brothers with—"

"JoJo!"

Great, now it was me shouting. I lowered my voice and continued, "The only reason I didn't tell Mason about Tim was...was..."

Shit. I knew I'd made a mistake the second I started. But it was too late. I was in it. JoJo smiled smugly and waited. Let me hang on the rope I'd strung up myself.

"Dammit," I hissed. "No. No. Stop it. Stop smiling like that. I don't want Mason. I absolutely do not. The only reason I didn't tell him about Tim was...was...fuck!"

"Was because you want to keep that door open," JoJo said, wriggling around merrily on the floor, falling back to kick her rainbow-socked feet gleefully in the air. "Because you want to keep that sexy, hunky, tattooed, Irish door wide, wide, *wide* open!"

I tried my best to ignore JoJo and her little victory lap as I finished packing up all my clothes in my suitcase. It wasn't as simple as my supposed best friend was making it out. There were hearts at stake. Emotions to protect. Mine. Mason's. Tim's. I didn't want anyone to get hurt. That was all.

Nothing had changed. I still wanted a divorce. I still wanted to get back to America. I still wanted to marry Tim. I still wanted to put Mason and Vegas and dancing and performing and the life I once lived and loved behind me. Firmly behind me. Nothing had changed.

Seeing Mason for the first time in years hadn't changed that. Certainly not him with a woman's ass against his cheek. And then later a woman's lips against his. And then later still with a woman's naked tits pressed up against his side.

Sure, he had a nice cock. No one was denying that. Sure, seeing it may have reminded me of a good lay or two. But that was no reason to throw away the perfect life. The safe life. The secure and quiet and easy life.

I'd been reminded of a good memory or two over the past day with Mason, but none of those were reasons to change anything either. They were like old stories. Old fairy tales. You don't throw away something guaranteed for something make believe, now did you? You don't risk a roof over your head for a pair of glass slippers that surely don't fit anymore anyway. That would be stupid, now wouldn't it? Naive. Reckless. Ridiculous. You don't take a perfectly good this-will-do ever after and go chasing after happily. Because happily doesn't exist. The Mason of my memories was not real. He was just something I imagined when I was lonely. When I needed to get off when Tim's tongue wasn't enough. That was it. That was *it*.

"Hello? Hello? Earth to Rachel!"

I was startled out of my thoughts by JoJo's voice. My suitcase was packed. I was ready to leave. And yet I had been standing there. Frozen. Lost.

"Huh?" I stammered stupidly. "Sorry, what did you say?"

"So what are you going to do?" JoJo asked.

"Oh, um..." I shook my head and dragged my fingers through my hair. "Well, there's no way I'm going to stick around waiting thirty days for Mason to sign the divorce papers. No way. That's ridiculous. That's stupid. I'm going to force him to sign sooner. *That's* what I'm going to do. He wants a wife? Well, I'll give him a wife. I'll give him the worst, most horrible, most annoying and bitter and vengeful and terrible wife he's ever seen. I'm going to make him rue the day he ever married me. The day he ever decided to stay married to me. I'm going to make his married life a living hell. He thinks he can last thirty days? Ha! With *this* Mrs Donovan, I give him a week. A week, tops. Then I'm going to hand him the papers he's begging to sign. I'm going to get on a plane. And I'm going to marry Tim. *That's* what I'm going to do."

I was kind of out of breath after all that. Panting like a war general after a big speech to motivate the troops.

It was suddenly hot in the hotel room. I tugged at my shirt and fanned myself. All the while JoJo remained silent. Staring at me. The only sound came from the drumming of her fingers against the side of her wine glass.

"What?" I finally said, annoyed by her silence and unwavering look.

"I *meant*," JoJo said slowly, "what are you going to do about your feelings for Mason? For your hubby dear? For Mr Donovan?"

I laughed, but it sounded strained even to my own ears. I was sure that JoJo picked up on it. She was a fucking bat when it came to that.

"Feelings?" I said, trying to sound casual and mostly failing. "What feelings?"

JoJo grinned and nodded. "Emhmm."

I pointed a finger at her.

"Don't 'emhmm' me," I said.

She just replied with another, "Emhmm."

"JoJo."

"Emhmm. Emhmm. Emhmm."

"I'm warning you."

JoJo grinned. "Look, Rachel, just let me know which of Mason's sisters I'm taking as a date to the wedding, okay?"

"I don't want Mason, JoJo."

"I think I'll dye my hair green to go with those Donovan eyes."

"I. Don't. Want. Mason."

"Irish green."

"JoJo!"

JoJo blew me a kiss with a wink and then was gone. Call ended. I growled in frustration and stuffed the phone in my bag before storming toward the door.

JoJo was wrong. Dead wrong. And I was going to prove it.

I was going to be the worst wife.

Ever!

18

RACHEL

hen...

THE THEATRE WAS ONCE AGAIN empty.

Earlier that afternoon the theatre staff had filed in with their cold coffees and overdrawn bus passes and begun setting up for that night's performance. The other dancers and I had arrived a couple hours before curtain call to run through stretches, practise this element or that, and devour the day's gossip over greasy burgers and limp fries. Then it had been slapping on makeup, struggling into fishnet hose, and emptying half a bottle of hairspray into my root all while the audience and their low hum of excitement made their way to their seats. The lights went up, the burlesque show began, and the theatre rose to a standing ovation as sweat dripped down my back. There had been the usual mingling with creepy old men who wanted pictures, Midwest families who were in town for the spectacle, the all-you-can-eat buffets, and the runaway girls who wanted to be just like me (the poor things). Drinks with the girls backstage.

Lifting up our glasses and bottles for the cleaning crew. Goodnights all around.

And just like that it was over. The theatre was once again empty.

Empty save for Mason and me.

We sat across from each other cross-legged on the stage, our bare, dirty toes pressed up against one another's. Only the low half circle of lights that ringed the outer edge of the stage were on, but the old wooden floor still kept some of the heat from those big, blinding spotlights. It reminded me of the beach. Of the sand. Of long afternoons with nothing to do but lie there and soak up the sun.

"What do you think of a seaside wedding?" I asked Mason before plopping a dumpling into my mouth.

After the show Mason had arrived with a horde of food for us. Takeout from half the Asian places on the strip. Doggie bags from his hotel's complimentary breakfast: muffins and assorted fruits and cold pancakes sticky with maple syrup. He'd brought baguettes and wine, half of McDonald's menu, Frosties from Wendy's, a steak and pomme frites from one of the nicer steak houses in Vegas, a vegan lentil curry, what I was certain was a trough of fettuccini alfredo, and a stack of pizza boxes, each with two different topping combinations. He'd practically needed one of those carts hotels use for luggage to haul it all in. When I'd asked him why all the food, he just shrugged and said he didn't know what I liked. I told him the answer was all. All of it.

Mason picked a pineapple piece off a slice of pizza with a turned-up face. I snatched it from him with a roll of my eyes as he said, "You're not going to make me wear khakis, are you?"

Mason had brought the world of food to my stage, but he hadn't brought much in the way of glassware. I sipped my rose from a mug I'd snatched from the gift shop with a picture of yours truly pasted across it.

"Khakis and bow ties, obviously. Seersucker, I think," I said. "And I'm going to have twelve bridesmaids and they're all going to wear the same beige-coloured dresses that wash them out."

From the end of wooden chopsticks, Mason wrangled a dumpling into the little plastic cup of sweet and sour sauce. "Sounds horrible."

I wiggled my toes against his and he looked across at me with a grin.

"Well, what do you think then?" I asked. "What kind of wedding should we have?"

"A drunken one," Mason replied.

I dipped low, as if in a bow and said, "Naturally."

We clinked our stolen mugs together, cheap wine spilling out over the sides and dripping onto our half-finished steak. We continued in silence for a little while. It was all just for fun, really. Us talking about silly things like marriage and weddings. I mean, the whole situation was ridiculous when you thought about it. If I was out there in the audience right now, looking onto the stage, this is what I would see:

A little runaway trailer park girl dressed up as a burlesque dancer. An Irish stranger. Tattoos. Big muscles. Sharp green eyes. A man pretending his home isn't far away. His life isn't far away. Way too much fucking food between them. Way too much fucking unknown between them. A nice little dream. A sweet little moment. A snapshot. Not a forever. Just a now.

And yet, as I was staring out at the dark folded-up seats, row after row, and imagining that person out there, seeing us, seeing the truth about us up there on that stage, Mason dipped his finger into the Frosty and said, "I'd marry you just about anywhere."

I turned to him in surprise. We'd been playing around, but

Mason didn't sound like he was playing around anymore. I laughed because what the fuck else was I supposed to do? We'd danced around something real, Mason and I. Something lasting. Something forever. But it was a fire neither of us was willing to walk across. Afraid to get burned, I guess. What else was new?

I held up the finger where I'd apparently had a candy ring. I'd scrubbed at it, but still some faint colour remained. I wiggled it at him. "We can go to the Little White Chapel right now."

Mason smiled and ducked his eyes before replying, "I'd do it, you know."

I bit my lip. Hesitant. There was that fire again. There we were dancing around it. Or maybe it was just me who was avoiding its heat. Maybe Mason had walked right through it and was already on the other side. Waiting for me.

The tone of his voice frightened me a little. The sincerity. The earnestness. I mean, for God's sake, we'd just met. And half the time we'd shared together, as wonderful and thrilling and fucking hot as it had been, we couldn't even remember! Or at least I couldn't. God knows what insanity we'd gotten into. But none of that meant it was anything more than a fantasy to think we could stay together. Be together. None of that except Mason's voice. Right there. On that stage. His words soft as he circled his finger round the lip of his mug.

A part of me wanted to say, "Fuck it." A part of me wanted to stand up. Shake off the crumbs from all the food. Extend a hand down to Mason. Tell him it was time to put his money where his mouth was. A part of me wanted to go do what all those couples on the lash do when in Vegas: find an Elvis, squint an eye closed to make the signature line on the marriage certificate stop spinning all around the page, slur some vows, and get fucking hitched. A part of me wanted to give a big ol' middle finger to that faceless person out there in the audience watching. To yell at him or her. To scream. To scream, "We can make it, you know?! This can be real! We can be more than play pretend! This, *this* can be us! Forever! *Forever!*"

But I was afraid.

I'd always been afraid.

So I said to Mason, "I'd be a damned good wife, you know?"

He raised an intrigued eyebrow over a bite of a Big Mac, sauce dripping down his chin.

"Is that so?" he said through a mouthful of food.

I nodded, pinkie raised as I slurped at a chocolate shake. "I mean, you haven't seen ironed clothes till you've seen me iron clothes."

Mason swept his hands over his rumpled t-shirt.

"Well," he said grandly, "as you know, having sharp creases is the first step to a successful career as a tattoo artist."

I laughed and he smiled. I liked that he liked the sound of my laugh. I liked that he seemed contented by it. Like a lifetime of making me laugh, of hearing the sound of it, would be enough for him. The thought of this brought a little blush to my cheeks and I quickly ducked my face.

"I will, of course, make you breakfast every morning," I said.

"As a good wife should."

"The works," I promised, looking back up at him. "Bacon, scrambled eggs, toast of your choice."

"White."

I clicked my tongue. "A whole grain would really be better for your cholesterol, dear."

I didn't know fuck all about cholesterol except for what I'd half listened to during commercials on TV.

Mason played along, moaning, "But honey."

I grinned. "No butts."

Mason set down his chopsticks, his face grave. "When you say 'no butts'..."

I threw a fry at Mason. He caught it deftly between his teeth. I rolled my eyes as he chomped down on it. He offered me a fry as a peace offering. I bit his finger.

As he nursed it between his lips, I twisted a forkful of fettuccini alfredo.

"I'll vacuum naked if you're good," I said, eyeing him mischievously.

He nodded around his finger, his eyes sparkling. "Oh, I'll be good."

"And if you're really good, I'll cook delicious dinners for you in just my apron."

"Praise Jesus."

I grinned.

Mason poured more wine into my mug. "You know we're going to be the happiest married couple in the world. We're not going to be like all those others who fight and bicker."

"We'll just fuck and order takeout instead."

Mason lifted his mug. "To fucking and ordering takeout."

I clinked my mug against his.

"To the happiest married couple in the world," I said. "One day."

It was all play pretend, of course. All just for fun. Two strangers enjoying a fantasy. We weren't actually going to get married, right? I snuck a peak at Mason while he wasn't watching.

Perhaps I wouldn't mind all that much. Being a good wife to Mason Donovan...

19

MASON

Now...

Some people like to wake up to the sound of birds chirping outside. For others it's the steady drum of rain on the roof. Or a soft melody from a favourite song. Those crazy enough to procreate might enjoy the pitter-patter of little feet coming toward them from down the hall. There might even be those who quite like a city coming alive to awaken to: pedestrians hurrying on their way, trams rolling by, the occasional good morning laying on the horn.

For me the answer is quite different: silence. You can keep your birds, your snotty children, your aggressive corporate asshole late to work. But any morning, any day of the week, I'll take all of that over the melodious roar of a vacuum cleaner.

Ah, so sweet. So gentle. Such a pleasant way to ease into the workday.

"Goddammit," I hissed into the pillow I'd wrapped over my ears. It helped. Sort of. Mildly. Not bleedin' enough.

I flung back the sheets and stormed across the room.

Out in the hallway the wretched noise only got louder. There wasn't even a hint of light to illuminate the glass window at the end of the hallway yet, but there was the back-and-forth roar of a horrible devil-monster. Pushed, surely, by an even more horrible one. Following the noise to the source would have been easy enough, but I had even further help: a trail of thick green gloop dropped on the wood floors.

Toes cold against the floorboards, I sidestepped the mess and continued toward the stairs. When I poked my head around the corner, I squinted in the harsh light at my dear wife there on the landing.

It was, as you can guess, everything I'd ever hoped and dreamed for. More than anything I could have ever imagined. Truly the heart-fluttering sight one would expect from the love of their life.

Rachel's face was covered in the same green gloop that was left in a cookie crumb trail down the hallway. It had not only fallen to the floor, but also the old house robe she wore like a tent over her body. I'd told her to use whatever she'd found in house, and she'd found the ugliest thing possible: a quilted old floral-print robe with lace trim at the neck and wrists with giant buttons in the shape of little kittens. I think it belonged to my nan, but from the state of it, it could have very well been *her* nan's.

Rachel's hair was greased with some sort of oil and wrapped up in what I could only guess was cling wrap. She wore thick grey-coloured socks with holes in them and apparently hadn't bothered to shave given what I could see of the tiny peek of skin under the robe. She yanked the vacuum roughly over the stairs, the end banging loudly against the wall with each pass. As I watched her, the attachment slipped off the edge of the landing and crashed all the way down the steps to the front door.

Rachel dropped the vacuum, leaving it still roaring, and leisurely went after the attachment. I sighed and unplugged the vacuum from the wall.

She turned as the machine went dead.

"Oh, shoot," she said, placing her hands on her hips as she looked up at me, pushing a pair of giant old glasses up her nose so they didn't slip right off. "I didn't wake you, did I, dear husband?"

I smiled down at her and I leaned against the wall, arms crossed casually over my chest.

"Not at all, my love," I said through gritted teeth. "How can I possibly sleep when such a beauty is so close by?"

Rachel's jaw tightened.

"Well, good," she said. "Because I would have hated to wake you. Hated to be of any kind of annoyance to you. Hated to give you any reason whatsoever to want me gone."

Rachel smiled sweetly. Or at least, as sweetly as was possible with a chunky green face and glasses that made her eyes bulge out like a cartoon character's.

She might have smiled sweetly, but it was more than clear what was really going on: she was declaring war. The battle line was drawn with the cord of a vacuum. The rules of the game written on the floral wallpaper just to the side of us. She was going to make my life a living hell as long as she was forced to be here. I was to be under siege for thirty days.

Rachel smiled sweetly like she'd won the first skirmish, but she'd forgotten something very important: I was excellent at games. In fact, I quite enjoyed them. I was, in fact, quite good at them. Ask Miss Last Night. Any Miss Last Night.

I hopped down the stairs to where Rachel was standing. She eyed me warily as I approached. Her head jerked back when I placed both my hands on her cheeks. It was my turn to smile sweetly.

Eyes close to her giant ones, I said, "Wife, there is nothing, absolutely nothing, you can do that will make me want you gone."

I squeezed her cheeks a little tighter. Pressed out her lips a little farther so they puckered out like a fish.

"Absolutely nothing," I said with a grin before smacking my mouth loudly against hers.

I ran back up the stairs and left her to lick her wounds. If Rachel thought it was going to be that easy, she didn't know me well at all. If anything, she made me feel more alive.

I paced my room and planned my attack. It wasn't even—I glanced at the bedside clock—four in the morning yet and I was wide awake. Heart pounding. A wicked grin tugging at the corner of my lips.

We were playing, Rachel and I.

And I was going to win...

20

MASON

I'd laid a trap for her.

The next morning, she came in just as I expected her to at the crack of dawn with a laundry basket wedged beneath her arm. I'd told her the night before, casually, over an ice-cold frozen dinner she'd plopped down in front of me, that my sheets hadn't been washed in God knows how long. I'd lain awake for her practically the whole night waiting for her to take the bait.

It was quarter to five when the door creaked open. It all went beautifully. Perfectly. Could not have been better. Rachel attacked the fitted sheet without preamble. Wrenched it from beneath the mattress. Yanked it up. And sent my Miss Last Night rolling right off the edge of the bed!

"Darling," she said later over breakfast (an English muffin burnt to such a crisp that the whole thing disintegrated the second I tried to butter it).

"Yes, darling," I replied.

"Maybe you can tell me when you plan to have company over," she said, scraping a plastic plate in the sink so hard that it snapped in two.

I grinned as I scooped up my English muffin ashes with a spoon meant for the marmalade. "I thought you knew."

Actually I'd made Miss Last Night play a fun little game where we couldn't make any noise at all just so that Rachel would be surprised.

"It's really no problem," Rachel said, "it's just that I'm not used to seeing a stranger's pussy before my morning coffee."

She came over to kiss the top of my head and in the process put her dripping wet yellow gloves on my shoulders. I hissed at the cold water seeping into my skin. One point to wifey.

"Oh no, did I get you wet?" she asked, sounding like innocence incarnate.

I replied by standing up and dragging the hem of my t-shirt up over my abs, over my broad shoulders and over my head. I caught Rachel, in her freshly stained apron, staring at me. Point, husband. I flopped the sudsy shirt over Rachel's shoulder and grinned.

"Not at all," I said. I added over my shoulder as I was halfway out the kitchen, "Did I get *you* wet, honey?"

Rachel was smiling, but her eyes were on absolute fire. "Dry as a bone...*dear.*"

And so the battle went on.

I made sure to have a Miss Last Night there every morning, and Rachel made sure to burn iron marks into every single one of my favourite shirts. I made sure to walk around butt-ass naked as much as possible, and Rachel made sure to cover every inch of herself in the thickest, woolliest, ugliest fabrics known to mankind. I made sure to eat up every little bit of food she put in front of me whether it be burnt, frozen, salted to hell, or dripping in grease, and Rachel made sure to keep it coming.

She replaced my spearmint toothpaste with baking soda quoting it was better for my teeth. She replaced my black briefs with oversized white grandpa boxer briefs quoting it was better for my balls. She replaced my silk sheets with some scratchy natural material quoting it was better for my sleep. I tried to replace her robe with a lacy piece of lingerie, but she found it out in the trash. Point, wife.

Rachel vacuumed multiple times a day, usually when I was tattooing a client. She'd come round right when I was working and say, "Lift." "Other foot." "Oh, let me get your stool while I'm here." I smiled through it all, though with increasingly clenched teeth.

"Thanks, hun!" I'd shout after her as she disappeared into the kitchen, vacuum still whining.

"How long have you been married?" my clients would ask.

I'd sigh and say, "Too fucking long."

It was all fun and games in the start, but soon tensions began to rise. I wasn't getting much sleep because of all the extra work I was doing. Yes, work. It was work to go out every night and find a Miss Last Night. It was work to keep her up through the night so that *I* could be the one to wake Rachel up for once. With moaning. With wall banging. With light fixtures shaking. It was work keeping everything groomed down there so I could wander around the house butt-ass naked. To cross in front of the TV with my cock swinging while she was watching Derry Girls. To plop onto the counter next to her while she was scorching another egg. To scoot a little too close behind her while she was using that goddamn ice pick at two in the fucking morning. It was work replacing all the clothes she ruined. It was work even finding something to wear sometimes since everything was always "being washed". And it was fucking work trying to smile all the fucking time.

By the end of the first week, I was exhausted. My cheeks hurt (both the ones on my face and the ones on my ass). Rachel was finding new ways to annoy the shite out of me and I was finding new ways not to be annoyed even the tiniest bit by it.

I invited Conor and Rian over for poker night in the hopes that she wouldn't purposefully ruin dinner, but she burnt the popcorn so bad that she set off the smoke detector. I told her it was fine. Just fine. Fine. Fine. Fucking fine. When I upended the poker table with all its chips, I told her it was an accident and would she mind picking it up like a good wife. And she said it was fine. Just fine. Fine. Fine. Fucking fine.

Her hair was everywhere so the next time I shaved, I left *mine* everywhere. She was always running the washing machine into the middle of the night, so I fucked Miss Last Night on it and left her panties in the dirty hamper.

But we kept smiling, my wife and I. Through it all we smiled and smiled and smiled. Every morning Rachel chased off Miss Last Night and every day she tried to chase me off.

It felt almost sacrilegious to think this, but I was tiring most of having a different woman each night. Knowing Rachel was down the hall, it was hardest of all to resist the temptation to imagine her in my bed instead. Her in place of Becky or Tina or Lara or whatever her name was. I never thought sex would be the end of me, but I feared it might be.

I jumped eagerly into this war with Rachel, but I soon realised that I hadn't figured out what I wanted. What spoils would there be for me if I was the victor. For Rachel it was obvious: a divorce. But what about for me? What did I want?

What if it was the one thing I couldn't have?

Really that's how wars are lost. The opponent loses first not the battle, but the will to fight. That only happens when there's nothing left to fight for.

Was that what I was doing?

Fighting when there was nothing left to fight for?

21

RACHEL

You know what they say about the best laid plans… they don't mean shit all if you're not the one getting laid.

I'd tried everything. I swear to God, I'd tried everything I could think of. And when I ran out of things I could think of, I turned to the internet. I read all the blogs about divorces. What sent people over the edge. What made them finally crack. I searched out every straw that broke every camel's back. I asked JoJo for ideas. When she ran out too, I asked my accountant. When he came up empty, I asked the lady at the checkout counter at the grocery store.

"I don't know, my husband hates when I talk about celebrity gossip at dinner."

I sighed. I'd given that a go days ago, and Mason had just jumped right in at the first mention of Jamie Dornan.

All my attempts to be such a bad wife that my husband would kick me straight out of the house, straight onto a plane, straight back into the life I was supposed to be living with my fiancé back in America failed. Absolutely failed.

Because no matter what I did, no matter how loud I was, no matter how ugly I made myself, no matter how much I annoyed Mason, at the end of the day (or beginning of the morning) *he* was the one who was having sex with other people.

I was the one who had to come in when it was all said and done. Who had to see her there in bed with him. Who had to yell and wave my hands like some crazy lady. Who had to pretend day after exhausting day that it didn't bother me. That I was fine. Just fine. Fine. Fine. I said I'm fucking fine!

I wasn't fine.

I was fairly certain I was losing it. Every night I lay awake waiting for Mason and his little Miss Last Night to return. There I was in bed with a face covered in mud mask and coconut oil-slicked hair and there he was stumbling against the walls with another woman's lips locked with his. I was bundled in a quilted robe three sizes bigger than I needed and Miss Last Night was losing clothes by the second. I knew because I'd find them. A pair of jeans on the stairs. A bra in the hallway. A thong tossed over the door handle.

I'd lie in bed and listen to her giggling. Her giggling that turned to whimpering. Her whimpering that turned to moaning. Her moaning that turned to panting and screaming and calling out his name (which more times than not, wasn't even the right name).

No amount of stuffing my ears worked. No amount of cramming a pillow against my head worked. No amount of vacuuming at any hour of the day could get those noises out of my head.

What made it worse was that I knew it was coming again. I knew the next night would be exactly the same. Sure, it would be a different pair of jeans on the stairs. The bra would be a different cup size. The thong would be mesh instead of lace.

The giggles would be higher maybe, the whimpers louder, the screams a little shorter as she maybe came faster, this new Miss Last Night. But there *would* be a new Miss Last Night. And I *would* have to face her in the morning. To face her and to face the fact that it wasn't me. It wasn't me in Mason's bed.

"That was a brilliant," Mason said one morning toward the end of my first week as Mrs Donovan.

He was sprawled out in bed. Again. Naked. Again. Satiated from the night before and throwing it in my face that I was most certainly not. Again.

"In fact, it was such a good performance," he continued, "that I almost believe you."

I snatched his pillow from under his head and didn't feel bad at all when it cracked painfully against the headboard.

"Need to clean these," I grumbled.

Mason continued unperturbed.

"You really will do well in this new role of yours, because you've almost got me believing that it does bother you," Mason said. "Me fucking these women with you next door."

I stripped the pillow of its cover a little too roughly.

"Well, it doesn't."

"Right, right," Mason said. "Of course not. But it almost seems like you do, you know? You're that good, is all I'm saying. Like when you were yelling at that chick before, I really almost believed that you were upset your husband was slipping his cock into some pussy that wasn't his wife's."

"Well, I wasn't." With a mighty yank of the fitted sheet, I sent him and his stupid cock, that I didn't care about one tiny little bit, sprawling onto the floor.

As I stuffed the sheet under my arm, Mason's head popped up from the side of the bed. He rested his chin on the edge of the mattress and grinned up at me, his dark mohawk messied slightly. If I hadn't known the reason for that messiness, I would have found him charming. A little boyish. Sweet. Innocent even.

But I knew better. Fuck, did I know better.

"There's no telling what's been on that mattress," I said before stalking out of the room.

Mason laughed and called after me, "Well, I think we have some idea, now don't we, dear?"

Me slamming the door of my bedroom only made him laugh harder.

It couldn't go on like that forever. I just knew it couldn't. Something was going to have to break.

I just hoped it wasn't me.

"GET out and don't you ever come back here!" I shouted at the latest Miss Last Night.

And then again the morning after that, "Get out and don't you ever come back here! *Ever!*"

Miss Last Night was a busty girl with a shaved head. Or she was a tiny thing in fishnets and latex. She had a shaved pussy, a bushy pussy, a pussy trimmed into a tidy arrow. She had a nose ring, a WWJD bracelet, a chain between her pierced nipples. She had a tattoo of cherries on her neck, a tattoo of some guy's name along her lower back, a tattoo of a cartoon character on her ankle. She had no tattoos at all. Miss Last Night had freckles across her tits, a birthmark on her hip, a scar on her long tanned thigh. Miss Last Night was every girl and no girl at all. Miss Last Night could be anyone, anyone at all.

Anyone but me.

"Is this getting to you?" Mason asked, pausing that morning's "acting notes".

He'd begun to jot them down on a little notepad that he always seemed to find no matter how expertly I managed to hide it.

I was folding a new stack of t-shirts I'd ironed a scorched hole into, and I paused too to glance back at him over my shoulder.

"Getting to me?" I repeated.

"I mean, it seems like it's getting to you a little," Mason said, drumming his fingers along his notepad. "Like me and all my fucking and all my *not* fucking you is kind of...I don't know, getting under your skin."

The neckline of Mason's shirts stretched between my fists, the threads straining, popping loose.

Mason's smug face. His merrily wiggling toes. His cock lying there against his stomach, spent and emptied and content as a goddamn alley cat on a sun-warmed tin trash can lid. I could wipe that smirk off his face. I could make his toes freeze. I could make him drag the sheets over his proud, exposed body in seconds.

I could tell him the reason it wasn't, absolutely *wasn't* getting under my skin. I could tell him that I was engaged. Finally tell him about Tim. Tell him that I got cock, good cock, whenever I goddamn wanted (mostly true). I could tell him that I had someone in my life who I didn't want to chase off every fucking morning (also mostly true).

Looking at him and his little grin over my shoulder, I knew it would be so easy. So quick. Then it would be over.

Maybe that's why I still didn't tell him. Maybe that's why I stuffed the remainder of his ruined shirts hastily into his dresser drawer and left his bedroom. Maybe that's why I didn't do anything but scream into the pillow in my room.

Because I didn't want it to be over.

This arrangement with Mason was driving me mad. Absolutely mad. The desperate mews coming all goddamn night from his room were filling me with almost unbearable jealousy. That jealousy was filling me with almost unbearable self-loathing. And what did I want to do with that self-loathing? Get it fucked right the fuck out of me.

But I couldn't because I had a fiancé and I wanted a divorce. I was able to remind myself of it only till I heard the front door open and whispers on the stairs and that first little gasp and then it was the whole cursed cycle all over again.

And again...

And yet I never used the biggest weapon I had. Never pulled the pin from the grenade that was in my back pocket and tossed it right onto Mason's exposed lap there in bed. Never told him the fucking truth.

I don't know what I thought. That one morning I would walk in and Mason would be alone? That he would pull back the covers and there would be only space for me? That he would open his arms wide and tell me this was all stupid, all silly? That he'd hold me and be honest with me about what happened between us when he left and be honest about how he felt now? That I'd like what I heard? That I'd believe him? Believe in him once more? That I'd tilt my chin up to kiss him? That it would be my moans filling the hallway? My sweat soaking the sheets? My hands gripping the bedframe that was putting holes in the wall behind it?

It was madness really. But it was my madness.

The days were passing and my plans were failing. It wasn't that I feared I couldn't wait the full thirty days to get divorced. To return to America. To return to Tim. It was that increasingly I feared I couldn't *last* the full thirty days. That if Mason didn't break and sign soon, I'd do something stupid.

Like throw myself at him.

Like fuck the shit out of him.

I had a couple more tricks up my sleeve, but I was getting desperate. I was having a harder and harder time believing that I truly wanted a divorce. That I didn't want something else. Someone else.

Him.

22

MASON

I moved Miss Last Night's arm from across my stomach because I wanted to torment Rachel with an unobscured view of my very nice abs indeed. I edged away from Miss Last Night's ass because it was blocking the glory of Mason Jr. I twisted slightly in the opposite direction from Miss Last Night's naked body simply because the angle was better for my own ass.

None of this, I repeat none of this, was because I didn't want Rachel to see me wrapped up close with another woman. None of this, and really this is important, none of this was because I had some demented idea that if there was room between us (Miss Last Night and me), Rachel would more easily imagine herself pressed up against me. And none of this, absolutely none of this, was in regard to Rachel's feelings.

I knew, and understood, that Rachel was there for thirty days to scare away my Miss Last Nights, to give me a reputation around town that could facilitate friction-free fucking, and to leave. To take her signed divorce papers in hand. To finish what she started all those years ago. I knew all that. I understood all that. I was *fine* with all that.

Really.

A little drizzle fell on the roof as I waited for Rachel to come in for her morning duties as enraged wife. I strained to hear anything else through the pitter patter, but the house was silent.

I squinted at the clock on the nightstand. It was late. Rachel didn't exactly adhere to a strict wife-yelling schedule, but she normally came in before this time of the morning.

Downstairs was quiet, too. With the rain, Conor would be doing his physical therapy. Aurnia with him. For all I knew Rian was halfway across Ireland, having found a specific raindrop on the bus window particularly beautiful and finding it absolutely necessary to draw it right then and there in perfect detail.

If Rachel didn't come in soon, I was on my own with Miss Last Night.

Slowly, so as not to wake my sleeping beauty before the big surprise, I grabbed my phone and tried texting Rachel.

Me: Kind of waiting over here.

I listened for the sound of an incoming text message across the hallway. But the door was closed and there was the rain and who knew if Rachel even had her sound on. A few minutes passed and I was really starting to get impatient. My mind was going a little crazy imagining what Rachel was doing. What was so pressing, so important that she couldn't come scare off my shiny new fuck toy?

What annoyed me the most, or maybe scared me the most, was that Rachel was sound asleep. That she hadn't stayed up practically the whole night for this moment. Not like I had. That it didn't bother her to see me like this. With a hot, naked chick and empty balls. With an amused grin and a warm bed. With my perfect sex and my perfect, perfect life.

What if Rachel had even stopped caring? What if I were to slip out of the room and into hers to rustle her awake, and what if her response was to sleepily rub her eyes and mutter, "Oh yeah, right, right. Yeah, later."?

"Oh, you want to do what we did last night?" I asked loudly, really loudly. Practically shouting, really. Truth be told, I'd worked myself up into some kind of almost panic.

Miss Last Night jerked awake beside me, but my attention was fixed on the door.

"I mean, we did some pretty nasty stuff, babe," I added even louder. "Are you sure you want to do all that *again*?"

I was still looking at the door when long fingernails suddenly dug into my chest. I yelped in pain when they dragged down my abdomen, taking half my skin with them.

"What the fu—"

Teeth were sinking into my earlobe and a giddy voice was whispering hotly in my ear, "You were a dirty boy, weren't you? Momma *likes* that."

I pushed Miss Last Night away from me. I vaguely recognised her from the night before. To be honest I fucked around, there's no denying that, but not nearly as much as I had been fucking around since Rachel arrived. At a certain point, all the women and all the nights kind of blend together.

This Miss Last Night had her raven-black hair tied up into two buns atop her head. A blue lipstick had faded over the course of the night and its...activities and now gave her the look of having just sucked on a popsicle. The sugary, icy kind. She had high cheekbones, pale, flawless skin, and a cute button nose. She was gorgeous and kind of scary.

"Um, hi," I said.

"Hi," she drawled before leaning forward to lick a long, wet line from my belly button to my throat.

Her long, blood-red nails were wrapping around my cock and I quickly grabbed her wrist.

"Hey, maybe you can wait to do that for just a second?" I said.

Her pointed lips curled up devilishly.

"Wait till we get a cock ring on you, you mean?" she whispered, nipping painfully at my lower lip between words.

I pressed her back a little more on the bed.

"No, no," I said, glancing again toward the still closed door. "No, no, I just meant till we got into the hall."

Miss Last Night giggled. Without any warning she flipped herself over me so that her knees were wrapped behind my head, her pussy was at my chin, and her mouth was around my cock.

"Carry me wherever you want, Daddy," she murmured. "Take me to the candy shop."

The heat of her little mouth and her flicking little tongue was starting to get me hard and I wriggled away from her before it became impossible. Her lips were moist as she looked back at me, thighs slipping across my cheek.

"What's wrong?" she asked.

I scooped her up into my arms and carried her toward the door. "Nothing. Nothing at all. It's just we need to be out in the hallway and there was no way I was getting up once you started all that."

Miss Last Night kicked her feet and let her head fall back, biting her lower lip.

"We also need to be louder," I added, peering down the dim hallway toward Rachel's room.

"I can be louder," Miss Last Night purred.

Shifting the girl around in my arms, I pressed her noisily

against the wall right outside Rachel's room. My fingers went to her clit and she proved true to her word: Miss Last Night could, in fact, be louder.

"I sure hope we don't get caught," I said in that voice that was practically a shout over Miss Last Night's high-pitched whines.

"Caught by who?" Miss Last Night moaned. "Caught by the police? Oh my God, let's do this in a park. Or on the freeway!"

"What, no," I said as I pressed Rachel's door open with my toes, "no, by my—"

I'd craned my neck, which was presently being sucked on by Miss Last Night, into Rachel's room to find it...empty. The bed just a rumpled mess of sheets. The lights off. The bathroom unoccupied.

"What the fuck," I muttered.

"Yeah, what the fuck?" Miss Last Night said, bucking her hips impatiently at my stilled finger on her clit.

She repeated this even louder when I dropped her.

I stalked down the hallway and would have completely forgotten about Miss Last Night except for the fact that she ran after me and launched herself onto my back. When she went to wrap her feet around me, her heel collided with my half-hard dick. I fell to my knees at the top of the stairs, groaning in fucking pain. Miss Last Night slipped off me and got on all fours on the stairs, bare ass to the door, mouth to my ailing, throbbing prick.

It was then, as Miss Last Night was "kissing it better" and I was groaning either like I was having the best fucking sex of my life or like I was never going to have the chance to have kids anymore, that Rachel walked in through the front door.

Miss Last Night was so preoccupied with swirling her tongue around my aching cockhead that she didn't even notice till I tapped her on the back and said in a fake panic, "Oh, no, oh my God. My *wife*!"

Miss Last Night whipped her head around to look over her shoulder. Despite the pain (and despite my now quite unavoidable boner), I sighed in relief. All Miss Last Night saw was my wife, with an armful of shopping bags, casually assess the scene at the top of the stairs, slowly close the front door behind her, and then walk away without any comment at all. Miss Last Night and I were silent and frozen on the stairs for a moment, both of us doing nothing but listening to Rachel in the kitchen, unloading her bags.

Miss Last Night looked up at me with confusion. "Your wife?"

"That's what she does when she's mad. When she's really fucking mad. My wife."

Miss Last Night glanced toward the bottom of the stairs and then back up at me and said with a sheepish, slightly hopeful grin, "I don't know. She didn't seem all that upset to me."

"You better go," was all I said.

I slipped past her, leaped down the stairs, and crossed the parlour shop toward the kitchen in the back.

"Honey, I know you're mad," I said. "I know that even though you're not showing it like a good wife is *supposed* to do, you're enraged. That you're just waiting till that chick sticks her head in here to completely lose it. That you're about to fly off the handle and who knows what you could end up doing with all these knives around."

Miss Last Night had not gone as I'd suggested. Instead, she squirmed her head beneath my arm as I tried to push her back and peered curiously into the kitchen at my wife. My wife, who was holding up a new dress to turn this way and that in the kitchen light. My wife, who was unpacking a baguette, a wrapper of cheese, and a jar of olives from the market. My wife, who was trying on a pair of earrings and asking, quite fucking calmly, "Chinese or Indian tonight, do you think?"

Rachel looked over at me and put on a goddamn award-winning smile. Miss Last Night dared to wriggle in against me even further and I gritted my teeth.

"*Wife*," I said, trying to keep my cool. "You've just caught me *cheating* on you. Cheating on you with this woman here. This naked woman right here who just moments ago had my cock all up in her mouth. You can even still see the precum on her lips, I'd bet."

Rachel smiled at Miss Last Night and said, plopping an olive into her mouth, "Hello."

What the fuck? Should I just go ahead and buy name tags for everyone? We'll all just get together and get to know one another, my wife of ten years who I didn't know was my wife of ten years till not even ten days ago and *all* the women I've fucked in the meantime.

"*Wife*," I tried again. "Isn't there something that you would like to say? Isn't there some emotion that you would like to express right now? Like right now?"

Rachel, now leafing through a magazine, only glanced up to say, "I hope you two have fun."

"You don't care?" I said with a clenched jaw that might snap right in two.

Rachel shook her head. "Nope," she said. "Not at all."

Well, well, well. Rachel had a few tricks up her sleeve after all. I narrowed my eyes at her. I had to admit, I was impressed. She played the game better than I would have expected. I noticed a flicker of amusement in her eyes as she licked her finger and flipped the page of the magazine. She was the devil. And I wanted nothing else. No one else.

Goddamn her.

"Did you hear that?" Miss Last Night whispered, tugging on

my cock like normal people tug on an arm to get someone's attention. "She doesn't care."

"Is she *sure*?" I asked, gaze fixed on Rachel.

Rachel didn't even look up. Just shrugged.

"Who am I to deny the world someone so charming," she said. "So attractive. So good in bed. I mean, that would be selfish, wouldn't it?"

"I don't know," I said. "Sometimes it's good to be selfish. Set healthy boundaries and—"

I hissed when Miss Last Night pinched my ball sack with those nails of hers. I tried prying her wrist away, but that just tugged my sensitive skin more.

"That's sweet of you, darling," Rachel said, admiring her reflection in the toaster. "But really I just want you to have fun."

That was it. I'd lost the battle, the war was over. She'd outsmarted me. Outfoxed me, my clever little thing. With the fun gone, I'd have to sign. With the pretence stripped away, I'd have to give her what she wanted. Or admit what *I* really wanted. Both to myself. And to her.

It was over. Our little fun and games were all over.

Or at least they were until the brilliant, wonderful, ever so lovely Miss Last Night swept in and with three simple, oh so simple words, saved the fucking day!

"Then join us!"

I wish I had a video camera so I could have captured Rachel's face in that moment. To see her eyes wide in the reflection of the toaster. To watch her head whip around, tangles of hair falling over her face. Then as she pushed them behind her ears...

"Join you? I—no," Rachel laughed. Nervously. Very nervously. "I mean, I couldn't, I—"

"You did just say you wanted me to have fun..."

I said it slowly. Enjoying every word. Each like a fine wine.

Each like a perfectly aged scotch. I pinched Miss Last Night's nipple as Rachel watched in horror. The horror of someone who knows they have lost.

"Unless there is a reason why you wouldn't want to?" I added, grinning in sweet, sweet, sweet fucking victory.

Rachel's hands were in fists. I could see the veins popping in her taunt neck. Flames jumped from her eyes.

She faced Miss Last Night and me, each more naked than the next, and smiled. Spread her hands wide. Then she did it. Rachel actually fucking did it.

"Sure," she said, choking on the word, "let's have a threesome."

23

RACHEL

I'd gone ahead and snatched victory from the jaws of defeat.

More specifically, I'd gone ahead and snatched victory from the cock-clenched fist of a chick with blue lips and sex-crazed eyes.

I followed the two of them, my husband and Miss Last Night, up the stairs. My husband leading the way. Miss Last Night between us. One hand pushing him up. One hand tugging me along, her perky ass in my face. I was pretty sure she'd had her asshole bleached.

"This is like, really good for a marriage," she said, pushing Mason up faster at the same time as dragging me behind her. "You'll see. It's like spice, you know? It's like licking someone's tits covered in chocolate sauce for the first time. Plain tits are nice and all. But then you have the chocolate sauce and you're like...*wow*."

"Did you hear that, honey?" Mason called back to me. "Are you ready for 'wow'?"

He stopped at the top of the stairs. His cock already hard.

Miss Last Night's ass in his palm. His other hand extended toward me.

"Do you think you can handle 'wow'?"

He was daring me to back down. To end this. To fly off the handle. To curse. To shout. To send Miss Last Night on her way. To prove him right: that I couldn't handle this. That it did get under my skin. That I did, after all these years, still *want him.*

Keeping my eyes fixed on his, I slipped my fingers between his.

"Bring on the chocolate sauce," I said.

Mason bobbed his head from side to side.

"Her sexy talk can use some work," he said, looking down at Miss Last Night. "Don't you think?"

She took my other hand and smiled at me.

"We'll work on it," she said. "You can just start with stuff like, 'My pussy is wetter than the Liffey' or 'Choke me with your cock, Daddy'. Those never fail, sweetie."

"I'm going to choke you with your cock, Daddy," I said to Mason.

"Yeah," Miss Last Night purred. "That's so hot."

Mason and I exchanged a look over Miss Last Night's head as she closed her eyes in the hallway and groped my tits and Mason's cock. I was giving him what he'd given me: a chance to back down before the games really began.

I lifted an eyebrow at him which said, *"Are we really going to do this?"*

In the dim light of the hallway, he blew me a kiss. *"Babe, we're already doing this."*

Fine. He wanted to play chicken. I'd fucking play chicken.

Back in his bedroom, Miss Last Night hopped onto the bed and asked me where I kept my dildo.

"I don't have one," I told her.

"I'm plenty for you, aren't I, baby?" Mason said with a stupid grin.

"Oh, yes," I said advancing toward him. "All four inches of you."

Miss Last Night was rifling through Mason's nightstand, apparently not believing us.

"But what do you do for Double Penetration Tuesdays?" she asked, obviously disappointed when she just found a shit ton of condoms.

"Cucumbers," Mason said.

I glared at him before saying in a monotone, "Yes, cucumbers. Sometimes zucchini."

"Kinky," Miss Last Night squealed, writhing a little on the bed. "We're going to have fun, the three of us. Aren't we?"

"So much fun," I said, eyes narrowed at Mason.

"So. Much. Fun," he replied.

"You two start," Miss Last Night said.

This drew my attention away from glaring at Mason to staring at her. She was propped up on the pillows. Legs spread like she was at the gynaecologist. Fingering herself with her bottom lip held between her teeth.

"Oh," I said uncertainly, "oh, I thought you'd want to like do something to him first?"

"Yeah," Mason said. I was surprised at the hesitation in his voice. "I kind of thought that the girls always start things off, you know? Like you could, like play with each other's tits? Or kiss? Or like you could go down on Rach—on my wife here? And then I could like, I don't know, join in later."

Miss Last Night mostly just ignored the two of us. She shook her head and said, "You two are so cute together," before slipping her middle finger into her pussy and adding with a slight groan, "and so fucking *hot* together."

Mason and I both watched her pleasure herself at the sight

of us. From what I could tell neither Mason nor I were doing anything particularly sexy. I was standing straight as a board, petrified into good posture. While Mason was at least moving, it was only to scratch at the back of his neck.

"Grab her," Miss Last Night said to Mason, gazing heavily at him from beneath hooded lids. "Grab her and pull her to you. Rough. Like you haven't been married for ten fucking long years. Like you just met her. Like all you want to do is fuck her and fuck her hard."

I was relieved that the first move wasn't to be mine.

I turned to face Mason. Challenged him by lifting my chin. Stared him down, to dare him to back down as we listened to the wet sounds of Miss Last Night's fingers slipping in and out of her pussy.

Mason met my gaze. Jaw tight. Eyes bouncing between Miss Last Night and me. Cock twitching.

"Come on," Miss Last Night whined needily.

I raised an eyebrow. Was it that easy? Had I already won our little game of chick—

Mason reached out and grabbed me, his hands strong on my arms, his fingers digging in almost painfully. Deliciously. He wrenched me to him like he was drawing me back from the edge of a cliff. I lost my breath because hitting his chest was like a brick wall. I lost my breath because there was his cock, hard against my thigh.

I almost leaned in. Because his lips hadn't been that close to mine since Vegas. Since he took me as his own. Since *I* was the one in his bed. The only fucking one in his bed.

"Yes," Miss Last Night groaned.

It snapped me out of myself. Mason pulled back but he still held me close. So damn close. Too damn close.

I could hear her finger moving faster. It made me self-conscious. Not of her. But of Mason. His desire. His rapidly rising and falling chest. His eyes on mine, saying, "Your turn."

"Now, you, wifey, unbutton your blouse," Miss Last Night commanded.

I looked over at her as if only just remembering she was here.

"You're behind, in case you haven't noticed," she said, playing with her own breasts. She grinned wickedly.

"You don't have to if you don't want to," Mason whispered, his voice too close. Too fucking close.

Even as he said these words, I could feel his cock twitch against my thigh. I could feel the heat of his body. The need. I could feel it just like I could feel my own. I looked up into Mason's eyes. There was nothing but lust. To step down now would be to admit that my needs weren't just physical. That I couldn't just take a good lay and move on. That there was more here than just a good time.

I reached between Mason and me and unbuttoned my blouse. I could feel Miss Last Night's eyes on me.

But it wasn't for her that I was moving slowly, revealing inch by inch of my skin, slipping my breasts from the cups of my bra. Their exhales came together at the sight of my erect nipples, but it was only Mason's that I cared about.

My breath hitched as I pressed myself against Mason's naked chest, his skin searing hot. First there was the brush of skin against skin, then the delicious press of them against rock-hard muscle. When we were as close as we could be, I looked up at Mason.

I wanted there to be nothing but defiance in my stare, nothing but a challenge, a stubborn dare. But I feared there was more.

Because in his eyes I could see it. More.

"Kiss her," came Miss Last Night's voice.

This time neither Mason nor I glanced over toward her. His eyes were on mine. Mine on his.

"Kiss her," Miss Last Night whined.

I knew he would. I knew from the determination in his eyes that he would. The will not to lose. The stubbornness that wouldn't allow him to be the first to back down. To admit more than his hungry cock and his blown-wide pupils ever could. No, I knew he would obey Miss Last Night's instructions. He would continue the game.

But what I didn't know, with my nipples yearning against his chest, was *how* he would kiss me. Just enough to satisfy his turn in this game of chicken? Or just enough to make me regret the years, the distance, the loss of us?

Mason's hands slipped beneath my blouse which had begun to slip from my shoulders. His hands were fire against the small of my back. I inhaled at his touch and his lips were there, already there to catch my exhale. He stole my breath and at the same time gave it. Gave it tenfold. Mason's mouth closed on mine, his tongue sweeping at the seam of my lips, begging for entrance.

I blame the shock of it. Yes, the shock. That's what made me groan, making my mouth open so he could slip his tongue inside.

It had nothing to do with the full-body shivers or the electricity coursing through my veins. Nothing to do at all with the way his nearness, the feel of his skin, his scent of musk and man, turned my bones to liquid heat.

With his lips against mine, my whole body came alive. I leaned into him and felt my ribs expand against his. I pressed tighter and felt my lungs full. Chest full to the point of bursting.

It scared me. If Mason's kiss made me feel so full, so alive, how I had been living without him? It frightened me, the surge of passion that his kiss brought, because that meant I'd been lifeless without him.

I trembled against Mason not just because of the goosebumps he elicited when he twisted his fingers around the curls at the nape of my neck, but because I was scared as fuck. About who I was with Mason. And more importantly about who I was without him.

"Push her onto the bed."

I was no longer sure if the words came from Miss Last Night or was beat out through my heart with my own searing blood. My coursing need making me hear voices. All I knew was that there was no hesitation anymore in this game of chicken. The rules had changed. The clock was winding faster and faster and our turns blended into one another's as I grappled for purchase along his back and as he yanked at the button of my jeans.

I fell backwards onto the mattress, my breath knocked out of me as Mason claimed the space between my legs. My back arched off the sheets as he drew his tongue in a long, hot line along my pussy.

"Devour that pussy," came the words, but whose words, I didn't know.

Mine.

Mason's.

Miss Last Night's.

It didn't matter.

My heels scraped against the strong muscles of Mason's upper back. My fingers curled into the sheets like I was plummeting off a cliff and they were my only chance to catch myself. Mason's fingers dug into the flesh of my thighs, my hips, scraping his nails across my erect nipples, scraping them again and again like he was falling too. Like I was his only chance to catch himself.

"Good girl. So fucking responsive."

Mason's voice rumbled through my core and I was smashed back into a place of just *being*. Somewhere between here and there. Hanging among the stars.

The world had faded away. Mason's bedroom. The rain on the glass window down the hall. Even the bed that I'd dreamed of being in, longed to writhe in the way I was writhing now. It was all gone.

Behind my eyelids it was dark like it was behind the theatre curtain. All-consuming as the theatre curtain when it closes on the audience and I was left alone with nothing but my panting, gasping breaths and Mason's voice, saying all those dirty things to me that drove me crazy.

"Such a sweet pussy. I could eat this fucking pussy all day."

There was me. And there was Mason's tongue. Mason's fingers slipping inside me. Mason's desire which I could feel in the roughness of the way his fingers curled and rubbed, in the desperate way he worked his tongue against my clit.

"Who owns your orgasm?"

Mason's words there, but far away. The words there, but close. Echoing in my chest. In my groans. Between my legs.

"You." It slipped out too easily.

"That's fucking right."

For a moment I feared he would torture me like he did all those years ago. Like I'd be punished for playing chicken with him, with pretending I didn't care about him, lying to him that our "marriage" was fake.

His wet finger slipped down between my ass cheeks and circled that sensitive back hole. Bastard. He knew exactly what he was doing. Knew exactly where to touch me to set me off. He slipped his finger in my ass and I let out a cry. With his finger in my back hole and his thumb in my pussy, he pulled and rubbed at the sensitive flesh between both holes, playing my body like an instrument.

"Come."

He sucked my clit into his mouth. I screamed as I came, my hands above my head, gripping the edge of the mattress, my fingers digging into that little seam like it was a crack in a cliff face, gripping it so tightly that my nails might crack. My back arched off the bed, taking the sweat-soaked sheets with it, rising like I was being exorcised.

Just as I was melting into the sheets, feeling like I could lose myself forever, there was Mason kneeling between my legs, pinning my hips down like I was his prey. His hungry eyes told me everything. He wanted to rip me apart. To destroy me. To make me a meal and to devour every single last bite.

I felt Mason's cock at my entrance, urgent and pressing. I felt me pressing back against him, just as urgent. Rising back up from the bed to meet him. To challenge him. My trembling thighs straining as I hitched my hips to urge him closer. My body was already aching again. Already hungry again. Already wanting again.

He plunged into me, hard and fast. I was so wet I accepted him fully, our twin groans echoing as he rammed into the hilt.

No hesitation. He pulled back and thrust into me again, the pressure already building back up inside me.

"Fuck, I love this tight little cunt."

He was merciless. Fucking me like he hated me. Like he was punishing me. Throwing my legs up over his shoulders so he could fuck me deeper. And fuck, his dirty mouth...

"Such a greedy little slut. *My* dirty little slut. Look at the way you're milking my cock. You're going to come for me again, aren't you?"

"Yes," I cried out.

He reached out, wrapped his hand around my throat and squeezed. A rush filled my head. Spots danced in front of my vision. My entire body buzzed.

"When you come, who are you going to come for?" he growled. His cock was relentless as he rammed into me like he was trying to break me apart.

"You," I croaked.

"Who do you belong to?"

"You," I chanted, barely a whisper on my numbing lips. "You, only you."

"Then come."

His hand loosened around my throat and the rush of blood flooding into my head made my whole body electrify, sending me over the edge.

I screamed his name. Heard him scream mine. Felt his warmth spill into me. We held onto each other as we rode our orgasms together.

We sagged together, and it was like the last ten years—the time, the distance, the hurt—were exhaled along with our breaths. He gently placed my legs down then lowered his forehead on mine as he rested forward on his elbows. For a few long moments, it was just our breaths tangling just like our bodies were still tangled. Like our souls were. There was no *then* and *now*, just us.

"Rachel," he whispered, his voice breaking, "I—"

There was a high-pitched moan. *A moan?*

I turned my gaze over to see Miss Last Night, sagging against the pillows.

Oh my God. She was here. She was *still* fucking here.

And she'd just come from watching *us* come.

We'd fucked in front of her. Our intimate moment, destroyed by the reminder that this was just a fucking game.

"Bravo! Bravo! So *fucking* hot!"

She brought her fingers, wet from her cum, to her swollen lips. Her grin turned my stomach as she sucked them into her mouth, choking herself on them as she pushed them deeper inside.

I turned to look at Mason and just like that, the world came crashing back. The past ten years and all their emptiness. The blackmail. The lies. The game. *This* fucking game.

What the fuck did I just do? Mason was above me, chest heaving, wide eyes like he'd only just woken up, too.

"Get off me," I mumbled.

"Rachel—"

"Get off me," I screamed.

Mason pulled back. "Rach—"

"I have to go," I muttered in a sort of state of shock as I climbed out of the bed and ran from the room, Mason's come dribbling down my thigh.

I didn't care if I lost. In fact, I wanted to lose. I wanted to get as far away from there as I could.

I didn't want to play games anymore.

24

RACHEL

hen...

I TRIED PUSHING at Mason's shoulders, but it was no use. It was like trying to push against a boulder. Or a brick wall. Or a—oh God, you pick your own analogy if you want. I was far too preoccupied to focus.

"I've got to—no, no, I've got to—"

Mason's tongue paused only long enough for him to lift his head between my legs, lips wet with me, and grin. "You've got to come all over my face is what you've got to do."

He nipped at that sensitive skin at the inner thigh, a reprimand, and my head fell back with a groan as he kissed it. And then kissed farther up. I dragged my fingers through my hair as Mason's tongue went back to work on my pussy.

"I've got to go," I whined, already losing the will as Mason circled his tongue over my clit. "I'll be late for my show if I don't leave now."

Mason murmured something against me. I propped myself up on my elbows to see him. Good God that was a mistake. How the fuck was I supposed to pull myself away from *that*? The muscles of Mason's back rippled beneath his tattoos like the goddamn tides at midnight. Smooth as silk. Powerful as the ocean itself. His bare ass was clenched as he rolled his hips against the sheets, getting off as he got me off. Unable to stop himself. The greedy bastard. His legs were a fucking mile long on the crumpled sheets (sheets we'd crumpled) and as thick as logs. I'd felt their strength over and over again in the last few days. As he held me up against the wall. As he pounded into me against the glass shower wall. As he hoisted me up onto his cock and thrust his hips up into me.

The final nail in my coffin was seeing his eyes. Those bright green eyes, filled with lust and flashing with desire, boring right into me. *Fuck.*

"What did you say?" I managed to ask as I gripped the sheets on either side of me.

"To go," he said between licks, "you need to come."

"No, no," I groaned as I flopped back, fingertips tingling, lips buzzing like he'd smeared them with whiskey. "Mason, I'm going to be *late*."

"Do I have to punish you again?"

"What?"

"When I say come, what do you fucking do?" came Mason's mumbled reply.

Mumbled because he was sucking on me. Licking me with such a fury that there was going to be nothing left of me.

"But my show," I muttered, already knowing that I was halfway gone. "I'm going to—I'm—"

"This fucking body is mine." He pushed a finger into my pussy and curled it round. "This pussy is *mine*."

He could have kept reminding me, but he didn't need to.

He'd release me when I released myself. There was no getting around it. I didn't *want* to get around it.

I sagged against the pillow.

"Good girl."

He added a second finger. And I melted further for him.

In another world he was making my dinner so that I wouldn't be late. He was checking the bus schedule for me or offering to drive me or reaching my costume from the laundry for me. In another world, he was wrangling up the kids to kiss me goodbye for the night. Or promising to help them with their schoolwork as I darted out the door. In another world he was at the kitchen table. "Yes, yes, I'll talk with our tax attorney. Just go. You'll be late."

The thought almost made me laugh. It was silly. Ridiculous even.

I didn't laugh, because I wanted that. Wanted that more than anything. Wanted to be running around trying to balance everything, wanted Mason to be the one running around with me.

"You're going to be here when I get back, aren't you?" I asked.

I'm not quite sure why exactly. My body was so hot with pleasure that I shouldn't have been able to think about anything but the fire consuming me. But the thought came and the words spilled out.

Everything inside me held tight. The muscles along my abdomen. My thighs. My forearms as they bunched the sheets even further. Even along my throat. I was waiting for my release. I was waiting for Mason's answer. They'd become one in the same. If I knew he would be there, I could let go. If I knew he would catch me, I could fall.

I stared up at the ceiling of the hotel room, our image reflected in the sparkling mirror. I looked at us sprawled out on the bed. Drunk on ecstasy. High on carnal pleasure.

But then I focused on the woman up there on the ceiling and saw a woman afraid. She was too naked. Too exposed. Everything there to see. Everything there to leave. To abandon.

The sheets suddenly seemed thin. Too cold to give the woman warmth. It was only he who could warm her, the man between her legs.

There up on the ceiling I saw Mason's naked body between mine. His toes scrambling for purchase as he bucked against the mattress. His fingers thrusting in and out of me. His head moving as he ran his tongue up and down in long, hot streaks.

I watched as my hands reached for him, suddenly afraid I wouldn't find him. That the woman in the reflection would keep stretching and stretching and not find flesh. Not find muscle. Not find his fingers to intertwine with. To lock into. To hold onto and not let go.

I reached for Mason as I waited for an answer. As I stared up at the woman. At myself. As I trembled with pleasure, as I shivered with fear. As my orgasm loomed on the horizon, hot and white. As it all balanced on a question I wished I hadn't asked.

Mason lifted his head. To get my answer I would have to look down at him. I couldn't look at this painting on the ceiling. I couldn't look at this projection of him and me, of the woman and the man, the actress and the actor on the screen.

I had to be there. In the moment. I had to look at Mason. Be there with Mason. To look into his eyes. To see him. To hear him. The real him. The real me.

My hand, still reaching, found his. He weaved his fingers through mine. I held on tight and drew my eyes to him down across my body.

Mason spoke one word and I could feel it against me. Against the wet heat of my folds. Against the raised bud of my clit. I could feel it *inside* of me.

"Yes."

I heard it. But I felt it, too. I *felt* it.

I squeezed his hand and he squeezed mine. We breathed heavily across one another. Eyes locked. Bodies rising and falling in time.

"And you?" Mason asked between licks. "You'll come back?"

Mason swirled his tongue around my clit. I groaned, resisted the urge to let my head fall back again. With his mouth on me, with his tongue in me, with his eyes on mine, I answered in return.

"Yes."

I'd wanted him to hear me. Of course I'd wanted him to hear me, just like I'd heard him. But I wanted him also to *feel* the word, the promise, the vow I'd made. I'd wanted the word "yes" to echo in my lungs, to travel through my veins, to crash over my body like an unstoppable wave. I wanted him to feel its power. Its strength. Its truth.

I had just enough time to think that this was how a marriage ceremony should be. Promising one to another through one's body. The ultimate connection. The most honest of vows. I had just enough time to think that any ceremony we had in the future (and I stupidly, ridiculously I believed we would) couldn't possibly be as meaningful as the one we'd just conducted between each other there on that bed.

Mason sucked my clit into his lips hard, gripped me tighter, pulled me closer, and sent me hurtling off the edge.

I wasn't sure I'd ever come like that before. So fully. So completely. It emptied me and filled me in ways that I hadn't known were possible. I tore at the sheets above my head and tried to buck away from Mason's fingers and tongue, but he just held me there, sending wave after wave crashing over me.

When I finally collapsed onto the bed, soaked and shaking, Mason was there beside me, caressing my cheek, running his fingers through my hair.

"I'll be here," he said, his voice echoing inside of me.

"I'll come back," I said, and I swore I could hear the words beating through my chest and into his heart.

After I'd dressed, I crossed the room on wobbly legs. When I paused at the door to smile back at Mason still there on the bed, I felt I finally had solid ground beneath me.

In a few hours' time I would learn just how wrong I was. It wasn't solid ground. Mason wasn't solid ground.

It was quicksand.

He was quicksand.

25

MASON

ow...

CLOTHES HAD BEEN the last thing on earth I'd cared about while Rachel was here. In fact, the general rule of thumb had been the fewer clothes, the better. The naked-er, the merrier.

But then, in the one moment when clothes should have mattered the absolute least, when it was actually necessary to forego the time it took to find a pair of boxers or pants on the floor and yank them hastily on, when it was better to run out the bedroom door with dick waggling free, then, *then* was when I decided I needed to clothe myself.

Rachel and I had fucked like we'd never been apart.

We'd made love like we'd never be apart.

Then Miss Last Night had come. And Rachel tore herself away from me with this look of horror and pain that struck straight at my heart. There had been a second's pause. Only a second. Not enough time to catch my breath. Not enough time to realise what was happening. What *had* happened. Not even enough fucking time to reach for her. To gasp out a panicked, "Wait." To make some noise, any noise, any form of protest. There had been a second's pause and then she had been gone.

Blouse left on the floor. Jeans left cast over the side of the bed where I'd thrown them uncaringly. Bra God knows where.

Clutching her exposed breasts and doubled over as if she'd been sucker punched in the gut, Rachel ran from the room. Instead of running after her I sat on the edge of the bed and swivelled my head back and forth, looking for something to cover myself up with.

I could hear her footsteps down the hall. I could hear the finality of them. The hurry in them. I knew that something had snapped. Something was broken. Something I wasn't sure could be fixed. I could hear the closet doors get slung open. Could hear them rattle against the walls. I could hear the screech of hangers. Metal against metal. I could feel it, that noise. In my body. In my bones. In my blood. I could hear the screech of hangers and the stuffing of clothes and the wrenching of zippers and I knew what was happening.

There I was, frozen, immobile, looking over the floors for clothes.

It wasn't just a numbness that made me certain that I couldn't face Rachel again naked. It wasn't a form of shock that kept me from running after her right that instant. I think it was something more like shame. Embarrassment. A part of me wanted to hide from Rachel. A part of me feared being seen by her. Exposed in front of her. A part of me knew it hadn't been fair. What had just happened. The reason something was now broken.

I hadn't meant for things to go so far. But when does anyone ever, in a game of chicken? You keep saying just a little further, just a little further. You keep thinking they can't go on like this, no, they can't go on like this. You feel alive and scared out of your fucking mind and you convince yourself nothing will go wrong if you push on that accelerator just a little more, just a little bit more. You don't expect how it could end. With shards of glass in the moonlight. Steam rising in the steady rain. Shattered headlights cast across a bloodied body. Unmoving. Broken beyond repair.

Rachel's body had been a drug. A trip. A memory I got to relive in vibrant colour, with searing heat, in real time. I'd been vaguely aware that I was crossing a line. That the game was losing its rules. That winning and losing were beginning to mean very different things. That the very game itself was no longer a game.

I should have pulled away. Should have stopped us. When I was still at least a little conscious. When I could still remember which bed I was in. Which year. When I still had some presence of mind that Miss Last Night was there. Getting off on us. Getting off on our train wreck. Our car crash on that one-lane road.

But it was Rachel. It was her. Her taste. Her body. Her moans.

And I couldn't stop. I wanted us to crash. I wanted us to collide. The goal was now to not let her turn away, to not let her swerve off at the last second, to hear her screams once more.

Maybe that's why I only hurried down the hallway once I'd yanked on the first pair of boxers I'd found. Because I couldn't be naked in front of her. I couldn't let her see all of me. All my desire for her. All my yearning for her. All the pain she'd caused me when she left. All the wounds she'd torn open again by coming back. All the pain I wanted to inflict on her. All the pleasure. All the lifetimes of fucking pleasure.

"What are you doing?" I asked as I stood at the doorway to Rachel's room.

She hadn't taken the time to put clothes on. She was still

naked as she tore like a hurricane through the room. The eye of the storm was the suitcase in the centre of the bed. Opened. Overflowing with clothes. All her clothes. Rachel was a torrent of fury as she darted between the dresser and the bed. Panties getting flung onto the stack. Panties falling onto the floor. It was chaos and Rachel was at the heart of it all.

Fuck, even as a hurricane she was beautiful. Honey curls wild as stalks of wheat in a summer storm. Breasts shaking in anger. Lips drawn tight. Eyes flashing like lightning. Her heaving breaths like thunder. Beautiful and violent like a passing storm. There then gone. Leaving a mess in her wake.

I hated her. Hated myself for loving her. God. *God.* I still fucking *loved* her.

"What does it look like I'm doing?" she snarled.

She looked like she was doing CPR on her suitcase. Tits flying. Hips thrusting. Hair wild. It certainly wasn't us that she was trying to save. Of that I was goddamn sure.

"Come on," I said, leaning against the door frame, trying for casual to cover up my inner panic. "We were just having a little fun."

Rachel's eyes stabbed straight through me. She said nothing. Just stared. Just ripped me apart and left me bleeding. She turned away like it wasn't her problem at all.

"You used to like a little fun," I tried. The words sounded lame even to my own ears.

"Um, are you guys coming back?" Miss Last Night called from my bedroom just down the hallway.

"Rachel doesn't think it's fun anymore," I called back to her, trying to keep my voice casual, easy.

I didn't think it was fun anymore either. Except I didn't know how to say it. I didn't know how to be anyone but the horny asshole who just wanted his "wife" to come back to bed and continue the threesome.

I didn't know how to walk over to Rachel. To place my hand gently on her arm. To whisper, "I'm sorry. Please. That was real for me. I love you."

Rachel tugged a sweater over her head. I was fairly certain it was backwards. Fairly certain she didn't give a damn. The pants she pulled on, stumbling from one leg to the next, were the first she'd grabbed off the heap from the suitcase. She didn't bother with socks before yanking on her boots. I guess that should have said everything about how she felt about me: she'd rather rub her feet raw than stick around two seconds longer to pull on socks.

"You started it," I tried again. Giving a little laugh. Hearing it fall flat. "I was just playing along."

Rachel zipped her suitcase till the zipper snagged on a pair of hose. She'd made it halfway. She decided that was good enough. Good enough to get out of there at least. I imagined her at the airport trying to fix it as her gate was called. I saw her disappearing down that tunnel toward the plane.

She shoved past me with her suitcase.

"What about that divorce you want so bad?" I blurted out.

I hadn't meant to sound so desperate. But reality was sinking in: Rachel was leaving. There was nothing I could do to stop her. Or at least nothing I was willing to do. Able to do: a hand on her arm. A plea. "I'm sorry." "Please." "I want you." "I need you." "I love you." "Don't go."

Don't go.

I followed Rachel down the hallway. Miss Last Night stuck her head out the doorway, calling after us as we passed. I didn't bother to listen. Rachel certainly didn't either.

"What about your sparkling new role?" I said at her a little too angrily.

I'd put on clothes to hide myself, but there I was letting my emotions expose me anyway. I tried to wrangle it all in, but it was like trying to harness a storm.

"Huh, Rachel? What are you going to do about that sweet, perfect, shiny little image you want God knows who to see? Huh? What are you doing to do about the bit of dirt still stuck on your Barbie doll's foot?"

At the bottom of the stairs, Rachel whipped around to face me. She was just as angry as I was. She wasn't trying to hide it. She wanted me to see it. To remember it. To remember why she was leaving.

"You think you can ruin my life?" she hissed in my face. "You think you can go out there and tell the world just who I am? Just who I really am? There's one little problem with that. Just one teeny-tiny little problem. You don't have a clue who I am. Who I *truly* am. You don't have a fucking clue, Mason!"

Her finger jabbed at my chest as she spoke. Each stab harder than the last. But they all hurt. They all fucking hurt. So I wanted to hurt her back. It was that simple. And stupid. But I wasn't thinking clearly in that moment. All I was was petty revenge and tit for tat.

I leaned in close to Rachel. Close enough that she could have stuck out her tongue and tasted herself on my lips.

I whispered, "And you think you do?"

Rachel flinched. Just barely. My strike had struck. I didn't even have a second to celebrate before she was gone. I was left standing there in front of an open door, the rain splattering onto the entryway.

She was gone. I could hear her suitcase wheels rattling on the sidewalk for a minute or two. Then that was gone, too.

I cursed her name as I stormed back up the stairs. Miss Last Night called me from the bed. I ignored her. I went past my room straight to the one at the end of the hall, the one Rachel had just vacated. I didn't want to see the emptied, open drawers and the hangers scattered across the floor. I was about to slam the door shut but—

A mess of my nan's shoeboxes had fallen from the top of the closet. Half a dozen or so. A couple remained closed. A handful opened, their dainty little church heels or red velvet ballet flats tumbled out across the floor. And one shoebox that didn't have shoes. From the doorway I could make out amongst the scattered pages a few old photos, some yellowed tickets, and a thick set of letters bound with frayed twine.

The name written across the envelope with the letters was my name. In a scrawling, unfamiliar cursive.

My name in my nan's shoebox. Someone's handwriting I didn't know in my nan's shoebox.

I shoved everything back inside the shoebox and crammed it without further thought back onto the top shelf of the closet. I didn't bother with the shoes. I figured my nan wouldn't mind; it wasn't like she'd be using them any time soon. I then left the room without looking back. Closed the door. Closed it hard. Walked away fast.

The memories I had of my nan were painful enough. I didn't need to go finding new ones. You don't go searching for more knives when you're already bleeding.

26

RACHEL

The taxi circled round and round Dublin city.

The rain slashed at the windshield as city block after city block passed in smears of grey. I spent the afternoon hunched over in the backseat, stretching to keep my cell phone plugged into the USB port on the dash. The cabbie sent me the occasional questioning glance as the meter ticked up and up, but I just shooed him with a hand or gave him another nod.

"I'm sorry, ma'am, but that's our earliest flight available."

"I need to get out sooner."

"I'm sorry, but—"

"What about standby?"

"There's really no chance until tomorrow morning. Again I do—"

Then I was on hold with another airline.

"Tomorrow."

"Nothing earlier?"

"The earliest is tomorrow."

Round and round Dublin we drove. Airline after airline I called. All the same red lights. All the same answers. All the same streaks of rain. All the same truth: I couldn't run. Not yet anyhow.

"We have one more seat on a flight tonight—"

"I'll take it."

"Are you sure, ma'am?"

"Yes, yes, book it."

A little longer. A little longer to run. To escape. I took a taxi round and round Dublin. I ended up, of all places, at The Jar.

It was still an hour or so before opening but "Thor" let me in. Okay, fine, his name was Noah as far as I could remember.

I was fairly certain Noah was afraid of me. In better times I might have taken it as a compliment. But it wasn't better times. In all probability he just thought I was crazy. A mad woman. Just another one of Mason's scorned Miss Last Nights.

I guess I couldn't really blame him. I must have looked like an absolute mess. If I dared to lift my chin enough to check my appearance in the grimy mirror peeking out between the line of liquor bottles, I would have been a little wary of that woman as well. Hair frizzed from the rain. Messy from the sheets. Makeup smeared from the humidity. Patchy from the sweat that covered my brow, covered my body while my fingers twisted in Mason's hair. Clothes rumpled and unmatched. Buttons done wrong. Sweater on backwards.

And my eyes... I couldn't imagine what they looked like. Dull and empty. Vacant. Not angry. Just...nothing. No me left at all. Rachel...gone.

Noah, as he pushed a beer down the bar top toward me with his fingertips, wanting (understandably) to stay as far away as possible.

"What's all of this?" I asked, nodding my head toward the staff who was working on setting up a small stage over by the DJ booth. Two girls, one with auburn hair and the other with black curls that made mine look limp and lifeless in comparison, were hanging a bright red sequined fabric across two poles. All around the stage were boxes with mics and cords, costumes and go-go boots, instruments and batons, lyric books and fire extinguishers.

"Talent Night," Noah answered. "It always brings in a rather amusing crowd. We provide a bunch of costumes and props and shite so people who swear they don't have a talent can remember their talent after a pint or two and still get on up there to give it a lash."

I watched him smile at the girl with the auburn hair. His eyes followed the swish of her ponytail as she stretched to pin the sequined fabric in place. I heard her laugh. Saw the reaction in his face as he heard it, too. An ache bloomed in my stomach and I drowned it with a big swig of beer.

"You know," Noah said, looking across the bar at me, "I don't know what you and Mason are up to, but if you want to—"

"I don't have a talent," I interrupted curtly.

Noah poured me a shot and nudged it closer with a wink. I rolled my eyes, but took the shot nevertheless. With my suitcase in one hand and my beer in the other I found the darkest, quietest corner of the bar. The one with the stickiest tabletop. The one with the wobbliest chair. The one with the column positioned awkwardly in front of it. I didn't want to hear laughter. See smiles. Sense love like a stirring breeze.

After my second beer I decided to call Tim. Maybe it should have told me something that it was only once I was a little tipsy that I even thought of my fiancé. Before that there had only been one man in my mind. One face behind my eyelids. One voice I mistook Noah's for time and time again...

"Babe, I'm so glad you called," Tim answered.

He was breathless. The sounds of New York City surged around him on the line: cars honking, pedestrians chattering as they passed the opposite way on the sidewalk, hot dog venders and ticket scalpers and old rappers still handing out mixed CDs on the corner. A wave of homesickness passed through me.

"Hold on, hold on," Tim said, making me realise I hadn't even answered back. I'd just been listening. Taking it all in. Remembering.

"Hold on, yeah, hold on," Tim said again, and then the noise of the city was gone.

Silence fell over the line like a blanket dousing a fire. Tim was home. I knew this. At the apartment. Taking off his shoes. Putting them properly back in their place.

I realised that the home I felt sick for was not those big bay windows overlooking the park by the grand piano. Wasn't the wood floors polished to sheen by the cleaning staff morning after morning. Or the crystal chandelier that hung over a deadly silence.

It was the sidewalk. It was the noise. It was JoJo and whatever colour hair she had that day. It was life. It was people trying, struggling to find their way. To do something. To be something. To be *seen*.

Clearing my throat, I said, "Um, you said you were glad that I called. It's, um, it's been a little while, hasn't it?"

I was grappling for something. Reaching out to catch something that I felt was slipping through my fingers. I wanted Tim to reignite a flame in me I feared had dimmed. Had gone out. Had been snuffed out by a tattooed thumb, callused and rough. I shifted uncomfortably because I needed Tim to remind me why I'd loved him. Why I *loved* him.

I wasn't empty, I realised in that moment. I was afraid. Afraid that I'd had something and lost it with Mason. Afraid that I'd never had anything with Tim and was going to give up everything for it. That thing that never was.

"Yes, yes," Tim said as I held my breath, on the edge of my

chair without realising it, biting my nails without realising it. "Yes, I made it work. I got us tickets for opening night!"

"Opening night?" I asked.

Tim went on to say what and when. He went on and on about what connection he'd used. And how. He went on about who would be there. Where they could get him. Each meaningless word seemed to carve more and more out of me. Each word hollowed my chest. Each word dug a little deeper, took a little more.

I don't know if I interrupted him. I don't know if he was already finished, breathless like he'd just jerked himself off onto the cashmere rug draped just so over the back of the couch. Frankly, I didn't fucking care.

"Tim," I said with an urgency that almost frightened me and almost certainly frightened him, "what if I wasn't who you thought I was?"

I imagined Tim pausing in the kitchen. Holding a crystal water glass. Purified water falling from the tap. I imagined him turning the tap off. Stepping back to lean against the marble countertops.

He laughed a little. Maybe nervously. Maybe not.

"Rachel, what on earth kind of question is that?"

I stood up because I needed to walk. Needed to pace. To move. To feel like I still could.

"It's just—I don't know, it's just, I mean, do we ever really know someone?"

"I know you," came Tim's reply.

I ignored it. Ignored it completely. Because he didn't.

"And if you were to learn something about me, something *more* about me." It sounded incoherent, I know, even though in my heart, in my mind, in my soul it all made perfect sense. "What I'm trying to say is, if you found out something about me and it didn't fit this image you have of me...would you still love me?"

I wanted to ask him more. Press him further. I wanted to ask if he had room in his heart for more of me. For a bigger image of me. For a messier me. A bolder me. A more complicated me. A me that wanted more from life. A me that stumbled in drunk in the middle of the night, laughing and singing and shedding sequins.

But I found those words didn't come out. Wouldn't come out. It wasn't something I wanted Tim to answer. Because I already knew another's answer. I already knew Mason's answer.

"Rachel, darling, you're perfect just the way you are. Really, I don't know where this is coming from. You're the sweetest little thing. An angel really. Something to be protected. Something to be held close and cherished. Something that deserves all the nicest things in life. All the comforts. All the simplicity. All the refinements."

Tim went on and on. I had stopped walking. Stopped pacing. Stopped moving.

"I know who you are and nothing you can tell me will change that," he continued. "I know you're as innocent as the snow. As sweet as candy. I mean, why else do you think I fell for you that day in the cafe where you were waitressing? Why else do you think I kept coming back when that cheap coffee was so horrible? I mean, where were those beans even sourced from?"

Tim laughed, but I was too preoccupied to laugh. I stared at the stage there by the DJ booth. It was a small thing. Kind of charming in how pitiful it was. But I knew it was the audience that would make it grand. Make it magical. The applause. The faces in the dark. Yeah, the fucking booze, too. I knew in a few hours' time there would be no difference at all between that little makeshift stage and the grandest theatres in the biggest hotels on the Vegas strip.

"Everyone loves you," Tim said, his voice sounding far away. Very far away. "It's nice, you know? In my circle, to have someone not from money. Someone real, you know? Someone who never had a chance in life, but now gets everything. It's a nice story, you know? People like it. Actually, at the opening I'll have to introduce you to Mr Livingston. He's the chair of—well, I won't bore you. But he'll love you. And your story. Our story. He's a good person to know if we want to get an invitation to that gala at the end of next year. Did I tell you about that one? It's really quite exclusive..."

There were more words but they faded as my hand fell from my ear. I stalked across the bar and stopped in front of the girl with big black curls. She glanced up at me, stooped over a box filled with nothing more than clown wigs.

"Um, hi," she said. "Can I—can I help you?"

"I'm Rachel," I said.

She eyed me curiously.

"Candace," she said slowly, glancing at the phone at my side where Tim's voice still came faintly.

"Candace," I said, "would you happen to have any makeup I could use? I think I have a talent."

Candace's face lit up. She dusted off her knees as she stood. I smiled when she stuck out her hand for me to take. I raised a finger to her before raising the phone to my ear.

"Tim, I've got to go. I've got a performance to get ready for."

I hung up and took Candace's hand.

"Are you a sparkle kind of girl?" she asked as she led me up the back stairs.

With a grin, I answered, "Yes."

27

MASON

Rachel left.

I shoved my nan's shoebox and whatever secrets were inside it back into the closet. I slammed the door on that godforsaken room.

After Rachel left, I yelled at Miss Last Night to leave. To get out. When she laughed and suggested we wait for my wife to cool down and come back, I shouted at her.

"Get the *fuck* out!"

Miss Last Night left after that. Left without a longing glance back over her shoulder. Left without asking for a number. Left without trying to set up a second date. Left and was glad to be leaving.

Turns out I was perfectly capable of getting rid of my Miss Last Nights all on my own. What a goddamn surprise, eh? That my ruse to keep Rachel around was bullshite from the very beginning. Maybe she'd seen through me this whole time. Maybe she'd always known my excuse was as flimsy as they came. Maybe she'd ignored it because she wanted to give me a chance.

A chance I'd just thrown away.

The divorce papers were where they'd been since that first night: under the bed. I'd come home with that woman I picked up in front of Rachel at the bar. I was about as close to blackout langers as you can get, but I was sober enough to still know that it wasn't her I wanted to fuck. I still had enough presence of mind to get those divorce papers out of sight. Under the bed seemed like the easiest place to make them disappear. So under the bed they'd gone. Off went Miss Last Night's clothes. And, as they say, the rest is history.

I don't know if that meant I was digging up history, lowering myself to my hands and knees and crawling beneath the bed. It certainly felt like there was a shovel present as I stretched my fingers, grunting as I searched. There was a shovel and it was scooping out my heart.

I emerged with my hands full and my chest empty.

Signing the papers wasn't difficult at all at that point. Something I would have refused to do that morning I did without hesitation. Something I couldn't imagine ever doing, I did in seconds. A flip of a page here. A flick of a pen there. And it was done.

A part of me had been sure that it wouldn't come to this. I'd agreed to thirty days, sure, but only as a way to buy time. A part of me had been certain that I'd buy more time after the thirty days if necessary. I'd buy more time after that. And after that. A part of me was determined not to ever sign. Not to ever give Rachel up. Not to ever let her get away a second time.

I'd killed that part of me. Because that part of me hurt Rachel. And that was worse than losing her.

So I signed. Whiskey bottle in one hand, pen in the other, I signed.

The tattoo parlour was quiet. Empty. The rain fell and I sat there alone staring at the stack of papers. All that was left to do was mail them back to the States. I didn't have Rachel's address.

But there was the one for the attorney. He'd figure it out. There were stamps in the supply closet. Or Aurnia could go grab some the next day. That would be the biggest complication left: Aurnia bristling at having to do a menial task, no longer seeing herself as the shop apprentice.

Other than that, there was nothing. No snag to keep Rachel and me tied together just a little bit longer. No error that would force her to come back. To come back to me. No mistake that would give me just one more chance...just one more chance...

I crammed the papers into the envelope. They sliced at my fingers but I didn't even feel the cuts till blood bloomed along my fingers. I sucked them between my lips. Then I bit down on my skin.

Bastard. I'd hurt her. Hurt Rachel. And this was my fucking penance. My signature on a fucking legal document that said I relinquish her. I give her up. I set her free.

The table overturned. Crashed to the floor. Splintered. I hardly realised it had been me till I saw the little smear of blood on its edge. Till I felt my feet beneath me. Till I struggled for breath as my heart pounded, as my lungs constricted.

I didn't want to give Rachel up. I didn't want to give her the divorce she came here for. But I was doing it. I *had* to do it. Because I'd hurt her. I'd fucking hurt Rachel. And I couldn't stand it. Hurting the one who'd hurt me first. It was fucked. All kinds of fucked. And it was threatening to drive me mad.

My knees collided painfully with the floor. Despite the old rugs I could feel the cold seeping up. I curled over myself and tugged at my hair. I couldn't get her face out of my head. The way she'd looked when she'd opened her eyes. The way she'd looked at me. The way she'd *seen* me.

I replayed it over and over again in my mind. Our little game. Pushing too far. Pushing farther. Miss Last Night's voice fading. Rachel on the bed. Her taste on my tongue. Her hot wet pussy around my cock. Her fucking reacting so beautifully to my dirty words. Everything. We'd had it again. Everything. Everything. Everything. Rachel coming on my tongue. Me lapping her up like her body held the very last drop of pure, clean water on earth. Me believing this was it. That we'd found our way back to one another. Me overcome with such desire, with such need that I plunged into her without restraint, as if I was trying to break Rachel in two with my cock. Then us coming together. Her name is a scream fading to an emotion-choked whisper.

Then her eyes. Her eyes. I remembered her eyes. Her eyes finding mine when we realised we hadn't been alone. The horror. The disgust. The pain.

I rocked back and forth on the floor there in the parlour of Dublin Ink. Gripping my head. Clenching my eyes shut.

"I signed, goddammit," I muttered in that hot, humid cave. "I fucking signed, so go! Leave me alone!"

But she was there. Rachel was there. In my head. Imprinted into my soul. Her pussy around my cock. Her warmth like a balm. Everything I'd missed for all those years just right fucking there.

I tore through the shelves in the supply closet for a stamp. I was out of my mind. Out of my goddamn mind, panting like a rabid dog as I made an absolute mess. Ink bottles falling. Shattering. Paint smearing beneath my boots. Her accusatory eyes would leave me alone once the papers were in the mail. Once they were out of my control. Her pained eyes would fade once I found those fucking stamps. Her hurt as she looked at me, *me* would be erased from my memory once I gave her what she wanted. A divorce. A separation from me, from *me*. An end. A fucking end.

"Go away!" I shouted as I yanked boxes of stencil papers from the shelves.

But Rachel and those piercing eyes were harder to get rid of than my Miss Last Nights. I couldn't scare those eyes away with my roaring voice. They didn't shrink from my imposing height. From my tensed muscles. I couldn't threaten those eyes.

We were out of stamps. Or I'd made such a mess that they were now impossible to find. I swore and pounded my fists against the metal shelving.

I needed a bar. I needed a drink. I needed a crowd. I needed to get lost amongst noise. Amongst people. Amongst faces I didn't know. I needed a Miss Last Night.

It was a solid enough plan:

Go to The Jar.

Get plastered.

Fuck some woman for the twenty minutes of peace that carnal act could give.

Hope for a rainy morning the next day to prolong unconsciousness.

Find stamps.

The rain hadn't let up. So by the time I got to The Jar I was soaked. The place was crammed. People stuffed all the way up to the foggy windows. I'd forgotten it was Talent Night.

It was the first good thing that had happened to me all day really. To pick up a chick, it didn't get much easier than swearing that she sounded just like, no really, *just* like Whitney Houston. Easy fucking pickings. Perfect for my foul mood.

In fact, a potential candidate was just finishing up a screeching ballad as I pushed and shoved my way to the bar. Noah and Aubrey were working double time to keep up with the drink orders. I caught Noah's eye after a little while and he nodded. He came a few seconds later with a beer.

"You're just in time," he shouted over the noise.

I frowned.

"Just in time for what?" I shouted back.

Noah jerked his chin over toward the stage at the back of the bar. It seemed impossible that in that exact moment I could have seen her. There must have been a hundred people between her and me. But I turned my head and the goddamn sea seemed to part for me. For us. There she was. On stage. The woman I thought was gone. The woman I thought I'd never see again.

Rachel.

And she was going to dance just for me.

28

MASON

hen...

"YOU GUYS DO KNOW they have strip clubs here?" I grumbled as we made our way to our seats. "You know, places where girls dance *on* you? Not just for you?"

After bumping into a dozen knees in that crammed little aisle, I collapsed moodily into the plush chair.

"There's leg room at strips, you know?" I complained as I squirmed like an impatient child. "They don't pack you in like cattle at strip clubs."

"You know, Conor," Rian leaned across me to say, "I think Mason would rather be at a strip club right now."

On the other side of me, Conor gave me a raised eyebrow.

"Is that so, Mason?" he asked in that gravel voice of his. "Because I wouldn't have guessed myself."

I slouched down even further in my seat and gave the two of them the middle finger, one each.

"We're in Vegas," Rian said as the announcement to silence

all phones came over the speakers. "It would be a waste if we didn't experience the local culture while we're here."

I crossed my arms moodily over my chest.

"I'd let a stripper tell me all about the history of the West while she shook her titties in my face," I said. "Would that count?"

"Didn't you fuck that flight attendant on the way over?" Conor asked as the lights went down.

"Yeah," I said, looking over at him. "So what?"

Conor shrugged. "Just thought that would keep you happy for a bit longer than it has."

I caught sight of his eyes before the theatre went dark. He wasn't joking. He'd meant it. "Keep me happy."

I should have been offended. That wasn't all my life was. Fucking around.

But I couldn't be offended, because a part of me knew he was right. That *was* all my life was. All I'd allowed my life to be. Fucking around. Woman to woman, day to day. Living the dream.

The irony was, I wasn't happy. Something was missing. It was times like these that I knew it. Saw it. Was forced to face it. The times when I didn't have the immediacy of hips in my hands, a nipple between my teeth, or an ass smushed against my cheeks. The times between saying goodbye and saying hello. The empty times.

I stared out across the pitch black of the theatre and saw my life. There was no pain. No, I hadn't been hurt. I'd made sure of that.

But there had to be more than that, right? Something more than a lack of pain? Something more than an absence of hurt? Something to fill me up. Something to overflow between my fingers. Something bright and lovely.

The lights along the stage flared up suddenly. They rose to

the heights of the velvety curtains. They cascaded down over the audience like torrents of water. They flashed in my eyes. Brighter than the sun. People around me blocked their eyes momentarily, but I stared at them. I stared through them. I blinked and there she was.

Alone on the stage. I saw her before everyone else. I was sure of that. Everyone else had their eyes closed. Had their eyes turned away. But I was looking right at her.

And she was looking right at me.

The theatre had to have had five hundred people in it, but I looked right at her and she looked right at me through that impossible light.

I saw surprise in her eyes. I'm sure she was used to staring out at the audience like a splatter painting, not picking out anyone in particular amongst the crowd. Maybe she saw surprise in my eyes as well. I expected the dancers to be far away. To smile blandly, generally. To move like puppets on strings and then get dragged away to the sides of the stage. I didn't expect to catch her eyes like we were across a bar. Like she could walk right over to me. Like she was about to whisper into my ear, "How about a drink?"

We looked at each other, looked at each other in surprise, and then the blinding lights were rising again, sweeping toward the ceiling, falling backwards to illuminate the stage. To illuminate her.

She stood there on stage in the ensuing silence, one heel up on a single chair. She wore fishnet stockings that ended mid-thigh. Her bustier was gold. Her honey-coloured hair fell around her bare shoulders in big curls.

The silence stretched on as she stood there. A few people in the audience cleared their throats. There was a cough or two. Some scuffling, some shifting in chairs.

The woman on stage looked picture perfect. Nothing out of

place. She was exactly as she was supposed to be. But the silence extended too long. The show should have started. Why was she still not moving? Still frozen there with her heel on that chair, top hat hanging loose at her side.

Only I knew, I thought with a shiver that trailed down my spine.

She was looking for me. Blinking through the lights that blinded her there on that big stage. She was looking for *me*.

The single spotlight shifted around her like it, too, was growing impatient. Eager for something. Eager for her to perform. Just like the audience who had come, paid for their tickets, waited in line.

I understood: she wasn't going to perform for them. For the audience. For the spotlight that circled her the way I wanted my tongue to circle her. She was going to perform for me. For me alone.

The girl stared into the blinding floor lights and a hiss came from the side of the theatre. We were careening toward a breaking point. She'd strained the audience too thin. People were going to start complaining. Walking out. Demanding refunds. The manager of the show was seconds away from storming the stage and animating the girl's frozen limbs like a puppeteer. "Look, everyone, no, look! She's performing! She's performing for all of you!"

Only I would know it was bullshite. She was here for me. And I was here for her.

Another hiss from the eaves of the theatre. More shifting. More creaking of the chairs.

Rian leaned over to whisper, "I want whatever she's on."

I thought I heard a name hissed this time from just out of sight. But I couldn't quite catch it. It was like a passing breeze. Perfumed with flowers. Beautiful, but quickly gone.

"You might get your strip club after all," Conor grumbled next to me, folding his big arms over his bearlike chest.

"Shut up," I whispered, eyes still transfixed on the girl.

The whole audience went silent when a short man in all black stalked down the centre aisle toward the stage with balled fists and a sweating forehead. The girl eyed him, saw how fast he was approaching, searched once more futilely against the stage lights, and then almost angrily threw back her head.

From the band in the orchestra pit came a snare. The director paused mid-step. The snare went on. Soft. Low. The audience held its breath. We all watched, transfixed, as the girl, in time to the building snare, lifted her top hat, slowly, slowly, slowly. When it was all the way over her head, she shook it as the snare went faster, faster. She was beautiful, her figure graceful and elegant, but there was frustration in the lines of the muscles of her arms. Her knuckles were white, trembling where she gripped the edge of the black top hat. With a sudden clash of symbols, the girl dropped the top hat onto her head and mounted the chair.

The theatre was once again silent as she stood up there, facing us. The director still hadn't retreated. He wasn't sure yet what she was going to do. How much money he was going to have to give back that night. What her next move would be. No one did. No one but me.

I was the only one not on the edge of my seat. The only one not turning my head from neighbour to neighbour, asking confused questions with the lift of an eyebrow, with the widening of dilated pupils. The only one unsure whether this was planned or not, a part of the show or not.

Because I understood. Just like I understood the sun would rise in the morning. Just like I understood storms would come and storms would go. Just like I understood that fire should not, ever, be touched, no matter how beautiful. No matter how alluring.

I understood she was going to dance for me.

The brim of the top hat shadowed the girl's face, but I knew her eyes even then were still searching. I knew from the tremor that shook her frame. She was still angry. Still frustrated. She still wanted to find me. And she still couldn't.

The girl's foot collided with the stage floor in time with a bang of the gong. As her hands rose over her head, she slowly slid her heel forward, extending into the splits. At the sight of this the director spun on his heel, probably cursing low under his breath. The theatre audience sank back against their seats, assured that everything was fine. Everything was the way it was supposed to be. Nothing had changed.

I alone leaned forward. I alone knew that nothing was as it was supposed to be. I alone knew the truth: everything had fucking changed.

The girl began her routine. She shocked the audience, content in the silence, by kicking the chair over. By sinking all the way to the floor as its rattling echo filled the theatre. Shocked everyone but me. I leaned even further forward as she spun her back leg around to meet the front. I was transfixed as she slumped over her legs. A broken doll. Eyes concealed by the shadow of her top hat, crooked on her shining curls. Again the silence fell over the theatre like a heavy blanket. Suffocating. Inescapable.

No one else around me was breathing like I was. Heart pounding. Somehow both panicked and assured. No one else was struggling to keep from gasping, because the director had gone backstage. The girl had begun her performance. The band was following her cues. Everything was alright for them. But nothing, absolutely nothing, was alright for me.

When the music started and the girl arched her back,

pushed up into a bridge, kicked her legs over, caught the top of the fallen chair with her toe, hoisted it up into her waiting hand, spun it round, and came to sit on it with a coy smile, forearms folded across the back, the audience cheered because this was what was supposed to happen. Only I saw the girl's eyes. Searching again. Their intensity not matching at all the sweetness of her smile. That was for the rest of the theatre. Her eyes. Her eyes were for me.

The dancer drummed her feet in time to music as the chorus girls in sparkly, glittery costumes filed in from the sides of the stages, dragging behind their measured steps chairs of their own. The stage was soon busy with spinning chairs, with fingers sliding slowly, seductively down outstretched legs, with feathered butts wiggling against one another, with music and singing and chorus lines. But at the peak of it all, always in the forefront was her.

I remained leaning forward. Elbows on my knees. Heart pounding. And she, always, remained separate from the rest. Not just because she was the showrunner. Not just because she was the most beautiful, the most magnetic, the one that sparked with a special kind of energy. But because she was the only one not performing for several hundred people. The only one not sharing her bright eyes with the whole theatre. The only one not going through the motions, not aware that this was a show in Vegas.

The only one who was dancing on an empty stage. In front of a theatre of empty chairs. Empty all save one.

The one I was sitting in.

The burlesque show went on. In a whirl of bright colours, of flashing sequins, of billowing feathers, she was the only fixed spot. She was the North Star that all the other constellations spun and twirled and dashed around. Or maybe she was Mars.

Burning red. Angry. Frustrated. Furious. Because she hadn't found me again against those blinding lights.

But I would find her.

I was sure of it. Just like I was sure that when the girl bowed at the end of the show, just before the curtain swallowed her whole, she already hated me. Hated me the way I would one day hate her. Because I'd been there in the first place. And to be there and then be gone, gone forever, was always worse than to have never been there at all.

Another blank face in a sea of blank faces.

That was my sin without even knowing it.

And it would one day be hers.

29

RACHEL

The little back room of The Jar was a far cry from the full-service dressing room I enjoyed in Vegas when I had my own show.

It was half the size, for one thing. If not less. The soft lamplight which filtered a soft pink all those years ago was more of a bright glare at The Jar: a mirror, some bare bulbs lining it, nothing more. The couch was older, dingier, patchier. I knew there wasn't going to be a knock at the door. An intern with a clipboard, a headset, and an eager smile to stick her head inside. Anything I can get for you, Miss Garcia? Anything? Anything at all?

The noise from outside the little back room of The Jar was different too. Not the demurred, respectful buzz of the Vegas theatre. But loud, brazen, drunk. It seemed to press on the flimsy plywood door like unwanted guests. Trying to cram inside.

There was not an antique dresser to hang my cheap polyester costume I'd borrowed from the boxes set up around the stage. There was not a glass of champagne waiting on the rose gold side table by the chaise. There was not a line of fans waiting for autographs out in that back alley lined with trash bins and illuminated by the red glow of bummed cigarettes.

In almost every way possible it was different from Vegas. From the show. From the crowd. From the pay, God knows that. From the little back room where I stood breathing heavily. Bent over at the waist. Hands on my knees. Hair hanging loose. Gasping. Everything was different, except for the way I felt.

I remembered with such clarity the moment I left the stage after that performance where I first locked eyes with Mason. When I hadn't even known his name. Hadn't know the time we would share together. Bright and fast and burning and gone. Hadn't known that he would be the one who would carve a hole in my heart and leave me with nothing but the shovel.

I remembered hurrying to my dressing room just like I hurried to the little back room of The Jar tonight. The way the door knocked the breath from my lungs as I fell against it, slamming it shut, had been exactly the same. I remembered pacing as I had just paced. Dragging my fingers through my hair. Tugging. Yanking. Staring up at the ceiling of the little back room with a tingle in my fingertips. Exactly like I did in my dressing room back in Vegas.

Staring as I tried to hold onto the image of his face. Trying to figure out why he had rattled me. Trying to figure out a way to get him out of my head because I was sure, absolutely sure, that I wouldn't be able to find him. Not amongst hundreds in the theatre. Not amongst thousands in the hotel. Not amongst hundreds of thousands on the strip.

I remembered that desperation, that confusion, that love. That hate. Because of all the people in the audience, I had to look at him.

In the little back room of The Jar, I started yanking at the zipper around the back of my costume. It was poorly made and I wasn't doing it any favours, tugging at it so recklessly. It caught.

I growled low in my throat as I twisted my arms around trying to free it. To free me.

Seeing Mason there in the crowd...was it a blessing? Or a curse? Or was that the cruelty of Mason? The cruelty and the beauty? That he was both. And would always be both.

He drew me in like a moth to a flame, only to watch me fall with singed wings. He caught me only to brush his fingers along the scars and assure me I could still fly. He threw me from his hand and turned away before he witnessed what I already knew: I couldn't, I couldn't. I *couldn't*. Not without him.

My heart was racing. Racing like it had been that very first night. Back then I'd been trapped in luxury. In fine silks. In expensive leathers. Constricted by the finest lace lingerie. It made no difference that it was now polyester and rayon and faux feathers. Because trapped was trapped. I wrenched at the zipper and it wouldn't release. It wouldn't just fucking let me go.

All Mason had to do was not show up. That was all he fucking had to do. Was I not worthy of even that simple kindness? Not fucking showing up? Hell, he could have stumbled into The Jar just thirty minutes, an hour later than he had. I would have been gone by then. I was sure of it. I would have danced. My zipper wouldn't have gotten stuck. I'd be in a taxi to the airport. Waiting in line at the terminal. Boarding. I'd be landing in the States. Getting drunk with JoJo. Getting my divorce attorney to deal with Mason like I should have from the very start. I'd be standing across from Tim in a white designer dress (the best money could buy) and I'd be saying my vows. And I'd be fucking sober enough to remember them this time!

"Goddammit," I cried as the zipper absolutely refused to budge.

All Mason had to do was stand a few feet to the right. A few feet to the left. The Jar was packed. Crammed from corner to corner. If he stood anywhere else, there was no way I would have seen him, *could* have seen him. Anywhere else and the stage lights (small compared to Vegas, but still bright enough) would have blinded me to him. Anywhere fucking else and Mason would have remained a faceless shape in the dark. An anonymous audience member. Nothing to remember him by. Nothing to sear onto my fucking heart.

But he hated me that much apparently. He had to come in right then. To stand right there. To not turn his eyes away when ours met. Locked. Connected like they'd connected all those years ago. On a different stage. In a different time. In a goddamn different continent.

But in the same way. In the same fucking way.

I tore at the zipper with all the strength I had left, but it did not relent. Panic and anger rose up in me till I was red in the face and struggling to catch my breath. It was then, when I was seconds away from collapsing to the floor, seconds away from trashing the whole goddamn little back room, seconds away from storming back out there, half clothed, and finding him and shoving him against the wall and—it was then that the door opened.

Mason.

I saw him over my shoulder in the mirror. There was me: one shoulder bare, costume tugged down, caught. There was me: an animal snagged in a snare. An animal whose thrashing only made it worse. I'd only managed to dig the teeth of the trap deeper into my flesh.

There was me: eyes on fire, cornered, but ready to fight. And there was Mason: slipping inside the room without a word. There was Mason: coming to stand in front of the door as it clicked shut with almost no sound at all. Mason: staring at me in the mirror with his emotions hidden.

Was he here to set me free? Or had he come in silence just to watch me struggle? To enjoy my pain? My cruel lover. My blessing. My fucking curse.

My hands remained where they were on the zipper at the back of my bustier. I pinched at that little metal zipper till my fingertips went numb. Till pins and needles came in to stab and prick at me. My arms shook from the effort. Was I shaking because I was strong? Or trembling because I was weak?

Mason and I locked eyes like it seemed we were fated always to do. We had as much choice in the matter as magnets. I loved it. And I fucking hated it.

He stood there against the door as the noise outside pounded its fists louder and louder. The glare of the bulbs around the mirror stabbed into my eyes, stabbed into Mason's. But he stood there, still. And I stood there, shaking. Trembling.

"I hate you," I said.

Meaning every fucking word. Filling each word with venom. Loving the bitter taste of it. Loving the sting of it. Each word like striking fangs on a snake. Death before you even realise the coiled thing has struck. I loved it. I loved saying it. I already wanted to say it again. I wanted to say it to his face. Against his lips. I wanted to say it with his cock in my mouth. I wanted to say it while taking him all in, while swallowing his cum, while choking on him. Wanted to shout it beneath him as I pounded my fists against his chest. Wanted to scream it as my tits bounced and I rode him, rode him hard. Wanted to—

"I hate you, too."

Just as quickly as I'd struck, he struck back. And so it was, we would fucking die together. For just an instant, I saw in his eyes that, like me, he meant it. Behind his back, I heard the lock turn. He kept his eyes on me and I saw: he wanted to say it again, too.

I whipped around to face him. He advanced.

Back, back, back I stepped. Forward, forward, forward he came. The room was only so big.

My shoulders collided with the wall. The bricks snagged the fabric of my costume. Mason's hips pressed me tighter.

He loomed over me. Tall. Imposing. Dangerous.

"I fucking hate you." My chin jutted up at him, defiant.

His chest crushed my lungs. My hard nipples wanted me to move, wanted friction. I stayed perfectly still, crushed beneath him.

"I hate fucking you, too," he whispered.

His hands came to either side of me head, boxing me in. I pressed mine flat against the brick. Told myself I could still escape.

"I hate you," I said through gritted teeth. "I hate you, I hate you, I—"

He kissed me. Hard and furious, his tongue demanding entrance at my lips.

Crack!

His face turned to the side at the force of my slap on his cheek. I sucked in a breath. I barely realised what I was doing before I did it. "Don't kiss me."

I expected him to be angry as he turned back. But he flashed me a wicked grin. "You fucking want me as much as I want you."

"I don't."

"Then what was that back there—?"

"A game. A fucking game."

He pressed me into the wall even further. My hips tilted to meet his barely restrained cock.

"Liar," he growled.

"I'm not—"

He shut me up with a hand up my skirt. A mutinous moan escaped my lips as his fingers edged my panties. Slipped underneath.

He let out a low chuckle when he found me wet. "You're already soaked for me, dirty girl. Tell me again you don't want me."

Stretched up onto my toes and smashed my lips desperately against his. Inhaled breath from his lungs. Whispered against his teeth, "I hate you."

But it was me I meant.

I hated myself.

Hated that I didn't hate him at all.

30

MASON

If Rachel's mouth on mine was the spark, then her teeth sinking into my lower lip, drawing blood, was the flame.

They say there's no escaping a wildfire and whether Rachel knew it or not, there was no more chance of her escaping me. I had her pinned to the wall again and the heat that I pressed against her bucking, wild hips was all-consuming.

There was a fury to the way I tore at her hair just like there was a fury to the way she wrenched at my jacket. I'd meant what I'd said. I did hate her. I hated her with my whole fucking being. I hated her more than I hated anything else in the world. It wasn't with kindness that I yanked at the hair at the nape of her neck till her head stretched back and exposed her neck to my tongue. It wasn't with gentleness that I bit at her delicate skin there where the neck meets the shoulder. It wasn't a sense of tenderness toward Rachel that made me grip the front of her costume and tear at it.

"Bastard," she hissed, as she stared down at the costume.

Don't let me make myself out as some kind of vengeful predator. As some asshole being too rough with a delicate, helpless woman. As a hateful monster taking it out on a defenceless fawn.

Because Rachel said it, too. Rachel said she hated me. And everything about what she was doing made me believe it. If I was rough, she was rougher. If I was brutal, she was demonic. If I bared my teeth at her, it didn't fucking matter because her fangs were already piercing my jugular.

Rachel's fingernails were like daggers in the small of my back as she dragged me closer to her. If my whole goddamn body wasn't already inflamed, I would have felt the heat of drawn blood trickling down my back. She yanked at the back of my t-shirt till the collar choked me, bit into my flesh. I saw in her kiss-drunk eyes that she liked it: seeing me gasp for air, watching me claw at the material there at my throat, struggling against her till I did the only thing I could do to escape: rip my own fucking shirt in two.

There we were. Two enemies pressed up against one another. Each breathing raggedly. Each shaking in tattered clothes. Each with eyes filled with hatred. Each with eyes filled with lust. This was our only break from one another. The sizing up of the opponent after the initial round. The testing of wills. The blood-thirsty trail of eyes, from head to toe; my gaze catching on her breasts barely held back by her half-torn costume, eager to be free, eager for my mouth. And hers on the almost painful bulge against my pants, the only thing she hadn't torn off of me.

Rachel dragged the back of her hand against her red mouth, eyes on mine, a boxer in the corner between rounds. The adrenaline only made her want to fight harder. To hit faster. To hurt me more. I grinned wickedly at her as we panted against each other. Because it just so happened that I felt the exact same goddamn way.

Rachel's hands fumbled with the button of my pants and

mine clawed like a caged animal at her fishnet stockings. She used her hands, her toes, everything but her fucking teeth to push down my pants. I did the same for her underwear. Neither of us bothered to free ourselves completely. It was like we were shackled at the ankles, but we didn't care. Maybe we liked it: the bondage. I mean, what had we been doing to each other over all these years if not locking one another up and throwing away the key.

Rachel's costume came away from her with one final tug and I groaned at the sight of her naked against the wall, nothing left on her but tattered fishnets and underwear-bunched heels. I slipped off the remains of my ruined t-shirt and lunged for her.

I got Rachel round the hips, but it was like wrestling an alligator. She thrashed in my arms, beat against my chest, dragged her fingernails down the back of my neck. I hoisted her in my arms and together we fell back against the wall, her lungs colliding with the bricks, my lungs colliding with hers. Slicked already with sweat, our bodies slipped against one another's. I could feel her hard nipples brush against mine. I could hear the catch in her throat just like I was sure she could hear the catch in mine. The pounding music outside the locked door was loud, but Rachel's mouth against my ear was closer. And closer will always be loud, closest always loudest.

"Dirty girl. You want to play rough?"

"Fuck you, asshole."

She was all I could fucking hear. Her angry, snarling breaths as I struggled for her wrists. Her low cursing as I grabbed them, her victorious exhales as she wrenched them away. Her frustrated whine when I encircled them once more. Her pained gasp when I squeezed them, bone grinding against bone. Her involuntary moan as I pinned them together up above her head.

"It seems to me like you've forgotten who's in charge."

Rachel kicked off her panties and locked her ankles around

my waist. Her thighs ensnared me. I might have gotten her held down, but she wanted me to know that I wasn't any freer than her. We were both fucking trapped together.

"Let me fucking remind you."

Without the use of her hands, Rachel snapped her teeth at me like a cornered, rabid dog as I guided my cock toward her pussy with my free hand. I held her wrists against the bricks with the other. But she didn't stop. Not the biting. Not the thrashing in my arms. Not the bucking of her perfect tits against my chest.

My dick was so hard I feared that just the brush of her wet lips against my head might send me over the edge. It was twitching in my trembling fingers. Twitching between my strained, trembling thighs. Rachel's teeth found the lobe of my left ear when I was off-guard. I howled as she whipped it back and forth like a chew toy.

I drove into her pussy with such a violent thrust that Rachel's teeth were ripped from my earlobe, her back scraped up against the bricks. The noise that came from her mouth was the only thing that made me stop: if I hadn't, I would have come right then and there. Buried balls deep inside of her. Knuckles bloodied against the bricks as I held her wrists. Lips against her throat. The noise was half pain, half pleasure; half hate, half love; half desperation, half passion; half desire, half loathing. It was everything fucked up about us. It was everything fucking goddamn perfect about us.

Rachel's nails dug into the flesh of the back of my hands as I remained stilled against her. Eyes clenched shut. Trying to regulate my breathing. Trying to fight back against the overwhelming desire to just spill everything inside of her in that very moment. Her nails dug and her hips bucked and from her throat came a low, desperate whine. Her heels kicked against the broken skin at the small of my back. The music pounded outside. My heart pounded in my chest. Rachel's pussy pounded against my cock, around my cock, into my fucking cock.

"Don't fucking move."

Pinned to the wall like that, without the use of her hands, Rachel was helpless. I could feel her desire in the twitch of her inner thighs against my waist, in the unevenness of her breathing, in the sharpness of her nails as she pierced deeper and deeper. I tightened my grip on her wrists. Any further and I would have broken them. I held her there against the wall, with me as far inside of her as I could possibly go and just stayed there.

"Fuck you."

She fought against me, but I took the pain. Took the frustration. Took the temptation of her nipples against mine, hard and peaked and perfect to lick, to suck, to coat with my cum.

"I said. Don't. Move."

I held her there as she quivered needily against me, quivered yearningly around me because a part of me did hate her. I wanted her to know, to get a tiny little taste of what it felt like to be helpless. To go in search of the one true thing you'd known and find it gone. Find it missing. Find it forever out of reach. I fought against the overwhelming need in me to move myself, to fuck, to get off, to finally fucking breathe, because I knew it was just as painful for her. That it was tearing her up just like it was me.

I'd been falling all these years. And I was still falling, but it was nice to drag her down with my, even if just for a tiny moment in time.

What I didn't expect was these trembling, airy words exhaled from Rachel's glistening lips, "I'm going to come."

I opened my clenched eyes. I looked at her face. There she was: pupils blown wide, mouth parted as she held her breath, cheeks flushed. There it was: ecstasy written all over her fucking face.

She'd been getting off on it. The whole goddamn time I'd held her there with me buried inside, nipples pinned against mine. She'd been getting off. Twitching around my cock. Tightening around my cock. My hands were cuffs around her wrists and she liked it. Rachel was going to cum and there I was holding myself back like some goddamn fool.

Well, fuck her.

Pulling out of her was like slapping Rachel in the face. Her eyes refocused. Her lips slammed shut. She glared at me with a fury as I cut off her orgasm.

"Bastard."

"You will *not* come until I say so."

"Fuck you, I'll come if I want." She yanked a hand free from my hold and pressed her fingers to her clit, rubbing furiously. "Oh God."

"No, your orgasms are *mine*."

I tore her hand away from her pussy and she let out a furious shriek. I wrestled with her as she tried to punch me, her anger making her strong. She wasn't strong enough though.

I got her hands back over her head and thrust back into her.

"Mine. My pussy. My orgasm."

It only made her madder. I glared right back at her. The harder I fucked her, the madder she got. The madder she got, the harder I wanted to fuck her.

Our bodies dripped in sweat and our lungs burned and we hit each other with our eyes because our hands were preoccupied. Mine squeezing tighter, tighter as I fucked her harder. Hers struggling to free themselves harder, harder as I fucked her madder.

If I would have turned my head, even just a few inches, I would have seen us in the reflection of the mirror. I would have seen my ass clenched as I drove up into her. I would have seen Rachel's ankles slipping and relocking, slipping and relocking and squeezing me closer. I would have seen her hands and mine above her head, interlocked. I could have believed that it was ten years ago and I was fucking the woman who hadn't broken my heart.

But I didn't turn my head. Didn't wrench my eyes away from hers. Couldn't.

All I saw was her hatred for me. The only reflection, my hatred for her. I couldn't see it, but as I rushed toward the edge, I could *feel* it. The woman I'd loved. The woman who'd once loved me.

I could feel it in the way she couldn't stop herself from bucking back against my hips, driving me further, deeper inside of her. I could feel it in the hum of her frustrated growls against my chest, like a bird trapped in her ribcage. I could feel it in the way she melted not against the wall, but against me.

My hips thrashed up into her. The muscles along my thighs were spasming like I'd run a marathon. I could hardly breathe. I was drenched, absolutely drenched in sweat. I was close, so fucking close.

"Dirty girl, you will come around my dick."

I fucked her so hard her hair snagged against the bricks behind her. Even as she tried to tear her wrists away from my hand still above her head. Screaming in frustration because she couldn't get away. Because she couldn't get closer. Cursing my name because I was going to force her to come around my cock. Even as she lifted up her hips to meet mine. Even as she clamped her legs around my waist to hold me to her.

I could feel her anger in the way she came, in the fury of her pussy clenching around me, the hatred in the way she screamed my name. I came hard, shuddering against her. She took it as I sank my teeth into the fleshy part of her neck.

We fell together to the floor. We collided painfully. There'd be bruised elbows the next morning. Sore shoulders. Knots on the sides of our heads.

As I lay there panting, Rachel rolled over beside me. She drew her fingers through her hair as she stared up at the ceiling. Her face was unreadable to me. The pounding of the music outside the little back room came back into focus.

"I still want a divorce," Rachel said after a moment or two.

She didn't turn her head to me. Didn't look over to make sure that I was listening. That I could even hear her. I wondered even if she said it more to herself than anyone else. Because I'd felt the way she responded to me, even if she thought she merely hated me. She wanted to come around me. She wanted me to come inside of her. I knew it. And I think Rachel goddamn knew I knew it.

Still I said, "I know."

I didn't tell her that I'd already signed her fucking divorce papers. Didn't tell her that I'd been a little more sober and a couple of stamps away from sending them.

Because for the first time I didn't quite believe her when she said she wanted a divorce. I didn't know what the fuck Rachel wanted. Hell, I wasn't even sure if Rachel knew.

But there was love in our hate. I knew that. Even if it was the light of an already dead star in an otherwise pitch-black sky.

I knew that.

31

RACHEL

Aurnia had flowers in her hair. Origami cherry blossoms woven into a spattering of dark, almost black braids. Tiny. Delicate. White. One petal brushed against her cheek as her hair fell over one eye.

Her head rested sweetly on Conor's big shoulder. Like a tiny canary alighted on an imposing boulder. Her hands were hidden beneath the white tablecloth, but I knew nonetheless what they looked like. Pale. Chipped nails painted black. Small and cupped tenderly in Conor's palms.

A part of me envied her. Envied this easy love. This new love. A part of me wanted to stand up from the table, rattling the fine glassware, knocking over the overpriced bottle of wine, and shout, "Run! Run while you can! This, *this*, it's all a lie!"

A part of me hated her. Really hated her. And a part of me loved her. Really loved her. Because she was me: fallen, falling, goddamn fucking doomed.

"So tell me, tell me," Aurnia said with eager eyes as she nestled even closer to Conor, who turned to kiss the top of her head, "I want to hear everything about you two. How did you meet? I've been begging Conor to set up a double date since you arrived, Rachel. There's so much I don't know!"

"Aurnia," Conor said patiently.

She turned her head to him, origami flowers swaying with her sleek black hair.

"What?" she asked him, eyes wide, confused.

Conor eyed Mason and lowered his voice to say, "Remember, it's...complicated."

Aurnia laughed. A sweet laugh. A laugh that didn't know it was all fucking downhill from here.

"What love isn't?" she declared boldly, the way only someone in love truly could.

I cleared my throat and Mason choked on the wine he had been guzzling like it was the last gallon of gasoline. Like without it he'd have no way to fucking escape.

"We're getting a divorce," I said, my own nails digging into my palms beneath the tablecloth.

Mason and I sat in chairs just about as far from one another as was possible without our knees being exposed on the sides. We might have even separated that far, but the restaurant was busy and we'd likely end up with a chest full of spaghetti if we tried. Hey, that might not be a bad excuse to bail out of this shi—

"You say that," Aurnia said, wagging a finger between Mason and me. "But are the papers signed? Are they turned in? Do you have some sort of official stamp or whatever shite you get?"

I sighed and muttered, "They'll be signed in a couple weeks. We're just waiting on...some clerical details."

I glanced over at Mason but found his face lowered, busy spinning his steak knife on the edge of the table.

"Right?" I pressed.

He looked up with a strange look on his face.

"No, yeah, right, right." Mason sat up so straight he looked pained as he contorted his lips into a smile and said, "Look, Aurnia. This is really sweet. This like double date shite. And we're obviously so happy that you and Conor found each other. And haven't left one another. But Rachel left me and she wants a divorce and that's that."

I was about to call fucking bullshit on whatever the fuck *that* was, but Aurnia swept in with an impassioned plea for giving it "another try". So I resorted to kicking Mason under the table. I didn't spare him any kindness either. He got the pointed toe of my heel. And he got it hard.

Wine sloshed out of Mason's glass onto the white tablecloth as he gritted his teeth to keep from shouting. Maybe gritted his teeth to keep from whipping around angrily and giving me a piece of his mind, too. Who knew. Either way, Aurnia looked at him with concern.

"Everything alright?" she asked.

Conor's response was to lift his empty whiskey glass to the passing waiter and tap it with his forefinger.

"No," Mason replied after collecting himself. "No, Aurnia, everything is not alright. You'll understand one day. You'll understand the pain another can inflict on you. You'll understand just how terribly someone can hurt you."

I gasped in shock when, unknown to anyone but me, Mason ground the heel of his boot over my toes. He pushed harder as I struggled to maintain my own composure, smile easy and casual as Aurnia argued back.

"But we hurt the ones we love, you know?" she said, bringing the back of Conor's hand to her lips. "Because all we really want is someone to trust, someone who won't run at the first sign of trouble, someone who can handle our pain. It's like we're testing the ones we love, the ones we think we can love."

I slipped my butter knife under the tablecloth and jabbed the butt at Mason's intruding thigh.

"Well, some fail that test," I said to Aurnia, but really to Mason. "Some really fucking fuck it up."

"But—" Aurnia's phone went off. She held up a polite finger, cheeks reddening as she said, "Sorry, sorry, I have to take this real quick."

Mason and I both smiled like the goddamn queen of England and nodded like obedient dogs and said, "Sure, sure, of course. Take it. Take it."

But the second she was gone we were scooting our chairs in toward one another's, fingers getting pinched as we got as close as our chairs would allow. And then we got closer.

"Don't lie to Aurnia about what happened," I hissed, face right up to Mason's.

His was twisted with as much frustration as I was sure mine was. He whispered harshly back, "The truth hurts, baby."

I glared at him. "No, your fucking *boot* hurts."

Mason smiled wickedly. "Why don't we save the bruise-measuring competition till we get home, dear?"

I laughed bitterly. "I'm not sure it's much of a competition, *dear*."

Across the fine white tablecloth, across the romantic flickering candlelight, across the reflection of red wine that danced seductively, Conor pinched the bridge of his nose with a tired sigh and muttered, "Well, this is going just about as well as I expected."

Aurnia returned just as the big plates of spaghetti and meatballs did. I stabbed the plate so hard that I thought it might crack in two.

Aurnia adjusted herself back in her seat. "What did I miss?"

"Mason and Rachel kissed and made up, baby," Conor said, eyeing the two of us like naughty children. "Didn't they?"

I made a big show of patting Mason's thigh only to sink my

fingertips into that sensitive inner flesh when Aurnia looked down to twist pasta round her fork.

"We'll, of course, give it a try, hun," I said. "I mean, things were so terrible when Mason bailed all those years ago. Who can blame him? It wasn't like we were madly in love or anything, and he just up and left."

Mason patted my back kindly only to then clamp his hand down too tightly around the back of my neck. I bit back a hiss and smiled around my bite of meatball.

"And don't worry, Aurnia, Rachel here has such a terrible memory that she can easily forget all the pain she caused," he said. "Overwhelming guilt and shame will never, ever be a problem for her."

"Jesus, Mary and Joseph, help me," Conor muttered into his whiskey glass.

"Believe me," Aurnia said, "nobody forgets. Scars make us, you know? The ones we have ourselves. The ones we *gave* ourselves."

Conor smiled down at Aurnia, and that just about broke my heart. I knew little of Conor. Less than little really. But I did know this: Conor didn't smile. So to find the one thing that made him do so and to find that it was Aurnia with her origami flowers and persistent faith in love, well...it sucked.

Mason's fingers weren't clamped so tightly around the back of my neck anymore, but the sting of his words still hurt.

I wanted to hurt him back. It was our "thing", apparently.

My hand, the one that had been on his leg, fingers brushing his inner thigh, moved slowly but determinedly as I said, "Aurnia, we don't have scars. A scar comes from a big wound. A gaping wound. But Mason and I, well, we got drunk, had some fun, did something stupid, and parted ways. If he sliced me at all, which he didn't, it was surface level. It was a mere paper cut. It was nothing. Nothing."

Mason had hold of my neck, but I had hold of his cock. I squeezed it till Mason leaned forward for his glass of water. I was trying to hurt him, to really, really hurt him, so why was it turning me on? His cock in my hands. Why was it bringing me back to The Jar? To that *mistake*?

I forced myself to grip him harder because otherwise I was going to start stroking him. Otherwise I was going to slip beneath that fancy white tablecloth. Otherwise I was going to do things that would get me banned from the restaurant, hell, banned from the whole fucking city.

It certainly didn't help matters that Mason was getting hard. And fast. I flicked his cockhead with an angry scowl and he hissed, hiding it with a quick cough, pounding at his chest.

Conor's eyes were suspicious as he glanced between the two of us, but Aurnia was preoccupied with her spaghetti and meatballs.

"I've seen the way you two are together," she said around a big bite, "and nothing about you two is surface level. There's a bond. I can see it. I know it."

I had to wrench Mason's hand from the back of my neck, he was clamping down so hard. I patted his fingers which I laid flat on the tablecloth between us.

"Rachel doesn't want to see it, Aurnia," Mason said with clenched teeth as he tried to pry my fingers from his dick. "All she wants to see is a lie. This perfect little life for herself. This stupid role for herself. She doesn't even want to see her own fucking self. So why would she want to see us? See me?"

We were slapping each other's hands in Mason's lap. Trying not to make it obvious as we fake-smiled. Smiled angrily.

"You two haven't touched your spaghetti," Conor said pointedly just as Aurnia's phone rang once more.

She excused herself again.

Conor waited till she was out of earshot to hiss, "Hands above the table!"

I shoved Mason's hands away and he shoved mine away and we both pouted silently as we picked at our plates. Forks screeching horribly. Tomato sauce flying. Teeth biting roughly.

"Jesus Christ," Conor sighed, drawing his hands over his face, pushing the loose strands from his bun up out of his eyes. "I can't tell if you two are going to murder each other or fuck."

"Murder each other," Mason and I both said.

"This was a bad idea," Mason added. "The mess between the two of us is already bad enough without Aurnia getting all these crazy dreams about 'saving' us."

Conor practically snatched his new glass of whiskey from the waiter. "Yeah, about that. I should warn you that—"

"Sorry! Sorry!" Aurnia said, kissing Conor on the cheek as she retook her seat. "Everything's ready now— I mean, good now. How's everyone liking the food?"

The tenting of Mason's pants distracted me as I smiled at Aurnia. I blocked it from view by unhooking my hair from behind my ear.

"The food is perfect, hun," I said. "It's wonderful and delicious and probably the best food Mason has ever had, and he's probably going to throw it all away before the night's over."

I think we were all rather stunned when Mason stood abruptly. Half the wine glasses were knocked over. The plates jerked so violently that half the food went onto the tablecloth. It silenced the restaurant. We were all stunned, but I think no one more than Mason himself.

Clearing his throat, he said, "I'm going to wait in the car."

I should have kept my mouth shut. But I was mad. Embarrassed maybe. Uncomfortable that I'd probably taken it too far.

It was a mistake to mutter, "Told you so."

It was my fault that Mason backhanded the bottle of wine as

he stormed past. That it shattered and fell. That there was no saving this night. I exhaled shakily and returned to my pasta as the restaurant stared.

"Um," Aurnia whispered, wincing as the chair she scooted back made a horrible noise in the horribly awkward silence. "I think I need to go make a call."

I forced myself to chew the meatballs. To not look up. To act like everything was fine. Just fucking fine.

I only heard Conor say to the waiter, "We'll need some 'take-away' boxes."

Heard him sigh.

Heard him mutter across to me, "She's young."

I was once, too. A long time ago, it seemed. A long time ago.

32

MASON

I should have known something was wrong by the number of cars outside the shop.

Dublin Ink wasn't exactly in what one would call the trendy part of town. Nor what one would call the desirable, nice, clean, safe part of town. Most the people in our neighbourhood didn't own cars. They pushed shopping carts, they pushed kegs of beer, they pushed needles into their arms. So the cars lining both sides of the street should definitely have been a warning. I didn't even think for one minute that they were customers (and the reason was not because it was nearing ten at night).

It was silent as we approached, Conor and Aurnia insisting to come over for a "nightcap". Silent enough to make me wary as I slipped the key into the lock. Silent enough to check over my shoulder at the line of cars, dark beneath the burnt-out streetlamp. Aurnia was chewing at her fingernails, eyeing warily the inside of the tattoo shop. Conor was staring up at the star-less night, muttering what I could only think was a prayer of some kind. Rachel was the only one looking at me. She gave me the middle finger.

Dinner had been a disaster. A shite show. A fecking train wreck.

Rachel and I fucked at The Jar and it seemed something might change, but nothing changed. We pulled apart like we'd done something wrong. Something dirty. Like we'd made a mistake.

So I lost it at the restaurant. I couldn't stand it any longer. The one step forward, three back. The desire, the need. The shut doors. The questions without answers. The hate when we were maybe, just maybe moving toward love. Another Miss Last Night. Another Miss Not Rachel. Another Miss Not, Never Would Be and It Was Driving Me Insane Rachel.

"Are you going to open the door or not?"

Rachel stared at me. Arms crossed. She'd seen me lose it. Had she known it was her fucking fault? All her fucking fault.

"I'm not used to so much hostility when I return home," I grumbled.

"You're not used to the woman you go home with knowing you," Rachel retorted.

I returned the favour of the middle finger and then went back to the key in the lock.

Slowly I turned the key. I pushed the door open. I stepped inside. Then not slowly at all, actually all at fucking once, the lights went on, balloons descended from the top of the stairs, and two dozen people jumped up from behind the old furniture, shouting, "Surprise!"

"What the fuck?!" I said.

Rachel said, "Good God."

Conor groaned. "I knew I should have had more whiskey."

Aurnia whimpered, "No one answered."

The mood of the room plummeted as the four of us remained frozen in the entryway. All of us stared at the big banner hung on the opposite wall that declared in big bold letters that Aurnia had obviously painted herself: Happy Engagement/Marriage/Wedding Party Rachel and Mason! Balloons bounced round our feet and then stilled. Hands extended up into the air in excitement lowered awkwardly. A few people cleared their throats.

I suppose it was obvious on Rachel's face and mine that this was not a time for celebration.

"The whole cab ride back I tried to get ahold of someone to tell them to cancel it," Aurnia explained in a small voice. "I'm sorry. I really thought I could convince you two. To, I don't know, try again... You know, because of me and Conor and... I'm sorry, I'm sorry."

I glanced at Rachel, who was staring at her feet. She lifted her eyes to mine and there wasn't the anger that had been there just a few seconds earlier. I drew Aurnia to me and ruffled her hair.

"Squirt, you wanted to throw a party and that is never something that should be apologised for," I said, holding her cheeks, squishing them together. "I assume you have booze?"

From the kitchen I heard Declan shout, "Enough to tranquillise a zoo."

"And a drug or two?" I asked Aurnia next.

Her response was to shift her eyes to Rian hunched over his canvas in the corner of the room. That was answer enough.

For the past two weeks Rian had been obsessively drawing the same mysterious young woman with that thick, dark hair and eyes that wouldn't leave you. He drew her on every conceivable surface: paper, canvas, the margins of the magazines littered about for waiting customers. I even found her face in the tattoos he did. He insisted she was real. But he also insisted that she visited him in his dreams. And that her soul tasted like autumn on the tip of his tongue, so...

"Music?" I asked.

Diarmuid, Aurnia's JLO, said, "I brought some records."

I rolled my eyes.

"*Good* music," I clarified.

"I'm here, aren't I?" Danny, lead guitarist of The Untouchables and reliable source of good music, said.

I drew Aurnia into my side, one arm over her shoulder. "Now all we need is someone to tear that sign down."

A pair of hands reached up to yank down the sign. I extended my hand to Rachel, who took it reluctantly.

In a loud voice, I said, "Hello everyone, thank you for coming to this wonderful party arranged by Aurnia here."

A couple cheers went up, Conor's the loudest of them.

"Rachel and I are so happy to see you all, as you could probably tell by our tears and big, big smiles."

Some laughter.

"We're really looking forward to celebrating with you all our big ol' wonderful, life-changing, fantastic, best-thing-that-will-ever-happen-to-us...*divorce*!"

This declaration was met, perhaps unsurprisingly, with a resounding awkward silence. Everyone looked from neighbour to neighbour. It was clear that some thought it was a joke. They were waiting for the punchline. Well, me fucking too!

Just when the silence was getting too much to bear, Rachel stepped forward and said, "So who's getting me a shot?"

An arm extended from the semicircle of friends with an open bottle of Jameson. Rachel took it, turned, and lifted it up as she smiled at me.

"To our divorce, baby."

Everyone watched, still stunned and confused, as Rachel tipped the bottle back, guzzled it, and then wiped her hand across her shimmering mouth. Her eyes sparked as she glared across the parlour at me. She dared me to challenge her. Dared me to say something.

I gritted my teeth and lifted my arms.

"Fuck yeah," I said, staring Rachel down. "Let's get this party started."

It didn't take long for the night to devolve into a drunken mess. Or at least for Rachel and me. We circled the small crowd gathered at Dublin Ink like lions stalking a herd of zebras on the Sahara. Our eyes meeting through the maze of people. Our bellies hungry.

Alcohol seemed to be the answer to our frustrations. A glance meant a shot. Caught in the middle of a lingering gaze? Well, that meant a full pint. Thrown back in one go like a fucking nineteen-year-old. The music was loud enough to shatter the windows, but I always heard her voice. There were enough people packed in as the night went on to get lost in, but I never lost her. I wanted to escape her in the chaos. I wanted to escape the chaos and have only her.

The awkwardness of everyone around us was soon gone. Or maybe I just got too locked to see it anymore. There were cheers for divorce. People shook my hand. "Happy Divorce! Happy Divorce!" I'm pretty sure there were ballads to divorce. Poems to divorce. Drinking songs to the beauty and grace and inevitability of divorce.

At one point, Aurnia was locked enough to lean against Conor and dreamily sigh with her beer bottle at her lips, "I hope *we* get divorced one day."

There was yelling and dancing and singing and neon lights spinning and I'm not sure which of us kissed someone else first. Whether she saw the smear of red lipstick on my lips first and went to retaliate. Or whether I sought out that juicy red apple because I'd seen someone else's fingers carding through her hair. It was all a blur at that point. Time and space and the fragility of hearts all fucking relative.

All I know is that I devoured that girl's mouth. The sweet

little thing with cherry lips and needy hands. I remember hoisting her up on the tattoo chair. Tilting her chin up. Seeking out Rachel's eyes in the crowd before pressing my lips to the girl's pulsing throat. All I know is that I fucking loved it. All I know is that I never would have kissed her if Rachel hadn't been watching.

Watching like she'd been when that asshole rutted his hips against her on the makeshift dance floor. Her eyes fixed on mine despite everyone moving between us. Her lips curled cruelly at me as he slid his hands down to her ass. Watching me like she did to make sure I saw when she pulled the asshole's face to hers.

Rachel and I didn't say more than two words to each other the entire night. We didn't dance together. We didn't drink together. We didn't even find a quiet moment in the line for the bathroom to curse each other out. To taunt each other.

And yet, for her and for me, there was no one else. Everything I did was for her. To her. Because of her. And it was the same for her. She moved one direction because I was coming from the same way. She took a drink because I'd caught her looking. She trapped me, made me believe she hadn't noticed I was looking, so that I would reach for the bottle myself. I performed for her. She performed for me.

The red lips were a prop. That man's hand on her ass was exactly the same as a lacy black bra, a brush of a finger along the thigh, a whisper in the ear. It was meant for me. It had nothing to do with that ass. Nothing at fucking all. It was all for me. Me.

Because she wanted me.

And I wanted her.

Or at least that's what I told myself before passing out in my bed sometime in the early morning. Alone. Not even having the wherewithal to take off my shoes.

33

RACHEL

I hadn't heard Mason leave the next night.

I'd spent the whole day beneath the sheets. Groaning. Moaning. Cursing my life choices. Promising to never, ever consume a drop of alcohol never, ever again. I heard every goddamn creak in the house like nails on a chalkboard. I heard every door open and close like a hammer to my skull. Even my own breathing, in and out, in and out—oh God, Rachel, don't throw up—had been like a cruel, howling wind to my ears. But I hadn't heard Mason leave.

I did, however, hear him return.

It was like a nightmare that I'd tired of having. That no longer scared me, but exhausted me. Annoyed me. Irritated me to hell. The high-pitched voice. The girlish little giggles. The heels on the steps. The silence which was worst of all because I knew what it meant: it meant Mason had stopped Miss Last Night to kiss her. To press her against the railing. To slip his hand inside her shirt. To find her clit so she gasped, unable to say a fucking thing anymore.

I heard them come up the stairs. Falling over each other.

Laughing. Mason trying to get her to be quiet. The girl just getting louder as he pinched her ass at the top of the stairs.

I knew what was going to happen. I knew exactly what kind of sounds I was about to hear. I knew exactly how loud they were going to be, how long they would last, how they would end. I *knew*. Knew like the back of my fucking hand.

And I was sick of it.

I wasn't sure what I was going to do when I threw back the damp sheets atop me. The chill of the air bit at my fevered, flushed skin, but I never once considered returning to the humid warmth I'd cocooned myself in all day. Hiding from the light. Hiding from the pain. Hiding from Mason. I didn't have a plan, not even anything remotely close to one, but I had a direction: out of the room. Down the hallway. Toward the noise on the stairs.

My bare feet smacked on the cold hardwood floors. My heart beat in rhythm. All I knew was that I had to do something.

I was propelled by this anger that had been building and building in my chest. Anger that all I had at night was my hand when these other women had all of Mason. His strong arms. His muscular chest. His cock splitting them in two.

I rushed forward down the hallway toward that faint pink neon glow because I was hurt. Hurt that Mason knew I could hear him. Hurt that he probably liked that I could hear him. Could hear the pleasure he was giving to someone else. Could hear the pleasure he was withholding from me. A shiny, juicy apple just out of reach.

It would have been smart to slow, to hesitate, to think fucking straight for once. I had a fiancé back home. I had a life back home. I had the promise of stability and comfort and ease and maybe if I'd slowed down just a bit, just a tiny bit, I might have been able to convince myself that I wanted all of that more than I wanted to do whatever the fuck it was I was about to do. That I wanted all that—everything I ever wanted, ever thought I wanted—more than I wanted to scream at them. At Mason.

And fuck. If I could have just stopped to think for two seconds, I would have seen this was madness. Madness, throwing it all away. Giving it all up. Sacrificing forever for just one night in Mason's bed. Just one night as Miss Last Night.

But maybe if I'd been able to slow, if I'd given myself a second to breathe, to think, I would have realised that it was madness to wait so long. That this was what I was always meant to do. That this, *this* was the smartest thing I could possibly be doing, storming down that hallway in the middle of the night.

In the end it didn't fucking matter. I would never know what I would have thought, what I would have decided. Because there was no way I could slow. No chance in hell I was going to hesitate. Not now. It was absolutely impossible to think. I was like a car barrelling down a mountain without brakes. There was only one way it could all end.

It took a second or two for them to realise that I was there. Standing at the top of the stairs like a wild-haired ghost. White pyjamas blowing in the breeze from the open window at the end of the hallway. Face haunted like I'd been wronged during my living years. And now I was out for vengeance.

They had fallen halfway up the staircase. The girl was on top of Mason. His hands were on her ass. Beneath the waistband of her jeans. Her high-pitched giggle caught in her throat when she saw me.

Mason had to twist his head around to see what Miss Last Night was looking at, the reason why she was squirming away from him. At first he looked just as surprised as she had. Then his face changed as I began walking slowly down the stairs toward the two of them. I'm not sure what it was. Intrigue.

Excitement. Relief even. A bit of frustration. Always that undercurrent of anger and hurt. The lifeblood of our relationship. His face seemed to say: what the fuck took you so long, goddammit?

"Um, what the hell?" Miss Last Night said as she tugged up her shirt to cover her breasts. Breasts that had been pressed against my man. Dirty tits that had been longing for the mouth of *my* husband.

Calm as the grave, I said, fingers light on the handrail, "What the fuck indeed?"

"Look, um...who is this bitch?"

I smirked. Miss Last Night didn't even know Mason's name. How was she supposed to know how to swirl her tongue around his cockhead to get his hips to buck? How was she supposed to know when to pinch his nipples, that he liked it right before he was about to come? How was she supposed to know that he fell asleep almost instantly when you cuddled him from behind, like he counted your steady breaths on his back like sheep jumping over a fence? How was she supposed to know what only his wife could know?

What only *I* could know?

"Rachel," Mason said.

But it wasn't in answer to Miss Last Night's question. His eyes were fixed on mine. Not hers. His attention was on me. She, for all he knew, had already left. Disappeared. Never fucking existed. He said my name to me, not her. Said it as a question. The question? What are you doing, Rachel? What do you want, Rachel? Rachel, your move.

My fingers suddenly tightened on the handrail. Before my touch had been as light as a feather. Now I was going to splinter the wood. Break it. Split it in two. My smile was cruel, vindictive, assured as I turned my head slowly toward Miss Last Night. She was looking desperately at Mason. She didn't know that he couldn't help her. Wouldn't help. Didn't want to fucking help her.

"This bitch," I said slowly, savouring every word like honey drops, "is his wife."

Miss Last Night laughed.

"You're not fucking married," she said to Mason. When she found his eyes still on me, still fixed on me, she said, a little less surely, "You didn't say you were fucking married."

Mason's lips curled at the corners. His eyes flashed darkly.

His voice was thick, lustful as he said to me, not to her, not to fucking her, "I wasn't sure whether I still was."

Electricity sparked between us. I was surprised the neon light on the wall reading "Dublin Ink" didn't spark. Didn't shatter. Didn't cascade down on us drops of glowing pink rain.

In his eyes I could see the darkness I used to stare into from my bed as Mason fucked his Miss Last Nights. I could see the way the chandelier rattled, feel the ceiling dust on my tear-stained cheeks. I could feel my desire, my lust, my panic, my fear, my anger as I remained there, frozen, as I imagined what he was doing, choreographed by their cries.

But I could also see that tonight would be different.

I would not remain down the hall staring into the darkness, fingers trembling over my wet panties. Mason would be there to brush away the dust from my cheeks. The bed would be empty of any desire, any lust, panic, fear, anger.

Because tonight I was going to be Miss Last Night.

"I think you should leave," I said, not bothering to look over at the girl.

She tugged at Mason's arm. Whispered, "Come on, let's go."

The poor thing didn't realise I was talking to her. Didn't know the decision had already been made. That she was already an unwelcome guest. That Mason and I, that my husband and I had already moved on. That she wasn't even there anymore despite her tugging on his shirt like a pathetic little kid.

"I think you should leave before things get ugly," I said, eyes still fixed on Mason.

He licked his lips, pupils widening. She should leave before she saw my naked body, saw how my husband salivated over it. Saw how he would never react to her naked body the way he did to mine. I spared her the details that things getting ugly meant rough, violent sex. Meant holes in the wall. Meant sweating bodies moving against one another in a way that only two as close as my husband and I together could know. Primal. Instinctual. Loud. The girl should leave before she witnessed a kind of passion that she would realise with crushing certainty that she would never experience, never know.

"Now, bitch," I hissed, taking all the hate I felt for Mason and directing it at her.

It wasn't fair. But fuck, when the hell was life ever fair? If it was fair Mason wouldn't have left. If it was fair, I wouldn't ever be in a position where I was unbuttoning my pyjama shirt in front of some random chick who thought she was going to get her brains fucked out by my husband.

When the final button was undone, I turned on the stairs. My hand trembled as I released the handrail. My knuckles were white. My fingers red. I turned and without another word, I climbed the stairs. I slipped the shirt from my shoulders. Let it fall behind me. At the top of the staircase I leaned over and pulled down my underwear. Slowly I stepped from them. One foot. The other. With a toe I pushed them off the top step. I could hear my panties, like the little flutter of a dove's wing, falling to the stair below.

Naked there in the soft pink glow at the top of the stairs, I hesitated for just long enough to say, "Are you coming?"

As I turned down the hallway with all its hidden shadows

and dark corners, I heard the door downstairs close. But I didn't stop. I didn't look back. I knew who left.

And I knew who stayed.

I walked toward my bedroom. Not the one down the hall. Mason's. *Our* bedroom.

Without asking, I went inside.

34

RACHEL

Mason kept me waiting.

His footsteps up the stairs had been slow. Painfully, agonisingly slow. I'd listened to them like I'd listened to his pants when he fucked those women. Like I'd listened to the pounding of the bedframe against the wall. I listened with trembling breath. With a frustration that made me tear at the sheets. With fingers brushing against my nipples and then pulling away like I'd touched fire. Because it was wrong. Wrong. *Wrong.*

I was naked in his bed when he arrived at the door.

I was already wet when he paused there. Filling the doorway. My nipples strained already for contact, for friction, for his lips. I was struggling to keep still. Fingers balled in the sheets. Nails nearly piercing through the thin cotton. Mason came to the door. Filled it like I wanted to be filled. Like my escape was blocked. Like the cave entrance had fallen in and I was trapped.

It took everything inside of me not to groan. Not to writhe. Not to fucking beg.

I drank in his darkened silhouette in the door frame. The width of his broad, muscular shoulders. The length of his toned thighs. The slight quirk of his head. I couldn't see him. Couldn't make out his shadowed features. But I knew he could see me. Could see my struggle. Could see my need. Had I already soaked the sheets between my quivering thighs? Were the muscles of my lower stomach already twitching in expectation? Were my hairs raised along my forearms, everything inside of me excited, ready, eager?

Mason stood there. The sound of the closed door was long gone. Miss Last Night was long gone. It was just him and me. Alone. No one coming to interrupt. No one coming to stop us. No one coming to fucking save us.

Just when I couldn't hold out any longer, thought that I was going to scream at the top of my lungs just to do something, *anything*, Mason spoke.

"What do you want, Rachel?"

Mason's voice was steady. Gentle, but clear. Pained almost. Fearful, in a way. Because it could mean anything, his question.

And my answer? My answer could *be* anything. He could be asking whether I wanted to be on top. Or he could be asking whether I really wanted a divorce, whether there really was no mending us, no fixing us.

I could answer that I wanted him to tie my hands to the bedpost. Or I could answer that I believed in us. Even if it was stupid, I believed. I believed we could find our way back to one another.

It was as close to honesty as we'd gotten. This open question. This endless possibility of answers. Mason and I, since falling apart, we'd hidden so much from each other. We'd avoided the hard questions. Ducked the even harder answers. We'd skimmed the surface of the water and ignored the impending storm with its towering waves on the dark horizon. We'd touched each other everywhere but the heart, working around it like a game of Operation. Like we knew we'd get electrocuted. Because we would, I suppose.

Mason was silent in the doorway. Still in the doorway. I had my chance. My chance to tell him what I really wanted. To be honest. To be open. To take the shock that I knew, that he knew was coming.

And I couldn't. I just couldn't.

There was a sadness in my voice that I was sure he heard.

"I want you to do what you would do to me if I was one of those other women. I want you to fuck me like I really am your Miss Last Night."

I was sure that he heard the sadness because I heard it myself. Because it was as clear as day in the dark.

Mason, or at least his silhouette, hesitated a moment in the doorway. Then he moved toward me with a fury. He ripped off his jacket. Tore off his shirt. A streak of fear jolted down my spine at seeing the violence with which he threw away his jeans. The brutality with which he mounted the bed. The roughness with which he flipped me over.

I gripped the bars of Mason's bedframe as his fingers dug into the flesh of my hips. There was no longer any hesitation in how he moved. He gripped me like it was the only way to grip me: hard, painful, sure. His knees spread my legs apart. His cock found my wet folds and I cried out as he drove into me. His thrusts were different than I'd ever felt from him. Mason had always been powerful in the way he fucked me. But there had never been this kind of urgency. Not urgency to come. To get release. To feel that white-hot bliss. But an urgency to be done. To have it over with. To collapse to the side of me and pass out. To find a different kind of escape.

The bed rocked just the way I imagined it would when I squeezed my eyes shut down the hall. His grunts were exactly how I thought they would be when I heard hints of them behind my closed door, between the pillow stuffed round of my head. The sounds coming involuntarily from my lips even mimicked perfectly the sounds that came from all those Miss Last Nights. I mewed like a kitten. Gasped when Mason choked me. Moaned and groaned and whimpered like all I wanted was for it to stop, like all I wanted was more, more, *more*.

The noise of our bodies filled the room. Our heat made the window fog. The air became heavy, stale, claustrophobic even. I realised that I was trying so hard to hold on that I wasn't sure I could come. It was all so frantic. All so fast. All so brutal and faceless. I bit into the sheets when it was Mason I wanted to sink my teeth into. I clawed at the pillows, at the bars of the bed frame, at my hair, but none of that was Mason. None of that was him. His flesh. His body. His soul.

I could tell from the way the rock of Mason's hips grew erratic that he was close. I imagined the long, drawn-out groan I would hear when he came. When he shuddered against me. When he sank his nails into my hips. I tightened around him at the thought. He would come for me now. Not some Miss Last Night. Not some random girl. Me. His wife.

I cried out again because he drove into me with such anger that it was very nearly painful. I don't know when the switch happened, but I found myself with a mouthful of sheets. I didn't tell him to stop, please, stop. It was too much. I was too invisible when he fucked me like this. I clutched the bars to keep myself from disappearing completely.

I told him this was what I wanted, but it wasn't. I didn't want to be fucked like them. I wanted him to see me. I wanted him to *love* me.

Mason screamed, loud and angry and violent, and I thought he must have come. He must have let himself go. He must have allowed me to be just anyone else. Just another warm body. Just another Miss Last Night.

So it surprised me when he growled out, "*No*."

Before I could stop him, Mason pulled out and flipped me over like a rag doll. He pulled me up to him, held me on his lap, cock twitching against me. He shuddered as he buried his head against the crook of my neck.

I found my fingers carding through his mohawk.

"Mason—"

"They weren't you," he said, clinging to me, drawing me in tighter to his chest atop his knees. "They were never you. None of them."

My heart skipped. I stared over Mason's shoulder at the darkness of the wall. This wasn't what I'd imagined when I'd stared up at the darkness of the ceiling down the hall.

I thought I could take those women's place. Slip into the role they played for Mason. Become one of them. Take the pleasure they received and leave like one of them. But it was never going to be like that. Not between Mason and me.

I saw that. I could never be his Miss Last Night. But I could never be the wife he'd loved for more than ten years, the wife he'd agreed to spend his life with and stayed for. If I was going to be anything to Mason, play any role with him, it would have to be something else. Something new. Something we created together.

Softly, uncertainly, I whispered in the hot, unmoving air, "And if they'd been me…all those women…?"

Mason's hands moved hesitantly up the small of my back. He splayed his fingers wide. From pinkie to thumb, thumb to pinkie, he spanned my entire back. With his hands braced just below my shoulders, he lowered me back. Pulling away from the warmth of his chest was like a sudden grey cloud on a perfectly sunny day. I longed to go back to him. To drag him toward me. To fall back with him. To cover myself with his heat.

But Mason kept me suspended away from him. Holding me

like I was falling back from a cliff's edge. His arms shook even though I knew I couldn't be heavy. Mason's eyes met mine in the dim light. He was looking at me with a sort of disbelief. Like he couldn't quite believe that I was there. Like it hadn't been him who'd thrown us away. Like all the years we'd lost hadn't been because of him. His fault. Fucking *his*.

An anger so deep it was nothing but pain welled up in my chest till I couldn't breathe. I hated Mason because we'd had it. We'd *had* it. I hated him because this could have been us for all these years. Bodies quivering against one another. Muscles strained. Desire swelling. This closeness. This intimacy.

He stole it from us. He robbed us. And yet there he was with this look of disbelief, like *I* was the one who left.

Mason rocked his hips, sending his cock slowly, but deeply into me again. I nearly sobbed. It was the most intense pleasure and the most brutal pain all mixed into one. It was hate and it was love. It was devastation and it was hope. It was wanting to get away, to flee, to run; it was wanting to sink even further onto him, into him. To give all of myself. To give absolutely nothing.

I clung to Mason's biceps like there really was a chance of falling. Like I didn't trust his hands on my back. Like I was afraid. Because I was. As Mason thrust into me, that's all I was: afraid. Afraid of how much I loved it all. The feel of him. The strength of him. The restraint of him as he measured his pants and clenched his jaw. Afraid that I couldn't stop loving this.

That's what sheer terror is: knowing the thing you need is the thing you cannot ever have, will not ever have. I'd fallen into the temptation of my favourite drug while knowing there was no more of him. Just the one hit. Just now. Just tonight.

Every time Mason pushed all the way in, he reached a place that only he knew. It made my toes curl. My fingers dug into his skin, burying into his muscles. It made me twitch in his arms. Buck against his slow, steady, excruciating pace. I realised I was sobbing, this desperate, pathetic sob. Miss Last Night had never made that kind of noise. And yet I was no different from them. Was I?

I looked across the small space between my naked chest and Mason's. His eyes were locked on my face. He hadn't looked away yet.

But I didn't want to look at him. Didn't want to see him seeing me. And yet it was everything, everything that I'd ever wanted.

He reached out and wrapped a possessive hand around my throat.

"Mine."

"Yours," I gasped as he held me atop him, held me as he reached that spot deep in my body, in my heart. As he squeezed my neck, holding my life in his hands.

I came with a gasping shudder against his chest. He followed right after me, crushing me so tightly against him that my ribs might break.

My lungs struggled against his lungs. My heart ran to catch up with his. We stayed there, me on his lap, him still inside of me, our arms wrapped around each other. We stayed there for a long time.

I breathed in the scent of him, my nose pressed against the tight muscles of his neck. He had his face in my curls. Each of us hiding. But maybe it was okay if we were hiding in one another. Concealing ourselves with the other's body. Maybe it was okay that we hid the truth from one another if we hid it with warm skin. With wild curls. With strong chests and supple breasts.

Maybe we could keep our secrets and keep each other. Maybe it would be okay if we just kept holding one another. Maybe we wouldn't have to face the morning if we kept our eyes closed...

35

MASON

hen...

WHY DID I RUN?

In no way did it make sense to. I had been gone from Vegas for over a week. Saving thirty or so seconds certainly wouldn't make a difference. Running was ridiculous. Duffel bag bouncing on my back. Sweat from the brutal Vegas sun dripping from under my arms. Lungs struggling in the arid desert air like I'd been fucking for hours as I took the stairs two, three at a time. And why? Why? Why did I run?

I knew why. Of course I fucking knew why. Because I didn't believe that she would stay. Because I knew I'd given her a chance to get out and she'd taken it. Because I didn't trust one bit that she would be sitting there inside her apartment, worried and concerned and confused and, sure, a little pissed off, but *there*.

Because I didn't believe that she believed in me. In *us*.

So I ran like some idiot who thought he could catch her. Catch her as she locked the door for the last time. Catch her as she got into the cab without a glance back at the flashing lights we'd fallen in love under. Catch her as she drove away. I'd be the eejit standing in the middle of the street. Screaming her name. Believing, stupidly, that I could catch her if I just ran. If I just ran a little faster.

I yanked on her apartment door handle so hard I'd nearly torn it from the door. All to find it locked.

There was no answer when I rang the bell. No answer when I knocked. No answer when I pounded. I'd run so far, so fast all just to stand outside a locked door with no answer. There was no answer when I shouted her name. No answer when I shouted for so long, so loud that I was again breathless. Again bending over at the knees. Again dripping with sweat that smelled this time like panic.

Eventually the super either heard me or heard someone's complaint about me. He arrived at the door after walking at a snail's pace down the hall. I'd watched him. I remember being curious how he could move so slowly. How he could care so little. How it wasn't a big deal at all for him that the world was falling apart around me.

In the end I think he let me inside out of pity. And because the unit was empty. Maybe because he saw me as a potential rental. Or he just didn't give a fuck and it was the easiest way to get me to shut the fuck up, to go away, to restore the goddamn peace.

I called her name as I ran inside the apartment even though I'd been told she was "gone". But I ran like an eejit. I ran.

I called Rachel's name and ran like a dog through the few small rooms. Anyone could see they were empty. Abandoned. Nothing more left but an old mattress on the floor in the bedroom and a half-used bar of soap in the bathroom.

"When?" I asked the super, who was leaning against the door frame.

He gave a bored shrug that made me want to grab his throat and shake him.

"Couple days ago," he said.

I shook my head. That's all she'd given me? A couple days? Less than a week? Less than we'd even known each other? I grabbed at my hair. Yanked at it till it hurt.

"A number," I said, a stupid ray of hope flaring in my chest. "A note. She left me something. Anything. Surely she left me something. A way to find her."

The super stared at me, looked me up and down like he was trying to recognise me.

"And you are?" he finally asked.

The question hit me harder than it should have. Because what was the answer? I was the man the previous tenant had been fucking. I was the one-night stand who turned into a week night's stand. I was one she was going to spend forever with. No, really. I was. I was. She told me. She promised. We promised. It was more. More. I swear.

Fucking hell, I would sound insane.

I sank down against the kitchen island. My head fell into my hands.

"I don't know," I muttered. "I'm the guy she was seeing for a while."

The super scuffed his toes at the yellowed linoleum.

"You know, son," he said gruffly, "sometimes it's best to know when to let someone go."

I laughed bitterly as I raised my head.

"'Let someone go?' 'Let someone go?' What about this looks like I can let her go?"

I waved my hands wildly around the place. The empty, abandoned, forsaken place.

"No," I said angrily. "No, sometimes it's best to know when you've been *left*. That's the answer here. Because she took that from me. Took the 'letting go' from me. I'm *left*. I'm always the fucking *left*."

My heel kicked out before I could stop myself. The super hollered as my boot went through the drywall across from me.

"Now don't go doing something you might regret," the super shouted as he grabbed me by the collar.

I had a foot on him. Probably fifty pounds of muscle on him. And I was younger by about twenty years. There was no way he could have dragged me out of that empty apartment if I hadn't let him. Lead-footed. Dead-hearted. I sank against the wall in the hallway as he locked the door.

He waggled a shaking finger at me. "Destroy anything else and I'll call the police, son."

I waited till the jangle of his keys had disappeared around the corner before pounding my head back against the wall. Again and again. Do something I might regret? What the fuck did he know about regret? I laughed bitterly. It came out as more of a cough. Like I was choking. Like I was being choked.

At Rachel's work the director had the same question for me: who are you?

From the moment he laid eyes on me, hands clutched at my chest, pleading for answers, begging for help, the question had been written across his face, clear as day: and who the fuck are you?

"I'm the one she saw in the audience," I could have said.

"I'm the one she searched for," I could have said.

"I'm the one she wanted to dance for," I could have said. I could have fucking said, "For me, goddammit! For me and me *alone*!"

But those words wouldn't come. None of them. I stood there

with slumped shoulders. With shadows beneath my eyes that had nothing to do with the red-eye international flight. With all the sleepless nights before that. With the crying and aching and dying before that. I stood there with a week-old beard. With desperation. With a fucking pathetic shrug.

The director sighed and patted me on the arm. "It's Vegas, honey. That stupid saying is bullshit, you know? Nothing fucking stays in Vegas. And certainly no one will."

He left me there on the stage. The empty stage. The empty stage where Rachel and I had shared dinner. Shared silly dreams. Shared ideas for the future. A little cottage on the seaside. A restored theatre in a small village in France. A tattoo parlour with a dance studio upstairs. Weddings. Marriage. Babies. Everything.

And in the end, nothing.

I tried all the bars we'd been to. At each one I got the same question: who the hell are you? At each one I got the same answer: people leave. That's what they do. No, she didn't leave a note. No, she didn't leave a number. No, I have no fucking clue where she is. At each one I got a drink.

I followed our mad dash along the strip as if I could pick up the scent of her. The scent of us. As I stumbled along the sidewalk, I heard laughter and whipped around thinking that maybe it was us, Rachel and me. That I'd found us. That we still existed somewhere, somehow. But inevitably it was another couple. Their arms draped over one another like ours had been. Their bodies colliding against lamp posts like ours had. Their mouths sloppy and eager over one another's just like ours had been.

What a fool I was to think we were different. That I was different. Different for her.

People left. That's what they did. Rachel left.

So why was I running to the Denny's at God knows what time in the morning? Why was I climbing up on the empty table and shouting at the top of my lungs for her? Why was I spilling coffee over the edge of the table like she could be summoned back to me with remnants of that night we fell in love?

Fell in love! What a joke. What a goddamn joke. Love was just denial. Love was all of us telling ourselves that we'll stick around this time. Love was just what we called the space of time before truth. Love was hiding, lying, pretending. Love was playing a role. Because in the end everyone would leave. In the end the masks came off, the curtain closed, the game was over and everyone went home.

We all were left.

If I knew this, if I fucking knew this, then why was I running, still running back toward the theatre? Why was I yanking on the locked front doors till the glass rattled? Why was I falling down in the alleyway? Pushing back to my feet? Falling again against the back door she said was always open? Why was I letting it give me hope once more when I found it open? Open like she said.

I ran down through those dark corridors. Nothing to light my way but the green glow of the Exit signs. I'd only been to her dressing room once, but I knew the way as if by heart. I ran to it. Why? Why did I run to it? I ran to it and I wrenched the door open.

She wasn't there. Of course she wasn't.

The couch where we'd first made love was still there. The antique armoire. The mirror in the dark. I panted like a dog there in that little room. Sweat dripped down my back. Rachel was gone.

That's when it really hit me. When there was nowhere else to look. When there was nowhere else to find her. When there was nothing to face but the truth.

She left me.

I think I destroyed that little dressing room. There in the dark. I tore at the cushions. Maybe with my fingers. Maybe with my teeth. I screamed. Screamed till my throat was raw. But there was nobody to see me. Nobody to hear me.

I was what I always feared: alone.

36

MASON

Now...

I SWEAR a psychologist would have a fucking field day with me.

Just downstairs, just twenty or so stairs away, there was a fully stocked kitchen. Aurnia was to thank for that. Apparently a diet of whiskey and Cheez-Its could be improved upon. I knew for a fact that there was toast, eggs, bacon, English muffins, jams of several varieties, butter, frozen waffles, raisin muffins, and fresh fruits including strawberries, raspberries, blueberries, kiwis, and cantaloupe. I knew this because after Aurnia's weekly grocery deliveries there was no fucking room for whiskey and Cheez-Its.

What I'm trying to say is that there was no reason to even leave the house the next morning. Within crawling distance was a plethora of breakfast options. A veritable feast at our feet. Anything and everything we could possibly want practically at our fingertips, if our fingertips simply rolled out of bed.

Maybe you can explain the fact that I decided to ignore the

fully stocked kitchen and set out into the early morning dawn because of laziness. It's true that the closest I would ever get to being a chef was prying open a can of Batchelors beans with a switchblade because I never bothered learning how to use a can opener (I mean, you can't defend yourself in my neighbourhood with a can opener...). Fine. Sure. Reasonable enough.

But it doesn't stop there. Because despite the fact that our neighbourhood is crime-riddled and poor as shite, it has some damn good food. Within walking distance was a pub that served all-day Irish breakfast, an all-night restaurant with melt-in-your-mouth crepes, and a hole-in-the-wall bakery that served these criminally wicked cinnamon donuts. I could have picked any of these places and been back to Dublin Ink, back upstairs to Rachel in less than thirty minutes.

So find me a shrink to tell me why I instead felt the need to cross over to the bus stop at the end of the street for a bus I knew wasn't coming for nearly twenty minutes. Find me someone with an advanced degree who can tell me why I hauled my ass all the way across town. Figure out who out there can solve the riddle of why I was gone almost three hours just to bring back home breakfast that wasn't even very good. And cold by the time I turned the key in the lock.

Or maybe I don't need a shrink at all to tell me. Maybe you don't need any education at all to put two and two together. Maybe a fool knew exactly why I was being such an eejit. Maybe I knew full fucking well what the shite I was doing.

If only I could be honest with myself...

With the bag of cold, soggy breakfast food, I climbed the stairs slowly. My ears strained for any hint of a sound. I paused on each step. Waited for the creaking to stop. Leaned forward, trying to hear something. Anything. I thought I already knew. I thought the silence was already my answer.

Because it could be the only answer.

I continued up the stairs with memories of the night before haunting me. Taunting me in the silence. I shifted the plastic bag to my other hand just to hear something other than that terrible silence.

I'd given Rachel time. Time to leave. Just like before, time to leave. Time to take her out. Time to escape. Just like before. I was sure, absolutely sure that she had taken it once more.

That's the kind of twisted fuck I was. Because the five minutes it would take to go downstairs and toast, butter, and jam an English muffin wasn't enough. She'd know. I'd hear her at the door. I'd catch her as she tried to slip through unnoticed. She'd have to face me. She'd have to see my face as I asked without a word, "Why?"

Thirty minutes was right on the fence.

Thirty minutes meant she would be unsure. I knew. And she knew. I could see her: tense in the bed. Ears straining like mine were straining down the hallway. Thinking, "Had he just gone down the block? What if he was already on his way back?" Not wanting to run into me out on the sidewalk. Not wanting to bump into each other around the corner, me with an armful of breakfast burritos, her with a suitcase dragged behind her. Not wanting to have to see me. To explain to me. To fucking explain to me.

But three hours was safe. After an hour she'd crack open the blinds. Check the street outside. She'd pace for a bit. Chew at her fingernails probably. A bad habit. She'd hesitate for another fifteen minutes or so. Unsure. Wanting to be sure. I knew. And she knew. But even if she waited till the two-hour mark. Just to be sure. Just to be safe. Even if she was so cautious as to wait two hours, I'd still left her with nearly fifty minutes. Nearly fifty minutes to leave me.

Like she'd left me before. Like she would leave me again and again. Like she would always leave me.

The hallway was silent as I tiptoed down it. I didn't move quickly because I was sure what I would see. I didn't move slowly because there was no avoiding it now, now was there?

I stopped just outside my bedroom door. Just out of eyeshot of the bed. I remembered the stripped mattress in Rachel's abandoned place. Left on the floor. Crooked. Pathetic without sheets. Cold without her. I told myself that I knew what I would see when I rounded the corner. I told myself it was alright. I hadn't set myself to be hurt the way I had all those years ago.

I'd protected myself...hadn't I?

Maybe that's what made me hesitate. Not that I was afraid of what I would see. But that I was afraid of how open I'd left my heart. It frightened me how quickly I'd let down my guard the night before. How easily I'd bared myself to Rachel. I was afraid that I'd let her in too much. Enough to feel the emptiness in my stomach when I laid eyes on the empty bed in the empty room.

I sucked in a breath and turned into my bedroom. There it was. Just as I knew. There it was. Just like before, I'd left her time to leave and she'd taken it. Jumped at it. Refused to miss her chance.

I resisted the urge to throw the bag of breakfast across the room. I clenched my fists to keep myself from punching a hole into the wall. I wanted to kick things, break things, tear things in two. But I couldn't. I absolutely couldn't. Because if I did, it meant that it was just like before. I'd have to admit she'd hurt me again. That I'd *let* her hurt me again.

And I couldn't. I just couldn't. I had to tell myself I was stronger this time. Even if I knew it was a fucking lie.

I was shaking against the door frame, straining to control my twitching muscles, when the bathroom door opened.

"I'm glad you're back," Rachel said around a toothbrush. "I'm fucking starving."

I stared at the empty bed. Stared at her. Rachel raised a

quizzical eye as my wild gaze darted between the two: the empty bed and her. The cold and the warmth. The absent and the present.

"You're still here," I said, almost laughing in disbelief.

Rachel frowned. She looked startled. I'd thrown her off guard. She'd expected me to assume she would be there, that she would stay. I hadn't. Now there was that chasm widening between us. All those unspoken words. All those unrealised expectations. Rachel shifted awkwardly. She averted her eyes.

Her voice sounded different, farther away, as she said, "Well, I mean, yeah. The thirty days isn't up yet, is it?"

I looked across at her. Again, there it was. Another moment to be honest with one another. Another moment of vulnerability. Another moment to trust.

But we'd failed. I'd failed. She'd failed. We failed. If there even was a "we". If there could ever be again a "we".

"Um, I went out and got breakfast," I said lamely in the end, holding up the plastic bag as if I needed to show proof.

Rachel tapped her fingers along the toothbrush. She was wearing one of my shirts. Open down the middle. One foot was on top of the other as she leaned against the door frame of the bathroom. I could see her toes curling atop one another.

"Hey, um," she said hesitantly, a little flicker of a smile on her lips, "do you remember...no, never mind."

She waved her hand at me and disappeared into the bathroom. I heard the faucet squeak as she turned on the water. I crossed the room and took the place she had had in the door frame. Her eyes met mine when she lifted her head, hair held back at the nape of her neck with her hand to keep it from her face.

"Denny's?" I asked.

Her smile was beautiful but fast. A bloom that has only one

morning. It was like she wouldn't allow herself more. More openings. More mornings. Her eyes went to the plastic bag.

"Is that?"

I shook my head. "It's the closest I could get in Dublin."

Rachel turned around. Her hands rested on the pedestal sink. She leaned back.

"Shitty pancakes?" she asked.

"Cold bacon."

"Burnt coffee?"

I nodded, our eyes lingering over one another. Rachel drummed her fingers against the aged porcelain.

"I guess we both remember then," she said softly.

I didn't tell her that I remembered it every night. And wished I hadn't every morning.

We ate our food in silence. Somehow the fact that it was cold was made alright by how close Rachel's toes were on the bed. Criss-cross apple sauce just inches from mine.

When I plugged my nose to down the last of my coffee, I found Rachel fiddling with her Styrofoam cup. I didn't want the morning to end. Me to work. Her to...her waiting for Day 30 I supposed.

So I went on a limb. Took a daring plunge. Put myself out there more than I should have.

"Now what?" I said.

I thought I might die when Rachel looked up at me, eyes sparkling.

And grinned.

37

RACHEL

Mason was grumpy, which was perfect. Just perfect.

"Look," he said as we weaved through the crowded shopping district of Henry Street, shuffling forward like cattle to the slaughter, "I love playing hooky as much as the next guy. I really do. Add in a smoking-hot chick and what could be better? There's fooling around on a blanket at St Stephen's Green with a bottle of champagne. There's lying in bed all day fooling around. There's fooling around at the National Museum or the bank—"

"You'd rather be at a bank than here?" I asked.

I leaned back to avoid getting smacked in the face by an armful of shopping bags. Mason was not so lucky. He set his jaw and inhaled to steady (sort of) his breathing.

"I think you missed the common theme," he said, looking miserably down at me.

I smiled innocently up at him. "Which is?"

Mason's hand slipped down to squeeze my ass and he leaned down to whisper, "Fooling around, love."

I swatted his hand away and pushed his chest back. We got

off the elevator and were hit with the wafting aroma of stale pretzels circling in a heater, chain curry, and teenage hormones. I grinned.

"It's just that I put in a favour with Rian and Conor to get today off," Mason said as we wound through the throngs of people, all carrying more shit than the last. "And it would have been nice to know beforehand that you intended for us to do this."

"Spending quality time together as husband and wife?" I asked.

Mason gave me a straight, unimpressed face. I smiled and tried again.

"Delving deeper into the depths of our relationship by exploring unexplored corners of domesticity?"

Mason scoffed.

Shrugging, I said, "Finding out who we are as a couple by throwing ourselves into the most high pressured of social situations to see if we fall apart or come out stronger?"

Mason rolled his eyes and pulled me away just in time so that I didn't get a mouthful of some trashy French eau de parfum.

"Go to Jervis fecking Centre," he said, dragging a hand over his face and groaning.

I reached down between us and intertwined my fingers with his. Mason just groaned louder when I swung our hands merrily back and forth.

"Ah! Here it is," I said suddenly, dragging him behind me into the department store.

We were greeted with a wad of coupons and I drew them to my nose like they were flowers or money, breathing deeply.

"I really did fuck your brains out last night, didn't I?" Mason grumbled.

I smacked him in the chest.

"This way."

The fluorescent lights were horrible. Those long, dirty bulbs. The flickering. The unflattering tone that made everyone look sick. It was perfect. Shopping carts crowded the aisles like bumper cars. Dangerous for the fingers. Perfect. Absolutely perfect. There was everything you could have wanted: a crying baby, a crazy lady with a dog in a stroller, a shrill-voiced Karen demanding to see the manager, a misbehaving toddler knocking over a display of china, and, the pièce de résistance, a security alarm going off at the entrance to the store that wouldn't shut off for God knows what reason. Perfect. Perfect. Perfect.

"Are you ready?" I asked Mason.

He looked like he was ready to puke, but I wasn't sure whether that was the lights or he really was ready to puke. Either way, it was perfect.

"Ready for what?" Mason asked, half bored, half annoyed. One hundred percent already over it.

I did my best to hold back my laughter. I was already having so much fun.

Without warning I stopped beside a wall of kitchen towels. A whole aisle, really, of kitchen towels. All different kinds of material. All different kinds of patterns. There were stripes, there were flowers, there were kittens and duckies and for some reason little golden turkey legs. And don't even get me started on all the printed slogans. "But First Coffee." No, no, no: But First Fireworks!!!

Mason was waiting to continue, because of course we didn't need kitchen towels. *We* didn't have a kitchen.

So it must have come as even more of a surprise when I said loudly, too loudly, "Honey, come on. I thought we agreed!"

I wrenched my hand from Mason's, made little fists at my side, stomped my feet petulantly. Mason just stared at me in bewilderment.

"You always *do* this," I whined loudly, too loudly. "We always agree to something and then you just go and change your mind without telling me. Without talking to me. Without remembering that we're supposed to be a *team*. You can't just pick the kitchen towels without me. Especially after we *agreed*."

A woman who was just about to turn her cart down the aisle we were in quickly decided against it. Mason's head swivelled around before turning back to me. He narrowed his eyes at me. I stomped my foot.

"We agreed!" I shrieked.

I imagined what Tim would do if I tried this shit at the mall. Not that he would ever be caught dead in the mall. We had personal shoppers at Crate and Barrel for our informal kitchen needs, darling. If I raised my voice in a public place, Tim would have assumed I was having a stroke. Losing motor functions. The only way I could ever be out of control according to him was if I literally was out of control.

I imagined Tim glaring. Hissing, "Stop it. I said stop it!" Dragging me into the nearest changing room. Wagging his finger at me as I grinned against the changing table. I imagined Tim walking away. Running even. Glancing around him in the hopes that nobody had seen us together. Nobody of note at least. I imagined Tim having me committed. Feeling for my temperature. Covering my mouth and telling those around us who were watching in shock, "She's an actress. It's for a role. She's not like this. Really. In real life she's quite polite. Calm. Sweet. Innocent. Pretty. I mean, isn't she such a sweet, innocent, pretty thing?" I imagined Tim howling when I bit his finger. I imagined him slapping me, but of course he never would.

Just like he'd never fuck me the way I wanted to be fucked. Just like he'd never see me the way I wanted to be seen. Just like he'd never, ever snatch a kitchen towel from the rack, wave it wildly, and shout at me, “No, no, love. *You* agreed. We never agreed. You confuse those two a lot, now don’t you?”

But Mason would.

Mason did.

I smiled so hard my cheeks hurt, there in that department store. Mason whipped the kitchen towel (the ugliest one they had) around and said, loudly, crazily, *perfectly*, “This is your mother talking, isn’t it?”

I forced back my smile despite how good it felt, despite how fucking *good* it felt, and stalked forward to jab my finger at Mason’s chest.

“Don’t you dare bring my mother into this,” I shouted. “You can’t blame everything on her, you know?!”

Mason threw up his hands into the air.

“Oh, so I just *happened* to be the only one who got food poisoning at Thanksgiving, huh?” he hollered, his voice echoing up and down the aisle, all the way to those horrible, perfect fluorescent lights. “Thirty people all crammed into your family’s house and I’m somehow the *only* one!”

I gripped my hair like I was going crazy even though I was really kind of having the time of my life.

I growled and then shouted back, “It’s not my mother’s fault that you have such a weak constitution.”

Mason scoffed and crossed his hands over his chest.

“Is that what we’re calling taste now? ‘A weak constitution.’ Well, I’m sorry, *dear*, but I wouldn’t serve your mother’s food to my dog!”

“We don’t even have a dog!” I shrieked.

“And who decided that?” Mason bellowed. “Oh, that’s right, that’s another thing we ‘agreed’ to, isn’t it? Funny, I don’t really remember that conversation.”

People were poking their heads into either end of the aisle. Half were concerned. Half amused. I’m pretty sure I even saw a phone or two. I figured I might as well give them a show. I was a performer, wasn't I? I grabbed some kitchen towels at random from the rack and threw them at Mason, who ducked behind raised arms.

"Well go on then," I cried, forcing up tears. "Go find the love I *obviously* can't give you in the flea-ridden arms of some dog. Go on, honey. If I'm *so* terrible!"

Retreating, Mason picked up some of the towels and hurled them back, a hint of a grin on his own face.

Between throws he said, "At least a dog isn't withholding if I don't pick the stupid kitchen towel he wants."

I screamed and then shrieked, "We had sex last month! What more do you *want*?"

Mason hurled a towel at me and shouted like a madman, "Fine! Have it your way. We'll take the ugliest one here if that makes you happy."

I gripped the towel to my chest and smiled, a giggle barely held back.

"Now, see, darling, was that really so hard?"

Mason stared across at me, panting, chest rising and falling a little too quickly. All I did was raise an eyebrow and he advanced on me. He placed his arm over my shoulder and I practically tripped, he guided us forward so quickly.

"I'm sorry, dear," he said as the crowd at the end of the aisle parted for us, a sea of agape mouths and wide eyes.

"No, *I'm* sorry," I insisted.

"We really shouldn't fight," Mason said distractedly.

His eyes were glancing at the doors that lined the back of the department stores. He hurried us past the bathrooms, the breakroom, the returns section. Behind us the entertained shoppers, no longer entertained, were going to back to their as-scheduled day.

"No, no, I hate fighting," I agreed.

I nearly yelped when Mason suddenly pushed me into the dressing room. I stumbled back on the bench as he fumbled with the lock of the door.

"Baby," I said as I spread my legs and let the kitchen towel fall to the floor, "I really think you need to look at that sex addiction pamphlet I brought home."

Mason's eyes flashed darkly as he advanced on me, fingers at the button of his jeans.

"Shut up. Right now, I have other uses for that mouth."

38

MASON

I'd never enjoyed blue balls so fucking much.

Next to me on the hard metal bench Rachel looked like a mess. Her hair was knotted, her wild curls practically feral at that point. Static made it climb up the corkboard above our heads like ivy up a brick wall. Her cheeks were still flushed, her pupils still dilated, her nipples still hard through the sweater she'd buttoned up all wrong. I think she'd managed to get her underwear back on. But I couldn't be entirely sure it wasn't still on the floor of the dressing room where we'd vacated rather...hastily.

Not that I could say that I looked much better. For one I was squirming around like a horny teenage boy with a boner in fifth period math. For another I'd somehow lost a shoe. It had maybe ended up in one of the stalls next to ours. In a pile of some housewife's pyjamas. There was a possibility that I'd thrown it somewhere. Again, I couldn't be sure.

I remembered locking the door, seeing Rachel there with her legs spread. The rest was just a race to get rid of as much clothes as possible. Then there was, perhaps most damning of all, the long, angry red scratches down my upper chest that

Rachel had managed to gift me before the security guard not so politely banged on the dressing room door.

Rachel giggled suddenly and immediately clamped her hand over her mouth.

"Don't you start," I whispered, keeping my attention straight ahead at the security guard's office as he filled out paperwork. "If you start, I'll start and if I start, I won't be able to stop."

"Sorry," Rachel whispered back, the word bouncing with laughter. She leaned forward to bury her head in her lap.

"Rachel," I hissed, sinking my teeth into my lower lip.

"Sorry, sorry," came Rachel's words buried in her lap.

Seconds later she was giggling. Back bouncing as she laughed. I forced myself not to laugh as the security guard looked up from his desk and narrowed his eyes at us through the glass.

"She's just really overcome with guilt!" I shouted to the security guard as I patted Rachel's back. This only made me buck more with uncontrollable laughter. "She never does stuff like this," I added. "Always such a good girl. Really, sir, it's eating her up inside."

Rachel elbowed me in the side and I bit back a grin. The security guard rolled his eyes and returned with a bored sigh to his paperwork. There'd be a fine, of course. And a stern talking to. Thankfully no charges were being pressed. The only other people in the dressing room at the time had been creeps with ears pressed against the walls.

Rachel lifted her head, tears streaming down her face. She wiped at them with the back of her hand and hiccupped. Our eyes met and she had to turn away instantly, cupping her hand over her mouth as she began giggling all over again.

I smiled because it was so obvious that she was happy. That the weight she'd been carrying around like a chip on her shoulders had been lifted, at least for a little while. It was almost the Rachel I remembered from Vegas: full of life, daring and bold, eager to grab every chance at happiness that she could get. I smiled because it was obvious that I was happy, too.

I'd searched for happiness for so long. Tried to convince myself that I'd found it, that I had it, more times than I could count. But when you were truly happy you didn't have to wonder if you were. You didn't ask yourself, "Is this it? Is this happiness?" You didn't feel that sinking disappointment when you tell yourself, "I guess this is it...this is it?" True happiness just was.

And this was it. Sitting there next to Rachel. In trouble for trying to fuck like horny teenagers in the dressing room at Jervis mall. Attempting to appear remorseful for our actions for a security guard who probably couldn't give a fuck. Knees brushing. Eyes avoiding one another's but only because we knew we wouldn't be able to hold it in if we caught hold of one another. Our laughter. Our happiness.

Rachel composed herself, managing to let out a long, shaky breath as she leaned her head back against the corkboard. It was covered with pinned pictures of shoplifters. Like a wall of shame. Our pictures would be up there. There was no avoiding that. Rachel with her wild hair, her sex-flushed cheeks, her teary eyes from laughing so fucking hard.

And me, with my eyes not on the camera, but on her standing behind the security guard as he took the photo. Biting at her lower lip. Toes on top of one another. Fidgeting with the wrongly done-up buttons of her thin cashmere sweater.

I'd wondered for a moment if you could see her reflection in my pupils still dilated from the image of her spread legs.

I'd like that picture. I wanted to hold onto that. The way she had looked at me in that moment. It was the way she had looked at me all those years ago.

"I can't believe I did that," Rachel whispered, her words still interrupted by soft giggles.

Her fingers were playing at her lips as she stared forward. When she glanced over at me, she found me looking at her. She smiled but this time did not laugh.

"I think that's a lie," I said.

Rachel's smile faltered a little. I hadn't meant to sound so serious when I said that. I didn't want to do anything to take away her laughter, to steal her happiness. Not ever. But the words came out and it was the truth of them that made them sound different. Because our truth, Rachel's and mine, it wasn't happy.

Rachel shook her head. She tried back on the laughter, but it was like a shirt that shrank in the wash: it no longer quite fit.

"I'm not that person anymore, Mason," she said.

She busied herself with fixing the buttons on her sweater. Her eyes remained focused on the task. Remained away from me.

"Because of this new role?" I asked.

Rachel looked up at me.

"What? No," she said, shaking her head. "I mean, what we had in Vegas was just a drunken couple nights. That wasn't— I wasn't—"

"That wasn't you?" I asked.

Rachel's fingers fidgeted on the top button of her sweater. She licked her lips. Hesitated.

"No," she finally said.

I stared at her in the silence. There was the noise of shoppers passing by out in the mall. There was the steady scratch of the security guard's pen in between his bored sighs.

And there were Rachel and me, breathing together.

"I think that's a lie too," I said.

"Mason," Rachel tried.

"Then why this?" I asked, throwing my hands up. "Why this?"

Rachel laughed, but it wasn't a laugh like before. It was uncomfortable. Nervous. Dismissive.

"I'm playing a role!" she said, trying to sound casual. Failing. Her fingers were moving quickly now, fixing her buttons. I caught a glimpse of the swell of her breast. She caught me looking and blushed. "A role, Mason. I mean, you know that. We're playing at husband and wife, right? I mean, come on."

Rachel's eyes darted to mine. There was something more there. There was fear now. She was begging me to sweep it all back under the rug. To let it go. To avoid it all, all the inconvenient truths, all the inescapable feelings, like we always did.

I didn't want to this time. I couldn't this time.

"Bullshite," I said.

Rachel's face clouded with anger.

"That's right," I said, leaning in closer to her face. "I said, bullshite."

Before she could say anything, I kissed her. Dragged her toward me. Pressed my lips to hers. Slipped my tongue against hers.

Rachel shoved against me, but I held her close. My fingers tangled in her hair, caught on her tangles. She hissed when I tugged, when I claimed more of her mouth.

She relented with a sigh. Her body melted against mine. Her tongue twisted around mine. She lifted her thigh across my legs. She started to pull herself up onto my lap when a loud pounding came from the glass window of the security office.

"Hey!" the security guard shouted, baton smacking once more on the glass. "Don't make me cuff you to opposite sides of the room, you eejits!"

Rachel slipped back into her own seat and wiped at her mouth, concealing her laughter again. The good kind. The happy kind. When the security guard returned to his paperwork, Rachel elbowed me.

"Asshole," she grumbled.

I grinned.

"And that doesn't prove anything," she said, keeping her eyes forward, arms crossed stiffly over her chest. "Except that you're hot and fuck well."

"Which we already knew."

Rachel rolled her eyes. I smiled when she laughed again. Hid it behind her hand. Masked it with a cough as the security guard looked up irritably.

We sat in silence after that.

I thought I'd won. I'd forced the two of us to face the truth, to not hide from it or run away from it. But as I sat there the smile on my lips sank. The happiness in my heart dimmed. I glanced over at Rachel, who gave me a small smile. Simple. Easy. Noncommittal.

Had I won? Or had Rachel just allowed me to believe I had?

I stared back at the security office in front of me. I called Rachel out on her bullshite, but had she really relented? Agreed? Admitted the truth? The truth that when we were in Vegas we were more ourselves than any other time in our lives? That the beauty of us, the rarity of us was that we didn't have to play roles with one another? That whoever I was here and whoever she was there, there in New York, was the fake us, was the actors on the stage?

I'd kissed her and she'd kissed me and now it was gone. The moment.

Yet again she'd avoided a confrontation. We'd fought in the department store and it had been fun as hell, but it wasn't the kind of fight we needed to have. That I *knew* we needed to have. It was just another fantasy. Like Rachel burning toast. Like me getting caught by my wife with another woman. The fantasy of a fucked-up marriage. The fantasy of us being messy and angry and fucked up, but *together*.

"I can't believe you asked the security guard for two more minutes," Rachel whispered next to me.

I gave her the same smile she'd given me. Small. Easy. Noncommittal. I think she saw it. I think she knew. Knew what she had done. Knew what I was letting her do.

Because I didn't want this to end either. Us having fun. Us fooling around. Us being us.

"That was for you," I leaned over to whisper. "You know I could have come just at the sight of you."

Rachel elbowed me again. After a second she whispered back, "Then you should have asked for five."

I put my arm around her and after a moment's hesitation she put her head against my shoulder.

A little while later we paid the fine. Hefty, but reasonable, I suppose. We made our apologies. We listened to the security guard's warning as he tacked up our photographs to the wall of shoplifters and flashers and child snatchers.

I should have wondered why Rachel would have risked such a potentially damaging public relations fiasco when the reason she was here in the first place, asking for a divorce after all this time, was to scrub off the last remaining stain on her record.

But I ignored that along with everything else.

Because Rachel was worth it.

Or at least whatever role she claimed she was playing was worth it. It was a painful truth, I supposed: that a glimpse of Rachel, a shadow, a part, a piece of Rachel was better than nothing.

But I ignored that, too.

At least, for as long as I could...

39

RACHEL

It was nice to sweep things under the carpet.

Nice to put on a sweet apron with little heart details and scalloped edges. Nice to get a kiss from your husband on the cheek. A pinch on the ass if he was feeling frisky. To hear him humming a song you'd just been singing in the shower. Nice to lift up the corner of the carpet in the bedroom you shared, sweep the dust right under it.

It was nice to be Mason's wife even if I wasn't. Even if I couldn't be. Even if we never talked about the reasons why.

It was nice to ask him which lipstick before dinner. Nice to watch his head tilt from side to side as he considered, to laugh when he inevitably said, "Neither goes with that dress, so really I think you should just go naked, darling."

It was nice to hold his hand on the sidewalk like any other couple. To have him pull out my chair for me. To have his fingers interlock with mine beneath the white tablecloth without either of us trying to break the other's knuckles.

"You two seem...*different*," Conor said at the restaurant we'd selected for our do-over double date.

He eyed us over his glass of whiskey. Apparently he'd

arrived early. Ordered a double. Threw it back and had another ready for when Mason and I showed up. To prepare, he'd said.

Aurnia swatted at Conor's chest. He narrowed his eyes suspiciously at the two of us across the table from them.

"It's called happy, you idiot," she said.

Conor shook his head.

"It's called strange. It's called 'I don't like it.' It's called 'I don't trust it.'"

I turned my head to smile at Mason and he turned his head to smile right back at me.

"We talked," I said.

This was a lie. We fucked and said dirty, filthy things to one another while fucking, but we did not, in any way, talk.

"Yeah," Mason said, squeezing my hand. Gently not murderously. "We had a nice long talk and really worked some stuff out."

Also a lie. We worked out some stress, sure. Going at it all night, I'm sure we worked out some calories, too. But the closest we got to a nice long talk was the nice long groans we purred into each other's ears as we rocked together on the bed. Me on top. Mason on top. Both on our sides. Him behind me. Me flipped over on top of him...it was a nice long list. Did that count?

Mason and I smiled at each other like we believed everything we said to be true. I guess we'd been doing that from the start, though. Believing we'd spend the rest of our lives together when we said it within an hour of meeting. Believing we were meant for each other when all we were meant for was a killer, brutal hangover. Believing that anything would last past the week like we ourselves could stop the dying of a star.

"So my party was a good idea after all," Aurnia said, more to Conor than to us.

Conor rolled his eyes. "They were all over other people the

whole night," he said. "I wouldn't exactly call that a success, baby."

"But it forced them to see what they really wanted," Aurnia insisted. "I mean, *who* they really wanted."

Her beaming smile was so charming as her sparkling eyes danced between the two of us. She lifted her glass of wine and proposed a toast.

"To talking it out!"

The clinking of glasses masked the obvious lie in Mason's and my voice. Or maybe there was nothing to conceal, nothing to hide.

I raised my glass to my lips. Maybe Mason and I just "talked" in a different way. Maybe our bodies could communicate what words couldn't. Maybe we didn't need to open our mouths except to claim lips, to wrap around cocks, to sink our teeth into that sensitive skin at the crook of the neck.

Maybe things swept under the carpet could stay under the carpet.

Because the truth was I was enjoying myself. The truth was my role as wife was feeling less and less like a role. With each passing day I felt less like a travelling stranger in this town and more and more like someone who belonged.

I knew how to get around the neighbourhood not like an actor knows how to get around a stage (stage left, stage right, exit left, exit right), but like someone who doesn't even think. Who just finds themselves where they meant to be. Who doesn't even realise they'd left the loft till they were putting away the groceries in the kitchen, black liquorice for the husband, peanut M&Ms for the wife.

Aurnia was chattering on about plans for a group vacation, and I found myself nodding along like it was actually something that could be in my future.

"And in August there's a gallery opening in Marseilles," she said, eagerly slurping up her spaghetti. "The artist is incredible, like really incredible, right, Conor? And I mean, we can get like a little beach house and bicycle to the gallery, don't you think? And Rachel, you and I can check out the shops. Doesn't that sound lovely. I mean, we'll have to take Rian, of course. He'll be a bit of a fifth wheel, but I'm fairly certain that girl he keeps drawing is his imaginary friend anyway, so we'll just count it as six!"

August. August! The plan was to leave in a week. There I was nodding along to plans in August. With the Dublin Ink family. With Mason. What was worse was that I could imagine it all. I saw a whitewashed stone villa with a view of the sea. I saw ripe tomatoes sliced atop thick slabs of buffalo mozzarella. I saw painting Aurnia's toes on the balcony. I saw fucking Mason on the sand beneath the moonlight, quick because the dawn was coming. I saw getting high with Rian. Getting drunk with Conor. I saw my tongue at the corner of my mouth, eyebrows furled in concentration, as Aurnia tried to teach me how to draw. I even saw the balled-up paper of my thousandth failure soaring out the window onto the avenue below. I heard Mason's amused chuckle.

And I liked it. I liked it all.

"I'm going to get ice cream every single day," I said, sipping my wine. "Chocolate churros for breakfast every morning. A shit ton of tapas for lunch. And paella. And for dinner, dinner every day, ice cream. And I'm going to get fat and you're going to have to roll me back to Dublin at the end."

I felt Mason's eyes on me. I could sense his hesitation. His uncertainty. I could practically hear his inner thoughts: what the fuck is she on about? Day 30 is just around the corner. But then Mason was slinging his arm over my shoulder and pulling me toward him in a warm embrace.

"Or we'll just stay forever in Marseilles," he said, smiling along with everyone (yes, even Conor cracked the teeniest, tiniest smile for our gratification). "The five of us."

"Six of us!" Aurnia interjected, laughing.

It was ridiculous really. We started mentioning dates. We went over budgets. We discussed what we would do with the shop. Close for a week? Find someone to cover the place? Oh, someone named Tommy could come over and do some tattoos while we were gone. He was fantastic. No, no, really good. Our clients would love him.

I mean, I should have laughed at it all. Because this wasn't my life. Dublin Ink. The boys. Little Aurnia. Mason. My life was back in New York. Those were the streets I knew. I had JoJo's toes to paint. If I wanted to learn to draw, I was certain she could teach me. I didn't *need* an amused chuckle from my husband when I chucked a balled-up piece of paper out the window. Besides, it was littering. That's what Tim would say. And he would be right, of course. He was always right. He was good for me. I behaved myself around him. I kept myself in line. I didn't order another bottle of wine for the table when we all clearly didn't need it just because I wanted the good times to keep going.

Because I wanted to hear more about the life I could have in Dublin. Because I wanted to dream Aurnia's dreams. Because I wanted to believe it could all be real, if just for a little longer.

"And listen, Rachel, if you need work over here, I'm sure we can find a place for you at Dublin Ink," Conor said. "Or Noah at The Jar is always looking for good staff. You've already met Candace..."

I don't know if it was the whiskey that warmed him to me or Mason's arm still around my shoulders, but I liked that, too.

"Oh, well," Mason said, "Rachel actually has a new role back in—"

I interrupted him with a hand on his knee.

"A new role in Dublin," I said ridiculously, stupidly. Maybe it was the wine. Maybe it was the fantasy. I added, knowing Mason's eyes were on me, "I mean, that's what I'd want. Is to find a role here. As a dancer maybe. Or a singer. And I act. I mean, I—"

"She can do everything," Mason said. "She's intoxicating on any stage."

I looked over at him. Both our cheeks were strawberry-red from the wine. We were clearly both far, far away from sober.

"Thanks, baby," I said.

Mason pressed his lips to mine. And for a moment it was all real. My husband and I out at dinner with our friends. Plans for the future bright and happy. For a moment I didn't cling so desperately to the present, because we would have loads of evenings like this. Mason would always believe in me, always find me so irresistible that he couldn't help but kiss me. We would always leave together and make love and wake up in each other's arms. And we would never know what day it was, never think, "One day less". Because for a moment Day 30 didn't exist. Because for a moment there was forever.

My phone vibrated in my lap, distracting me. I pulled away with a sudden jerk. Otherwise I think it would have had to have been Conor or Aurnia who tore us apart. I glanced down at the caller ID to see Tim's name.

This time the presence of Mason's eyes on me made me red with a different kind of embarrassment.

"It's my...producer," I said, putting the phone away a little too hastily.

"Does he need you?" Mason asked when my phone immediately vibrated again.

I smiled and shook my head. Tim didn't need me: the woman who ordered too much wine, the cheater, the girl stripping on stage, the mess who still had feelings for her secret husband of ten years who left her. Tim needed the promise of me. The promise of a sweet, innocent wife. Tim needed the woman he proposed to.

I just wasn't sure I was her anymore. Or if I ever had been her.

Conor and Aurnia were discussing continuing drinks at The Jar. But Mason's eyes were still on me. I put my phone on silent as Tim called again and leaned forward, elbows on the table, avoiding Mason's questioning gaze.

"Let's go," I said. "Really, let's not stop. We definitely shouldn't stop."

I was afraid if we stopped, the fragile fantasy I was living in would crack. Break. Shatter. The key was to just keep going.

"You know what?" I laughed. "Let's go to Marseilles!"

Everyone laughed with me. Even Mason. But a part of me was serious. Really serious. I wanted to run away with Mason. With Conor and Aurnia and Rian. With this little life that felt real. I wanted to run away and hide it. Protect it. Keep it.

Before it fell apart.

40

MASON

It was getting late. I'd had a long day. A new client. And a talker at that. Of course, he wanted a giant-ass tattoo across his shoulders. It took the whole afternoon. My brain was dead. My ears were bleeding. I was hardly paying attention to what I was doing as I barged into the bathroom up in my room.

It wasn't my fault.

"Sorry, sorry, sorry!" I said quickly as I jumped back from the bathroom as if the tiles had scalded my feet, the light had burned my eyes, and the person in there had exhaled fire from his mouth. "Shite, sorry!"

From the bathroom came a muffled laughter. As I finished dragging my hands over my face, I saw a toothbrush with a dollop of toothpaste atop it extend out into the bedroom. When I didn't immediately take it from the delicate fingers, it wiggled at me.

Rachel leaned back, her own toothbrush sticking out of her mouth. White foam giving her a little moustache. She had a raised eyebrow. An amused grin.

"It won't bite," she said out the corner of her mouth, jabbing my toothbrush at me.

I took the toothbrush slowly. I kept my eyes on her the whole time. Rachel stepped aside to make room for me to slip inside the little bathroom along with her.

"Are you sure?" I asked.

Rachel took the toothbrush from her mouth and said, "Am I sure that I want you to brush your teeth? Um, yeah, I think I am."

"No," I said, glancing into the tightness of the bathroom. The narrowness of the space between the tub and the radiator. The smallness of the pedestal sink. "No, I mean, are you sure you want me in there with you."

Rachel blinked at me.

"What's up?" she asked.

"I don't know," I said, glancing down at the toothpaste she'd obviously put out just for me. Probably done it when she'd done hers. Maybe even hadn't thought about it. "I just...brushing your teeth together is like..."

Rachel laughed and guessed, "Scary?"

"Normal," I said, scratching nervously at the back of my neck. "I mean normal for a couple. Normal for like...committed people."

Rachel laughed again.

"Let me guess," she said, "you never let your Miss Last Nights brush their teeth?"

"How did you—"

"You hide your toothbrush," she answered. "You weirdo."

I laughed myself. For some reason that was the line for me: brushing your teeth together. That meant something even more than fucking meant something. I could circle my tongue around a girl's clit while she moaned my name, and that was less intimate than circling my toothbrush around my mouth while she did the same. With her toothbrush. With her mouth. In my bathroom. Together. Side by side.

"Get in here," Rachel said and stepped back up to the sink.

She spit some of the foam down the drain as I inched hesitantly inside.

"Boo!" she suddenly shouted, and my back collided painfully with the towel rack inside the bathroom.

"That's not funny," I said, slowly inserting the toothbrush into my mouth.

Had she poisoned it? Was that what this was? Had Rachel spiked my toothpaste? With what? Probably not with anything deadly, I didn't think. She needed me alive to sign the divorce papers she still didn't know were already signed, all ready to go just inches from where she laid her head to sleep at night. No, not anything like arsenic. Probably. Maybe a relaxing agent. Something to make me pliable to her will. Something that would kill any resistance to signing...

Rachel watched me in the mirror as she scrubbed at her tongue. Her hair was drawn up into a bun atop her head with a neon scrunchy. On the little shelf above the sink was a bottle of her makeup remover. I could point it out in the shop now, when I walked down that aisle. It was Rachel's makeup remover now. If she one day asked me to pick some up, she wouldn't even have to tell me which one. Because I knew.

I kind of liked that. Being the one who knew her.

I began to brush my teeth and Rachel grinned.

"See? Not so bad, huh?" Rachel leaned back over to wash out her mouth.

I listened to her gargle water. It was with a strange fascination that I heard her swish it from side to side. If we had stayed together, if Rachel hadn't left, I would know that noise by heart. I would have her whole routine memorised. We probably would have fought a dozen times about how loudly she cleared her throat. She would get on my case for how much water I was wasting.

I stepped forward and leaned over the sink next to Rachel. She lifted her head just enough for our eyes to meet. This wasn't the closeness of sex. The closeness of her on top of me, hips bucking against mine. And it wasn't the closeness of fighting. Of getting into each other's faces and yelling at the top of our lungs. It was a quieter closeness. A simpler closeness.

My eyes followed the faint freckles on her nose. I noticed the way some toothpaste remained in the hollow above her cupid's bow even after she wiped her mouth with the back of her hand. And I could feel Rachel's eyes trailing over my face with just as much attention. She laughed when I let the foam slip from my mouth slowly.

She shoved at my shoulders and stood to wipe her hands on the towel.

"You're gross," she said.

"You asked for it," I answered.

I finished myself and followed Rachel back into the bedroom. We stood on opposite sides of the bed and changed into our pyjamas. For Rachel that meant carefully removing her clothes. Folding them nicely on the mattress. Slipping into flannel pants. Buttoning up a flannel shirt. Stretching her arms overhead. Leaning from side to side. For me that meant yanking my shirt over my head, jumping out of my jeans, throwing it all across the room, and standing butt-ass naked with my hands on my hips, rocking back and forth on my heels, cracking my back.

Taking her hair down from its scrunchie, Rachel looked at me from across the bed.

"Ready?"

"For what?" I asked.

"For bed."

I frowned slightly. I'd never had someone ask me that

before. If I was by myself, I just passed out when I was good and ready. If I was with Miss Last Night, I...also just passed out when I was good and ready.

"I guess," I said slowly, almost warily.

"Grab your side."

Together Rachel and I tugged down the comforter. This was also not something I usually did, as making my bed in the morning was definitely not something that I ever did.

We crawled up and under the sheets at the same time like we were performing some kind of ritual. Side by side we laid flat. Hands resting on our stomachs. Eyes facing the moulded ceiling.

"What do we do now?" I asked in an almost reverential whisper.

"Now we turn out the lights."

Her voice was also soft. Like the kind of breeze that only comes at night.

I reached out for my bedside light at the same time as she did for hers. I mirrored the movement of her arm in the pale yellow light. The crook of her elbow. The fumbling fingers. The slow twist of the little brass knob. The lamps went out at the same time. Synchronised like a clock. Darkness didn't flash or twitch or jerk onto us but fell in one gentle swoop like a blanket lifted high and then left to fall. It fell upon my eager skin. Connected first with the raised hairs of excited goosebumps. Then sank. Moulded to the lines of my thighs. Pooled like water in the contours of my stomach. Caressed my cheek like a cupped hand.

"And now what do we do?" I asked.

I resisted the urge to turn my head toward Rachel. I kept my eyes focused on the darkened ceiling. I counted the lines the blinds cast across the wall behind me.

Rachel was silent for a moment. I could feel how close her

body was next to mine beneath the sheets. I sensed that her pinkie was just a hair's breadth from mine. If I breathed in a little too deeply, our fingers would touch. Would there be sparks like when you rub your socks at the foot of the bed as a child? Heat lightning silent and beautiful? Weaving like delicate lace between us?

"Now we close our eyes," came Rachel's whispered response after several silent moments.

This time I did turn my head. Rachel had already done the same. We looked across the crumpled pillows at one another. There was a stretch of light from the streetlamps outside across her face. There was a shadow across mine.

We never agreed to close them together, our eyes. Nothing at all was said between us save what Rachel had already said: Now we close our eyes.

I mean, we weren't little kids anymore. It would be stupid to count down. To say, "Let's close our eyes on three." To laugh when neither of us actually closed our eyes like silly teenagers who wouldn't hang up the phone as they whispered in the cover of dark, racking up the phone bill in secret, "No, *you* hang up." We weren't even the old us, the Vegas us, who struggled against exhaustion to keep our eyes open just a few minutes more. To keep talking a few minutes more. To keep running our hands along each other just a few minutes more. To know that the other was real and not just a dream to be gone in the morning just a second or two longer.

In those times I never even remembered closing my eyes. I just remembered waking up and not believing she was there, still there. Not even when I breathed in deep the scent of her hair. Not even when I wrapped my arms around her. Not even when I pressed into her as she murmured softly and snaked her arm back to tangle in my hair.

But as Rachel and I looked across each other, not as children, but adults, not as frantic lovers, but as scarred humans, I was conscious of her fluttering eyelashes. I watched intently as her blinks grew heavy, dreamy. I paid attention to the focus of her pupils like she was participating in a sleep study and I needed to take note of everything. Every little detail of Rachel. And how Rachel, not anyone else, but only Rachel closed her eyes.

Like the comforter rolling back, like our bodies slipping beneath the sheets, like the lights going out, I followed Rachel as she closed her eyes. Like I'd never done it before. Like I needed teaching. Like if I didn't close my eyes when she closed hers that I would never be able to. Never ever again.

I would lie awake all night. Eyes glued open. Nothing but the darkness of the ceiling to see.

The darkness behind my eyelids was warm. Soft. Comforting. The brush of Rachel's pinkie against mine didn't startle me. Because I had been moving toward her, too. Seeking hers as she had been seeking mine. Just the same. At the same time. A reflection. A perfect reflection of her.

"This is...nice," I murmured.

Rachel hadn't guided me to say that. I heard the echo of those words nonetheless in the easing of her breath. Heard it in the stillness of her little pinkie against mine, callused, rough, stained from ink. Heard it in the soft rustle of sheets as she scooted just a little closer.

I did the same. I liked the idea that this was what husbands did with their wives. I liked the simplicity of it all. How ordinary it was. Liked that I could paint in the years we'd spent apart with nights just like these. I'd learned a brush stroke that night. And I could fill the empty canvas of Rachel and me with it. In darkness. In quiet.

"What do we do now?" I whispered.

"We sleep."

Rachel wounded her arms round me. I enveloped her, drew her close. We breathed against one another. But my breaths, as first like gentle waves were gaining in height, building in speed, as Rachel's proximity caused a surge of energy through my body. I tightened my grip on her. Rachel's fingers curled against the skin of my back like there was something to grab ahold of.

"Fuck it," she said, abruptly tugging her arms away from me to undo the buttons of her pyjama top. "We're married. We're not dead."

It was a good thing, too. I was as hard as a rock.

"What do we do now, dirty girl?" I asked with a smile as Rachel caught herself in the arms of her shirt.

Her eyes found mine. They sparked deliciously.

"You know exactly what to do now...sir."

41

RACHEL

Sweat prickled my back as I sighed against the pillow. Mason lifted a damp curl to kiss the curve of my neck. I shivered when the lock fell back against my exposed skin. My eyes fluttered closed as Mason kissed along my shoulder blades. He set a wet trail along my arm all the way down to my bent elbow, all the way along my forearm tucked beneath my cheek, all the way down my fingers resting on the humid pillow. I giggled when he kissed the tip of my nose.

His cum was drying on my ass. I could feel where it dripped down on either side like I was a Bundt cake he'd frosted too soon. The sheets were wet beneath me. But neither of us seemed interested in cleaning up. I was sinking deeper and deeper into the mattress. And Mason seemed intent on covering every inch of me with the tenderness of his lips.

I inhaled deeply and felt such a deep sense of calm as I exhaled slowly. Mason was walking his fingers along the backs of my thighs. Swirling his pointer finger in his cum. Drawing dreamy spirals that threatened to send me right off to sleep.

This was something I had longed for. Yes, the passion and intensity of fucking was amazing. But sex wasn't rare. You could get it any time you wanted. On practically any corner. For almost any price. Sex was happening all over the world. On beds just the like one Mason and I languished on. Up against walls. Atop washing machines. On kitchen tables. There were animalistic grunts and the grabbing, grappling of skin in hotels and prisons, schools and conference rooms, graveyards and maternity wards. Sex was anything but rare.

But this, this quiet moment. This soft attention to my body, this wordless devotion to my form. This calmness and ease, this tenderness and slowness. This feeling that nothing ever had to be done ever again in life. This was rare.

I'd never had it with my past boyfriends who fucked me while drunk and immediately after passed out. Who fucked me while high and immediately after rambled at the ceiling about the butterfly effect. Who fucked me while nothing at all but horny and immediately after pulled out, ran out, peeled out the drive. Never to be seen again.

I'd never even really had it with Tim. There was always an important meeting in the morning that meant sleep. Or a couple more emails to send out which meant his hands were on a laptop, not me. Or a promotion he missed out on that meant huffing irritably, rolling over, and a half-hearted apology in the morning as he tapped the top of my head like I was a dog he spoke to a little too harshly.

I'd had it before, though. This rare time where your body drifted toward the clouds and your lover's touch dragged you toward hell and you wanted both. You wanted it all. You *had* it all.

It had always been with Mason. It had been in Vegas. After we fucked like animals. And it had been right then and there. After we fucked like husband and wife.

Mason was on his side beside me. His eyes were drawing the outline of my body as he trailed his finger up and down my spine. I watched him watch me for a moment and then closed my eyes. I never wanted this moment to end. Not ever. Not—

"Hey, what was our wedding like?"

Mason's question startled me and my silent reverie. Fear jolted through my previously jelly limbs. I squeezed my eyes shut so they wouldn't jump open. I knew Mason would see the terror as clear as day. The "oh shit"-ness I was feeling. I was about to get caught in a lie. A small lie, but a lie that could unravel everything.

"Um..." I mumbled, trying to buy time, "what do you mean?"

Mason's hand splayed flat against the small of my back. I wondered if he could feel the difference. How I'd gone from putty in his hands to set concrete. How I'd been floating and was now scrambling to catch myself before I hit the ground. How I'd been sinking into the mattress just moments before and now resisting the impulse to leap up and run. Escape.

"Well, I don't remember a goddamn thing," Mason said, his words just as soft as before. "And you said you remembered. So...I don't know. I'm just kind of curious, I guess."

From what I could tell there was no malice in Mason's voice. No suspicion. As he tucked my hair back behind my ear it wasn't to see more clearly the lies on my face. I wasn't stepping into a trap. Or at least, I didn't think I was.

I should have known it was a bad sign that there was still such mistrust between us. Still such lies. But I was so preoccupied with weaving more lies, to think it through. Because that was the way to keep Mason's hands on my body. That was the way to keep his heart beating beside mine.

I thought for sure, with a pang of sadness, that it was the only way.

"Like it's kind of silly, I know," Mason added when I remained silent for a little too long. His fingers moved a little more roughly across my back. "Like it was so long ago and who the fuck cares about all that like manufactured shite anyway and—"

"I want to tell you," I interrupted.

I could feel Mason's eyes on me, but I kept mine closed. Why had I said that? *Idiot, Rachel.* He was giving me an out all on his own and I went and blurted that out. I just asked the executioner who was staying my death to continue with the noose. Please and thank you. Why? Fucking why? I squeezed my nails into my palms.

"Um," I began awkwardly, just like any terrible liar does, "um, I mean we were pretty drunk."

Mason laughed. His mouth was at the back of my neck. His teeth scraped against the knots of my spine.

"Maybe that goes without saying," he said, nipping gently at my skin.

"Right," I said, hoping my own laughter didn't sound so obviously nervous. "Right, well, let's see. Um, I don't know. I...I wore a white dress."

Mason pressed a kiss to one hip and then, dragging his tongue from point to point, kissed the other hip.

"It's like I'm there right now, Rach," he joked.

"Okay, okay," I said as he smoothed his hands over the swell of my ass. "It was one of the costumes from my show. We, um, we broke in and stole it before we went to the chapel. It was, um, it was all white feathers. The skirt was one of those like high-low things. So it had this crazy train, but was almost like indecently short in the front."

Mason hummed against my ass cheeks.

"And the part that covered my breasts was just a feather each. One fanned feather for my right breast, one for the left."

I yelped when Mason's teeth sank into me.

"I said I had to wear my silver pasties with it and you said I would have to do no such thing."

Mason laid his cheek against my ass and walked his fingers between freckles on the backs of my thighs. I was beginning to like the lie. Maybe that was why I said I'd tell him about our wedding. Because I liked lies. Loved lies. Because a fantasy could be real if two people believed it.

"Yeah, the owner of that shitty chapel took one look at us, you in a bow tie, shamrock underwear, and nothing else, and me looking like a witch who'd been stripped naked, had feathers thrown over her, and was just awaiting the tar, and said, 'No. *Hell* no.'"

Mason had moved down the bed. His toes were by my head. My toes were in his mouth. I squirmed as he laughed.

"So we had the choice to change into clothes they had at the chapel—like this shitty Marilyn Monroe polyester dress and one of those tuxes that are really just a printed t-shirt, I'm pretty sure they were just left behind by some couple sometime in the last three decades—or bribe the Elvis priest into marrying us outside the chapel."

"We obviously just changed," Mason said, and I swatted at his ass.

"We didn't have any cash so we offered Elvis an Eiffel Tower if he married us beneath the Eiffel Tower," I said, grinning at the image of it.

Mason twisted toward me. I rolled onto my side myself to stare down the length of our bodies at him.

"An Eiffel Tower?" he asked.

I found myself no longer afraid for him to see my eyes. I didn't think he could see the lies there anymore. Because I believed it now. I wanted it now, this wedding I was writing. Besides, who was there to tell me I was wrong? Who was there to say that this was not exactly what happened?

I held up one hand, said, "This is you," held up another

hand, said, "This is Elvis," and extending my thumbs between my peaked fingers, laughed and said, "And this is me."

"An Eiffel Tower," Mason repeated, awe in his voice.

I wiggled my toes in his face.

"Anyway, we dragged some poor Midwest tourist who had too many Mai Tais at Caesar's Palace and passed out at the fountains to be our witness and we said our vows, said our 'I do's', and kissed to seal the deal beneath the twinkling lights of fake Paris."

I said Paris like the French and flicked my wrist. I smiled down at Mason, who was running his palm up and down the length of my thigh. His eyes were on my skin, focused. Like he was sanding a piece of rough wood.

"And our vows?"

His eyes were hesitant as he lifted them up to meet mine.

"Do you remember anything that we said?"

I sighed. Stared briefly up at the bars of light across the ceiling.

"I mean, we were really drunk," I said.

"Sure," Mason said. "Yeah, yeah, of course."

He was kissing my knees. I was a little kid with scraped knees and he was kissing them. Kissing them better. One. And then the other.

"I think yours were better than mine," I said.

Mason gazed up at me over the gentle curve of my naked hip.

"You might be remembering that wrong," he said.

I shook my head. Laughed softly.

"You always seemed to promise more," I said.

Mason was silent, his eyes distant. Without looking at me he said, again softly, again I was sure too softly, "Well, now I know that you're definitely remembering wrong."

Between his stomach and mine our fingers were twisting

around one another's. Not interlocking. We never stilled enough to hold one another. Never stilled enough for his fingers to rest in my palm, or my fingers in his. It wasn't exactly playful either. Just a sort of circling one another. Wanting to feel the other. Not wanting to stop. But also not wanting to stop moving. To sink. To be still.

"I think I said something about always being on the road," I said after a few quiet moments. "Something about running from home and feeling like that was safety: running. Something about how when I was with you, I felt like I was running with my feet in one place. And, like, how with you I was always panting and out of breath and there was always that thrill of being gone, being alive, being on the run, but, I don't know, how it was amazing because I felt all that in your bed. In your arms. When I wasn't even moving at all. I don't know, something stupid about how I ran all this way to you. And that you knew I wouldn't know how to stop so you just ran with me. And you'd always run with me, if that's what I wanted."

I laughed. I rolled onto my back as I dragged my fingers through my hair.

I said to the ceiling, "Something really stupid like that."

Mason made his way slowly back up to me. With his tongue. With his lips. With his fingers. He moved over me like that hot Vegas breeze. He was everywhere. So fully all around me.

"Do you remember what I said to you?" he asked.

I felt like he was searching me. Hands moving over my body in the dark like an archaeologist. Thorough, but careful. Wanting to find something, but afraid that the finding would break it. Afraid, then, of the finding.

I sighed deeply as his hands caressed my breasts.

"I think you just said that you love me," I said quietly, a little too quietly.

Mason lifted my arms, placed them over my head. His

fingertips tickled slightly as he ran them down the underside of my arms.

"That's it?" he asked, eyes darting to mine. Darting away.

I stared up at the ceiling. I considered what I'd wish for Mason to say to me, if I actually remembered our wedding, his vows. Mason moved his hands over me. Touching me. Holding me. I tried and tried to find more, to want more.

Finally, I just reached out, touched his arm, and brushing my own fingertips against him said, "It was enough."

Mason sat up and guided me up into a sitting position in front of him. My hands were held in his between us.

"Was it?" he asked, turning my hands over, drawing over the lines of my palm like he was doing a reading.

"Yes," I answered, the first truthful thing I'd said all goddamn night.

I wondered if Mason could hear the difference. I waited for his head to jerk up. Waited for the accusation in his darkened eyes. But he kept his attention on my fingers, turning them this way and that like he was trying to crack a code.

I thought maybe he hadn't heard me, but then he said, "If I married you today, I'd say more."

"I wouldn't want you to."

"I'd say I love you and—"

"And I'd cut you off right there," I insisted, curling my fingers around his. "And not let you say another word."

Mason finally looked up at me.

"Whatever we fucked up later," I said, "we got the wedding right. We got the vows perfectly right."

How silly how much I believed that, despite having not a single recollection of it happening. How silly that Mason seemed to trust me, despite not having any reason at all to do so.

"One thing I thought I remembered..." Mason began after a moment, frowning again down at my hands.

Again that jolt of fear. Again that need to run. Again that terror that always lurked beneath the surface like a black river.

Mason smiled and shrugged and said, "But I guess not."

"What?" I asked.

Mason laid me back down. Cuddled behind me. Wrapped me tight in his arms.

"Nothing," he said. "It's just that I kind of have this vague memory of tattooing you that night. Or some night."

I swallowed heavily.

"I must not have because all you have are these little dove wings right..." Mason wriggled his fingers between us to tap the small of my back, "...here."

"How do you know that wasn't you?" I asked.

Mason nuzzled his chin into the crook of my neck.

"Well, it's not exactly my style, though that's not it."

"What is it then?"

He inhaled the scent of my shampoo as I waited eagerly for his response.

"I don't know," he said. "They're not you. And...well, I think, at least for a brief moment in time, I really knew you, Rachel."

I didn't say anything in response. I just blinked the tear from my eye so it soaked the pillow and not Mason's hand tucked up with mine beneath my chin.

"Hey, so what happened with Elvis and the Eiffel Tower?" Mason asked long after I thought he'd fallen asleep.

I laughed.

"Oh, we ran," I told him. "Ran like the devil himself was after us."

Two true things that night.

42

RACHEL

hen...

I HADN'T EVEN NOTICED the bandage till my director freaked the fuck out.

"So let me get this straight," he'd shouted while pacing back and forth in the tight space of my dressing room while I popped another Advil. "Our audience tonight is going to get sparkler pasties in the front—hot, Little Miss America with her perfect tits—and in the back they're going to get burn victim? Little Miss Domestic Violence? Little Miss Skin Cancer Screening? What's hot about that, Rachel? Tell me! What is hot about melanoma?!"

I stretched my arm around to prod at the rather sore area under the bandage.

"I don't think it's a burn," I told him, craning my neck this way and that to try to catch a glimpse in the mirror. The sparkler pasties swayed about as I squirmed in the chair.

"What in the hell did you do last night?" my director asked.

"I have no clue."

My director sighed dramatically and stared up to the ceiling. "Lord, please give me strength to deal with these sluts I, for some reason, love so much."

I ignored him as I peeled back a corner, wincing. I squinted at the red, raised skin in the mirror.

"I think it's a tattoo..."

We dressed up the bandage as best we could. My makeup artist painted over the bandage and concealed it under this giant-ass eagle.

"I don't know," she said, stepping away from it and shrugging, makeup brush between her teeth. "America, you know?"

I didn't really care all that much. I was eager to see what it was. Eager to get back to Mason. Eager to try to piece together the night before with one another over sushi...or wings...or both... Yes, both, I thought as I threw my arms over my head, smiled, and shook my sparkling tits to a standing ovation.

I told the makeup artist not to bother washing it off. Mason could handle that in the shower. On the bus ride down the strip, I leaned my cheek against the hot glass as the bright lights slipped by and imagined it was the hot glass of my shower. It was quiet in the back of the bus. Dark. There was no one to see my fingers slip between my thighs as I imagined Mason pressing me harder against the water-streaked glass. Imagined the fear of breaking that hot, steam-covered glass as he fucked me from behind. Imagined my knees collapsing because it felt so damn good and Mason having to hold me as he finished, hold me there against that hot glass.

I laughed as I took the elevator up to my floor. I laughed because I was happy. Because I had someone waiting for me who I'd been waiting for. I laughed because I just couldn't believe it. That life could be so kind. That I'd be given something when all I knew in life was that good things were for being taken away. That I could actually *be* happy. I laughed because I was happy, which was funny. Really fucking funny.

I fidgeted with the corners of the bandage beneath my t-shirt as I unlocked the door. All the lights were on and I threw my stuff down in the entryway. I had better things to do than stay tidy.

"Mason," I called into the apartment. "Hey, so do you remember anything about tattoos last night? Honestly, I can't remember a fucking thing. But I kind of think we might have gotten tattoos. Do you have, like, a bandage on you anywhere?"

In the kitchen beer bottles were still spread out everywhere. Mason wasn't exactly tidy either. I grabbed one from the fridge. Laughed as I popped the top.

"I kind of hope you have one," I called out toward the living room. "'Cause maybe it *is* a burn. God, did I try to twirl fire-sticks? For some reason I always get that urge when I'm drunk and, like, why can't I want to, I don't know, cuddle with stuffed animals after drinking a big glass of water when I'm drunk, you know?"

I kicked off my shoes as I walked toward the living room.

"Mason?"

I was surprised to find the couch empty. The TV on, but no one there to watch it. I checked the balcony overlooking the strip. A cigarette still burned in the ashtray, but Mason was not out there either.

"Mason?"

I went toward the bedroom. If he felt anywhere near as bad as I did during my performance, a nap might have been a very smart thing. The sheets were a mess. Just the way we'd left them. A mess and empty.

The bathroom, too. A mess of vodka bottles, travel-size shampoos and my dildo. But empty of the one thing I was looking for.

"Hmm," I said and walked back out to the kitchen.

I said "Hmm" because it sounded like something someone who wasn't worried would say. "Hmm." It had an ambivalence I wished a felt. A carefreeness I longed for even as my heartrate quickened. "Hmm" seemed to say to the emptiness around me, "Everything is fine. Everything is going to be fine."

"Hmm" was everything I wanted to be. "Hmm" was everything I was not.

Seated on the edge of the kitchen counter, I sipped my beer and kicked my feet about and tried to imagine what takeout Mason was picking up for us to eat at a quarter past two in the morning. I sipped my beer and kicked my feet about and tried to pretend that was what I was imagining. Plastic containers. Grease-stained receipts. Crumpled brown paper bags.

Not a suitcase gone from beneath the bed.

Not a jacket torn from the hanger in the entryway closet.

Not a seat on a plane soaring over the country that was supposed to be empty.

I made it through one sitcom, God knows which one, before allowing myself to chew at my lip. There were plenty of places in Vegas far enough away to take longer than a sitcom to get there and back. There was traffic sometimes. Even at night. I mean, for fuck's sake, it was Vegas, what was I freaking out about?

No.

No, I was not freaking out. Especially because I hadn't even looked around for a note. I downed the rest of my beer in one gulp and hopped up from the couch. A new sense of purpose helped me swallow down the panic that I definitely was not feeling. I had a whole apartment to check for a note. That was potentially hours of searching. Hours of business. Hours of something else to think about.

There's no way Mason wouldn't be back by then.

But when the first dagger of morning light slipped between the ribs of the blinds and found my wide, unblinking eyes, Mason was still not back.

I sat like a forgotten rag doll on the floor in my living room. Back stooped over. Arms heavy at my sides. Palms facing up like a beggar who no longer even had the strength or desire to lift his hands to the passing crowds. My bare legs, extended straight in front of me, still had some glitter left over from the show. It sparkled in the light. A betrayal to how I felt.

The slight breeze from the cracked window shuffled the downy feathers around my ice-cold feet, toes pale, frozen like a white marble statue atop a tomb. I'd torn at the cushions of the couch when there was nowhere else to look. It didn't make any sense at all that Mason would have stuffed a note for me into a place only accessible by ripping, tearing, screaming, but it didn't make any sense at all that Mason would have left either. So I'd ripped the cushions. I tore at them with clawing fingernails and hot tears, screaming as feathers erupted all around like the grand opening of a burlesque show.

Drawers from my bedroom dresser were littered around me. They looked like little barges on the foamy white seas. I emptied them first in the lamplight of my bedroom. I went methodically at the start. My bra drawer made the most sense as a place Mason would leave a note, something like,

Thought you needed more of these for me to tear from you. Be back soon ~ M.

I made tidy stacks of my bras and then my panties and then my pyjamas on top of the dresser. I fought back my panic by focusing on keeping the straps tucked in, the thongs folded along the edge perfectly, careful not to snag the silk on the wood grain of the dresser.

By the time I reached my period sweatpants at the very bottom of the very last dresser drawer, I was flinging things out behind me like some kind of crazed wood chipper. When the drawers were empty, when there was no chance at all that there was a note in them, I took the drawers out and carried them in a towering stack to the living room where I told myself there was more light.

Trying to find a hammer made me feel okay for a little while. It was something else to think about. Something else to focus on. More time to occupy so that Mason would be back sooner and we would be laughing about this little mix-up sooner. Joking about how insane I went throwing my clothes everywhere. Arguing about where the appropriate place to put a note for someone is. When I failed to find a hammer, I used a meat mallet. I pounded at the corners of the drawer because sometimes little scraps of paper get caught there.

I could almost see it. Mason with a wry smile placing the note gently. Turning already as he closed the drawer. The little draught wafting the light piece of paper to the back. It getting wedged when I pushed everything around, searching.

But there was no trapped little piece of paper. No note. No note in the drawers. No note on the fridge. In the fridge. Behind or underneath the fridge. No note on any of the counters: bathroom, kitchen, living room, balcony. I even leaned out over the edge of the railing, hot summer night wind tangling my hair and imagined Mason's note fluttering away. It would be impossible to find. Just like he was. Just like he *wanted* to be.

There was no note in the cabinets. No *"You're out of soy sauce and how can you have duck without soy sauce. Be back soon ~ M"* in the junk drawer of rubber bands and takeout menus. No note on the mirror. Not in lipstick. Not even in the steam of a long, hot shower; I checked. In the madness of the middle of the night, I ran the shower at full heat and tore at my lower lip as I sat hunched on the edge of the tub.

There was no answer on his phone. The only time I stopped

searching was to try Mason's number again. And the only time I stopped praying on each and every ring was when I heard his voice, distant, unreachable at the very end, "It's Mason. If you know me, leave a message. If you don't, fuck off."

I never left a message. I could never quite convince myself that I knew him. At least not anymore. I'd been able to believe that there was no one else I knew better in the entire world. But I'd also been able to believe that he would be there when I returned. Like he said. Like he promised. So what the fuck did it matter what I believed or didn't?

As I sat there on the floor, in the mess, unblinking, unseeing, the bands of light from the blinds travelled across my face. Across my body. Hours passed like that. Nothing moving but those bars. Nothing changing but their shade as sunset painted them red and the flickering on of the streetlamps doused them with yellow.

Only the itch of my skin beneath the bandage at the small of my back stirred me. It was healing, this wound I hadn't even known I'd received. The pieces were stitching back together and yet I couldn't even remember getting torn in two.

My body was stiff as I pushed myself up from the floor, down feathers stuck to my palms. I gathered them on the bottom of my feet as I padded toward the darkened mirror. My stiff muscles protested as I twisted to see around behind me. I pulled at the bandage. I hadn't realised how numb I'd become till I felt the tape peeling off the fine hair there at the base of my spine.

It was a tattoo. A tattoo of a feather. The kind that topped my headdresses. The kind that extended out from the back of my corset like old-fashioned bustles. It lay across the top of the cheeks of my ass like it had floated down there naturally. Like my clothes had been torn from my body and it came loose and fell, fell, fell. It followed my curves seductively. It was somehow raunchy and tender and beautiful. It was somehow fully Mason. Somehow fully me.

This tattoo was evidence.

He *knew* me.

He would never just...leave.

My fingers trembled as I dialled Mason's number again in the dark. I prepared myself for the rings. Long and anguishing rings. The terrible space between them. The little catches in the noise where I was positive for a second that it was the sound of him picking up, only for another ring to come. I was ready for all that.

What I wasn't ready for was a robotic voice to declare before any of that that the line had been disconnected. The caller no longer available.

I didn't cry. Crying is for when you lose hope.

There was no hope to ever be had. I had been wrong. This was as definite an answer as I would ever get: Mason had left. He intended to leave. And what's more, he intended not to be found.

That was it.

I couldn't go on in Vegas after that. It felt like a rotten dream. A spoiled fantasy. It was the place where I'd had everything and lost everything. There was nothing more to do there. I'd finally been accepted as myself, only to be rejected completely, as myself.

It was time for a new place. A new start. A new role for me.

New York City wasn't kind. The jostling on the subway, the shouting on the streets, the rats and the piss and the smells from the steaming sewer drains. But there was a tiny tattoo parlour tucked between two skyscrapers and they were open late.

I showed the artist the feather. He looked shocked when I told him I wanted to cover it.

"But it's beautiful."

"It's not me," I told him.

He eyed me warily.

"And who are you then?"

I avoided the reflection of the feather in the mirror.

"I don't know," I said. "What can you make it into?"

The artist ran his thumb over the tattoo at the small of my back as he sighed.

"Well," he said at last, "I think I could make it into a pair of dove wings pretty easily."

And so I went from a fallen angel to dove.

43

MASON

Maybe Rachel was always meant to be a flash. A moment of brilliance so blinding she left an impression on the back of my eyelids so fierce, I didn't even realise she was gone until she was impossibly out of reach. A shooting star, a comet, a siren's call toward the rocks.

Day 30 of our "marriage" was fast approaching. With each day closer Rachel became more distant. I feared Day 30 she would be gone. I'd be left blinking at the burned image she left behind.

When we fucked, her eyes seemed to stare at something unseen over my shoulder. Her fingers still dug into my body, but not like she was falling, not like I was the only thing to keep her from death. More like she was on a busy city bus and was reaching up for a handhold. Jostled, off-balance, but certainly not in any sort of danger. When I came, she rolled away from me faster than before. Tugged the blanket up over her shoulders higher than before. She joked like usual about making my breakfast in the morning and fell asleep more quickly than before.

She rose before me. Some nights I wasn't even sure she'd

slept. I worried she'd slip out when I fell asleep, tiptoe to the room down the hall and in the morning make the bed there with such precision that no matter how closely I analysed it, I couldn't be quite sure whether it had ever been disturbed at all.

Rachel's time at the shop lessened. More and more, Rian or Conor or Aurnia would ask where Rachel was and more and more, I wouldn't have an answer. More and more, I wouldn't even be the first to know that she had left. Her excuses for missing beers with the gang after work came less easily over time. Or she tried less.

"I'm just tired," she'd say after avoiding my eyes for a few quiet minutes, busying herself with a receipt for groceries.

"You didn't sleep well?" I'd ask.

Rachel would then give me a weak smile and say something like, "How can I when my husband snores so terribly?"

We'd do what we always did: laugh, let it go, each pretend that there wasn't something heavy between us. Pressing between us. Unresolved between us.

I'd come back from beers at The Jar and Rachel would be by the window. Just staring out through the cracked blinds. Or sitting on the still made-up bed. Legs long in front of her. Back rounded as she gazed in a sort of unsleeping dream at the wall across the bedroom.

"You waited up?" I'd ask, slipping off my jacket, coming over to fondle her breast. I'd whisper in her ear, "Not so tired, eh?"

She'd fuck me like a sex doll. Drag her fingers through my hair like a comb. Make sounds like she knew those were the sounds she was supposed to make, were she feeling what she was supposed to feel.

Bit by bit, Rachel avoided my eye more. Waited till I was done brushing my teeth to slip quietly into the bathroom. Bit by bit she kept her clothes separate from mine in the dresser drawers. Easier to grab. More convenient to pack when she leaves.

She's going to leave. She's going to be gone. Day 30 would come and Day 30 would go and I would be alone.

One evening I closed the shop alone. Conor had taken Aurnia home, the two of them all chuckles and straying hands before ducking out into the rain. Rian had asked if Rachel and I were going to have dinner alone or if we wanted to go out. I told him dinner alone, because I had no idea where Rachel was.

I was thankful that the guys had left early. It meant more work to consume my time. There was the trash to be taken out. The tattoo guns to clean, to polish, to prep for the next day. The chairs to wipe down, the desks to brush clean of pencil shavings and eraser remnants, the floors to sweep from shaved arms or legs. There were the appointments to confirm for tomorrow. There was going over social media posts. There was tidying the storeroom in the back.

There was plenty to do and yet not nearly enough.

The rain increased, pattering loudly against the now dark windows. I stood in the noisy silence without anything to do. Without anything to do, but wait for Rachel. Or think about waiting. Wait to think about waiting. Think about waiting to think about waiting.

Pacing was good at first. Movement. A sense of progress even if it was just a back-and-forth illusion. I could also see down both sides of the slick sidewalk when I paced. First to the north. Then to the south.

But soon pacing felt like running. My heart was erratic, wild. My palms were sweaty. My shirt clung to my clammy shoulders. Sitting was better. A glass of whiskey was better. Relaxing, staying calm, remaining reasonable was better.

I lasted about fifteen minutes before leaping toward the stairs. I took them two, three at a time. I yanked at the dresser drawers in a panic.

No, her things were still there. All the tidy little piles separated more and more, bit by bit from mine were still there. Her passport was tucked under her sweatpants at the very bottom. I ran my fingers over them because I was fairly sure she'd had them since Vegas. They were buttery soft and they smelled like her.

Dragging my fingers through my hair, I sank wearily onto the edge of the bed. I was driving myself mad. I was so worried that Rachel left me when I *knew* she was going to leave me. What did a day or two or three more really matter? Sure Day 30 wasn't technically here, but it would be. For all intents and purposes, it might as well be. Because she was leaving. She said she was. A few good fucks and a trip down memory lane hadn't changed the fact that she came to Dublin for a divorce. Stuck around for a divorce. Was waiting around, at my insane insistence, for a *divorce*.

The truth was right there in front of me: I thought she might not. Might not leave me. Might not really want a divorce in the end. Might not go come Day 30.

I'd given myself this glimmer of hope. I'd allowed myself to believe that love was anything more than the thing that made the inevitable pain of being left all the worse. The heights you were dragged to before being dropped. You would always be dropped; I knew that. Love was what made it hurt. If I just stayed on the fucking ground...

I growled in frustration and went back downstairs. The glow of the pink neon "Dublin Ink" sign on the wall reminded me of Vegas so I ripped the cord from the wall. It sputtered and snapped as it died. Darkness fell on the parlour like a closing curtain on a stage.

Where the fuck did she go? I wondered at the window. Where the fuck did she always go? And for so long? More and more time each fucking time? Why couldn't she just stay? Why couldn't anyone just fucking *stay*?

I grew angry because it was the same feeling as when I returned to Rachel's apartment in Vegas to find it emptied, stripped clean, abandoned. I wanted to drive my fist through the wall because I was there again: heartbroken, devastated, ruined. I wanted to throw a chair through the glass of that bigger window overlooking the empty sidewalk because *I* put myself in a position to get hurt. *I* did this to myself. *I* let Rachel break all my rules, crash through all my defences, lay waste to the walls I'd so tediously built up through all my years of Miss Last Nights.

As the rain swept across the black street in lashing waves, I tried to imagine how I would get past this. Rachel being gone again. Me again being the one left. The last time it took years. The last time I fucked my way through Dublin to get over her. The last time I built Dublin Ink as a lighthouse for her to find me.

What was I to do now?

This time years would be decades. I was sure of it. This time there would be no pleasure to be had between faceless thighs. I was sure of that, too. I'd get hard, of course. I'd come. I'd experience that carnal flash. But I knew that it would be like a drop of water in an empty vase. Worst of all was the fact that this time I would know where Rachel was. I had her number, she had mine. Nothing would be keeping us apart this time.

Except for us.

This would destroy me. That I could not heal from.

I was hunched over on the edge of the couch, feet tapping madly, fingers digging into my skull, when the door opened. The little bell rang and I looked up. It was like seeing Rachel at the bottom of my stairs all over again. I was shocked. I was scared. I was flooded with hope, drowned with lust, choked with anger, paralysed by terror. I couldn't believe she was there, actually there.

I must have looked like a madman. Eyes bloodshot and wide. Whiskey on my breath. Crumpled clothes torn at like a shifting werewolf under a full moon. But then again, Rachel looked like a madwoman, there in the open doorway.

Her hair clung to her paled skin like river weeds. She dripped onto the floor, breathing heavily. She didn't seem to care at all that the door was open or that gusts of wind were sending in rainwater around her trembling form.

"Look," she said as I stared at her, "if we're going to make this work we need to talk. Really talk."

I barely comprehended her words. *"Make this work."* Make what work? What was she talking about? Why wasn't she closing the door? Wasn't she cold? Wasn't she freezing? Wasn't she chilled to the bone? Why weren't my arms around her?

Rachel sucked in a trembling breath, her chest still heaving.

"Mason," she said as the rain roared behind her, "we need to talk about what happened in Vegas."

44

MASON

hen...

IT HAD to be something spectacular. And unique. And sweet. And dazzling. And brilliant and sexy and intriguing. It had to be theatrical and it had to be from the deepest depths of my heart. And funny. And irresistible. And like nothing at all ever before.

It had to be like Rachel.

"Fuck!" I growled, balling up another sheet of paper and hurling it over the edge of the balcony at Rachel's apartment. "Fuck, fuck, fucker, fuck me, goddamn fuck, *fuck*."

The chair I'd been leaning back on crashed to the concrete. I pushed myself up, tossed the notepad on the little glass patio table, and stalked back inside. At the mirror in the living room, I stared at my reflection and tried to speak from the heart.

"Rachel," I said, an alright start, I supposed, "I know it's only been...damn, I don't even know how long it's been."

I tugged at my hair and shook my head, muttering, "It

doesn't matter, it doesn't matter. She's not going to say 'yes' because you got the dates right. Keep going."

Breathing in deeply, I tried to calm my thrashing heart and tried again.

"Look, I know it's been short, our time together, but when you know, you know, you know?"

I bellowed at the ceiling like a maniac and stormed toward the kitchen. *"When you know, you know, you know?" What kind of bullshite was that, you feckin' eejit?* The refrigerator door clanging noisily against the wall as I pulled it open. I grabbed a beer and popped it roughly on the edge of the marble island. I downed half of it before gasping at the air.

I needed to calm down, I told myself, palms flat on the counter, back heaving as my head dropped. I squeezed my eyes shut. A million different possibilities shifted through my head like sandstorms. Bits and pieces. Flashes that stung my eyes. Do I take her to a nice restaurant? Too typical. Do I stand up on a table in a nice restaurant? Rachel might like that. But it didn't scream "romance", screaming my proposal to her as I was dragged away by security. But maybe that was the exact kind of romance that Rachel would love. She'd probably hold an old lady at knifepoint just to get dragged away with me. We'd fuck in the back of the cop car. Red and blue lights whirling. Rocking on the strip. Batons banging against the plastic divider as the Vegas lights bathed her bare tits before my mouth did…

I pressed the ice-cold beer bottle to my forehead. Fuck, I loved that woman. Loved her more than anything. Loved her more than I thought was possible. Like I was mad, feverish, sick. Loved her like she was the impossible made possible, the unreal, real, the dream, a reality. Loved her like she alone was worth loving.

At first I was going to ignore my phone. I heard it ring from the bedroom. Buried somewhere under the sex-stained sheets. I had more important things to do before Rachel got back from her performance later that night. Proposing marriage to the woman you just met took hard work, you know? But I decided in the end to at least check it in case it was Rachel.

Maybe the rest of the show got food poisoning and the show was cancelled.

Maybe there was a pipe burst in the theatre and the show was cancelled.

Maybe the electricity on the Strip had gone out and the show was cancelled.

Maybe a tornado was heading for the city and the show was cancelled.

Maybe Rachel couldn't stand to be apart from me the way I couldn't stand to be apart from her and had demanded that the show be cancelled right then and there with a stomp of her little foot and a sexy pout.

I almost tossed the phone back onto the bed when I saw the Dublin area code. But I saw the name as I was extending my hand, fingers ready to unfurl. My palm moved slowly back toward me. I stared down at my phone as it continued to ring. Maybe I already knew then. Maybe I already knew what would have been impossible to already know.

"Hello?" I answered.

"Mr Donovan?"

"Yes."

I didn't want to say "yes". It was the last thing in the world I wanted to say. I wanted to lie. To say no. To hang up the phone and throw it across the room and run to Rachel where everything was alright, where everything would always be alright.

"Mr Donovan," the woman's voice came, "I'm calling because we've admitted your nan, Nancy. She came complaining of chest pains and..."

The rest of the words blurred and faded. Sentences became

indistinguishable from one another. Technical terms were no different in my ears from kind, gentle words of encouragement. The only thing that came clear was at the very end.

"I'm sorry to be the one to tell you, but I think it best if you get here as soon possible."

I didn't remember hanging up. I didn't remember the mad dash around Rachel's apartment. I didn't remember stuffing mismatched socks into my backpack. I didn't remember deciding to leave my suitcase, to leave the jacket in the hallway. I didn't even remember whether I called Conor or Rian. Or if I'd texted.

I did remember thinking of Rachel. I remember because it was what I regretted the most. I remember that moment, halfway out the door with my passport in hand, where I considered going back to write a note. I remember thinking of her returning from her performance and finding me gone. I remember not wanting her to think the worst.

In the end, I left without a note. Because the worst had happened.

I thought when I returned that Rachel would be able to understand. It never occurred to me that she would also leave. That she would take the opportunity to be gone. That I would never even get a chance to explain, to apologise.

Getting to my nan was what mattered most in that moment and so I didn't go back to write a note.

I remembered that. I remembered that all too well. The deciding. The closing of the door. The glancing back one last time and reassuring myself it wouldn't matter. A note. Just like it wouldn't matter when I finally proposed whether or not I got the dates right. Rachel wouldn't care.

Because she loved me. Because I loved her. And she would be there. Always.

The plane ride was split between downing whiskey and throwing it up in the tiny jostling bathroom. My nan had raised me. Taken me in when my mother left. And I was an ocean away the second she needed me. I wanted to drown that pain. But I knew, I guess in the depths of my stomach, that I deserved it.

I rode the whole cab ride to the hospital at the edge of my seat. I pounded the headrests for the driver to go faster till he threatened to kick me out if I didn't stop. I rocked back and forth after that. The driver had to tell me when we were outside the hospital. Then he had to tell me to get out. Then, when I still hadn't moved, he had to storm out, wrench open the back door, and grab ahold of my arm.

If the glass sliding doors hadn't been automatic, I might have stood there forever outside. A reason to not go in. A reason to stay where I was safe. Where I didn't know what I already knew. But the doors slid open and a wave of people behind me forced me inside and the woman at the counter asked who I was there to see.

There was no avoiding it. No way not to see her eyes scrolling down the computer screen. No way to miss the slight hitch in her breath. The quick licking of her lips. The little sigh before she looked up at me.

"If you'll just come with me."

I couldn't say no at that point. I couldn't run from her as she guided me slowly, too slowly to a dim, quiet side hallway. I couldn't refuse when she asked that I sit.

She told me that my nan had suffered a second heart attack that morning. That she didn't suffer. That she was gone.

"How much?"

"What's that, dear?"

I stared at the blank grey wall across from me as I repeated, "How much did I miss her by?"

The woman made a sound, something like, "Oh", something like, "Please don't make me answer that. No good comes of asking—"

I sent my eyes to her. "When. Did. She. Die?"

"Mr Donovan, I—"

"When? *Please.*"

Her shoulders sagged. She consulted her clipboard like she didn't already know. She didn't look at me as she said, "Miss Donovan passed about fifteen minutes ago."

I saw myself in the doorway of Rachel's apartment, pausing to consider a note. I felt those ticking seconds go by like freight trains in the night. Each impossibly long. Each unbearably loud. Each rattling the floor beneath my feet.

I saw the cab I missed at the foot of Rachel's apartment, saw it drive off, its headlights fading. I felt the restlessness of my feet as I waited too long for the next one. I heard the driver's voice, "Accident just happened up ahead. Might add a bit of time." I heard the man's voice behind the counter when I finally got to the airport, "Well, there's a connecting flight in ten minutes, but there's no way you'll make it." I heard the TSA agent's voice when I tried to explain, "Everyone's trying to make a flight, sir." I saw the closed doors. Heard a voice who thought they were being helpful, "It's no big deal. There's another one out on a different airline in no more than fifteen minutes."

In the end I heard my own voice, loud and clear in that dimly lit hallway as the nurse patted my arm.

"I will never forgive myself."

I didn't mean to scare the nurse. She was just doing her job. She was just trying to be as kind and gentle as possible while doing it. She didn't deserve to get frightened. To jolt back. To gasp and cover her mouth when I screamed and hurled my phone against the wall. When I decided that wasn't enough, I drove my fists through the drywall, crushing the shattered pieces of my phone beneath my boots. When I lost myself so completely in my rage and grief that I didn't even realise she was no longer there to apologise to. She'd run off to get security. I was being dragged away.

It seemed I blinked and I was in a chair. In an empty hallway. A different one from before. No holes in the wall. No shattered phone. It was the morgue. I blinked and it was another chair, another hallway. The funeral home. I blinked and it was another chair, another hallway. The crematorium. Plenty of holes in the fucking wall there.

I blinked and it wasn't a chair, but a bed. An empty one. Not a hallway, but a room. An empty one. I stared at the ceiling and hot tears poured from the corners of my eyes to stain the pillow. Because there was one person I wanted to call. One person I wanted to ask for comfort. For support. For love. There was only one person I wanted to call and it was the one person I couldn't.

Rachel's number was broken to pieces in my mind just like the phone had been on that hospital floor. I could grasp at a digit here and there, but it was as useless as half a phone battery, its edges sharp enough to slice straight through your palm.

It was days later (I wasn't sure how many) and I was just realising that I had no way to contact the woman I loved, an ocean apart, but it might have well been a whole lifetime away.

I couldn't hold the shattered phone in my hands. Couldn't even try to begin to piece it back together. It had surely been swept up by some janitor. Thrown into a black plastic bag. I imagined the shards of glass tumbling from the back of a dump truck. Rain splattering the dark, empty screen.

And Rachel's number there. Somewhere. But unreachable. Lost in the dark.

It was what I deserved. To be alone like my nan had been alone. To expect someone to be there and be proved wrong. To lie there and know it was my fault.

All my fault.

I will *never* forgive myself.

45

RACHEL

Happy endings aren't supposed to feel so shitty... are they?

Mason's fingers played gently with mine in the little space between our crossed legs on the bedsheet. Lamplight cast over us softly like the glow of that Exit sign on the stage where we sat surrounded by half the takeout in Vegas. Our knees didn't touch, but occasionally when one of us sighed deeply or reached for another biscuit, they brushed briefly.

The rain still pattered against the window in Mason's bedroom, but it was gentler now. It had lost all its rage. It fell peacefully. Dripped down the windowpane instead of lashing it like a whip.

My fingers shook slightly as I took up my saucer and teacup. The lemon ginger tea had been diluted with so many refills from the pot resting beside us on a handwoven coaster that the lemon had lost its bite, the ginger its spice. Still I embraced the warmth as I raised it to my lips. I swirled it round my tongue, searching out what I knew had been there before.

"Well, that's it then," I said in the silence. Mason had been chasing crumbs along the rumpled sheets; he looked up at me. I said, "I mean, I forgive you. And…and you forgive me."

I hadn't meant for the words to come out like a question. Like I wasn't at all certain of what I was saying. Just like I hadn't meant for my fingers to shake. My lip to tremble. My heart to doubt. I wanted to be sure. To believe. To grab ahold of my happy ending with wide open arms and never let it go.

But I couldn't.

Mason nodded in lieu of speaking.

I swallowed. I glanced down into my teacup. The teabag, stripped of its colour, hung limp in the hot water. Nothing left to give.

"Right?" I said when Mason's pinkie hooked around mine. It should have felt like a key turning in a lock. It should have felt like safety, security. But I couldn't help but feel that I was trapped on the wrong side of the door. That I was being locked out. That the waters were rising around my feet and the way out was being shut forever.

Mason smiled at me. I searched his smile. I searched it for any of the doubts I was feeling. Any of the sense of unease I felt. I searched to see if in his dimples I could see a shadow like the one over my heart. A foreboding that things weren't over yet. That we weren't past the storm. That we were smack dab in the goddamn middle of it.

But Mason's smile was the smile I remembered. Full of life. Full of love. Eager and allusive, playful and seductive. It was the smile I saw at the bar that very first night. It was the smile I couldn't remember from our wedding. It was the smile of my dreams.

"I forgive you," Mason said. I think I would have felt better had he not added after a quick, harsh breath, "I mean, how could I not? Knowing what I know now."

I'd told him everything. How I came back to find him gone.

How I discovered his number disconnected. How in my mind there was nothing to wait for. Part of me wished that he had yelled. That he had screamed. That he had accused me of not believing in us. Of not trusting him. Part of me wished that he said that I took the first chance I got to get out of there. That he asked how long I waited before cleaning out my apartment and skipping town. That he insisted that I was always going to leave, that I was never going to stay with him, that if it hadn't been then, it would have been some other time. Further down the road. But inevitable.

Part of me wanted him to break something. To put a fist through a wall. To shatter a lamp, overturn a dresser, tear a door from its hinges. Part of me wanted to cower beneath his rage, shiver in the trembling length of his towering shadow. I wanted the dam to break, to finally fucking break.

I wanted it to sweep me away. Maybe forever.

But it was my turn to smile. My turn to say, and believe it, really truly believe it, "And I forgive you." I too added, after a second's hesitation and an inhale like I'd forgotten something very important, "Really, how could I not?"

His nan was in the hospital. She raised him when his mother left. She was his rock in a world that kept knocking him off his feet. He'd had to go. Fear and panic throw thinking straight out the window. I believed him when he said he considered leaving a note but felt he didn't have the time. My heart broke with him when he told me how he just missed an earlier flight that could have gotten him there in time to say goodbye. I felt his anguish over that hesitation, over those precious minutes lost. And I went through the same what ifs that he had: what if he had just run out the door with his passport and credit card? What if he'd thought just to send me a message in the cab instead of pausing there, anguishing there at the doorway? Or what if he'd never met me? What if he'd gone back with his friends? What if he was fifteen minutes away instead of fifteen hours?

How could I not forgive him breaking his phone? How could I not understand the grief and anger and devastation that had to escape somehow, that had to get out? How could I not pity him that moment? How could I not believe that given that same situation, I would shatter my phone in the exact same way?

If I'd had a parental figure in my life, ever, they would have been my everything. But I'd never had everything to lose. Not till Mason. I understood the pain of losing him. Maybe it would have been healthier shattering a cell phone. Maybe it would have been easier than shattering myself instead.

"I mean, you came back," I said when Mason continued to look at me.

My fingers fidgeted almost nervously with the lip of the teacup beneath his gaze. I wondered if he was searching my face the way I had searched his. Was this little happy ending of ours failing him somehow, too? That probably would have been the thing to say. To say: *"There's still something missing. There's still something we've left unsaid."*

"You came back for me," I said, "and you built Dublin Ink for me and there's nothing more you could have done."

Mason's fingers interlocked with mine. He twisted my hand back and forth. I smiled till he dropped his gaze. We'd bared our souls to one another. Opened up about everything. Been honest about everything. Held back nothing. Or maybe that was just what we told each other. Maybe that was still what we both just wanted to believe. What was simpler to believe, easier to believe.

"And so you forgive me?" Mason asked.

I had a smile ready for him when he lifted his eyes to mine once more. I squeezed his hand. I tried to connect to him, to speak to him where words failed, to make him believe my answer.

"Yes."

Because I did. Something was wrong, something was off. But my forgiveness of Mason was not. My forgiveness of him was full and complete and real. Maybe the problem was he couldn't believe me. Maybe the problem was that I couldn't believe him.

But that was not the problem we were going to talk about. Everything but, it seemed.

"Well, that's it then," Mason said, repeating my words with a gentle smile.

We smiled at each other like two people in a tiny boat who see the shore on the left but not the giant wave about to crash over them on the right.

"I forgive you and you forgive me," I said.

Mason ran his thumb along my palm and said in turn, "I forgive you and you forgive me."

My smile faltered, but I don't think Mason saw.

"Come here," he said and drew me toward him.

The tea from my cup spilled and soaked through my bedsheets. Despite the strength of Mason's arms around me and the sturdiness of his chest against my heart, I couldn't shake the feeling that the ground was giving way beneath us. That it was rotted. That any second we would fall through the bed. Fall through the floor. Fall and never stop falling.

This was what I wanted. What I'd always wanted. A simple explanation. A stupid misunderstanding. An unfortunate twist of fate. To know that we'd never stopped loving each other. To know that it hadn't been us. To know that Mason was torn from me, but not his love. That I was torn from him, but not my love. That it had always been there: our love for one another.

I clung tightly to Mason. Maybe if I just held him closer, squeezed him harder, then the waves of vertigo would dissipate.

I clenched my eyes shut and buried my face in the crook of his neck and hoped that breathing in his scent would steady me, wake me from this dream I insisted on making a nightmare.

Was it that I was still engaged? Was it that I had another man who I'd kept a secret from Mason? Was that the gulf between us? Was that the earthquake rumbling beneath our feet?

I wished it was. I begged and prayed and hoped upon hope that it was. That it was that simple. That easy. That a trip back to the US would fix everything, would fix us.

Or fix me.

Because I had my happy ending and I hated it. I'd gotten the answers to all the questions I'd asked again and again over the years, and they weren't enough. I had Mason's forgiveness and I didn't trust it.

I could only think one thing as we held each other: it's not enough.

Why isn't it enough?

Something was wrong with my happy ending.

Or something was wrong with me.

46

MASON

I hadn't been sleeping well.

Ever since Rachel and I talked, cleared the air, explained, forgave, healed, I hadn't been sleeping well. Falling asleep was elusive. Staying asleep even more so. I started at every creak of the bed, expecting to open my eyes in the dark to Rachel sneaking out. In my dreams she did. In my dreams she slammed the door and it jolted me up in bed, back pin straight, breath coming in ragged gasps.

In real life she would ease the door shut. Careful to twist the lock back slowly. Careful not to even leave with a tiny click. I slept like the man at the edge of a cliff; expecting always to fall.

But that night before Day 30, I really didn't sleep well. Didn't sleep at all.

The decision had been made: Rachel was to go back to the US to deal with some theatre business before returning back to Dublin. For me. For good. We'd decided.

And yet I felt no sense of security. No feeling of solid ground beneath me.

I tossed and turned the hours away like I was awaiting a judge's gavel in the morning. Like a ruling one way or another was still hanging over my head. Like the executioner's blade was still inches above my neck.

I feared I'd wake Rachel as I shifted this way and that, throwing the blanket down off my sweating body, tugging it up against my chills, kicking my feet long, drawing them up to my stomach like a frightened child. When I heard Rachel's breath catch, I forced myself to stay still. But it only took seconds for me to feel like I was in a coffin. And the only thing to keep me from screaming was my teeth buried into my lower lip. It was torture, those long minutes waiting for Rachel to sink back into that deep, dreamless sleep where I could not follow.

When morning light of Day 30 came weakly through the cracks in the blinds, I was exhausted. My muscles felt weak like I'd not used them in years. Or like I'd not rested them in decades. I'd sunk into the mattress like it was wet cement. Like Rachel would go and I would be stuck there.

And yet her touch was the touch I remembered as she rolled over with a sleepy smile. The tickle of her wild curls against my bare chest was everything I'd wanted. She was there and drawing herself in closer and her eyes were sparkling as they met mine and I couldn't shake the feeling that something wasn't right.

"It's Day 30," I said, splaying my hand against the warmth of her skin at her lower back, there against her tattoo of a dove's wings.

Rachel craned her neck to give me a tender kiss.

She whispered, "And tomorrow will be Day 31 and the day after that Day 32."

I curled my fingers into her skin. Tried to grab hold of more of her. Tried to fill my palm with her like she was precious water in an endless desert. But the dove's wings were taut. I wasn't sure they wanted to be held so tightly.

"Do you want that?" Rachel asked, her eyes questioning on mine.

"Yes," I told her, and it was the truth. It was more than the truth. It was everything.

Rachel smiled. It was that smile. The smile before she left for her performance. The last smile I'd see before I had to go. The smile I didn't know was the last smile. It promised everything. It offered everything. It sparkled like a diamond. Or did it sparkle like a mirage? Were my cupped hands dry, there in that blinding desert?

"Me too," Rachel said, nipping at the line of my jaw.

Her rolling on top of me, naked. Her hands all over my body. Her heart beating through her breasts against my ribs. It was the only thing I could have asked for.

But I worried this was the dream. That I hadn't slept poorly at all. That I'd fallen fast asleep and was being tortured not with sleeplessness, but with the most perfect dream.

The most perfect dream that was always bound to end. As all dreams do.

It was a strange cruelty when I couldn't quite believe her when she whispered against the pulse in my throat, "I want Day 34."

Or when she kissed a hot trail down the centre of my chest, saying between each wet press of her lips to my scalding skin, "I want Day 35... I want Day 36... I want Day 37."

Rachel shimmied down the length of me and my grip on her dove wings fell away.

"I want Day 121," she groaned against my lower stomach. My fingers moved of their own accord into her tangled curls as she licked the length of my hard shaft and said, "I want Day 308". My head arched back and my hips yearned to buck up as Rachel paused with her mouth around my head, "I want Day 1,073," before taking me fully into her hot little mouth.

When I came and she swallowed everything down and looked up at me from between my thighs with heavily hooded eyes and said, "I want Day 4,920," I couldn't quite believe her.

I drew her up, slick body against mine, and claimed her mouth, tasting me on her lips. There was something wrong about her saying as my tongue swirled around hers, "I want Day 8,011".

I urged Rachel's pussy up to my mouth, thighs parted on either side of my face. All I wanted to do was lick her wet folds and hear her moan for the rest of my life. Rachel promised me exactly that as she gripped the bars of the bedframe and rolled her hips against my tongue.

"I want Day 9,282," she moaned, toes curling against my ribs. "Day 10,000," she gasped as her fingers clutched at my hair. "I want your Day 100,000," she screamed as she bore down on my mouth and my tongue pushed inside her. "I want..." she began before the words were stolen from her by a wave of pleasure that made her collapse against the bedframe, sink onto my face, melt onto me like she was ice on a hot summer's day as I lapped at the core of her. "I want all your days," she whispered when she came to lie beside me with her flushed cheeks and bright eyes.

I hated myself, because I couldn't quite believe her. Believe us.

We fucked till it was time for Rachel to pack. We laughed as she threw her clothes (new ones because I'd torn the old ones, new ones because the old ones weren't who she wanted to be anymore) into her suitcase. We were all over each other like horny teenagers on the staircase. We were still in each other's arms at the doorway when the cab pulled up.

"I won't be long," Rachel promised, her words muffled by my chest.

"I know."

"Just some things to sort out with the show."

"I know," I said again.

"Then I'll be back," she said.

It felt stupid to say "I know" again. So I said nothing. I'd heard it all before. We'd been talking about the plan for days. We'd made our decision to be together. I knew that. I did. I knew. I knew, at least, what we'd said.

When we finally pulled away from each other, I told her to wait. I almost forgot. Rachel looked at me questioningly when I handed over the signed divorce papers which had been signed from almost the start. She pushed them away. I urged them gently into her hands.

"I don't want them," she said even as her fingers folded over the edges. "We talked. We forgive each other. We decided. We..."

When her words trailed off, I said with a smile, "Hey, a deal's a deal, right?"

Rachel's gaze was steady on mine.

"I'm coming back," she said.

I know. I know that's what you said.

"Will you be here?" she asked.

I told her yes. But I saw her searching my eyes long after the word left my lips. I saw her thinking the same thing: I know. I know that's what you said.

Why couldn't we trust each other? Why couldn't we believe this was it? This was forever this time?

When Rachel stretched up onto her toes to kiss me, it was perfection. It was the Rachel who danced on diner tables and ran away from Elvis in a wedding dress that left her tits bare to be coloured with the Vegas city lights. It was the Rachel who held me in her arms, who held me tight. It was the Rachel I was sure, so goddamn sure would never let me go.

Her lips on mine were everything I wanted. And yet her "see

you soon" sounded like a goodbye to me. The goodbye we never had.

I watched her cab disappear around the corner and went slowly back inside. I lingered at the base of the stairs, remembering her miraculous appearance. Going over our thirty days together, our "marriage". Trying to convince myself that if it was all we had, it was enough.

The doorbell ringing made my heart leap. Because it was Rachel. Rachel came back. She'd felt the way I'd felt: that something was still off, something still not right. She'd demanded the taxi turn around. She'd run to the door.

We were going to fix what was still somehow broken. We were going to fight. We were going to yell and scream and curse one another long into the night. We would go at it all the next day if needed. We would hate each other for another thirty days if that was what it took. But we were going to do it because we loved each other. Because we believed in each other. Because we were done fucking leaving.

Except when I opened the door it wasn't Rachel. Her cab wasn't back. She wasn't there to yank inside, to push against the wall, to shout at: "How could you have possibly left like that? Left *us* like that? I hate you, I hate you, I *hate* you! Goddammit, Rachel, I love you."

It wasn't Rachel.

It was a man. Blonde. Blue-eyed. Prim in a tan suit. He told me his name. American accent. I should have known then, American fucking accent.

"I'm looking for Rachel."

"Who's she to you?" I asked.

Maybe I already fucking knew.

"Her fiancé," the man said, affronted.

I laughed darkly as I looked him up and down from gelled hair to shined shoes.

"So it's you then," I said.

"Me?"

I snickered. Because it was funny. It was really fucking funny. The man looked at me like I was mad. I probably was.

"You're her big, new, shiny role."

47

RACHEL

New York City no longer felt like home.

I guess it's possible that it never did. That I always found a way to convince myself it was home. That I was comfortable as a nameless face among millions, to blend in with the crowd. That the best place to be quiet was in a place where you couldn't be heard, no matter how loud you screamed.

The subway ride from the airport had me sweating. It was easy enough to blame it on the humidity. On the heat from miles upon miles of concrete. On the human bodies crammed into that metal box like sardines. It was easy enough to pretend I wasn't as nervous as I was.

This was the final cord to cut: my engagement with Tim. When I ended it with him, I was flinging myself fully into the void. Trusting Mason completely to catch me. I was giving up the security of Tim's money. The comfort of his loft overlooking Central Park. The ease of his cook and his butler and his assistant. The peace of mind of his name next to mine on a marriage certificate. A warm body in bed, promised. A hand to hold in the cold, guaranteed. A pair of eyes to catch in the mirror as you brushed your teeth each night signed, sealed, and delivered. I was giving up a nice life. A quiet life, a life that wasn't really mine, that probably wouldn't ever really be mine. But a nice life nonetheless.

Maybe that's why I hadn't told Mason about Tim. About our engagement. About the secret I had been keeping from the start. About the lies I told him during all those weeks because of it. I wasn't quite ready to cut that cord. I still didn't quite trust the arms that were to catch me when I did.

I got on the subway. I climbed the stairs at the stop near our building, walked with sure steps down the sidewalk. I breathed in deep and went straight up to the lobby door.

I already had my eyes on the elevator across those shimmering marble floors. Already saw my finger pushing the top button, already saw it glowing golden. Already heard the words from my mouth as I stepped onto the rug I once found beautiful, "Tim, there's something I need to tell you."

But I only got as far as the lobby door when an arm came out to stop me.

I stared at the arm barring my way. Frowned at it. Looked up in confusion as the doorman said, "I'm sorry, miss."

I followed the doorman's arm to a pile of hastily and carelessly stacked boxes by the trash bins.

Because I was standing beside my things which had been ordered out of the apartment. Sent out to be trashed.

Tim had somehow learned about Mason.

I wasn't sure how. Or when even. But he had. That I was sure of. There was no other explanation for suddenly getting tossed out of my home. There was no other explanation for my things boxed up and already covered in dog piss on the sidewalk. The doorman had already turned away. The door already was closing.

I was alone.

No. No, no. I wasn't alone. I had Mason. He'd forgiven me. I'd forgiven him. We were going to be together. We were going to have the forever we'd once promised each other. I believed that. I did. I trusted it. I trusted him. I had Mason. I had him. I was not alone.

But I had the same feeling that I did when I found my apartment empty that night I returned from my performance. I believed in Mason then, too. And yet I somehow already knew. I got that same feeling as I stood there on the curb, trying to telling myself I was not alone, trying to avoid what was right there in front of me.

With trembling fingers, I dialled Mason's number. As it rang I paced back and forth in front of all my life's belongings thrown out onto the curb. The longer the time went by without Mason answering, the tighter I gripped the phone.

The heat from the sidewalk seemed to burn through the soles of my shoes, scorching my skin, drenching me in sweat despite the pleasant breeze. My throat was parched by the time Mason's voice came on. It was the same message. The same message as all those years ago.

"It's Mason. If you know me, leave a message. If you don't, fuck off."

I had that same feeling as I slipped my phone into my back pocket. That same feeling but *worse* than all those years ago. Because then at least there was something to destroy. There were drawers to break as I yanked them loose to check them. There were pillows to tear open, fluff to litter the floors of my living room with, leather to scratch as I clawed at the couch cushions. There were glasses to shatter when I scrambled around the backs of the cabinets, praying to find a piece of him, begging to stumble upon a sign, an answer, yearning for just the tiniest glimpse of hope.

There, on the busy, ruthless city street, there was nothing to destroy. It was all already destroyed. My things were already broken. Already scratched and dragged and dirtied. There wasn't even me left to ruin. I was already ruined.

I called Mason over and over until my phone ran out of battery. I waited through all those hopeless rings as people left work, as couples passed by hand in hand to dinner, as teenagers wandered by in the middle of the night, buzzed from a couple of cheap beers. I waited there with my whole life on the sidewalk and tried to tell myself I wasn't alone until I literally was.

The streets were empty save a car or two with silent, rolled-up windows. No one crossed the sidewalks in front of the building where I was once going to live happily ever after. Even the homeless had found a place to lay their heads, a corner of the brutal world they could call their own, even if just for the night. The doorman of Tim's building had stopped peeking his head out at me, stopped checking to make sure I was alright.

He knew I wasn't. But he couldn't do a goddamn thing about it.

I collapsed onto my suitcase because it was the closest thing I had to Mason. His eyes had been on it. His hands. It had spent thirty days in his home. Thirty days beneath his bed. We'd fucked above it. Whispered late into the night with it tucked away beneath us. Made promises and told the truth, all the goddamn truth with it in earshot. I'd lied to Mason with it right there under me.

I don't know when I started crying. I just knew that the concrete had retained enough heat that by the time I stopped, the concrete was already dry of fallen tears. No trace of my pain. Not even something to point at and say, "Here, right here, was where it all fell apart."

I was just a girl without a home.

That was my lesson. I wasn't meant to be the girl with a Vegas show. I wasn't meant to be the housewife of a rich man in NYC. I wasn't even meant to be the girl heartbroken on the curb.

I was just meant to be alone. That was my role. My big, shiny, new role.

48

MASON

I'd moved into the room at the end of the hallway.

Rachel had stolen my room from me. Stolen it just like she'd stolen everything else. My happiness. My love. My security. My freedom. Her ghost stood in the doorway of my bedroom and there was nothing I could do to get her to leave. She just stood there. Arms crossed over her naked chest. Laughing. Fucking laughing.

I raked my fingers through my hair as Miss Last Night hopped up from the rumpled bedsheets with a giggle.

"How about now?" she asked, bouncing on her knees beside me.

She walked her fingers up my thigh toward my boxers, but I grabbed her hand. Her touch felt like ants under my skin.

"I need a minute or two," I said.

"That's what you said a minute or two ago," she whined. She placed her pouting chin on my chest and with puppy dog eyes said, "Maybe a coffee will help? Or a shower? A shower *together*? A nice hot shower cures whiskey dick."

"Your nan's cure?" I grunted.

She just laughed and slapped my chest.

"You're so funny."

"I'm really not," I grumbled.

I should have just explained that I was ruined. Completely ruined. That no amount of coffee or showers would cure my limp dick. That the problem was that I felt no attraction whatsoever to her. I hadn't even had all that much to drink. There was a ghost down the hall and she wouldn't leave and she was the reason I would forever need "a minute or two".

"I have an idea," Miss Last Night chirped, leaping off the bed with an annoying amount of energy. "Ice cream!"

"You want ice cream?" I asked.

She wiggled her ass in my direction.

"I want ice cream and *you* want ice cream," she said. "Ice cream with two little cherries on top."

Miss Last Night pinched her nipples and gave a high-pitched giggle.

"My business partners are downstairs," I told her before she wrenched open the door wearing nothing but the tattoo tiger between her shoulder blades.

"Oh," she chirped, completely unperturbed. "Well, I'm sure it's nothing they all haven't seen before."

She wiggled her little tits at me. Both nipples were pierced. She told me when I fucked her that her long, sleek black hair would get snagged in the little silver rings. She told me it was fine. She told me it saved money on nipple clamps. She told me if I wanted, I could thread her hair through them both. Tug it with my teeth, if I wanted.

Well, I didn't. And I hated it. Because I *wanted* to want.

I just...*couldn't*.

"Can you at least throw on a shirt?" I asked.

She giggled and I wanted to scratch my ears out. "You tore mine, remember?"

I repressed a sigh. "Grab one from the closet."

Miss Last Night shrugged, but she walked over to the closet as I tugged my pants back up and over my boxers.

I'd already received enough dirty looks from Conor and Aurnia and even Rian when I came in with Miss Last Night. For one thing it was hardly past noon. When it became frowned upon to get wasted in the morning, I had no fucking clue. Especially amongst my group of friends.

True, we hadn't exactly been quiet. Or respectful. Or anything other than loud and horny and nasty. Miss Last Night stumbled against the stairs as the front door I'd been grinding up on her against finally fell open and slammed against the faded wallpaper. She laughed and I pounced on her. It was only when I was fumbling with the button of my jeans that I realised they were all there. With clients. Miss Last Night greeted them with a cheerful "Oh, hello there" and didn't bother tugging the top of her dress back over her exposed tit.

I gave a half-sheepish wave and said, most likely slurring my words, "Um, we'll continue this upstairs."

It was better that way. Better that they all thought I was actually fucking this girl. I didn't want them to know that the second I got her alone all drive left me, my dick deflated like a fucking balloon, and her very touch made me want to tear out my hair. I didn't want any of my friends to know how much Rachel had messed me up. I couldn't admit to myself that I'd never be the same; I certainly couldn't admit it to them.

I'd take their judgement. But I couldn't fucking deal with their pity.

I hadn't told any of them what had happened. The man I had met at the doorway. The truth he revealed to me as my white-knuckled fist shook on the door handle. The calls I'd received from Rachel. Tentative, hesitant at first. Spaced out between hours. Then panicked, rushed. Sometimes I received several within just a few minutes. They didn't know why I'd changed my number after a few days so she couldn't reach me. I told them I was getting calls from telemarketers. I told them I'd lost my phone. I told them lies that contradicted other lies, which I didn't give a fuck about coming up with a lie for anymore. I hadn't told them the truth: that I was lying because I'd been lied to. Hurting them because I'd been hurt. Leaving them alone because I was terribly, horribly, inescapably *alone*.

Conor, Rian, Aurnia, they didn't know anything. So they judged me. They were mad at me, especially Aurnia, who'd believed—like the little kid that she was—in Rachel's and my love.

So they shook their heads and thought to themselves, "He was going to bollocks it up somehow." Conor sighed and dropped his head when he saw me with Miss Last Night. Aurnia looked wounded, a small woodland animal I'd accidentally felled with an arrow not meant for her. Even Rian glanced up from the drawing of that girl he'd been obsessing over and his eyes bounced between me and the unfamiliar woman in confusion.

They didn't know. They didn't know it wasn't my fault. They didn't know that this was just my curse in life: to be left. To always be fucking left.

Rachel never had any intention of coming back. It was all just lies. She gave me enough to get her divorce papers. She told me enough to have a good time while she waited for the thirty days. She promised enough to ensure it would hurt as much as fucking possible when she closed that door. Got in that cab. Boarded that plane. Left.

She hadn't forgiven me. She never would.

So Conor and Rian and Aurnia could all go fuck themselves. They didn't know shite. They didn't know Rachel like I did.

Miss Last Night yelped from where she stood by the open closet. A mountain of shoeboxes tumbled down around her from the top shelf. She covered her head as the last one slipped from the shelf and then turned to smile sheepishly at me.

For fuck's sake.

"There were a dozen shirts hanging right there," I told her angrily.

"Yeah, but I saw this up there."

She held up a cream cashmere sweater over her naked body. Rachel's sweater. Miss Last Night purred as she ran the material all over her skin. She nestled her cheek against it and smiled as her eyes fluttered closed.

"It's so soft and *luxurious*," she cooed. "It must have cost a fortune for whoever bought it."

"Don't touch that," I told her, voice dark.

She must have noticed the change in tone. She opened her eyes and with a half-smile still fixed on her deep-purple lips, laughed a little.

"What's that, boo?" she asked.

I must have stood with enough violence in my glare to scare Miss Last Night because she extended her arm forward, careful not to get any closer to me, and draped the sweater across the end of the bed.

"Get the fuck out," I said.

Miss Last Night looked around the room like there was some explanation somewhere for the sudden change in the mood. Her eyes trailed up and down my own naked body. Maybe to see if I was aroused. Maybe to see if this was some sort of kinky sex thing: the scorned lover, the abandoned soulmate, the sucker-punched sucker. Maybe it was my limp dick against my thigh that finally convinced her the anger I trembled with was real.

"You can choke me, you know," she said softly.

"Get the fuck out," I repeated.

"Whoever she is," she said, toes playing over one another in the mess of my nan's shoeboxes on the floor, "you can take it out on me. What she did to you. Revenge sex, you know, boo? Hot, rough, painful revenge sex. I'm totally into it."

"I'm married."

I managed to shock Miss Last Night. She took a little step backward. Reassessed the room. Reassessed me. She wagged a finger at me. Shook her head. She was laughing again.

"No, you're not," she said. "You know, I've heard there's this new thing that guys are doing. Having some chick roommate come in and scare off—"

I snatched up the cashmere sweater. I almost expected it to burn my fingers. I almost expected the faint linger of Rachel's perfume on it to poison my lungs. I almost dared to hope that she would appear there in the doorway, angry and indignant. *"What the fuck are you doing with my sweater? What the fuck are you doing with* her?"

But I wasn't burned. I wasn't poisoned. I was perfectly alive and well to see that Rachel was not there in the doorway. Perfectly alive and well to live the rest of my fucking life without her.

"This is my wife's," I told Miss Last Night, shaking the sweater at her. A sweater I thought wasn't "her". A sweater from a lifestyle I could never afford. A sweater I thought she didn't want. Not when she had me. "I'm married. And my wife is coming back and she can't find you here."

Miss Last Night huffed irritably and crossed her arms over her chest.

"So I'm supposed to believe that you just fuck around on your wife?" she asked, jutting her chin up at me.

I grinned darkly.

"We didn't fuck."

Miss Last Night glared at me.

"You just bring girls over and get them naked with the promise of fucking around on your wife?"

"My wife and I have a rather complicated relationship." I extended my palm toward the door. "Now, if you wouldn't mind," I said.

Instead of leaving, Miss Last Night ran her fingertips down my arm. "But she's not here right now, is she?"

I lost it. I screamed at Miss Last Night to get out. I stalked down the hallway after her, quick at her fleeing heels. I bellowed down the stairs as Aurnia, Conor and Rian's concerned faces appeared at the bottom.

"My wife is coming back," I shouted as Miss Last Night tripped down the last few stairs. "She's coming back and you need to get the fuck out! Because she's coming back! My wife is fucking coming back!"

Conor climbed the stairs toward me, but I turned before he could speak. I left the chaos on the stairs. Left Miss Last Night to cry. Left my friends to worry. Left the image of that doorway and the woman who walked through it, only to walk right back out of it behind me.

My footsteps rattled the ceiling downstairs as I stormed past my old room. I heard something crash to the floor in the parlour when I slammed the door of the bedroom at the end of the hallway.

I wanted everything back in the closet. Everything hidden. Everything out of sight. I threw the cashmere sweater, that smelled like the perfume I wished I could forget, into the mess of tangled hangers. I shoved empty boxes into the back, their cardboard cracking, bending, collapsing. Old pairs of shoes I hurled against the hanging sweaters and bulky fur coats. When they fell, I kicked them wildly, jammed them in violently with my heel.

I reached down for another box, my wild fingers knocking off the lid. I grabbed instead a fistful of envelopes. They cracked in my grip like logs on a fire. Their yellowed paper was brittle, not cutting. They might just turn to ash, should I squeeze just a little harder.

There was no shoving these into the closet this time. No scooping back into the box like spilled trash. No hiding the name written in an uncertain, trembling hand across the front:

Mason.

The ink was already against my skin. The lips that had sealed the edges were as close as they would ever be to mine as I brought an envelope to my lips. I breathed in the scent of that old paper, that old ink, shakily.

I'd run from the secrets inside my nan's old shoebox for too long. I sank to the edge of the bed, letter light in my fingers. I'd run away from a lot of things. I'd been running from Rachel for a decade and she hadn't even been within my reach. And when she had, well, I'd just run all the faster.

Opening the first letter felt like I'd stopped running for the first time in a long time. My muscles felt weak, my body exhausted. There was a weariness in my bones, a soreness in my heart.

Opening the first letter felt like the first real step forward I'd ever taken.

49

RACHEL

It was JoJo who kept me at the table.

She threatened me with rainbow-coloured fur handcuffs if I tried to get up "one more goddamn time". She was just crazy enough for me to believe that she had indeed packed such a thing into the tie-dye knapsack hanging from the post of the completely mismatched chair.

JoJo had a glass of water with lemon in front of her. I'd splurged on a coffee.

Leaning forward, JoJo whispered, looking around her, "People keep giving me funny looks."

I laughed a little as I played with a packet of sugar, spinning it this way and that on the modern concrete table.

"Maybe because we're in one of the nicest restaurants in the Financial District at lunchtime and you're wearing an upside-down bikini top," I told her.

She tucked her chin into her chest to examine her mostly naked torso.

"But I wore a tie," she protested, flitting a red silk tie back and forth with a grin.

I smiled back, but then butterflies twisted in my stomach and my toe started tapping erratically on the marble floor.

"Look," I said, "we can just go. It's awkward and we're under-dressed and—"

"I will tie you to the chair with this tie if you even *think* of standing up, Rach," JoJo interrupted.

Her petite hands went to the knot at her throat and she lifted a *go on, dare me to* eyebrow at me. I sighed and stole a sip of her water.

"This is what you've been wanting," JoJo reminded me. "All you've been going on and on about all these weeks on my couch is getting a chance to talk to Tim. Well, here you are. And now you want to bail? What is it with you and avoiding the fucking truth?"

That last part stung. My gaze fell to the swirl of milk in my overpriced cup of coffee.

JoJo's toe wiggled against mine beneath the table.

"You know I love you, bitch," she said, her voice softened.

I smiled at her.

"I just—I just don't know if I can face him," I told her, avoiding the irritated glare of a waiter passing.

JoJo reached across the table to take my hand.

"You don't know if you can face him or face *you*?" she asked.

Before I could ask her what the fuck *that* meant, she kicked back her chair with a loud scrape as she stood, drawing all kinds of stares from the restaurant. "He's here."

It was a whirlwind as she kissed my head, wished me good luck, stole a bread basket from the table behind ours, and darted out the emergency exit.

Suddenly, Tim was there, grasping my elbows, kissing my cheek, holding out my chair for me. Ordering both of us a glass of wine as he straightened his tie across from me.

"Tim," I said, voice fluttering, "Tim, I—"

It all came out. The truth. All of it. The truth about my past. The truth about who I was before I met him. The truth about who I'd transformed myself into when he'd fallen for me. The truth about Mason then. The truth about Mason now. I apologised more times than I could count. I cried and Tim, instead of chastising me about getting emotional in public, just offered his napkin.

At the end I was empty. At the end I was a total shit. I couldn't even meet Tim's eye.

"I'm sorry," I murmured again, shaking my head. "I should go."

I went to leave. Tim stopped me with a hand atop mine.

"Rachel..."

I sank back down into my chair. Slightly unwillingly. But at some point I had to stop running from things that made me uncomfortable. At some point I had to face the truth.

Tim tapped his fingers against the bottom of his wine glass for a quiet moment before saying, "I'm sorry I had your things taken to the street. I was...angry."

"I deserved—"

He interrupted me with a raised hand.

Smiling, he said, "I would have liked to meet her."

I frowned.

Tim shrugged and adjusted his tie once more.

"The girl you were," he said. "The girl who wouldn't say that there's nothing to apologise for. The girl who wouldn't go easy on me for being a dick. This loud, brazen, rude showgirl."

I laughed. Really laughed. The kind of laugh that draws attention in a place where attention is not supposed to be drawn. I laughed loudly. Brazenly. Rudely. I smacked my hand over my mouth, going red in the cheeks. Tim smiled gently and reached across the table to tug my hand away. He squeezed my fingers before placing them tenderly on the tabletop.

"I might not have proposed marriage to this girl," he said with a wry grin. "But I would have liked to have seen her. Would have liked to know that she existed in the world. Would have liked to know that when I let her go, she was truly and fully and wonderfully *herself*."

I swallowed heavily.

My voice was earnest and I hoped that he heard it when I said, "I never meant to hurt you, Tim."

"I know," he said, smiling sadly.

"I was on my way back to tell you and—"

"Rachel."

I was surprised by his interruption. By the tone of his voice: kind but strong. I stared at him in slight confusion.

"What?" I asked.

"Do you really think you would have?"

I sputtered out a shocked, "Of course."

"Told me?"

"Yes!"

"And gone back to Mason?"

I couldn't believe he was actually suggesting I wouldn't have.

"Yes," I told him, affronted as I leaned back defensively.

Tim followed up by saying, fingers bridged, elbows on the table, "Then you're going to be with him?"

I stared in silence across the table at Tim. For the first time since he'd arrived, the sounds of the restaurant filtered in. Waiters passing. People paying bills. The door of the bathroom opening and closing. Life going on. Time moving. The real world come for me.

"You're going to be with Mason," Tim said, pressing me even as his eyes held me softly. "You're going to fly back to Dublin. You're going to make things right. You're going to be with the one that you truly love, like you said you would."

I remained silent as the waiter asked if we wanted another round. Tim said we were almost done. He asked for the check. I avoided his steady gaze as long as I could.

I said to my fingers in my lap, "Mason would never forgive me. I'm not even sure he forgave me for leaving the first time. And this? No, there's no way. Mason doesn't forgive. He never forgives."

Tim sighed. "But neither do you."

A flash of anger flared in my chest and I looked up at Tim. He seemed ready for me. Ready to take a punch, ready to absorb it.

"I forgave Mason. I did. I truly and honestly did. It broke my heart when I heard what happened with his grandmother and it's the most understandable thing in the world, what happened. The moment he told me I forgave him. It was instantaneous. And complete. There is nothing but love in my heart for him. I forgave him. I'd forgive him over and over again. I don't think there is anything in the world that I wouldn't forgive him for."

I was gasping when I finished. I took a trembling sip of the last of my wine and sank back against my chair, lightheaded.

"So there," I said like a petulant child who'd just finished her tantrum.

Tim seemed content to wait me out. To let me have my say. To give me time to get it out of my system. But I think he knew exactly what he was going to say the moment I opened my mouth.

Calmly, he said, "I don't mean him."

My eyebrows flicked together. I shifted uncomfortably in my chair.

"What do you mean?"

Tim licked his lips. He drew his fingers through his perfectly gelled hair, messing it up a little. I'd never seen him do that before.

"Rachel," he said after a moment, "I knew about your past."

I frowned.

"I knew you'd been a showgirl in Vegas. I knew you'd danced. I knew you had a skeleton or two in the closet," he explained. "I went to that coffee shop you worked at all the time to try and talk to you. Well, when you weren't there, I tried to learn more about you. Your co-workers knew things. And then, well, it's easy enough these days. To dig things up on the internet."

I couldn't believe it.

"Why didn't you tell me?" I asked in a whisper.

Tim shrugged. "I was waiting for you to tell me. And when you didn't, I figured you had your reasons not to want to. I was going to respect that. I loved you, Rachel. Or at least, I loved whoever you'd become for New York. For me. For your heart, to get over him, maybe. I'm not sure. But whoever you were, *why* ever you were, I loved you."

In that moment I felt the same draw to Tim as when I first met him, that first tenderness in my heart. Not that I loved him, maybe I never had. Maybe I never could. But I trusted him. Even if he couldn't send me flying high, he would at least never let me fall.

Tim continued, "I figured the reason you decided not to tell me about your past was that you were ashamed of being that girl. But Rachel, what if the reason you never told me was that you were ashamed at giving that girl up? Of *not* being that girl any longer. Of changing. Of letting yourself, your true self down. What if the person you need to forgive instead of Mason is...yourself?"

Minutes later, Tim and I were out on the sidewalk. He blocked the late afternoon sun with his hand, shielding his face. I realised that I never really knew him. Never gave him a chance. It was always someone else's face I saw when I imagined forever.

When I went to return the engagement ring I'd kept hidden in my suitcase for a month in Dublin, Tim closed my fingers back around it.

He kissed my cheek and whispered, "The pawn shop on 60th will give you the best deal."

"I don't need the money, Tim," I tried to tell him.

He pushed my hand toward me and walked away. Looking over his shoulder, he smiled against the sun.

"Flights to Dublin aren't free."

50

MASON

If I'd found the three dozen or so letters from my mother before reading my nan's letter first, I probably would have burned them without opening them. Coaxed up a hearty flame. Tossed the whole stack in without a second's hesitation. Enjoyed a stiff glass of whiskey as I watched the edges shrivel, the pages blacken, the ash waft up the chimney to stain the night sky.

If I'd learned that my mother had been trying to contact me for years all the way up until her death before everything went down with Rachel, I would have laughed. I would have revelled in the fact that she'd suffered. I would have praised the universe for the blissful irony of that woman who left me as a child failing to find her way back to me.

If I'd stumbled upon that shoebox any other time in my life than that very moment and opened any other letter first than my nan's, I would have shoved everything back inside. Closed the closet doors. Locked the bedroom door. Shut down Dublin Ink. Moved to a different city. Run and run and run. And never stopped.

I would never know for sure, of course, could never possibly know for sure, but a part of me believed it was Rachel. It was her chaos like a hurricane. Her anger like a thunderstorm. Her turmoil like a tornado destroying everything in its path, but so beautiful to behold. A part of me believed it was Rachel first knocking over my nan's shoebox of secrets as she gathered her things in a fury to leave that shifted my nan's letter to the top. Like a miner shaking his pan to bring the flecks of gold to the surface. A part of me believed if Rachel hadn't made such a mess, then my nan's final words to me would have remained hidden, buried beneath my mother's final words, final words I would have rejected out of hand.

Like I said, I would never know, could never know. But I believed nonetheless. Believed it was Rachel.

Dearest Mason,

Oh, how to start, how to start, I don't want to start, how to start when it's the last thing in the world you want to do, start.

I READ my nan's tidy, neat hand. I'd never known her to hesitate. Not once. She took me as her own when my mother left. From that moment on she was my rock. Sure. Certain. Never wavering. I drew my fingers over those first few lines like they were my nan's hands, hands that I'd never known to tremble because they couldn't. Because they always had to be strong. For me.

I almost stopped there. I almost stopped reading after those first few lines as I sat there on the edge of my nan's bed in my nan's old house. Because I'd failed her. She'd been strong her whole life for me and the one chance I had to be strong for her...it was almost too much. It was her next line that prevented me from stuffing the pieces of paper back into the envelope and shoving it along with the others back into the shoebox, back into the closet, back into the recesses of my mind where I did not dare go.

Well, I love you. I guess that's the only way to start, now isn't it? I love you, Mason. I always have and I always will.

These were words I could hold onto. Words that could keep me steady. Words that I could follow in the dark as I plunged into the rest of my nan's letter.

Please believe that everything I've ever done was because of this, because I loved you. Because I wanted to do the right thing for you. Because I never wanted to see you hurt or in pain or suffering, even just a little bit. That's what I thought I was doing...protecting you because I loved you...

Maybe I should really start now. With the beginning. With your beginning. With mine, too, maybe.

The day your mother walked out on us was one of the most horrible days of my life. You were just a child. Hardly old enough to speak more than a few simple words, though "Momma" was, to my dismay, already one of them. I knew that you were unlikely to have any real conscious memories of that day, which was a blessing. But for me it was like a dagger through the heart.

To hold such a perfect little thing in my arms, to stare into those bright green eyes, so full of life and joy and potential, to feel your tiny fingers wrapped around my thumb with such ferocity, oh, my dear, dear Mason, I didn't know how I was going to do it. To one day explain to you that the woman who was supposed to love you more than anything, the woman who brought you into this world, something you never once asked for, the mother who was yours, your one and only, had left. Something so sweet, so tender, so precious and I was the one who had to break his little wings before he'd even taken flight?

It was almost too much for me to bear. The anger I felt. The indignation. The overwhelming, crushing, inescapable feeling of injustice. Unfairness. Meanness. Ugliness. I was angry at the world. Angry at humanity. Angry, above all, at my daughter. My own daughter!

I suppose it's ironic that the fuel for my anger and the dousing waters for my rage were one and the same: you.

If you hadn't been in my life there would be nothing to be angry about, and yet, if you hadn't been in my life there would be nothing to keep me from burning the whole damn place to the ground. Please forgive me such language. You know I never allowed it. Nor condoned it. But we're both adults now. And we're being honest. Or at least, trying to.

Okay, okay, here is the start, the real start: one day I received a letter from your mother. From my daughter. I'm not even sure I remember how many months (or was it years) later that it arrived in the mail. I can't check because that first letter didn't survive. The rest barely did. I flipped through junk mail, some bills, a postcard from my sister on a vacation in France, and there it was.

It was addressed to you. But I didn't even need to open it to know who it was from. What it said. Why it was sent. It must have been winter when your mother sent that first letter because I remember I threw it in the fire. Though, maybe we don't even know that for sure. Maybe I built up a fire in the middle of summer, on the hottest day, just to make sure not a trace of that damned thing survived.

I didn't even think twice about it. Didn't pause to consider whether I should give it to you, let alone even open it myself. The answer was so clear and obvious to me that burning it, destroying it seemed the simplest thing in the world: your mother had made her decision. She had left. She had abandoned you. And she could live with that decision. That sin. That pain.

The letters kept coming and I'm really not all that sure why I didn't do the same thing with those that I did with the first. It's possible I caught a glimpse of her in you from time to time. Heard a bit of her laughter in yours. Noticed that you crinkled your nose the way she did when she was just a baby, just a teeny, tiny precious baby in my arms. It's possible that I searched out those links, those links between you and her, those links between me and her, mother and daughter. It's possible those letters became a link as they piled up in a shoebox in my closet. I probably scorned this softness in me. I probably cursed myself for not being stronger, for not just tearing them up, ripping them up, burning the whole goddamn lot of them.

Would you look at me, dear, cursing like a sailor? Your grandfather would be proud, I suppose. Smiling up at me from Hell.

I started reading through them one day. Your mother's letters. She wanted back in your life. Wanted a second chance. Wanted forgiveness and mercy and grace. Ha! Let me tell you, I felt quite good reading those letters. I'm not proud of it now, but I revelled in it. Rolled around in her grovelling like a pig in the fucking mud. Excuse me. I wanted her to feel pain. To suffer. Like she'd made you suffer. Like she'd made me suffer.

The years went by and the letters kept coming. You grew and the letters kept coming. Your childhood come and gone and the letters kept coming. I told myself I was doing the right thing. You were fine without her. Better without her. It would be too much to ask you to forgive her. To put that burden on your young shoulders.

I thought I knew that weight, because I *couldn't forgive her. Just couldn't. Wouldn't. Didn't want to. Didn't ever want to.*

Ah, I see we've at last come to the real start, my dear. The start that we can put off no longer. The real beginning of this letter:

I was wrong.

Perhaps that's always the start. Admitting we were wrong.

You're a grown man, now, Mason. I see it. And a part of me is sad. Sad that I can give you nothing more, but these three words: I was wrong.

Mason, I see you and I see the way you keep love at a distance. I see the way you never hold onto anyone too tightly. I see the way you move through people like water through rapids, just passing through.

You're a grown man and I'm an old woman. You're at the start of your life and I'm at my end. But one day you too will be old, you too will be at your end. And I pray you take this advice before it's too late:

Forgive yourself, my dear.

For so long, I withheld my forgiveness toward your mother. But it was never her who needed the forgiveness: it was me. For so long, I concealed in anger what I was really feeling: guilt.

Guilt at not being a good enough mother to convince my daughter to stay. Guilt at not loving her enough that she knew what love was. Guilt at not being there enough for her that she knew she had to do the same for her child. Guilt at just not being enough. Because a good mother raises a good daughter and a good daughter doesn't leave her baby. So guilt at not being a good enough mother myself.

Forgiveness for myself has been hard. And I'm not sure I've fully reached that point. Maybe that's why I've put off giving you this letter, these letters, for so long. I've promised myself to give them to you when you return from Vegas with the boys. I've promised a few times before, but I mean it this time. It's that important, Mason. It is.

If you can't forgive yourself, you can't ever forgive anyone else. If you can't forgive yourself, you can't ever love anyone else.

So this is me loving you, Mason, or trying very hard to, at least. This is me forgiving myself. Forgiving my daughter in turn. And praying that when the time comes, you forgive yourself as well, for whatever it is.

If I've kept my promise and you're reading this after your trip to Vegas, I've put two aspirin and a glass of water for your hangover on the bedside table. (You always do drink too much.) The bottle of whiskey is for when you read your mother's letters, knowing she is gone now. (I do see the irony of chastising you for your liquor consumption and then supplying it, but I'll make this exception. Because it's hard. But it's necessary, my dear.)

I love you. I've made plenty of mistakes, but I've always tried my best to love you.

Let's make that the start, shall we? I love you, Mason.

- Nan

I TRIED to remember what happened to that bottle of whiskey. I wouldn't have been surprised if I downed it in one night after her death. If I shattered it against the wall. If I poured it out over her grave as I cursed myself. Hated myself. Vowed to never fucking forgive myself.

Whatever its fate, it was gone now. That was for sure. So when the tears dried well enough to drive, I went to the liquor store and bought another. Then I went home and cracked it open, not even bothering with a glass. I kept my nan's letter beside me, there against my thigh like a comforting hand as I opened my mother's first letter.

And began to read.

51

RACHEL

I didn't have a penny to my name, but my name was echoing in the theatre. I was about as homeless as one could get and yet I felt about as at home as one could ever hope for. My future was undecided, unclear, confused and complicated and, honestly, a fucked-up mess, but my next five minutes weren't.

Because for the next five minutes, at least, I would be dancing.

My heart raced as I walked across the empty stage draped in darkness. But it wasn't the racing heart of someone who wanted to escape, to flee, to get away. It was the racing heart of an athlete at the starting block. A racing heart ready, eager, willing to race.

My towering heels clicked against the well-worn wooden planks as I walked toward the centre. This was something I'd done a million times in Vegas, but it was like the first time all over again.

I wobbled like a colt. Sweat like I was having a heart attack. I ran through my choreography with a jittery panic like I hadn't been running it over and over again for days. Nonstop. Because this was what I wanted to do. This was where I wanted to be.

I found my place in the centre of the stage. My place. *My place*. I'd found my place. I raised my trembling chest, because I was proud of the little sequined number clinging to my curves. My skin was mine and no one else's. I breathed in deeply. Smelled all the old smells: the old wood, the luxurious velvet, the pillars of marble. It smelled like an old church I never got married in. It smelled like a warm home I never had. It smelled like a theatre I fell in love with, fell in love in, fell away from, fell to my knees in front of, fell for again and again and again. It smelled like where I was supposed to be.

The spotlight slipped over my body like a yellow silk dress. I wore it like it was fitted just for me. Tailored in to nip my waist. Sewn tight over my hips. Dripped over my thighs like honey from the comb. I bathed in that spotlight like it was scented with lavender, speckled with rose petals, drawn just for me. I lifted my chin and batted open my eyes like it was a lover to challenge, a lover to dare, a lover to push away as he wrapped his arms around me, to draw nearer, nearer still, as he tried to get away.

The music began and I danced the way I'd danced when I first came to Vegas. I'd run from home. Escaped that hellhole where there was nothing for me, no one for me. I'd stumbled into those bright lights like a deer on a highway. Blinded and shocked and scared. Back then I'd danced for my life. Danced to survive. Danced because it was the only thing I knew, the only thing I loved. I moved my body because if I didn't, I would die. I moved my body because that was who I was. I moved my body because it was my way to life, my path to love, my only chance in this godforsaken world.

It was just five minutes, but it was the most important five minutes of my life. I'd asked forgiveness from Tim, but he'd been right: it was never him I needed forgiveness from. It was me, myself. *I* needed to forgive *me*.

When I ran away from Vegas, I left the city I loved, the career I lived for, the woman I'd become and grown, at long last, to be proud of.

I'd learned the wrong lesson from Mason leaving. I thought it meant that the *me* I was wasn't enough. I thought I needed to change, to become someone different, to become a woman who could be loved, cared for, stuck around for. But it didn't mean that at all.

So I danced for myself, for me, for my life, the way I'd first danced all those years ago. The way I always wanted to dance. Now and forever. The way I deserved to dance. The way the woman I left behind deserved to dance. The way the woman I was today deserved to dance.

The only kind of losing myself I wanted to do anymore was losing myself in the music, losing myself in the sensuous movement of my body, losing myself in self-expression and joy and love and happiness.

Five minutes to forgive myself. Five minutes to let it all go. Five minutes to free myself from the binds I'd wrapped around myself.

I won't say it was easy. Forgiving Mason was easy. As easy as falling. But forgiving myself required sweat. Required hard work. Required pushing my muscles to their limit, straining all the tendons in my thighs, beating my heart harder and harder and harder. Forgiving myself meant putting it all on the line. Emptying myself completely. Exposing everything, all of myself, my body, my heart, my soul, there in the spotlight, there in the vast dark. Forgiving myself made me gasp. Every second of those five minutes I considered stopping.

How easy to shout, *"Stop! I can't!"* How easy to run off

without a word, to dart to the dusky eaves, to hide myself, all of myself. How easy to cut my performance short, to not show everything, to hold myself back, just a little piece of myself.

Forgiving myself meant fighting myself. My arms thrashing. My legs kicking high. My back arching as the light spilled over my chest. Forgiving myself meant remembering. I couldn't curl in on myself as I was dragged back to my empty apartment that night. I had to stand tall. I couldn't lie down on the floor as I felt the prick of that tattoo gun that covered up Mason's feather. I had to leap, to spin. I couldn't tear at my hair as I ran through all the times I sacrificed myself to become Tim's sweet, innocent wife, his little orphan to save. I had to save myself. To dance for everything I wanted, everything I'd always wanted.

Forgiving myself meant crying as the music ended, as I stood with arms high over my head, as I lifted my head to the spotlight which snapped off, leaving me alone. Beautifully alone with myself.

I wiped at the tears hastily as the audience lights went up. They kept falling but I didn't care. I smiled through my tears and stepped forward. I laughed a little as I tried to catch my breath. I'd done it. I'd actually done it.

Three people were seated in the fifth row back, bent over clipboards positioned on their knees. The first to look up at me was a middle-aged man. Black turtleneck. Circular spectacles. Everything you'd imagine a director would look like. He drummed his fingers along the top of the clipboard.

"Very nice, Rachel," he said. "We'll let you know soon."

I thanked him. Thanked the other two. My heart was still racing as I left the stage. And I was still crying. I didn't know if I'd landed the role or not.

It wasn't exactly the most over-the-top positive reaction to my performance. But that wasn't always what mattered. Sometimes you just never knew. That's what made life so damned interesting, so worth living.

All that mattered was he'd said my name. A dancer. A performer. A failure or not, who gave a damn. A director had said my name.

And he said it in the most delightful Irish accent.

52

MASON

"What's the story?"

Rian looked at me over his drawing.

I flipped over one of my mother's letters and answered, "Reading."

It was a painful process, sifting through her words. Thousands and thousands of words. Difficult facing her pain, her hurt, her regret. Facing my own. The burden of not forgiving. The life and love that could have been, but never would.

Rian snorted. "You don't read."

I glanced up from my stack of old letters and noticed him drawing that same girl in the faint pink glow of the neon Dublin Ink sign.

"Yeah, and you don't draw real people."

This earned me a smirk over my friend's shoulder.

"So what are you reading?" he asked.

"So who are you drawing?"

Rian grinned and returned to his work. For a few minutes more I read on in silence. Then I set the letters aside, dragged my legs off the edge of my nan's old floral couch, and leaned forward, elbows on my knees.

"Hey, can I ask you something?"

Rian answered, "I'm not high on anything, alright? She just won't get out of my head. And...and I still haven't quite got her nailed down. Though, if you want get high?"

Again Rian drew his normally fixed attention away from his paper and raised his eyebrows up and down to tempt me.

When he saw my downturned face, he rolled his eyes. "I'm not dealing, alright? I see how you guys have been looking at me—"

"It's not that," I said.

"I know I've kind of been fixed on one subject for a while now, but—"

"Really Rian."

"And I told you where that cash came from, the cash I paid for my share of the Dublin Ink bills last week."

"I don't think you're dealing again," I said, though maybe that wasn't entirely true. I'd been so focused on Rachel that maybe I hadn't been paying close enough attention to my friend who had a troubled past with drugs.

I knew he wasn't sleeping well. I knew he was gone more often. I knew he wasn't quite himself: a little more distant, a little more moody, a little more tortured. But I didn't know why. I could only hope it wasn't serious.

"I'm teaching," Rian said. "Like I told you. And she's real. Whatever her name is."

I looked at my friend. His eyes were clear even if there were bags beneath them. He was sitting calmly even if his bottom lip was between his teeth. He was meeting my gaze earnestly even if I could see a whole other world just there beneath the surface of his green eyes.

"I was wondering if you could tell me about my wedding," I said with a gentle smile.

Rian frowned, then he pushed back his stool and stood. "I guess it's more of a whiskey night then."

He brought a bottle and two glasses to the coffee table. I took one and he cupped the other as he perched himself on the arm of a high-backed leather chair all scratched and faded. He drummed his fingers awkwardly and shrugged.

"What do you want to know?" he asked.

I laughed.

"I don't know," I answered honestly. "I mean, I don't remember shite. Like shite all. And Rachel said that she remembered and she told me about it, but..."

My voice drifted off as my gaze went to the dark sidewalk outside the parlour.

"You...want to see what she was lying about?" Rian asked.

I shook my head. The whiskey was hot against the back of my throat. The burn felt good. I took another drink. Rian, like any good boyo, was already reaching to refill my glass.

"No, no," I explained. "It's not that. The version of our wedding that Rachel told me...this sounds stupid, but I'm going to hold onto it."

"Even though it's not real?" Rian said.

My eyes trailed over to the half-finished painting on Rian's easel.

He growled, "*She's* real."

I held up my hands in surrender and said with a sad laugh, "Well, in some pathetic way that made-up wedding that Rachel told me about is real for me, too. I mean, I know it's not. But it is."

Rian told me he understood. I told him he did too many shrooms. He said I did too few.

"So why?" Rian asked after we clinked glasses across the coffee table and drank in quiet contemplation for a few moments. "Why dig up the past? Why now?"

I set my glass of whiskey down and leaned back on the couch. I stared up at the ceiling for a moment, got lost in its pink haze, got taken back to another time, another neon glow.

To the ceiling I finally answered, "I'm trying to find closure, I guess."

"Closure? Between you and Rachel?"

I didn't want to tell him between me and myself, though if anyone would understand of the friends I had it was Rian, so I just nodded vaguely.

"I mean, it was kind of a long time ago," Rian began. "But it was enough of a shite show that I do remember some things. Or maybe the better way to put it is that I can't—no matter how hard I fucking try, and believe me I have tried—*forget* some things."

I laughed despite myself. Laughed because I knew Rachel would have loved to be here. Loved to hear the shite we really got into that night. Loved to laugh with me as we shared a drink with a good friend.

Rian scrubbed at his eyes.

With his knuckles pressed into the sockets, he continued, saying, "I know for sure that Rachel wore a white 'I Heart Vegas' shirt that she cut the 'I' and the 'Vegas' out of."

"Oh," I said, imagining what little that left for the imagination.

"A pair of what I could only figure were your white boxers," Rian added. "And...and, oh yeah, these sparkly like go-go boots. They went up past her knee. The heel must have been a mile high."

Those boots winked at me from my past like a star on the horizon. I found myself smiling. Laughing when I remembered vaguely struggling to get them off of her, the only thing between her and complete nakedness, thong trapped round her kicking ankles as she laughed.

"I'm pretty sure she stole her veil from a tourist," Rian was saying as I drew my focus back to him. His hands circled his head as he explained, "It was one of those like hats with the net over the face. Like you wear on a safari or some shite. Or for beekeeping. Yeah, I'm pretty sure you two stole it somewhere. There was a lot of talk about something called Denny's."

I nodded.

"And me?" I asked.

Something told me I hadn't worn a fine tuxedo with my hair styled (or cleaned, for that matter). But even I was surprised when Rian hid his face and grumbled, almost incoherently, "Powder-blue cowboy boots, assless chaps, and, well, and that's it."

I shook my head as I laughed.

"And you didn't think for a second that I might not be in my soundest of minds?" I asked my friend. "I mean, you didn't stop even once to say, 'Hey, maybe we should save the "till death do we part" till we've all had some water and a good night's kip'?"

Rian stared at me like I'd asked him some complicated math equation. Who was I kidding? This was Rian. I'm surprised he stuck around for the ceremony and didn't wander off after some sparkling thing. Or some smoking thing more likely.

"You guys said you were in love," Rian said with a sureness that stirred my heart. "You said it and I believed you and that was that. I mean, what more is there than that? Nothing and no one should get in the way of love."

I glanced down at my fingers. That's all I did. All I'd ever learned to do: get in the way of love. I thought it had been to protect myself. But had I been hurting myself all these years? Hurting myself because the one person I'd never thought to forgive was the one person who needed forgiveness?

"And besides," Rian said, "your nan was so excited and crying and you know I came to love her like my own and—"

"Wait, wait, wait," I said, holding up my hands and scooting to the edge of the couch. "*What?*"

Rian rolled his eyes.

"Look, I know I can be a little...distant at times, but there's a lot of emotions down deep in here and only a feckin' robot wouldn't get just a little bit emotional when your nan is crying and saying how this was the happiest day of her life and all. I mean, it was beautiful. It really was."

I loved my friend. I really did. But there were moments, such as the present one, where I just wanted to grab him and shake him.

"Rian," I said as calmly as possible, "Rian, listen to me very carefully, because I don't know what you were on, heaven knows I was not in a place to judge, but there was no *fucking* way that my nan was there for my drunken Vegas wedding."

Rian stared at me for a second, blinking like an owl. I was going to scream. Or break something. Or break him.

Just when I was going to lose it, he said, "You rang her, you gobshite."

I was so stunned that I couldn't say anything. Couldn't say anything as I sank back into the couch. I drew my shaking fingers through my hair and tried to blink away tears.

"How much of a druggie do you think I am?" Rian raved on. "And, excuse me to your nan, but I don't think she'd be high up on my list of hallucinations. And, I mean, really, you eejits think all I do is paint imaginary girls, but some of them are fucking *real*! Jaysus, I—"

"I talked to my nan?" I asked.

"Yes," he answered grumpily.

"The night of my wedding?"

"Yes."

"When?" I said, leaning forward again. "I mean, where? What did she say? What did I say? Did she meet Rachel? Did she like Rachel? You said she cried? *My* nan? Are you sure? Nancy Donovan? *The* Nancy Donovan? Crying?"

I paced back and forth in front of the coffee table, no longer able to stay still. Rian's eyes followed me as I rounded on my heel.

"Um, okay," he said, squinting in concentration, "I'd say three-ish in the morning. Um, at this shitty chapel. Like really a shite hole. At the altar, if you mean specifically. She said that you're an eejit and she couldn't love you more. Yes, she spoke to Rachel. Yes, she liked Rachel. Yer nan said Rachel sounded like a spitfire and that she was a spitfire once. Said only a cowgirl could wrangle a bronco. Yes, she cried. Yes, *your* nan. Yes, I am sure. I cried, too. Yes, Nancy Donovan. Yes, *the* Nancy Donovan. Yes, crying...did I miss anything?"

My mind was whirling. I was swiping away tears and they were just coming faster. I could hardly think, but one question kept coming up. I rounded on Rian. He looked ready to dart away, like a startled, edgy cat.

"And I told my nan I loved her?"

Rian eyed me warily as he answered, "You got super soppy. Raved on about how much she meant to you. How she was your rock. How you felt like you could never repay her for taking you in as her own."

I sank back down to the edge of the couch.

"I heard your nan curse for the first time in my life," Rian added as I stared down at my hands, still unbelieving.

"Yeah?" I asked, looking up.

Rian nodded.

"Yeah, she said, 'You don't owe me a bleedin' thing but your happiness. Love. Do you hear me? Not a bleedin' thing.'"

I fell back against the couch. Stared up at the ceiling.

Just moments before I hadn't been sure how I was going to forgive myself, how I could possibly ever forgive myself for failing my nan, but she or Rian or Rachel or God knows who, maybe me, had given me one last gift.

I'd made myself so unhappy for so long, thinking I was settling a debt between my nan and me. But I'd been wrong. I'd been increasing the debt, digging a deeper hole, separating us further and further.

It was time to settle some accounts. Time to forgive myself. Time to allow myself to love Rachel. Time to make things right.

Time to, as my nan would *definitely* not ever say, get on a bleedin' plane.

53

RACHEL

The plan was to change after my audition. To take my time removing my makeup. The glitter, the sparkle, the bold lavender eyeliner. The full lips, the bright cheeks, the star sequins I'd stuck to the corners of my eyes. The shimmer I'd dusted across my collar bones. The plan was to take off my costume. Pack away the feathers. Fold the fishnets. Gently arrange the dramatic corset with its velvet cords. Tuck in my top hat so it didn't get crushed, didn't get scratched by the costume jewels that were...well, everywhere. The plan was to change into jeans, a white tee, sneakers instead of towering stilettos. The plan was to go back to the hotel, sink into a bubble bath, calmly, slowly, carefully think things over.

The plan was to wait till the morning to take the bus over to Dublin Ink. When I was ready. When I was prepared. When I wasn't still shaking with post-audition adrenaline, still blinking indigo mascara from my eyes, still making sure that my tits hadn't popped out of my costume as I paced the small back dressing room with an uncontainable joy.

Well, you know what they say about the best laid plans, and believe me, none of the plans for my life had ever been particularly "laid". But fuck it. They're all the easier to throw out the window that way. Fuck best laid plans. Fuck plans. Fuck doing anything well-thought-out, well-reasoned, well-judged.

I was laughing and crying and shaking and telling myself this was probably not a great idea and not giving a single fuck as I dialled Aurnia's number. Mason's number had been disconnected. But I had a way back to him this time. And I had the courage to take it.

"Aurnia, hi, hey, hello, it's me," I said the moment I heard the phone line pick up, not even letting her have a chance to say anything.

"Rachel?" Aurnia said. "Oh my God, Rachel!"

"Oh my God, Aurnia!" I laughed back.

"Look, I've been trying to tell Mason what a feckin' eejit he's been and how he's such a fucking gobshite for letting you go and—"

"Aurnia," I tried to interrupt, but my young friend was kind of bullheaded when she got going; that's what I liked about her, she reminded me of someone I knew.

"And Mason had all these excuses about finding out that you were engaged to someone else and how you were never coming back, how it was all a scam, a lie, and I tried so many times to tell him to trust you, to trust your love for him, because I saw it, I *saw* it, you know?"

I paced the small back dressing room, still fully in costume, as Aurnia rambled.

"Yeah, Aurnia—"

"Like for weeks I tried to get through to him and he was just so angry and it was like talking to a wall, like a fucking angry wall, but I swore I wouldn't give up, because I didn't give up on Conor and—"

"Aurnia."

"But I must have finally gotten through to him!" she said.

When silence finally came I suddenly had nothing to say.

"Rachel? Rachel, you still there?"

"You got through to him?" I repeated her words. "What—what does that mean?"

I'd never heard Aurnia so bubbly as when she said, "Yeah, all that beating my fists against that brick wall must have finally made a dent somehow because he just called to ask if I can cover his clients for a while."

"What?" I asked.

"Yeah, can you believe it?" Aurnia said. "I mean, shite, I hope I'm not ruining his grand romantic gesture. Ah shite, am I ruining it?"

In the background I heard Conor's gruff voice murmur, "You're fine, baby. Mason is probably just going to show up to her place with grocery store flowers and Taco Bell."

I'd stopped pacing.

"Aurnia?" I said. "Show up where? Why does Mason need you to cover his clients?"

But Aurnia was stuck in conversation with Conor.

"You don't really think he'd do it like that, do you?" I heard her say, clearly cupping the phone as she held it away from her.

I couldn't help but laugh, despite the racing of my heart, as Conor replied, "I know for a fact that it's how he's going to do it."

"Aurnia!" I shouted, but she didn't hear me.

"Conor, you have to talk to him!" Aurnia insisted in an impassioned plea.

"Aurnia!" I tried again, a little desperately. I was pacing the room once more, but this time with a sort of nervous panic.

"What am I supposed to tell him?" Conor said in that low monotone voice of his. "I got you by dragging you onto my motorcycle and locking you in a closet."

"That is *not* how you got me and you know it," Aurnia said as

I tried not to lose my mind. "You got me with that big, massive, monster of a co—"

"Aurnia!" I shouted, shouted so loud a theatre assistant poked her head inside the room.

I quickly assured her I was fine and then whispered into the phone, "Aurnia, are you listening to me?"

"I mean, yeah," she said with a tone of voice that reminded me she was just eighteen years old. "You kind of yelled my head off, Rach."

"Aurnia," I said as calmly as possible. "I need you to tell me what Mason is doing."

"But it's like I was saying, I'll ruin it and—"

"Aurnia, where is he?"

"But Rach—"

"Aurnia, you tell me right now or I'll come over there right this second and shake it out of you!"

Aurnia snorted. "Right, I'll see you in twenty hours," she said. "*Real* threatening, Rachel."

"I'm in Dublin," I said. "Aurnia, I'm in Dublin."

I heard the shock in her voice as she said, "You're in Dublin? You're in Dublin?! But— Rachel, Mason's going to New York! He's on his way to the airport right now."

"Aurnia—"

"Oh my God, if you miss him by like however many seconds it took me to tell you I don't know what I'm going to do."

"Aurnia—"

"I'm such an eejit!" Aurnia wailed as I gathered up my purse and bag.

Conor comforted her in the background and I tried again to get her attention.

"Aurnia, I—"

"How many years is it going to take this time?" she moaned. "Because I screwed it all up and you missed each other again."

"Aurnia—"

"Why couldn't I just shut up for two minutes? Just like two minutes!"

"Aurnia!"

"Yeah?"

I laughed, smiling from ear to ear as I said, already running out the door, "I have to go!"

"Yes, yes, oh my God, I almost did it again!" she said. "Go, Rachel! Go!"

Running through the airport already draws plenty of unwanted attention. I mean, it's practically all set up like a theatre anyway. People with nothing to do, sitting around waiting. Lines of seats just like a theatre. Tickets drummed against knees just like a theatre. Eyes seeking any form of entertainment, any entertainment at all, just like a theatre.

I can't say I blamed anyone who gawked openly at me running past. I'd certainly done my fair share of watching. At the single mom trying to drag a screaming child along as she juggled three suitcases and screamed ahead for them to hold the gate. At the businessman in his clearly uncomfortable shoes, slipping and sliding on his leather soles as he tried not to pant into his Bluetooth because he's on a conference call with Tokyo. At the teenage backpackers who left a trail of dust and body odour in their towering wake as they sprinted through the crowd on scrawny legs. I'd looked. Shamelessly. Everyone had.

So it was only fair that they got their turn, the single moms, the businessmen, the globetrotting kids. The airport theatre. Row upon row.

And boy did I give them a show.

At the very least I was a woman in high heels, a full face of dramatic makeup streaked with happy tears, and a feathery sequined burlesque costume running past. At the worst (or perhaps best), my tits had bounced out since I didn't have time to worry and I was a hooker chasing after my bill-skipping John. Either way, I had the whole airport at the edge of their seats.

And I loved it.

This was who I was meant to be: loud, abrasive, perhaps slightly inappropriate at times. Okay, pretty much at all times. Colourful and bright and sparkling. I was meant to be the one who drew your attention and didn't let go. Who danced because she would die otherwise, who showed her tits way too often because they—like all tits—deserved to be celebrated and "fuck the patriarch, free the nip" and because she goddamn wanted to. I was meant to be too much for some and just perfect for others. I was meant to love and to be loved, fully, completely, crazily.

In the end I didn't have to catch Mason as he was boarding his plane. Didn't have to beg the flight attendant to let me on board once the doors were closed. Didn't even have to run all that far down the terminal.

Because Mason came running to me.

I saw him from a long way down and he saw me.

If you think running through an airport draws attention, try colliding into someone. Throwing yourself into their arms. Breaking down into tears as they do the same. Kissing each other's necks and breathing in each other's hair and digging into each other's backs with greedy, earnest fingertips. Drawing their lips to yours like water from the well. Cupping their cheeks and staring down into their eyes and muttering a million words a minute, "I'm sorry— I love you— I'll never leave— I never should have left— I was stupid— I was wrong— I want you— I need you—I'm never leaving— I'm staying— I'm *staying*."

Try hearing them say all the same things right back.

Try letting them lower you slowly down, stilettos tapping gently on the floor.

Try sucking in a breath as they get down on one knee.

Try laughing through the tears as you say, “Sorry, but I’m already married.”

You’ll have an enraptured audience. You’ll have something they can’t look away from. You’ll have a show worthy of any Vegas stage.

You’ll have love.

EPILOGUE

MASON

Aurnia told me I absolutely could not marry Rachel at city hall. She was still pissed that I proposed to Rachel right then and there at the airport, in front of the KFC, without a ring, and to use her words, "without anyone to take a picture of it, save those asshole security guards who *still* won't let me have access to their fucking cameras."

I tried to tell Aurnia that Rachel and I didn't need the whole wedding thing, we were already married. I tried to have Conor tell her that. But Conor just said he was staying out of it, only adding with a sigh that I should probably just give Aurnia her way. To use *his* words, "It's just easier that way, man. Believe me, I know."

"Every girl has a dream wedding," Aurnia kept saying.

She'd been a pest for days, buzzing from one ear to the next as I tried to work.

"Not Rachel," I told her.

"*Every* girl has a dream wedding," she insisted.

I spun around on my stool. "Look, Rachel has never, not once, ever mentioned even the tiniest detail of what she would want for a..."

My words trailed off.

Aurnia beamed in victory. She flicked my forehead and said, "*Every* girl," before skipping merrily away.

We managed to keep the details mostly a surprise. Rachel still thought we were heading to city hall exactly a week and a half after I proposed at the airport. It was the closest we could estimate from when we'd met each other to the first time we got married; it felt fitting, even if we couldn't be sure it was entirely accurate. Rian was, of course, no help in the matter.

At first Aurnia didn't believe me when I listed the things we would need to get in secret for Rachel's wedding "dress". Sitting across from me in the parlour, clipboard across her knees, she tapped her pencil against her temple and said with obvious mistrust, "So let me get this straight...you want me to get a high-low white feather burlesque costume that fans over the breasts—"

"Almost like indecently short in the front," I said, remembering Rachel's words like she was there whispering them in my ear.

Aurnia eyed me warily as she said, "'Almost like indecently short in the front'. Um, silver pasties?"

I nodded. She just sucked her teeth.

Convincing her to paint a massive Eiffel Tower on the big wall of the parlour was a bit of an easier task. It was a bit tricky explaining why there was suddenly a big sheet of canvas covering the brick wall, but I told Rachel it was mould and maybe it was a sign that the house needed some work, and she easily bought it. Aurnia insisted that she get to marry us since it was her consistent badgering that got us back together. I didn't have the heart to tell her about my conversation with Rian, about him revealing that I'd talked with my nan before her passing.

"It would only be right," I told her as she flipped open her laptop to get licensed to perform wedding ceremonies online.

"Aurnia," I tried to say, "Rachel and I are already married. You don't need—"

"Shut up and go find me an Elvis wig," she said.

With Aurnia's...*careful persuasion*...Conor even agreed to dress up like the Midwest tourist from Rachel's made-up wedding. We gave him a big Mai Tai glass, a fanny pack, high-waisted cargo pants, and an I Heart Vegas t-shirt we ordered online that ended up being a *child's* size large, and therefore a midriff shirt after we cut out a bigger hole for the neck and sleeves. He was pissed and it was perfect.

We invited everyone. Even Rachel's friend JoJo made the trip over. Dress code was Vegas trashy. The invitation said, "If you look even remotely elegant, you're getting a pint of the black stuff spilled on you. You've been fucking warned." I tried to tell Aurnia the "fucking" was too much. She told me it was "fucking perfect".

When Rachel and I left for city hall the madness began at Dublin Ink. All the flashing neon lights our friends could round up were brought in. The place was packed with Marilyn wigs and polyester pink boas and lots and lots of black vests with no shirts, just inked-up pale Irish abs. I'd paid the cabbie ahead of time to get us a little lost in the direction of city hall, stall for time, and then double back to Dublin Ink. Rachel and I had been fooling around so much in the back seat, not so discreetly slipping hands where hands shouldn't be, that she didn't even notice when I opened the door and held out my hand at the curb outside the shop.

"Wait, why are we—" Rachel stopped when I unbuttoned my black slacks there on the sidewalk.

She watched with a mix of concern and intrigue as I kicked

off my shiny shoes, tugged off my socks, and pulled down my pants to reveal shamrock underwear.

"Oh...my...God..." Rachel murmured, smile growing on her perfect lips as I loosened by bow tie just enough to slip my collar from underneath it.

"Oh my God, oh my God," Rachel said.

She was chewing at her lips and watching as I tossed my suit jacket and then my white shirt to the sidewalk. I held out my hands in my wedding "suit" and she screamed, loud as hell, "Oh my God!"

She ran to me and leaped into my arms. I held her as she kissed me, smearing lipstick all over my face. Wild curls curtaining our locked eyes, Rachel looked down at me and whispered, "But I'm in this stupid dress."

I jerked my head to the side and she wrangled her hair out of her face just in time to see Aurnia, dressed head-to-toe as Elvis, peeking her head outside the door of Dublin Ink. She lifted a hanger with a white feather costume and wiggled it back and forth, grinning stupidly. But we were grinning stupidly, too.

Rachel changed and we all got locked on Jamie' and gingers downstairs. I thought she might need to catch up, but judging by the way she and Candace, Aubrey, JoJo and Aurnia stumbled down the stairs, giggling stupidly, and by the way their lips were all stained a bright blue, they'd been doing plenty of catching up already.

Doing her best Elvis impression—which between the bad American accent, the booze, and the massive wig that kept sliding around her head was absolutely, wonderfully terrible—Aurnia began the ceremony. Between the shouting and the drinking and the constant interruptions for cheering it was quite a shite show. Judging from Rachel's beaming smile and the way she kept squeezing my hands and pulling me in for preemptive kisses, it was exactly how she would have wanted it, there beneath the spray-painted Eiffel Tower.

When Aurnia asked us for our vows, Rachel was ready.

"This isn't at all what I was going to say at city hall," she warned me. "What I was going to say at city hall was beautiful and thoughtful and sober."

I grinned.

"Fuck city hall."

Then Rachel repeated the words she'd said in our bed. The words that I wrongly saw as lies. They were never lies. They were always the truth. They were true then, in Vegas. True there, with our naked bodies against one another. And they were true now, professing our love for one another in front of all our family and friends.

"I ran all this way to you," Rachel concluded, laughing as she started to cry, making a complete hames of her already messy makeup. "And you knew I wouldn't know how to stop, so you just ran with me. And you'll always run with me."

Rachel accepted a tissue from Conor's fanny pack.

It was my turn and I knew the words to say: "I love you, Rachel."

Rachel nodded. Nodded and whispered, "That's enough."

I repeated, squeezing her hands in mine, "And that's enough."

We kissed. We spilled shots of whiskey on each other as we took them with arms snaked through the others. We lifted our arms up in the air and smiled as a packed Dublin Ink cheered.

We partied like it was fucking Vegas.

At some point in the night (or was it already morning?) Rachel and I were kissing up against some hard surface. Who can really pay attention to whether it's a bed or brick wall or kitchen table when you've got a handful of a perfect tit, nothing between you and buttery-soft skin but a sparkly pasty and some feathers, and pillowy lips between your teeth?

Turns out it was a door. A door I was grinding my hips against hers against.

We were already pretty fucking locked so it took us a second to realise why the hard surface we were getting hot and heavy against was bucking back against us. The music was loud, the neon lights were flashing everywhere, and there was my fairly sizeable boner all to distract me.

"Door!" Rachel was shouting as she laughed.

"What?" I shouted back at her.

She thumbed over her shoulder as I heard a pounding fist.

"It's the door!"

Rachel adjusted the feathers of her bodice as if they'd ever do anything more than just hint at coverage over those tits of hers and pushed me back as I tried to advance on her again. Can you really blame me?

We scooted aside enough to let in a young girl, probably about twenty, with thick dark hair that curtained scowling, angry, determined eyes. She was so focused on something, or someone, that she hardly gave us a moment's glance. She elbowed past and stormed into the crowd muttering under her breath, "B minus! Fucking B fucking minus! That fucker!"

The two of us watched her go, parting the crowd with her little cloud of bottled fury. People turned to watch her disappear just like we were. She had something about her. Something magnetic. Something familiar. The music pulsed around us, the lights flashed, and slowly Rachel and I turned to look at one another. We frowned at one another, each not willing to be the first to speak.

I thumbed over toward where the girl had disappeared, leaving nothing more than a trail of turned heads behind her.

"Um, was that—"

Rachel shook her head. “It couldn’t—”

“But she looked so much—”

“I mean, almost exactly, but—”

“But no,” I said, laughing, shaking my head. “Definitely not.”

“Yeah,” Rachel said, dismissing the thought with a wave of her hand. “Yeah, no, definitely not.”

“Right. ’Cause she’s not real, right?”

“Right.”

Still we both turned and searched the crowd. Searched for the girl. Searched for Rian.

"It looked so much like her though...right?”

“Right.”

“But there’s no way that was her, is there?” Rachel asked, now sounding utterly unsure.

I squinted, trying to see only one of everybody I looked over.

At that moment Aurnia and Conor came by with shots for both of us. The four of us raised our glasses and downed what I think was whiskey, but who the hell knew. We coughed and pounded our chests.

Rachel and I looked at each other.

“Either we’re way too drunk,” I said slowly, “or Rian’s mystery girl is actually...”

A grin broke out over Rachel’s lips. “Oh my God. She’s real.”

The End

DUBLIN INK

OUT NOW

He can't give in.

Grumpy bad boy tattoo artist, Conor Mac Haol, doesn't trust anyone. Least of all the new juvie apprenticing at his beloved Dublin Ink as part of her probation.
She is way too pretty and way, *way* too young.

Coming from a broken home, Aurnia has had to grow up faster than most girls. She doesn't need anyone telling her what to do. Least of all Conor, her new (very hot, very muscled, very tattooed and very, *very* rude) boss who obviously hates her.

But Aurnia's troubles reminds Conor too much of his dark past. He becomes obsessed with keeping her safe. Keeping her protected.
Even from him.
Especially from him.

Soon sparks and insults turn into broken rules and forbidden moments—until one final mistake seals their fate.

IRISH KISS

OUT NOW

Saoirse

I wanted him since the day I met him. Bearded, tattooed and tall as an Irish giant. He was more than just handsome, he was drop-dead gorgeous. It didn't matter to him that my father was a criminal and my mother a whore. He was my best friend.

I could be anything I wanted.
Except *his*.
Because I'm too young and he's my Juvenile Liaison Officer.

Diarmuid

It's been years since I last saw her. No longer a girl, she has the body of a woman. When our eyes met again, I saw the only one who ever broke through my asshole mask. I saw my best friend.

She could be anything she wanted.
Except *mine*.
Because she's only seventeen and I'm too old for her.

I'm so screwed.

Cause I'm so f**king in love with her.

Irish Kiss is a slow-burn, angsty love story with a Happily Ever After, but damn, it is going to hurt along the way.

BOOKS BY SIENNA BLAKE

Dublin Ink

Dublin Ink

Dirty Ink

Dark Ink ~ *coming soon*

Irish Kiss

Irish Kiss

Professor's Kiss

Fighter's Kiss

The Irish Lottery

My Brother's Girl

Player's Kiss

My Secret Irish Baby

Irish Billionaires

The Bet

The Fiancé

The Promise

Billionaires Down Under

(with Sarah Willows)

To Have & To Hoax

The Paw-fect Mix-up

Riding His Longboard

Maid For You

I Do (Hate You)

Man Toy (Newsletter Exclusive)

All Her Men

Three Irish Brothers

My Irish Kings

Royally Screwed

Cassidy Brothers

Dark Romeo Trilogy

Love Sprung From Hate (#1)

The Scent of Roses (#2)

Hanging in the Stars (#3)

Bound Duet

Bound by Lies (#1)

Bound Forever (#2)

A Good Wife

Beautiful Revenge

Mr. Blackwell's Bride

Paper Dolls

ABOUT SIENNA

Sienna Blake is a dirty girl, a wordspinner of smexy love stories, and an Amazon Top 20 & USA Today Bestselling Author.

She's an Australian living in Dublin, Ireland, where she enjoys reading, exploring this gorgeous country and adding to her personal harem of Irish hotties ;)

tiktok.com/@siennablakeauthor
facebook.com/siennablakebooks
instagram.com/siennablakeauthor

Printed in Great Britain
by Amazon

18218745R00233